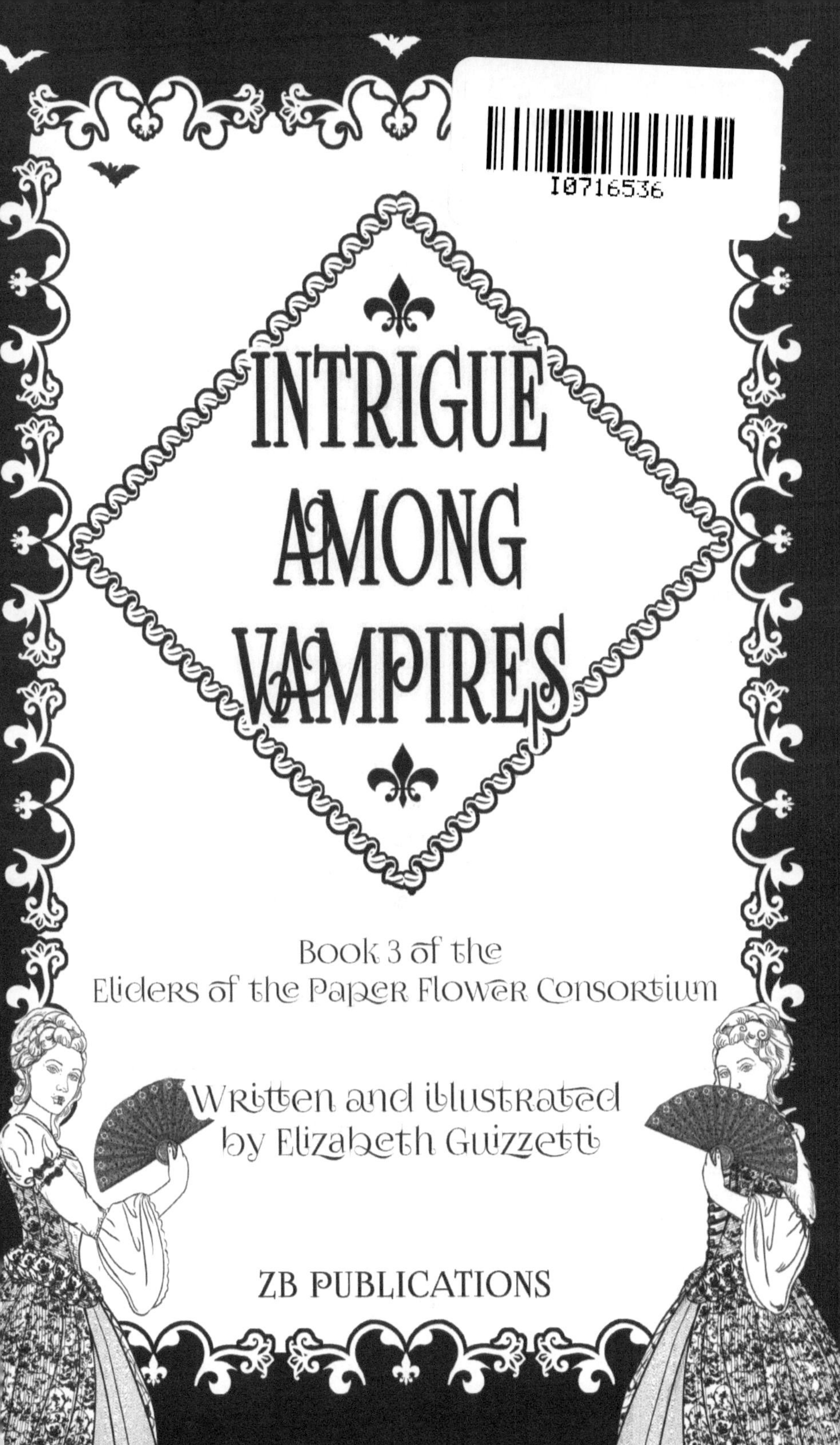

INTRIGUE AMONG VAMPIRES

Book 3 of the
Elders of the Paper Flower Consortium

Written and illustrated
by Elizabeth Guizzetti

ZB PUBLICATIONS

Intrigue Among Vampires
Copyright Elizabeth Guizzetti, 2024
Published by ZB Publications same year

Edited by Denise DeSio
Cover and Illustrations by Elizabeth Guizzetti

Printed in the United States of America
Hardback ISBN: 978-1-950708-36-9
Paperback ISBN: 978-1-950708-37-6
Ebook ISBN: 978-1-950708-38-3

*Dedicated to Gretchen
in hope we may
storm many castles together in
the most gentle way possible.*

Preface

Dear Readers,

Thank you for reading Intrigue Among Vampires. Pascaline and Loretta's book took me the longest to write—nearly five years! I appreciate your patience. Writing this book, I learned that authors should not fight their stories—the novel will be told how it wants. I originally wrote over 200,000 words, meaning several scenes were cut for a future book or podcast.

I initially planned for each elder vampire to have their own books, but Charles, Loretta, and Pascaline's stories overlap. I tried a few different methods to combine them. As sisters, the ladies begin life and undeath together. Ultimately, it makes sense that Pascaline and Loretta remain together for this book's narrative, setting, and bloodline. This book may reveal different faucets to their characters than commonly known; I hope you find their evolution as captivating as I did.

I invite you to witness the world of intense luxury and terrible poverty of seventeenth-century France. A few notes on my research: Louis XIV was the longest-reigning monarch and a brutal dictator. He stripped away religious rights. To ensure young widows would be forced to remarry and produce more children, Louis XIV abolished the 1/3 inheritance laws - a medieval way to provide for widows and younger children. Despite misconceptions, this era had a strict and stringent moral code. As Louis needed young men to fight in HIS wars, not each other, dueling was illegal. Women of all classes were expected to be virgins when they wed. Adultery was unlawful, but wealthy men had mistresses.

Louis XIV was also a great lover of dance, art, music, and food. Nearly every night, Louis XIV insisted upon the Grand Couvert, a massive banquet with 30-40 dishes. The art of sculpted cakes, sugar glass, and other fanciful cookery came from this era. He was served first, and a course ended when he said it ended. Whether or not, they were invited to the table, Louis XIV was seated to see who came into the room and was watching his courtiers.

Health crises plagued Europe during the early modern era. Much of this era's health data comes from Norway because they kept better birth and death records compared to France and Germany. Infant mortality was between 20 – 25%. Without antibiotics, scarlet fever killed 15% of infected children under 5 – as it develops from strep throat, it is widespread. People still believed in the four humours – including the vampires!

I am immensely grateful to my meticulous editor, Denise DeSio, and my diligent proofreader, Tim Marquitz. Additionally, heartfelt thanks are due to Evan Witt, Vivian Burrows, Stevie Rae Causey, Gretchen S.B., Raven Oak, Amanda Cherry, and Jennifer Brozek, who patiently endured my musings/rantings on the characters' questionable decisions over the past five years. My most profound appreciation goes to Dennis Roberts, the best husband in the world.

With boundless love and gratitude,

Elizabeth

LIMOUSIN
1685

Prologue

My destrier raced into the forests where my words might be lost in the night wind. The russet gelding's hooves dug into the deep earth in rhythmic movements. Like his predecessors, his spirited nature stole my heart when he was a colt. No one knew how to train a destrier anymore now. Jousts were simple games or reenactments. Though many war horses were trained and died on the battlefield, they were not destriers.

Though my lands remained at peace, I could depend upon Castor's speed and spirit if danger happened to fall upon us. I was not the only undead thing who lingered deep in the night. On a ridge that overlooked my border, I observed the movement of the horde—peasant vampires reborn with Black Death and other maladies that ravage their weak bodies. Yet, our treaty held. They had not attempted to cross my lands.

Once utterly alone, I spoke freely to Castor VII as my dearest friend, for he was. I've existed too long to trust any human to be privy my thoughts. in their entirety.

"The letter holds a hidden threat. If I don't answer correctly, the king may take my estate. Most likely, my head. And what of my wife? News from Versailles put fear in dear

Agata's heart. France changed the law regarding widows. If he takes my head, she would no longer be guaranteed a third of the estate. According to law, even lands she purchased and raised her sheep upon are mine alone. She would be set upon the road with no son to protect her. I must discover a way to answer this damnable king."

Castor neighed as he always did and tossed his head. As a horse, he had little knowledge of such things.

My corner of rural France was largely ignored by the last nine kings as I paid my taxes, occasionally went to war, and sent willing men for the Royal Army. However, Louis XIV wanted nobility in his Versailles pleasure palace. He grew impatient with a few decades of excuses of illness. I wondered if enough time had passed for me to replace me as a son replaces his father. However, Louis XIV's mind had not faltered, nor his eye for beautiful women. He might recognize Agata.

It was questionable which kings had known my wife and I were vampires. Louis XII, François I, and Henri II recognized my ability to heal from wounds that killed other men. As long as we remained on the right side of the law, perhaps, they did not care.

"I suspect Louis XIV simply cares that my beloved wife and I are Catholic," I said to Castor. "But was it enough that I ensured the completion of the Cathedral in 1570 and put on a new roof in 1670? Probably not. Both God and King Louis always want more supplicant hearts."

I dismounted in a wooded grove where only Castor, insects, and God, if He existed, could hear me. "What do You want? Another cathedral? A convent? My prayers at Your feet?"

No answer.

I knelt on a patch of cold earth. The pebbles shifted under my armored knees. "Is this what you want? I will give anything for my wife's safekeeping."

I cocked my head and listened. Nothing happened. The night was still.

"That's what I thought. You never concern Yourself with humanity's plight. Your Catholic followers are raping and killing your Protestant followers. Do You care for either?"

"You took my Agata's life, forced her to outlive our children. Now, You sent a long-lived king to change a law which would take her lands if I fall.

"Her goodness makes me a better man, a better count. My people thrive. Ought they suffer under someone who does not care for them?"

Still, nothing happened.

"Perhaps, You are no God any more than I."

I waited to be struck down for my irreverence, but I was not.

Blasphemy complete, Castor and I returned to our château and my wife. Agata never blamed God for our curse, even though she ought. She did not blame me either, though she ought. She loved me with the pure innocence of any bride rather than a woman married these two hundred years. I would never hurt her sweet and gentle heart, but this damned Louis the XIV, by the Grace of God, the most Christian King of France and the Navarre, might.

PARIS
1685

Chapter 1

Loretta

4th of March

Cher Journal,

I dared not commit these words to paper until I arrived in Paris. When I was young, I fancied my future husband might love me as gentlemen loved ladies in ballads and poems. At sixteen, I am able to comprehend the futility of that dream.

My intended is handsome enough but holds a mercenary cruelty in his demeanor.

Thankfully, my brother-in-law invited me to stay this year to provide companionship for my sister. My father and future father-in-law allowed this debut as they trust my musical talents to sway the king. My father complained about the cost of gowns but requires my triumph at Court. My future father-in-law hopes I can gain a court appointment for my betrothed. A lady is not supposed to know such things, but I listen.

I shall be brave.

In two days, I shall be presented to King Louis XIV. My only hope is to seduce him or perhaps a duke. They will use me for their purpose, but better to enjoy the soft touch of a man as his mistress rather than being a callously used wife.

My room in Andre's house is nice. But we are in Paris, not Versailles proper. Worse, there are theaters, symphony, and ballet outside, but Andre denies such diversions, claiming the expense. "There will be music at Court," he said.

Though the city and life with my sister and brother-in-law are not all I hoped for, I shall endure it until I arrive at Versailles. Still, at least, Andre never seems to get angry as long as I ask questions, he deems suitable.

Over the past week, I questioned him extensively on court fashions. Pascaline helps by studying society dailies but has little firsthand knowledge due to an extended confinement after having suffered an unfortunate miscarriage, followed by another pregnancy and the birth of her daughter. Andre practiced the new dances with us and listened to Pascaline and I play our instruments on the off chance someone would request us play. Though, outwardly, he seems gentle, something covetous resides in him, too.

I hate it when I hear them quarreling through the wall.

My sister's marriage had been an advantageous match, but I wonder for whom. Though I am not supposed to know, Andre's father squandered the family estate. Andre needed a noble girl with more than a few coins to rub together. Pascaline will one day be a marquise, not just a viscount's daughter. Yet that doesn't protect Pascaline when they fight. She obeys her husband in every way. Never says a cross word. Why do they argue?

Still, Andre does not go out of his way to find fault with Pascaline. Better to be in Paris with my sister than alone in the country manor where our father does nothing but bluster over the most trivial things Maman does. Worse, our eldest brother, Claude, finds fault in everything and everyone: Papa, Maman, his wife, his children, the amount his three sister's dowries pulled from the family estate—as if Helena and Pascaline's marriages had not aided our brothers in other ways.

I must be perfect for the plan to succeed. I worked diligently on my posture and grew taller than my sister by a finger's width. My ivory taffeta gown with golden lace underskirts is trimmed with pale blue ribbons that match my eyes. I won't wear a wig, and my hair design is nearly scandalous with its simplicity. In sunlight, my hair looks more blonde than auburn, but it ought to appear redder in the shade of my chambers and court candlelight. I shall intertwine blue and gold ribbons between my braids to match the gown, gather the braids into a bun and form a bow at its base. Perfection.

I will simply pat my cheeks with translucent face powder and, though a lady is supposed to be beyond beautiful, powder will be enough. I shall not use paint simply because most men and women do.

While I am not such a fool to think the king would keep me for long, such a respectable position as his mistress would influence my husband to protect and cherish me into my birthing years. The dailies claim King Louis XIV is the rarest of gentlemen...

Pascaline

I must return to court. Still in a dressing gown, I pore over *La Gazette de France.* I suck in a breath as my eyes alighted upon yet another story of King Louis XIV's Dragonnades terrorizing an unnamed Huguenot family for the glory of the Kingdom of France. I fear for my parents, eldest brother, his wife, and their children. Unlike his predecessors, Louis XIV enforced Catholicism as a national religion to strengthen the crown's authority. There is even talk the king might revoke the Edict of Nantes later this year.

I scan the details and call to my husband, "Andre, my love, the Dragonnades march to Poitou."

Sponging ivory paint onto his skin, Andre gazes at me in the mirror's reflection. "Surely, families who served the king in honor will not be harmed. Your father's and brothers' military service protects them."

"But, my love—"

Andre waves his hand. "These wars of religion have gone on for hundreds of years and will go on for hundreds more. Think of happy things such as Loretta's debut and your return to court."

Across the room, Andre's valet, Paul, brushes Andre's embroidered velvet justacorps to ensure the nape of the fabric lay correctly. He cleared his throat. "The blue or the green waistcoat today, Monsieur?"

"The blue, I think. Let's save the green for Madame's return."

"Yes, Monsieur."

"But I fear with—"

"Pascaline! Your fears do you credit, but we're members of the Court. I have military service. Ensure you read the fashion section. If we need anything else, we can send out Paul this afternoon."

"You're not dining at court?"

Andre frowns. "I wasn't invited today."

Fear settles into my stomach, but I must persist. "I wish you'd listen, my husband. The king has been stripping away religious rights for years. Perhaps we should convert."

He slaps his sponge on the dressing table. "You haven't been at Court for eighteen months."

Andre rarely chastises me in front of the servants. However, he expects complete fealty and, clearly, I overstepped; I whisper, "Yes, Andre. I apologize."

I must admit, what Andre said is true. I became pregnant too quickly to become well-known at Versailles. After my first bout of morning sickness, Andre insisted upon a long confinement away from the palace's filth. After I miscarried, he maintained I remain in confinement to "strengthen my humours." Once I became pregnant again, and after our little Celeste was born, he wished for me to remain at home to "protect her from loathsome air."

Mercifully, Andre has relented on my continued confinement now that my sister Loretta has come to debut. Yet, he dreads the cost of fast-changing fashions: the paniers, layers of underskirts, garlands, fans, high wigs, and white and rouge paint. Paul looks away.

Andre rises from the dressing table. I do not breathe for a moment as he walks toward me.

"A lady mustn't quarrel in matters she knows little about."

I apologize again. My mind races with words I am too frightened to speak. I want to tell him about the story in La Gazette. It describes how Madame de Maintenon whispers in King Louis's ear to unite the country under a Catholic banner. However, Louis XIV once said while his grandfather loved the Huguenots, his father hated them, and he had no use for them. His most gracious and Christian King does not abide anyone for whom he has no use.

My mouth dries.

When I say nothing more, he brushes his lips against mine without love in the kiss. "You must set a good example for your sister. She's an innocent."

Thankfully, Andre does not know Loretta well. He believes her to be a guileless, pretty girl of sixteen inclined toward music. In truth, Loretta is bold in a way I am not. We dare not tell Andre her scheme, but it will be good for the entire family if Loretta succeeds. Even if the plan fails, between Loretta's gifts in music and my understanding of politics, we might have influence we would not have alone.

"I will be a good example."

"Then, you're forgiven." He returns to his dressing table.

A whimper comes from our six-month-old daughter's bassinet beside the massive wooden marital bed. Andre used my dowry to pay for the Italian-made brass crib, as midwives and doctors alike now claim metal is healthier for babies than wood.

Even though Celeste is a daughter, Andre wants our child to have the best. After I miscarried, Andre held me gently and stroked my hair. He said, even the queen miscarried. *He's a good husband. He is.*

The whimper becomes a wail as Celeste fully awakens.

Glad for distraction, I reach for my child and rock her in my arms. My baby continues to weep.

"You ask me to listen, but you don't even think to call for the wet nurse." Andre rings the bell.

Jaqueline enters through the servant's door.

Feeling worthless, I smile. She gathers Celeste into her arms and, humming, takes the child into the other room to nurse.

A mother ought to know her child better than anyone. *I cannot even stop my child from crying. If I were not so focused on politics, perhaps I would be a better mother, a better wife.* Though I desire to return to Versailles, I must bear a son. The family estate, lands, and noble titles cannot be transferred to a daughter. Andre needs a son to cement his legacy.

I cannot fail again. I will not.

Andre finishes his paint and layers his velvets. He picks up his long-handled fan and leaves me, the staff, and our child. I listen to him move down the stairs and relax at sound of the front door.

Paul excuses himself with a bow. Only then do I return to the paper.

Shortly afterward, Loretta scratches at my door.

I open it quickly, happy for company.

Even Loretta's frown is pretty. "Were you hurt?"

"No. He just wouldn't listen."

Loretta whispers, "Which is one of the reasons I'd rather

be the mistress of a king than a lesser man's wife. What does the daily say?"

Though I am loath to do so, I turn the paper to the fashion section.

Loretta studies the drawings. "Most women still wear large wigs, but it's always best to be ahead of trends."

I open my wardrobe and inspect an old wig, which had not been to the hairdresser in eighteen months. During our parents' time, the king gifted lace and taffeta, but those days are long over. Andre's mother's gowns and masks were so far out of fashion, one might think I dressed for a masquerade.

"If we don't wear wigs, it will keep down the expense," Loretta says.

"Andre will appreciate that." I twist my wedding ring. "Lor, I can't stop feeling afraid."

"Of what?"

I turn the paper back to the front page. "Our sovereign continues to persecute Huguenots. I fear we ought to convert, but Andre won't listen. Maman and Papa are away from Court. The Dragonnades kill people, Loretta. If something happens..."

"Calette, fear not. When I succeed, I'll protect our family," Loretta says with the ultimate confidence of a young girl on the brink of her debut.

Even the slight faux pas of using my childhood moniker just shows her courage. Jealous of her assurance and freedom, I wish I could be as brave as she.

"Or if I convert, it will be easier for you to follow my lead. Or we could always throw ourselves upon the king's mercy. He's the rarest of gentlemen."

I met her eye. I must make someone understand my fear. "If that's true, why would the king allow the Dragonnades?"

Loretta points at my gown. "Your natural hair will look beautiful against the ivory and gold lace edging."

The transition is clumsy, but she will learn as I had.

I adjust the green sash of the gown I will wear for my grand return. The contrasting ribbon lacing and bows, which I harvested from one of my mother-in-law's old gowns, are dyed with a rare violet color only found in some rural province in France... Andre had been pleased when I asked if I might use the ribbons. They remind him of his dearly departed mother.

"You know what would look pretty with violet? My string of theater pearls," Loretta suggests.

I allow my younger sister to style my hair. She is correct. We can do the new English style and save on the hairdresser. If we scrimp, perhaps Andre will not insist on such a long confinement next time.

Chapter 2

Loretta

5th of March

Cher Journal,

Paris is burning! My debut has been ruined! My lovely harp is gone forever.

It all happened tonight while practicing the harp in my room.

Outside, I heard Andre's ragged voice and another man's.

I peeked out the door and followed the voices downstairs. Andre spoke to a messenger. He sounded worried. Holding a parchment, he slammed the door in the messenger's face.

"Andre?"

By the hard look in his eye, I understood why Pascaline feared her husband.

"Gather your jewels and silks. You're leaving," he ordered.

"But my debut," I cried.

His voice shot up an octave. "Has been canceled. Go."

When I didn't move, he pushed me toward the stairs. "You must hurry, do as I say. Pack any valuables. You're leaving Paris."

Pascaline

I smell smoke. Careful not to disturb my maid, Anne-Marie, and the nursemaid, Jaqueline, who lay on pallets on the floor behind a brass screen, I slip out of bed. My hands open the expanse of the lace-edged velvet curtains that hang at the windows. Something burns, but I cannot see it through the haze other than an orange light beyond the trees. I pray the fire does not approach the townhouse.

Outside, men's voices grow louder.

Andre rushes up the stairs in half-dress, his hand on Loretta's arm. His blond hair is loose and flaps against his shoulders. His face is a mask of panic, made more grotesque by white paint still in the creases.

Loretta has tears in her eyes.

I hope she has not caused injury to her reputation so soon.

He bellows, "Loretta, do as I say."

She runs into her room.

"Mon cher, what is it?" I ask.

"Get the baby and gather your jewels. I've called the footman."

"Where are we going?"

He keeps walking, leading me back into the bedchamber. "I expect things to fade away without serious consequences, but these soldiers...they aren't gentlemen."

"What are you trying to tell me?"

He pinches his eyes shut. "The king commandeered our

house as barracks. They'll be here soon. The stories I've heard. Take Loretta and the baby. You must escape Paris."

Icy terror in my chest halts my fury about feeling unheard. I knew what the Dragonnades had done...what they would do.

He kneels and shakes the servants. "Anne-Marie, Jacqueline, wake up."

They awake with a start.

"Collect the silver and wake the chambermaid. The women leave for the country."

"Yes, Monsieur," the women say in unison.

"I pray you'll be safe in Poitou. Your father is unimportant," Andre says.

I open the safe and grab my jewels. If Andre had listened, he would know I will not travel to Poitou. I must act quickly and speak in such a way as will not lead to a quarrel. With my best manners and sweetest tone, I ask, "My husband, would it not be better to go to Helena's? They are a Catholic family and closer."

"Yes, go to your sister's. Her husband isn't known at all."

I quickly dress in a travel gown, tie the jewelry bag to my waist, and place it under my middle petticoat. I grab my perfumes and most beautiful silks and shove them into my trunk. Andre grabs the baby's basket of diapers and swaddling.

Celeste makes a grumpy mewing sound as Andre removes her from the bassinet.

I have never seen Andre check an infant's diaper. Yet, he does. After he ensures our daughter's comfort, wraps her in a blanket and presses his lips to her downy head, he places her into my arms. Though he has also never done a stitch of physical labor, with a grunt, my husband hauls the trunk out the door.

"Loretta," I call.

Loretta rushes from her room, holding a bag of jewelry, a few silk dresses, her traveling cloak, and perfume. "Please, Andre, don't make me go."

Andre sets the trunk on the floor and tosses the lid open. He crosses the corridor in a single step and grabs the girl's wrist. The bottle of perfume crashes onto the floor and smashes into a puzzle of sparkling shards. The smell of lavender and roses tickles my nose.

"There's no time, ma chérie. You must get away." He seizes her things and heaves them into the trunk.

Loretta's lip trembles. "But—"

"I won't hear another word about it. Don't make your sister chastise you in front of the servants. A noble girl knows better."

Sobbing loudly, Loretta hurries down the stairs. Andre lifts the trunk with another grunt.

Anne-Marie sets a basket of silver next to the front door. She and the chambermaid hold bags of personal belongings. The footman opens the front door and helps Loretta into the carriage, then Anne-Marie, and Jacqueline.

We step upon the portico; the smell of smoke grows stronger. Andre transfers the trunk to the footman and, with his hand on mine, my husband puts me in the carriage.

"Things will get better. I once fought for the king. Even if we are Huguenots, he won't forsake us now."

"My love, come with us!" I cry.

Andre smiles sadly. He kisses my lips and presses a bag

of coins into my hands. "Am I your love?"

"You're the only man I ever loved."

"Fear not, then. I don't mean to be martyred, but if we're to have any future, I must remain."

Andre gives our driver directions to Helena's and passes him funds for the horses' care. He taps the carriage, and it sets off into the night.

Loretta cries softly and above, the chambermaid screams from the roof seat.

I open the carriage curtain. Our church burns. "Andre ought to have come with us," I say, pressing Celeste closer to my breast. She, too, starts to cry. Jacqueline opens her blouse "Should I take her, Madame?"

I hand my infant to the nurse and turn my attention to Loretta. Her tears make trails on her powdered face. "If only the king knew me," she whimpers. "My gown. My theater jewelry. I-I...failed."

Beside her, Anne-Marie whispers, "Don't cry, Madame. Monsieur is a good man. He'll make things right. You'll still debut."

The carriage sways and jumps as rocks crack against the metal-covered wheels on the bumpy road to the east. The smell of Paris and humanity evaporate into the smells of manure and spring pollen.

I shove the paralyzing fear into the abyss where I keep all things frightening. Yet, I cannot help but worry about my husband. Goodness will not save Andre.

For all I know, he is already dead. *Then, what will become of us?* I should never have been away from Versailles for so long. With beauty and grace, I might have whispered in someone's ear.

I know nothing of the man Father chose for Loretta. Only that he is a wealthy man from a petty noble family without court appointment. "Is your fiancé a Huguenot?"

Though Loretta's face does not change, she sits straighter and presses her fan to her breastbone. "Of course."

"Will he convert to Catholicism?"

"I don't know." Loretta flicks her fan open and cools her brow.

"Will your fiancé protect us?"

Loretta's eyes widen as if she met a sudden understanding of our situation. "Papa built my betrothal upon your marriage. My fiancé will probably recant our betrothal when he gets word of…"

"Andre stepped in front of the executioner's ax so Celeste could escape. Celeste might not have been a son, but he loved her," I say.

Loretta flashes a cold smile. "Did he love you?"

The servants turn their heads, pretending not to see the noble women quarrel.

I refuse to allow the barb to change my expression. A three-day ride on substandard roads between Paris and our sister's husband's estate, even if the weather holds, will be horribly long with quarreling sisters.

"He made love to me as if he loved me, but he never spoke words of love other than our marriage vows. By the look in his eyes, I think so. He loved you, too. When we spoke in our bedchamber, he always told me I must protect your innocence. He is a good man."

"But you warned Andre!"

"Andre never understood how or why King Louis considered his nobles dangerous." Such words are risky to speak in front of the servants. "My mistake was not fighting Andre when he insisted on my confinement. I might've seen this coming earlier. If our parents convert, we ought to be fine, but—"

"Papa won't convert." Loretta clenches her hands into fists. "No, this isn't right. Why would soldiers hurt us? What have we ever done?"

"The country has been divided for some time. The sovereign abides no dissidents."

"I don't want to be a dissident; I want to be a courtier."

I suppress my rising temper. "Loretta, we need a plan, and I don't have your boldness."

Loretta regards me. "The first thing we must do is to sew coins and gems into our corsets, perhaps petticoats?"

"Indeed, we should," I say. "Thank you, sister, for trusting me. Papa won't hear women, and Maman won't disobey him."

"That old cow follows the bull." Loretta rolls her eyes.

I take my sister's hand. "I know little of Helena's husband."

"Do you believe him not an ally?" Loretta asks. "He's bourgeoisie, but Helena's letters always speak highly of him."

Helena's letters are filled with tales of her children, mother-in-law, younger sisters-in-law, and Jean-Pierre, the man who dotes upon them. Still, as a married woman, I wonder. "Helena would speak highly of him whether or not he is worthy. He's her husband.

"We've time to think. Three days at least."

Loretta presses her lips together and nods.

Once fed, the baby falls back to sleep. Anne-Marie and Jacqueline snuggle with each other. I hope the chambermaid is all right above.

Loretta and I dress correctly as our tight quarters allow, ensuring our woolen travel gowns are in the complete state. With the energy of youth, Loretta watches out of the window while she sews coins into my and her third petticoats. I help for a time, yet I cannot keep my eyes open with the rhythmic rocking of the carriage.

Loretta

5th of March continued

Cher Journal,

We've been set upon the world without protection—all because we come from a Huguenot family. If we were braver, we would've converted without our father and Andre's permission. We should've gone to Versailles without permission.

The world is beyond evil, so evil it cast three noble-born ladies and their women upon it.

I don't know where the carriage halted. I peered out of the curtains into darkness. The stars twinkled above; the moon was but a sliver. The night is cold and deep. In the distance, there might be a fire, but trying to gauge its distance seemed impossible. Moreover, gendarme patrolled the roads. If Pascaline was right, who knew if they could be trusted?

"The road's unpassable, Madame," the coachman said as he dismounted. "I'll build a fire, tether the horses. We shall make the next town in the morning."

"Thank you, good man." I said, but thought: Why didn't we think to gather food?

Jacqueline could feed Celeste, but the rest of us would be hungry.

The charwoman came into the carriage and slept on the floor. The women leaned upon each other. I could hear the coachman and footman whispering. They worried about what it meant for their future to be escorting us. I sewed coins into our petticoats until the firelight died, then squished back into the carriage beside my sister.

Chapter 3

Loretta

Morning of 5th of March

Cher Journal,

Everyone's tempers were hostile this morning, as we all ache from the cold night and we have no food. Though the men were tired, they connected the horses to the carriage and set off again.

No one said much of anything as the carriage moved toward Thaisis, except Pascaline mentioned the city had a long history and stood since Roman times.

We've arrived, and it certainly looks it. We've fallen so far.

Pascaline

I fear Thaisis. The buildings are ancient brick and old timbers. Most do not have glass in the windows. We pass a few factories, farms, and deeper into the middle of the town, merchant homes. Loretta worked hard into the night to sew gems and coins into our petticoats and stomachers of our travel gowns. I thank God for that.

The town is not organized for the modern gentleperson. The carriage stops in front of the only inn—the type of foul place my women and I have never been. Outside, children in rags huddle against the darkness. Their snores are broken by coughs.

The footman helps us down.

I think it strange the footman tells Jacqueline to give me Celeste. Something passes between them. I foolishly think he wants a tumble. The driver takes the carriage to the stables to rest the horses.

I hold Celeste tightly as we open the door and witness the establishment's reputation. A crass woman, with pustules covering her lips, touches men without impunity or charm. But the men laugh. They enjoy it. In the corner, another woman leads two men up a narrow staircase.

The rotting wood walls smell of urine. It is warmed by a small fireplace with a sputtering fire, kept alive by bundles of sticks. Doves nest in the thick rafters and cover them with bird droppings. The tables and benches are covered in filth, too. The inn might stain our gowns but, at least, it keeps rain off our heads.

Celeste laughs and waves in ignorance, as babies do.

The landlady's face is caught in simmering rage. "Get out." Her eyes move over the crowd. A peculiar notion runs up my spine. There are spies or soldiers about.

"Please, could we purchase beer and bread for six and milk, if you have it, for the babe?"

Maliciousness grows in the woman's eyes. Her expression exposes that kindness and pity had been long seared away. "Four Louis."

Beside me, Anne-Marie curses under her breath. Her face tightens into a frown.

Four? I fish four single Louis coins from my pocket-purse and push them toward the woman. A jug of goat's milk, beer, and six small loaves of crusty bread are more expensive than I hoped. *How am I to pay and feed the servants?*

Unused to carrying Celeste, my shoulders burn under my daughter's weight.

When I turn back toward the other women, the expression on Anne-Marie's face articulates the truth of the matter before her words: "I'm a hard worker and a Catholic. Madame will attest to this before she leaves. May I have a job?"

My forearm muscles twitch. My vision blurs as I fight tears. This is no place to weep. Weakness will be a detriment here.

My heart feels the betrayal, but my head understands. If Anne-Marie stays with me, she might be raped and murdered alongside us. We know nothing of Helena's household. If the master of the Château Durrant is cruel, he might rape or beat her. He might release my servants. Where would they be?

"She was a good servant."

"Monsieur hasn't paid me," Anne-Marie says.

Loretta's ivory skin goes a shade paler as her eyes widen.

I hand Anne-Marie a two Louis d'or coin.

Her hard expression softens. "Madame, walk in caution. Tell your sister to do the same."

Not sure exactly what the maid refers to, I grip the baby more tightly to my chest. We shuffle toward the door with our supplies, set the beer mugs on the table closest to the door, and step outside to call the men.

Beside me, Loretta yelps. I turn to see our charwoman running down the street from the stables, a silver pitcher in her hand, and a smirk on her face. Jaqueline runs the other way. She glances toward us, and her eyes open wide. There seems to be a moment of tenderness. Then, braids and skirts flying, she, too, I realize, has been paid with silver from the trunk.

I watch our escaping servants dumbly. I never thought I might be betrayed.

Mon Dieu, why did Andre insist on a nursemaid? My breasts have dried; I have no milk for our daughter. Goat's milk would do, but we have so little coin. Confusion, fear, and hunger fog my mind.

My coachman mouths, "Run."

Only then, I see why.

Soldiers rifle through the carriage. I find myself in a strange place of understanding and indignation. The servants had taken what they could before all was stolen.

I grab my sister's wrist and pull her back into the public house.

Beside me, Loretta whispers, "How is this happening?"

Something about Loretta asking, enrages me. I am a lady. I obeyed my father and mother and elder brothers. I submit to my husband even when he is wrong as society dictates I must. I gave him my virginity and never took a lover. Yet, I am ousted with two girls who never harmed a soul.

"Shush. Loretta. Let us breakfast and be on our way."

We gulp the foul-tasting beer and take only our bread and milk with us. We leave the rest, as we have no way to carry it. The coachman enters, walking past us as if he does not see us. He will not look upon us again; perhaps he drank the beer after we left.

"We'll be safe once we get to Helena's?" Loretta's eyes are full of fear.

"We will. Don't lose hope."

We walk around the corner and hurry down another alley. Celeste whimpers as she has not been fed properly. I peer around the corner to find the coach stage building is guarded by men in regimental uniforms. Worse, according to the posted rates, a ride on the public coach cost more than our means.

Eyeing Loretta's gown and hat, I realize how exposed we are. Thankfully, no embroidery pattern screams we were Huguenot. Only quality announces our station. Women with means would have an escort and would not use a public coach.

"What will we do? How will we..." Loretta trails off.

We duck back into the alley. A three-day drive would take how long on foot?

Celeste squirms in my arms, returning my focus to my child. I create a sling from one of my petticoat skirts as if I were a common woman and bind Celeste to my breast. Loretta braids and wraps my hair into a tight bun and tucks it under my hat. I do the same to my sister's hair. I try to give Celeste a bit of milk, but she balks at the taste.

Another dark plume of smoke billows in contrast against the pale sky. In my heart, I know it is another Protestant church. We walk toward it to see it burn. The Royal Army's soldiers throw flaming torches through the windows, laughing in triumph. We walk on without stopping.

Loretta

5th of March continued

Cher Journal,

My sister and I have never been to such a foul place as this neighborhood. Dirty hovels spill smoke out windows and makeshift chimneys. Men roar at their women and children. We passed a toothless, old woman selling wilted cabbages. Another sold salted sardines.

A pimp asked if we wanted to join. "It's good-easy money."

We darted away, listening to his and his harem's laughter on our backs.

Still, we did not turn from our errand. Every type of goods lined the window of the brick brokerage house: jewels, plates, pipes, tools, sheets and gowns, old wigs, and last year's fashions.

Pascaline took care not to show too much and had our first sale at the ready.

I clutched Pascaline's hand as we walked into the dim hovel. In her other hand, she clutched the golden pendant shaped like a smooth tear with a sparkling sapphire.

A dirty child cried, "Baby!" from a broken cradle. The careworn mother rocking it, nodded.

"We wish to sell this necklace," Pascaline said to a greasy-haired broker who had long sold his incisors.

The broker examined it. He took a pick and tapped the

back. "Four, mademoiselle."

Pascaline did not correct him. "Please, it's real gold. It must be worth more than four?"

"Four, and it's a gift I don't call the gendarme..."

"It's not stolen," Pascaline said.

"Or perhaps the Royal Army?"

My sister accepted four Louis d'or, and we escaped the dirty little house.

"I fear selling too much at once. As things stand, we dare not throw ourselves on the king's mercy," Pascaline whispered.

We slowly wandered. I felt a lump grow in my throat that threatened to burst out as tears.

"In Paris, perhaps, I could sing, but this little town... How much does a street singer make, do you think?"

Though we spent years adjusting our posture for court, Pascaline's gait loosened in front of my eyes. She stared at nothing except the crumbling brick wall in front of us. For a moment, I feared she might faint into the manure and mud-covered street. Celeste made a yawning whimper. She looked at Celeste, at me, back to the baby.

As the Huguenot church was smoking rubble, we slipped inside the Catholic Church, hoping for sanctuary.

No one greeted us. The building seemed empty. We sank into a pew.

"Why do you think the servants turned on us?" I asked my sister in a hushed tone. I wanted her wisdom and assurance more than an answer.

Pascaline closed her eyes. "Because the tide has turned. I don't blame them." Except her voice betrayed she did blame them. Or herself. Or Celeste—for which she must have hated herself. She covered her eyes with her hand and rocked to comfort my niece.

I squeezed her in a quick embrace. "I won't leave you… or Celeste,"

"What are you Huguenot whores doing in here?" a priest shouted as he raised a cane above his head.

"We wish to con—" Pascaline began.

"Have you, whores, no respect for the True Church!"

The cane cracked against the pew. He lifted his cane again. We darted away. The clatter of the cane hitting the stone floor echoed after us.

Pascaline

Through the day's drizzle, we walk until we are far away from town. Our woolens grow wet from rain while our linens grow damp from sweat. When the sun falls below the horizon, we step off the road into a thick grove of pine. We pass bare branches with tiny green buds reaching for the sky like children reach for their mothers. Small animals flee from our footsteps like we fled from our enemies.

Before day leaves us completely, we find a bare and flat spot to lie.

I let Celeste out of the makeshift sling and allow her to crawl upon the ground while Loretta and I clear the debris away.

Celeste finds a small stick and snaps it in half. She laughs in delight at the sound. I wonder if a baby's laughter might bring someone evil upon us, but we are utterly alone.

My child puts a piece of stick into her mouth and chews. I laugh to imagine Andre's anxiety. In this darkened glen, the wood is probably the cleanest thing here. Though cold, one cannot deny the raw beauty of the place. The deep, heavy branches of evergreen trees stand sentry. These trees shelter us between verdant ferns, white fungus, and tiny golden buds pushing through the earth.

We split another loaf of bread and soak the softest pieces in goat's milk for Celeste. Though first, she turns away from the soaked bread, she is too hungry not to eat.

Footsore and exhausted from our exertions, we place the baby between us and fall asleep until Celeste wakes crying. I sit up with a start. I see nothing in the darkness. I reach for my baby and put her on my chest under the sling. She calms and nestles into me, but I cannot sleep.

Chapter 4

Loretta

10th of March

Cher Journal,

The worst thing happened today. I learned something about allyship I did not wish to learn. I'm so shaken, I'm not even sure if I can write about it yet, but I know beyond a doubt I can trust Pascaline. No matter how forsaken we are, my sister is my friend.

Pascaline

"The sun sets in the west, which means we shall generally be moving west if we use the setting sun as our guide." I try to sound confident about my direction. Closing my eyes, I attempt to picture the route we took when I came to Paris to be a bride.

The roads in Paris or Versailles are well-maintained, though many between smaller towns are no more than rotting paths. Many villages stand, pungent with loathsome air and fetid with smoke from the burning churches and homes.

"Are we near Chateau de Benefiel, do you think?" Loretta

asks suddenly.

I look around. "I believe you're correct."

The Benefiels had been a friend of my father and elder brothers for years. His son was at Versailles, but the elderly viscount had returned to the country for health reasons. As a gentleman and member of the court, Georges, Viscount de Benefiel, must give us sanctuary in our need.

At the border of his lands, we call to his gendarme, who hurry to us. I introduce myself, and one bows his head. A few men look familiar.

Loretta tears a page out of her journal and sends word ahead of our need. His guard apologizes for only having a wagon, but the wagon carries us to the great house.

His footman opens the door to expose Georges de Benefiel aged even further in the two years since I had seen him. He looks mildly unkempt in half-dress with an unruly white wig. Lead paint and several star-shaped beauty velvets conceal his aging face. The heavy bags under his observant eyes tell of exhaustion. Yet, he cocks his head at a jaunty angle as he appraises us.

He does not move us immediately into the parlor. Rather, we stand in the hall like common visitors. Benefiel playfully taps his walking stick in his hand. I do not like the innocent-looking affectation. I half-expect him to strike us. "If you're willing to convert, Mesdames, I will bring you into my home."

"We wish to convert but don't know how," I say.

"That can be done easily enough." In a cold voice, he asks, "Have you been virtuous?"

My heart skips a beat. I no longer trust this situation or

the look in his rummy eyes. "Yes, Viscount Benefiel."

"You came directly to me for aid?"

"We were waylaid on our way to Helena's. We hoped you might send a message to our brother-in-law or Papa. We'd be most grateful."

"How grateful?" He turns to Loretta.

I observe the darkened mark on his neck and slight tremble of his hand on the cane. *The pox?*

Loretta gives him a nervous smile and hides her face behind her dirty fan. A hot flash sears my heart and spreads throughout my body, pooling into my tingling fingers and toes. Andre warned me about men like this. She is still an innocent. I am not. I narrow my stance.

Ignoring our obvious discomfort, he reaches for my sister.

Loretta steps back with a cry.

Benefiel's gendarme do nothing. Would they not protect a lady?

"So, you've been a virtuous girl," he says.

I step in front of her. I fear the words I have to say but speak them for Celeste and Loretta's sake, "If love is required for your protection...for your help...for a letter to our brother-in-law and our brothers...I will—"

Benefiel bangs his cane on the floor to interrupt me. One of Benefiel's gendarme takes me by the arms. Celeste makes a shriek worthy of a banshee.

"No, I need a virgin," Benefiel says.

"You need a virgin?" I repeat dumbly. Andre told me about this myth. Benefiel wants to put his pain upon Loretta to cure himself. I cannot allow him to separate us. I must think quickly.

"Yes. You will be bathed, fed, and protected for her sacrifice until your brother or brother-in-law comes to collect you. The east rooms overlooking the garden will do."

Loretta weeps into her hands. My daughter whimpers, most likely sensing my sister's sorrow.

Benefiel does not react to the girls' tears. He rings a bell and speaks to his steward.

"Won't you help us?" I cry.

Their faces set in stoic frowns; the two gendarmes do nothing to assist us.

"Allow me to prepare my sister so she understands what's expected," I say quickly.

Benefiel nods and gestures at his men to escort us upstairs.

Loretta collapses and cries until her whole body shakes. The man lifts her in his arms and carries her as if she is a child. We are put into the east room. "A woman shall be in shortly."

Once alone, I press my ear to the door and hear retreating footsteps. I grab Loretta's hand and pull her to her feet. "We're leaving."

I loathe the distrust in her big blue eyes.

"We are?" she asks.

"Yes, so be quiet. I don't know how much time we have."

I hurry to the window and open it. "What luck!"

Beyond the thick stone window ledge stands a trellis, heavily laden with thick thorny rosewood and winter-browned leaves.

I look to the ground and wish I had not. I take a shaky breath. "Over the past days, we've grown stronger than we were."

"Yes," Loretta says.

I point. "Do you think you can make it across the ledge to the roses?"

"How will you escape?"

"I'll be behind you." I check the knots on Celeste's sling. I tie her tighter to me. "Go. Go now and don't look back."

Loretta climbs out the window. She crawls over the ledge, pressing herself against the stone house. Each movement seems to take forever. I pray for time. She grasps onto the nearest piece of the trellis and pulls herself onto it. It cracks under her weight, but she descends.

"Celeste, hold on to Maman with all your might," I whisper. "God protect my child."

Holding Celeste with one hand and my other on the ledge, I follow my sister.

Below me, the ground spins. I rock back and forth, before pressing myself against the wall, and scoot hand by hand to the rose trellis. I want to hurry because I fear the knots of the sling will not hold and Celeste might tumble to her death, yet I must go slow to ensure we do not fall. If I fall, Celeste falls. If I fall, I will fall on Loretta. *I must do this. I mustn't be afraid.* With sweat-covered hands, I seize the trellis. It creaks with every step. I grow dizzy. Another step downward. Another step downward, another groan from the rosewood. Another step. A thorn pierces my hand.

I gasp as hands grip my waist. I manage to bite my lip before I scream. It is not a soldier but only Loretta who assists my last steps to the soft, muddy ground. I press my lips into a weak smile.

Her sun-kissed skin is slick with sweat, glowing with life and something else I cannot place. My sister and I race across the garden to the wall. Celeste laughs as the sling bounces. We make it to the wall and follow it until we find a crumbled spot low enough to climb over, assisting each other.

We follow the road away from the château and on the long path to Helena's home.

"Will he come after us?" Loretta whispers.

"I doubt it. They'll likely search the house first, then the grounds. They would never believe we escaped through a window!" The bubble of fear in my chest rises to my throat. I giggle.

Mimicking me, Celeste giggles, too.

"I can't believe we did either. I'd never have thought we could. Papa and Claude and all the others wouldn't have believed it either. "

"Lor, we ought to hide from any gendarme we see."

She agrees. Seeing Celeste mimicking us, Loretta makes a funny face, which Celeste tries to imitate. My heart fills with joy at my baby's laughter. My sister is still innocent.

"How did you know it would hold?" Loretta's voice rises an octave.

In a singsong voice, I say, "I didn't, but better to fall than die from the slow pox that contemptible louse would've given you. Moreover, he would've thrown us out when your virginity hadn't healed him."

"Healed him?" By her expression, Loretta did not understand the danger she had been in. She knows she would be raped, but the whole truth is much worse. I quickly debate if I should tell her, but ignorance leads to danger.

In order to not frighten Celeste, who may cry or scream if we stop smiling, I explain in a singsong voice, "He thought a virgin would heal his pox. He would've left you ruined so he might live a few years."

Loretta follows my lead. "But his face wasn't marked."

"Many use beauty velvets to cover the marks. As pox remains in the body, it gives men the shakes and sometimes dark marks around the collar. The worst part is, ma chérie, you must drink quicksilver for life to keep the pox at bay."

"How do you know all this?"

"Andre pointed out a few men with pox at court so I might avoid their advances," I say.

"If I gave myself to him, I would've gotten the pox, too?"

"Yes."

The girl is silent for a time. I take one of the silver chains, removed the pendant for the next sale, put my wedding ring upon it, and put it under my collar.

"Callette? Why wouldn't the viscount protect us like he was supposed to?"

"We've nothing to offer."

"But he was friends with Papa, Claude, Alan, Pierre, Gabriel..."

Fearing she might name all our male relatives after she finished listing our brothers, I said, "Not anymore. Being noble-born won't help us. It shall be a long journey, but we must walk to Helena's. I don't know where else to find allies. I fear the costs for sanctuary are too high. Some will be kind, no doubt, but we don't know which ones."

Loretta takes my hand. Her eyes hold so much emotion; her cheeks sparkle with tears. "Thank you for telling me.

Maman never told me much about the pox."

"Gentlemen always claim how they'd happily die in service to a lady, but the gendarmes did nothing. We both have much to learn. I'm beginning to think Andre was a rare gentleman."

She squeezes me while we walk. "He is."

Chapter 5

Pascaline

I see the story on a discarded copy of *La Gazette*: **Marquis de Aubinet Makes Deathbed Confession; Heir-Apparent acknowledges father's Piety.**

My eyes blur as I scan the story. According to the state-run paper, Andre's father spent his last days on Earth appealing to God for his earthly sins. He succumbed to the "grief for his wickedness and those he led astray" on March Second...

I pinched my eyes shut. I feel Loretta shift as she reads over my shoulder.

"Andre is dead," she whispers. "He died a marquis, not the heir apparent. This paper is a lie!"

"When?"

"It says the sixth he succumbed to an old battlefield injury."

I shudder when I think of what Andre must have experienced in those two days. I hug my sister and daughter tightly as I realize what would have happened to us if we had been there.

I glance at the date. Something snaps inside me as I realize Viscount Benefiel would have read this article. He would have known that I outranked him. I was a Marquise for two days. Now I am a Marquise dowager and Benefiel still tried to rape my sister. My husband is dead, and I bore only a daughter rather than a son, so the inheritance will go to the next in line. There is nothing for Celeste. Moreover, I have too few coins and jewels to be anyone.

Tears stream down my face. I choke back a scream. I must get the girls to Château de Durrant, then get word to our parents before it is too late. "Come, Loretta, let us go."

Loretta

14th of March

Cher Journal,

I try to carry my niece, but Celeste cries unless in Pascaline's arms. The child is terrified of her new place in the world. I'm frightened, too. As Pascaline and I walked through these nine days, I have seen torments I did not know existed.

We were told if we acted in grace and obedience, men would protect us. However, we constantly run from soldiers and lecherous men who throw dirty words upon our persons for simply walking nearby. We stop to buy food and supplies but, otherwise, we keep moving toward Château de Durrant. We can find bread and wilted cabbages, but we cannot afford meat or butter at Lent prices, and fruit is non-existent. None of the trees have fruited, yet the sun is hot for spring.

Pascaline bought lumps of lanolin to rub into our hair and skin to protect us from lice. Other bugs bite at us. Everyone knows water is terrible for our complexions. Yet, without our normal toilettes, we wash in dirty streams as we skirt villages. We are never clean enough.

Worse, the jewels on our persons are too valuable to merit much. We can't sell them for anywhere near their worth in rural counties. Ornaments are nothing to the populace, especially at brokerage shops and other second-priced markets.

However, the worst is now the ground softens from warmer weather. We've passed many funerals, especially for babes who did not survive the winter's chill. They have no family plots and no money for priests to sanctify the dead. My sister weeps for each one and holds Celeste tighter.

I never gave a second thought to the life of the peasants until on the road. Farmers worked the fields. Factory workers went to their jobs with hunched backs. Bakers made bread. Yet, in every village, we see starving children, poor men and women huddling against the elements under eaves of buildings and bridges.

Without shelter, we are so cold at night and hot in the day.

Pascaline never complains. Her understanding and acceptance of our fate frightens me. She simply keeps walking. She looks toward the sky, attempting to navigate with the sun.

I've learned to mimic the movements of Catholics. We hide our religion. Yet, we cannot hide our identities. We never mention our noble names and titles, but we are reviled when the populace is famished. It doesn't matter that we starve with them. Every movement, every soft word practiced for the king betrays us. Our teeth are too white; our skin is too soft; the fabric of our gowns too finely woven to hide. My satin slippers are torn and stained by the mud, but they are still satin.

My feet are covered with oozing blisters. Our nails have grown stained with dirt and ash. Heat radiates through the torn lace on my hat. Still, in the day's hottest hours, we rest under the dappled shade of trees and let the baby play. I notice a denser sprinkling of freckles on Pascaline's nose and fear how my complexion fares.

15th of March

Cher Journal,

When Helena's family estate came into view, we believed we were delivered. We walked the cobbled drive with Celeste squirming in Pascaline's arms and generally making a pest of herself, as babies ought to do.

Though a manservant in a linen jacket opened the door, and cried, "Madame de Aubinet, Ma—"

Our brother-in-law, Monsieur Jean-Pierre Durrant, pushed the poor man out of the way and barked, "Leave my property, or I shall call my gendarme and have you thrown in prison, pretenders!"

Helena's husband was a well-off bourgeois rather than a nobleman. The man who stared at us with avaricious cruelty seemed not to be the man from Helena's letters. Indeed, Jean-Pierre had the same uncaring, stoic look when Benefiel reached for me.

"My brother, will you not receive us?" Pascaline asked. Her voice was small and defeated as if she already knew what the horrid beast would say.

"I am no brother of yours. There's a dragoon over that

hill. You think they won't hear I've given Madame de Aubinet sanctuary?"

Helena came from behind him. "But, Husband…"

He turned on Helena, who flinched from his hand. "I'm not taking in three useless women. We have my own people to watch over." He stabbed a finger toward Pascaline. "If your husband was truly a man of the Court, he would've seen this coming and converted to Catholicism like the rest of us."

"I have a little coin, my wedding ring, and a few pieces of jewelry, and we will convert," Pascaline said. "Please, let us in."

He laughed. "I have fields that need tending. Are those lily hands going to work? Think I care if you're Calvinistic or Catholic? The king cares, the dragoon cares, but the country is falling apart. We've no need for worthless women."

Beads of sweat formed on Helena's upper lip. She glanced at her husband and cast down her lids. "What about Loretta and the baby, my love? Loretta's gentle beauty should make a highly prized bride. We could make a good…profitable match."

"So she might be married higher than my sisters? I think not."

I felt a tightening of my stomach, a twisting of all my humours, trying to gather control. Anger and fear were winning. By the wild-eyed look in Pascaline's eyes, she felt the same.

"Please, take the baby," Pascaline cried. "Please, Helena. You can't want a babe to suffer. I'll pay you what I have."

Jean-Pierre scowled. "We have our own children. I don't keep a nursemaid. If you must, Helena, say goodbye to your sisters but don't let them step one foot into my house or I'll oust you, too."

The fear on Helena's face was apparent.

"Please go, sisters," Helena said. "Go home, if you can, or to court and beg sanctuary."

I finally found my voice. "How can you turn your own sisters away?" I asked, lips trembling.

"My husband's people became my people on the day we were wed," Helena whispered. Ineffectual tears formed in her eyes. "I must care for them or I will never see my children."

Hope left my soul as the hot sun beat upon my shoulders. "But your letters..."

Pascaline was crying and made one last attempt to save her child. "Take in the baby, please. Rename her. Let her be yours, just so she lives."

"I...have no influence over my husband; he means what he's said. I will lose mine if I take yours." Helena shook her head. "I'm sorry, but I must protect my own children."

"Your letters have all been fancy lies. All stories are lies," I cried.

Helena glanced behind her and removed the copper and silver bracelet from her wrist. "Loretta, before the sun fades your beauty, sell your virginity to some Catholic courtier who wants a pretty mistress."

Helena turned to Pascaline. "Go to a nunnery and raise your child there. You'll take a vow of poverty, but you'll be safe. The bracelet should pay to get you both away from here."

Though I wanted to throw the thing to the ground, I clasped the bracelet upon my wrist.

The door shut.

Pascaline held Celeste close. "We're in a country of strangers."

To calm myself and focus on anything other than the pain in my heart, I asked, "Do you think Helena's husband only wanted to protect her with that threat? Or was he angry the advantageous match hadn't turned out profitable?"

"Or he might be another windbag with fists and a thing between his legs which makes him the king of his house." Pascaline softly sighed. She sounded like Maman. Defeated.

She stepped off the portico and back onto the drive, though I did not know where she headed. I doubt she knew. Yet, she walked, and I followed.

"Think Papa ever loved us or were we beautiful cows to build his little empire?" Pascaline queried. Before I could answer, she said, "Never mind, these thoughts help no one."

"Yet, sister, these thoughts are also on my mind."

I spied movement of white cloth on a clothesline on the western side of the estate. "Wait...wait here. Hide under that tree."

Ignoring my blistered feet, I dashed toward the clothesline, crawled through bushes, and pulled a piece of ticking off the line. I also saw some linen, which might be used as swaddling, and grabbed those as well. Without looking back, I ran across the field, holding damp laundry in my arms.

No one followed.

"Run!" I called to my sister under the tree. Though walking for days, we were not used to strenuous exercise. We ran, gasping and panting. Pascaline held the baby close. Celeste laughed.

I turned around. "I don't think anyone saw me."

Pascaline's big brown eyes grew rounder. "You stole?"

"Think of it as a gift from the windbag for his infant niece."

I feared Pascaline might be angry, but she giggled.

"Now, let us catch our breath. I must know more about these edicts. I should've paid more attention to our governess, but I didn't."

Fight rose in Pascaline's eyes. "Before the Edict of Nantes, Catholics killed Protestants for owed debts, for refusal to do business. Henry IV made the Edict of Nantes to end the religious wars. Louis XIV wants to recant that. And he will."

"But isn't the Edict of Nantes good?"

"Yes." Pascaline paused to collect her thoughts. "Louis XIV dislikes, well, doesn't trust people who are not like him. But in my opinion, this is about money. King Louis has wars to fight. He needs to raise taxes. The French crown cannot raise taxes without consent from the nobility. We pay some taxes, of course, but many feel we do not pay our fair share. Moreover, many wealthy bourgeois, like Helena's husband, obtained exemptions."

"Exemptions?"

"That was why he married Helena. To send his lady-wife to Versailles and beg for exemptions so he isn't obligated to pay what he owes. I don't doubt Helena serves her husband in that."

Helena also bore the man eight children, yet he just threatened to cast her away. I wasn't sure what to say. "The world's much more mercenary than I expected."

"Don't feel bad, Lor; I didn't know these things until I married. When I first saw Court, I was dazzled. However, I started listening to whispers and saw the hypocrisy." Pascaline paused and looked to the sky. "Perhaps that's why Andre kept me at home. He feared I would speak my mind." Tears crested.

"Where do we go?" I asked.

"We must return to our father and convert to Catholicism. If we make it before a dragoon is billeted into the estate, we might save our family name yet."

"Let us begin."

Pascaline gently squeezed my hand. "I'm frightened but glad you're beside me."

"I'm glad you're beside me, too."

We took the first step north.

My elder sister further instructed me on taxation inequities, the most crucial reason France's peasants hated the nobility—though they still loved their king. She reminded me the king did not trust the nobility either, and if the beloved Louis XIV did not trust the noble class, how could the peasants?

Cher Journal, I did not know all these things. Everything I was told to believe in was lies. Most of all, I do not know if the king is "the rarest of all gentlemen" anymore. Even if he was, I no longer believe he will die in the service of a lady.

Chapter 6

Loretta

20th of March

Cher Journal,

We wear the ticking I stole from my brother-in-law during the day to offer some protection from the unrelenting sun. At night, we hang it from low branches to shelter us.

Our feet bleed as our slippers tear open, but we walk. Our gowns grow dirtier and even more ripped. Still, Pascaline ensures we remain clean enough to combat foul air and famished earth. I admit, once I broke into tears from hunger; Pascaline told me to just keep walking. We will be safe and well fed if we can get home.

Yet, I sense there is more that she is not telling me. She is scared, too.

I wish there was some way I could assist her.

Pascaline

A fragment of ripped paper tumbles down the road, drifting on the wind. I pluck the crumpled pamphlet off the road. It complains of luxurious palace meals for the nobility while the populace starves. I do not know how to use this information or even who it was for. Most farmers are illiterate. I note how the pamphlet does not explicitly blame the king for his meals—only the nobility. *No one could charge the publisher with treason,* I think ruefully. *Was this for high-ranking merchants like Helena's husband? Is this how he knew to convert before soldiers came?*

Why hadn't Andre listened?

"What are you doing with that?" Loretta asks.

"It's to be a cold night, perhaps we can start a fire," I say.

Celeste squirms in the sling. She must be wet. I wonder if I should let her crawl on the road for short periods of time. Perhaps, it's better to keep her clean. *How can I be such a worthless mother?*

My sweet plump sister had grown harder as her cheeks became hollow. She stopped talking about seducing the king or a wealthy duke after we lost our soft stomachs, the standard of a true French beauty. Each day we looked less the noblewomen we were. Perhaps that was for the best.

We sell another necklace for a pittance, but luck is with us as I spy a wig maker's shop.

Nothing feels more wonderful than a comb running through our hair, even though the clipping of shears made me wish to weep. Loretta sits bravely through the ordeal, tears in her eyes as her beautiful strawberry-blonde hair drifts into the basket below.

Our pockets are filled with fifty Louis d'or. I do not know how long it will last.

We buy bread, milk, and another lump of lanoline soap to wash with and leave the town following the road west. Thankfully, I see a sign at a crossroads. We head in the right direction!

Though walking slows us, it also offers us the opportunity to hide from gendarmes who patrol the roads and highwaymen who attack the coaches. We run from any group of men without women, especially soldiers. So far, that has kept us safe.

In rural areas, we gather early wood violets, one of the few flowers I know is edible since I have seen them upon cakes.

As we walk, Loretta asks many questions, which I

answer as I am able. Distress grows in her eyes as she learns about the world. I wonder if I am turning her unmarriageable. That will not do. I must find some way to see Loretta's and, one day, Celeste's happiness and security. Though unfair, a woman's security ultimately lies with her husband's position.

The husband, whoever he is, would need to be Catholic, and he must be kind. Yes. Kindness. That is the first thing I will look for in husbands for my sister and daughter.

I am assured we are alone, Loretta sings in her sweet, well-trained voice, an old crib song with repeating verses to please the baby. She fingers the air as if she recalls what her harp felt like under her hands.

Celeste mimics the tone. She cannot yet talk, so she is not quite singing, but I love the babble pouring from her lips. I feel as I once was and sing with them, but my voice sounds strange, unpracticed. Worse, it has been cracked by the pain of childbirth and weeping from the sting of an angry husband.

Remembering I loved Andre and hated him at times, I desire to understand why the world allows, no, encourages, violence to poison love—because I did love him. I had wanted to marry Andre from the first moment I saw his broad shoulders and perfect smile. I thought myself luckiest of women until the first time I angered him. I stopped singing after that.

Loretta slides her voice into another crib tale, a song best sung as a duet. With her bright blue eyes upon me, she encourages me to join her for the second part.

I do. It will not do to dwell upon what cannot be changed. Moreover, the road ahead of us is long.

Loretta

30th of March

Cher Journal,

Selling our hair was a stroke of genius on Pascaline's part. We finally have enough money when the opportunity comes to purchase food. Unlike our teeth, hair would grow back.

Each night, Pascaline prays to God for charity and mercy for Celeste and me, but I am not sure I believe there is mercy in France.

Two days ago, we passed a convent where nuns took pity upon us and gave us a loaf of bread. Most convents were overrun with street urchins and orphans. They cannot accept women or even offer them a night's shelter.

Today, I tried to sing for bread as we passed a village, but men and women alike called us slatterns, griselles, and whores. In their eyes, we are adventuresses who denied God's plan, reached beyond our station, and now suffer because of it. I suppose it's good they didn't know we are Huguenot as well.

Two younger men said something I did not understand.

Pascaline grabbed my hand and ran. I thought she might be cross, but she was simply sad.

"Until we arrive home, it's best that we don't draw attention to ourselves. There is something under this hot sun which seems to make everyone angry."

Chapter 7

Loretta

22nd of April

Cher Journal,

I awoke to the church bells. As custom, they have been silent since Good Friday.

I remember the story about how the bells fly to Rome to be blessed by the pope and come back with treats for the children. Our father never allowed us to listen to such folktales as he felt they were simply aspects of the Catholic idolatry, but we heard the tale from other children. We slipped into the next village and came across the mayor and a few members of the local gendarme cheerfully setting out red-dyed eggs in the bushes for the local peasantry.

Careful not to draw attention to myself, I snagged three boiled eggs and slipped them in my bundle. It is not really stealing, after all. They are for the community.

We hid under a tree and ate them. Pascaline carefully peeled Celeste's and broke it into small pieces. I am not sure how much she actually consumed, but she seemed to enjoy gumming the egg and making a mess.

We attended Mass, standing in the back with

commoners. After the service, the priests gave away more eggs and loaves of honey-sweetened bread. The church was full of people begging. Food in hand, we left.

7th of May

Cher Journal,

Food has become more abundant since Easter but still very expensive. Many are hungry. We do not know how long our money from the wigmaker will last. Pascaline has begun to barter as if she's a common woman. My sister is the bravest woman I know.

We arrived in our county without crossing the Dragonnades. Elation grew in my heart. Pascaline smiled often as we were but one day away. She even joked how Mother might need vapors when she cast her eyes upon us: barefoot, dilapidated, and covered in filth.

Before the light faded, we made camp in what we prayed would be our final night in the rough.

Howling lingered in the night air. It grew closer. The ground shook from a multitude of soft padded feet. Pascaline peered into the darkness. I was not ready to be yanked from our bedding and pressed into the nearest large tree.

"Climb!" she shouted.

I reached for the first branch. Pascaline pushed on my legs to get me up. From my perch, I saw movement in the underbrush. "Hurry, they're coming! Give me the baby."

My sister passed me the sling, and I scrambled higher once Celeste was safely bound to my chest.

My sister tried to lift herself onto the lowest branch,

but the wolves were too close to turn her back on them. She let herself fall and picked up a large branch. I heard a terrible cracking, and a howl became a shout. A naked man approached.

I had never seen a naked man before. My cheeks burned with embarrassment. Fear overcame me as he licked his lips. I tightened my grip on the trunk.

His nostrils expanded and he sniffed her with a terrible gleam in his eyes.

My sister shouted at the towering, hairy man. "Get away!" She started to shake. "I don't want to hurt you!"

Clutching the trunk, I stupidly shouted, "The loup-garous are real!"

The man took another step toward her, "You? Hurt me, pretty one?" He laughed a terrible, deep cackle.

From my vantage point, I could see that the loup-garou behind this first group wore belts with bundles of cloth. Some wolves even pulled carts with infants and tots asleep in piles of hay. Others transported goods.

"Leave me be, Goodman, or I shall swing; I swear by God I will." I heard rage and panic in my sister's voice, but I did not know how to help her.

He stepped even closer. "I like a girl with fire..."

Behind him, another wolf growled upon approach.

With another horrible cackle came another lean man with tawny eyes. Like the other, his muscular, sun-kissed body was naked. The man shrugged and howled as he turned into a wolf. It sounded as if a thousand hands cracked their knuckles. He loped away.

Pascaline continued to hold out the stick, but the

wolfman put his hands up. "Have you seen the Dragonnades, travelers?"

Pascaline did not change her stance, yet she spoke in her court voice, "We hope to remain behind the lines, Goodman, or far in front."

"As are we."

Pascaline bit her lip and ventured a question, "Tell me, did you pass Château de Fabron?"

"No, we passed to the south of the château."

"Any word of the family who lives there?"

"None. Perhaps..." he paused. "You might come with us as wives. My kinsman took an immediate liking to you."

Pascaline straightened. "No, thank you. May God watch over you and yours, Monsieur," Pascaline lowered the stick and curtsied. "I shall watch over my charges."

"God's Blessings be upon you, Mesdames."

The man bowed and retook his wolf form.

The pack raced into the night. In the short gap between the scouting party and the burdened wolves, Pascaline scaled the tree. She pressed me tighter to the trunk. We sat together, shivering, our dangling feet growing numb until we could no longer hear the echoing howls. We cautiously climbed down.

Celeste slept calmly, so I told Pascaline, "I'll hold her. No reason to wake her again."

Pascaline smiled. "Thank you."

I leaned on the tree trunk and listened to Celeste snoring under my chin. "Calette, how did you speak to two naked men without losing your composure?"

Pascaline shook out our sheet and tucked me and Celeste underneath it. "A lady of the court never hurts a person needlessly. The loup-garous run from the dragoons, or possibly the Royal Army, same as us. Mostly, I found myself wondering if they have their own religion or if they're Huguenots."

"They couldn't be Huguenot. He stood there naked and wholly unashamed." My cheeks grew hot, and I giggled in embarrassment.

Pascaline studied the horizon. "But, ma chérie, he's a wolf, and wolves don't wear trousers."

I laughed harder.

Chuckling, Pascaline cuddled beside us. Yet, she never stopped scanning the horizon. When I awoke, Pascaline had kept watch for the rest of the night.

Pascaline

Loretta, Celeste, and I laugh with such joy when we glimpse the roofline of our family's home in the distance. We run across our father's first wheat field to a large sycamore: where we stop laughing. I no longer know if I will ever laugh again.

Even if I rip out my eyes, it will not erase the memory of the sight before me. Squawking crows encircle the tree that my brothers used to climb. One step more, and a vulture fights with the crows over the rotting flesh of our father, mother, and Claude hanging from a low branch, dressed only in the inner layers of clothing. The outer layers and buttons had been snatched off their bodies and their bloody feet were bare.

Dried excrement spills down their legs and lay in piles on the ground where our sister-in-law lay, nearly naked.

Her chemise torn, blood staining the fabric. Our niece and nephews lie dead beside her.

Numbness spreads across my body; I tighten my grip on Celeste. I cannot breathe. Spasms traverse throughout the muscles in my legs.

I ought to pray for their souls, but I do not see the point. They are dead, forsaken.

Loretta starts to scream, "Ma—"

With the realization we must move, I slap my hand over her mouth and pull my crying sister close.

I hear voices in the distance.

Fearing we might be caught, I run, dragging Loretta by the hand.

"The crows... The crows ate their eyes," Loretta keeps repeating. "Maman. Oh, Maman."

I wish my sister would be quiet but say nothing. This time, I will not allow Loretta to know what I know of our mother, sister-in-law, and elder nieces' fate. That would be too cruel. I can never let what happened befall her or my Celeste.

With one arm on my baby and sister in hand, I run until my heart screams from exhaustion and terror. I don't know where we might go. Only that we cannot remain near the chateau or anywhere we might be recognized as daughters of Claude Fabron, the elder, or sisters of Claude, the younger. Are Alan, Pierre, and Gabriel also dead? They must be.

As Andre warned, the soldiers are not gentlemen— even those who might be gentleman by birth. No wonder Helena fears her husband; she and her children have no other protection.

I remember the wolf's offer. We know which way they

headed. Loretta and I can learn to be common women. Common wives. Might we catch up to them?

That night, we hide in a field, huddled together as we had for six weeks. I love my sister. *I might choose to die as a lady, but if I died, what would happen to Celeste? Perhaps I ought to drown both of us? Harm Celeste? Never.* Poor women feed their babies; I must learn to do the same, but Loretta does not need to suffer these indignities.

I whisper to my sister's back, "Helena was right. You should find a protector while you're still young and beautiful..."

"What about you?" Loretta asks, turning around.

I cannot answer her. I do not know. "It was cruel of me to keep you beside me. Forgive me." I squeeze her shoulder.

"Why will you not come?"

"Today, I learned the true nature of our situation. We've no protection. I'm a fugitive—wife of a dissident, and Celeste is the daughter of a dissident, but you're not. You only have one tie, publicly convert and get a written record. Kneel at the feet of the king and swear you saw a vision of the Holy Mother—"

"No!"

"Join the Paris Opera's orchestra and use your musical talents. Do whatever it takes to survive. Loretta, I should've told you before how much I love you."

Loretta presses her hands around me. The intensity of her gaze makes me believe the girl peers into my soul. Did she know I considered suicide?

"I shall not leave you. Either of you."

"But—"

"No, Calette. We've witnessed much violence, not just

today. We also witnessed acts of devotion, sacrifice, and loyalty. We will find a way together." The girl presses her lips together. "We still have most of the jewels. We simply must form a plan."

Chapter 8

Loretta

10th of May

Cher Journal,

When I close my eyes, I still see my noble parents hanging from the tree with feces along their legs. I still see the holes in my mother's skull where her eyes used to be.

I try not to dwell on their deaths but our situation. We have no friends left in France.

It took Pascaline and me a few days, but we formed a plan. We had laced our corsets with the necklace chains to keep them clean and untangled. Yet, selling a lovely pendent for a few days' food seemed a waste. As we walked away from another such sale, I asked, "How can we sell them for so little?"

"I don't know what else to do," Pascaline replied. "The king stopped providing passports to Huguenots years ago. Trying to cross a border is risky. Spain and the Holy Roman Empire wouldn't be safe for Huguenots." Pascaline's eyes brightened. "But the Teutonic city-states might be. What if we used the jewelry to bribe border guards?"

"Bribe guards?" I feared Pascaline had lost her sanity.

"Yes, without the king's permission, we cannot cross the border, but maybe we can if we tried to bribe guards. After all, we're only two women with a girl child in tow. What would they care if we left France?"

My lips trembled. "What if I—"

"If it comes to that, I'll sell my body. Your virginity has value, but I've already given my body to a man and had a child."

A rumbling giggle left my lips as inspiration struck. "Oh, mon Dieu! You know what might work?"

"What?"

"What if we covered our faces with beauty marks?"

"Pretend we've the pox?" Pascaline looked skeptical.

"Yes. Let us appear as low worth as possible."

As I searched her eyes to see if she needed more convincing, she threw her arms around me.

"That's brilliant!" she squealed. "They would be thrilled to see us leave France!"

15th of May

Cher Journal,

Though we walked north and east for many days, our ruse did not work. We did not even get close enough to the border to attempt it.

A contingent of the French Royal Army cut us off as they marched to "strengthen France's borders."

We tried to wait until the men, who should've been our protectors, moved on, but with their heavy carts and tents, the army trundled sluggishly. We feared the longer we remained behind the army, the more likely we would be discovered.

Fortunately, we were used to sleeping in the rough because, if we had been in the town, we might have been raped like many of the common women, girls, and boys. The Royal Army is a monstrous, many-limbed and mouthed beast. Soldiers stole men and strong lads from farms and factories. They pillaged and consumed everything in their wake. Food was devoured, and even the wheat in the fields was trampled.

As we traveled behind the army, I've stolen a couple more items of opportunity—a way-lain knife and a tattered straw hat snatched off a scarecrow. Pascaline never says a word about my thievery, but she prays to God for mercy upon my soul when she thinks I'm sleeping.

17th of May

Cher Journal,

It's been a few days of being unable to purchase food, so Pascaline and I have turned west, changing our course for Spain.

Pascaline

Loretta and I have been walking without sustenance, but a day south and we find a merchant willing to sell us bread. Celeste wants to be free of the sling more often. She cannot grow if she is tied to my chest.

Our situation cannot stand.

I should have taken the wolf's offer, but I did not even

consider it. Perhaps if it had been the gentleman who asked for my hand...but no, I am in no position to say no, even to a beast.

I am such a fool. I fear the night, insects that we barely keep at bay, and coming winter. If I were not such a coward, we would walk to Paris. I would get Loretta somehow into the opera. I would give Celeste to a kindly nun. Once my daughter and sister were secure, I would throw myself into the Seine. Unfortunately, I don't know who I can trust to protect them except myself.

Chapter 9

Loretta

1st of June

Cher Journal,

We arrived at another town untouched by the war. Pascaline says she shall try to find work again, but I ought to go to the church and ask for alms.

Pascaline failed and returned to us within an hour, her eyes bitter and desperate. We were not taught to spin, weave, sew, or use machines.

Even by dinner, something haunted her as she passed a loaf of bread to me.

Celeste fussed. Pascaline lost her temper and yelled at us for being ungrateful. Then, she cried, and the baby wailed with her.

I might've comforted my sister if I knew how, but all I could do was cry, too.

Once calm, Pascaline said she would try again tomorrow.

Pascaline

I tell myself I'm no longer de Aubinet, no longer de Fabron. I'm just a woman who needs to find work, same as common women. *I've done needlework; I can learn to sew garments.* With that thought in mind, I follow the line of people shuffling into the door of the garment factory. It is a dirty place, with people who look and smell as if they had not washed in weeks. Regardless, if I find a respectable job, I can keep the girls safe.

"Excuse me," I ask the large sweaty man at the door. I dare not look the foreman in the eye. I must seem a common woman. "I seek work."

"No work for the likes of you, griselle. Can't you read?"

He pushes me away from the door. The little faith I have in people shatters as I hit the gravel.

A woman sneers. "God's judgment is on you for what you've done, slattern." She kicks dirt in my face.

Another woman says, "Your kind of woman don't understand respectable work."

As he passes, a man in line blurts, "I know where you can sell your teeth—or your ass." He cups his manhood.

I rise to my feet, sullied but not broken, and race to the church where I had left Loretta and Celeste. I slip through the heavy wooden door. The pews are empty.

"Loretta?"

No answer. The idea I lost my daughter and sister sinks into the darkest place in my soul. The thought soldiers found them overtakes my good sense. I scream, "Loretta! Loretta!"

No answer except for an old priest brandishing a Bible and telling me to hush and have some decency.

"Have you seen my sister and my child?"

He just shakes his head.

I run back outside. "Loretta! Celeste."

"Woman, what are you doing here?"

My heart stops as two gendarmes approach me. I fear they might search me and find the jewels sewn into my clothing.

"I'm looking for my sister." Tears stream down my face. "She was just here, playing with the baby. Loretta!"

"I'm here," Loretta calls, walking up the embankment. Her threadbare dress drips.

I run to my sister and daughter and fold them into a wet embrace.

"I'm sorry. I didn't mean to frighten you. I thought you'd be longer. Somebody was stinky, so we took a bath in the river. And I washed our laundry," Loretta says too brightly.

A brittle laugh escapes my lips.

"Move along, woman. Next time, I'll charge you for disturbing the peace." The gendarme moves off, muttering about griselles having no sense of decency, and Loretta and I quickly turn the corner and hide in the shade of the church.

A sickly horror grows in my heart, weakening me. Loretta meets my eyes and, as I sink deeper, her ferocity grows. "We're sisters. Celeste is my niece. The others may've forsaken us, but I will never forsake you."

Her expression changes in an instant. "Mon Dieu, Callette, regimentals!"

I turn my head. The gendarmes are bad enough, but

several men in Royal Army uniforms walk in our direction. The men howl licentious words and hoot. My daughter is all the proof of dishonor they need to assume we are prostitutes.

We race toward the edge of town. The soldiers' horrid laughter echoes behind us. Miraculously, they do not follow us far.

Our coin is gone, but we still have some jewelry. It will hold us off a little longer, but winter will come. I need to get my loved ones somewhere safe. Once my sister and baby are sheltered, I will sell bits of myself for their upkeep. If I sell my teeth...my body...what does it matter as long as my daughter and sister might have a chance? But if I sell myself too early, I will contract the pox and the girls will still die.

A stale breeze slips between the trees and enters the cold hole in my heart. Andre would know what to do. I had vowed fealty to him. Yet, I ran when he told me to run. Perhaps I might have stood beside him. Perhaps I might have been a better wife in some way, and none of this would have happened. What is love if not a valiant husband? Had I ever completely become one with him? That is God's, the king's, and man's law, for two people to be one though marriage.

I want to remember his goodness, his loyalty, his tenderness, but I have no tears left to shed. Even with my child and sister beside me, the loneliest feeling settles in my heavy heart.

Chapter 10

Loretta

23rd of October

Cher Journal,

Pascaline picked up a discarded newspaper today and began to cry. She shoved it into my hands.

Yesterday, the king published the Edict of Fontainebleau. We don't know how not to be Huguenots, but I'm glad we've been pretending to be Catholic. Being a Huguenot is now illegal. It doesn't change anything. The Dragonnades have already destroyed our family, our good names. No one will hire us or let us cross a border. The edict just made it official policy.

We still wander. And we burned the paper to start a fire.

20th of November

Cher Journal,

The morning dew was frozen, as it has been for several days. Pascaline took inventory today of everything we have. If we can, she wants to splurge on a wool blanket. She prays we will have enough if we buy secondhand.

Pascaline

I cover my child's eyes. Loretta and I pass a dead gendarme in a shredded uniform. His skin looks strangely pale and bloodless. Worse, his eyes are plucked out. But the gendarme still has his incisors. *Why take the eyes but not the teeth?*

"There may be robbers about," I whisper.

"We must be careful," she agrees.

At the day's end, we've met no one, and night threatens to be cold.

Celeste's cough grows raspy and ends with a wheeze in her tiny chest. I am not much better off. I spit up something thick.

The full moon dips in and out of the clouds. The wind moves through the grasses next to the pitted dirt road. We need to acquire supplies in the next village for the coming winter.

I feel as if we were being followed but see no one behind us. Celeste coughs again. I cluck my tongue and cuddle the baby closer to my chest to provide comfort and warmth.

Loretta sings a soft lullaby.

"What a pretty voice you have." A tall, bony tramp appears in the middle of the road. His body is covered in dirty rags so thin and worn they're held together by nothing more than threads.

Loretta stiffens, but she says, "Thank you."

My sister and I glance at each other, trying to decide the

safest course. Drool slips out of the man's lip and drips to the ground. His teeth seem to grow.

The tramp gestures me closer. I do not want to, yet my feet step forward. I feel God's judgment in the tramp's sparkling eyes. *You left your providence. You sinned. You disobeyed the king. You made decisions against My law.*

Loretta clutches my wrist and cries my name, disconnecting me from the criticism of my maker. Celeste whimpers. I step back.

Shadowy silhouettes of several more people creep closer. As the vagrants draw nearer, I note something strange. Their stringy hair look as if it hadn't been washed in months, but none scratch or seem disturbed by fleas or lice. They wear rags over their too-thin frames, yet they do not shiver. Some do not even seem to breathe. Many are covered with blackened welts.

Loretta and I quickly turn around but, somehow, tramps moved behind us without our knowledge. There are more of them than we initially thought.

I pull Loretta off the road and push her in front of me. Grasses rip against our dirty skirts, and the muddy field soaks our feet.

Loretta grips the bag of supplies closer to her chest and runs. I trail her as fast as I can. The tramps' nimble feet seem to fly over the grass as they pursue us. With every step, they close the distance, laughing a horrible echoing sound. Loretta drops something from of the bundle, but the tramps are not distracted.

One grabs my shoulder. Without thinking, I turn and slap his hand. Fangs emerge from his open mouth.

Death approaches me in the tramp's luminescent eyes. I

cannot move, though death steps closer. *It is all meaningless. I had forsaken my husband. I will die, Celeste will die with me. The tramps will dine on our flesh. I can only pray Loretta will escape. But will God listen?*

Loretta screams, "Callette!" The sound echoes.

A tramp catches up with my sister. She slaps him with a glancing blow. Nothing happens. Then, a flash of metal. The tramp howls and grabs his face, shouting terrible words.

My mind rouses from this nightmare as I watch my sister stand her ground, staring at a streak of smoking, blistered flesh across the tramp's cheek. Around her knuckles is the heavy cuff bracelet Helena gave us.

They fear the metal.

In a strange calm, I knew as if it was old knowledge in the back of my mind. I yank a locket from my dress and swing it, missing his face. He shouts something to his companions as his foul-smelling hands rip at my collar. He jerks back, screaming. Did he touch my wedding ring? Is Andre protecting us from above?

"This way!" Loretta takes my hand and dashes toward a large pine grove.

I stumble after my sister as we enter the tree line. I'm sure they will kill us. I cover my child with my body and put the wedding ring around her neck. If I die, Loretta will take the child. But the four closest men don't come after us. Instead, they scatter.

I look up. My sister stands above us, knife in hand, swinging wildly at the air. The copper and silver bracelet flashes in the moonlight.

"What in the world? Why did they stop chasing us?" I

whisper.

Loretta reaches for my hand and pulls me to my feet. "Who knows? Come on."

As we scurry deeper into the wood, I wonder if I saw what I thought I saw or was it a trick of the darkness. Regardless, we lost much of what little supplies we had in the encounter. We will have to take inventory once we're secure. At least, I still have a bundle of ticking.

Hurrying down the wooded hill to get out of the wind, we find a road. We are deep in a rural county, but the gravel-covered thoroughfare is so smooth and flat it might be a King's Road in Versailles or Paris.

"The gendarmes who patrol this road have been busy," Loretta muses.

"Maybe that's why those tramps turned back," I suggest.

We follow the road until we find a large tree whose heavy boughs would offer us shelter until dawn.

Once the sun rises, we walk the well-tended road to a quiet village, which looks as if it hadn't changed for a hundred years.

Chapter 11

Loretta

21st of November,

Cher Journal,

Not only did we escape the tramps last night without injury, somehow we stepped into a fairy tale village. In the cold morning air, a whistling dairy wife pushed a cart. Two boys ran behind her, playing swords with sticks. She stopped in front of a cheesemaker's house according to the sign. One child hauled a large jug of milk to the house. The other, unburdened, collected the empties, jumping over the rows of woven branches that corralled the cheesemaker's goats.

"Excuse me, may we buy a bottle of milk," Pascaline called.

The dairy wife met our eyes. I feared a rebuke, but the woman said, "Quarter."

"I can give you a pearl. It's real," I said.

The dairy wife shook her head. "Seek the midwife once the sunsets and take this for your babe." She handed Pascaline a small bottle. "Fear not. She's a good witch and has good potions for the health of your babe. Look how strong my children are."

Pascaline nodded. "I'd sell my soul if Celeste would live."

"The midwife won't ask for that, chou." She sighed. "Pierre, Louis, show these women the baker's hut."

The two boys sighed with annoyance but did what their mother commanded.

The bakers were both older women, who clucked at Celeste and refused my pearl for day-old bread. Pascaline wept with gratitude for their charity.

One whispered, "See the midwife, Mademoiselles. She called you to her."

"My sister is a widow," I hissed.

"Loretta, don't be rude when they're being kind," Pascaline said through her tears.

My thoughts swooped between faith in their words and worry about the truth.

"I apologize, forgive my words. We were called many things on our travels," I said.

"No doubt," the baker said. "See the midwife; you're nothing but skin and bones."

After the surprising hospitality of the dairy wife and bakers, Pascaline and I moved to the center of town. Patches of bare earth showed where the farmer's market stood but, otherwise, the grounds were beautiful and green. We stopped to look at the stone statue of a knight fighting a monster with a sword. At the man's feet, another man lay dying but still trying to stab the monster.

"Men like him no longer exist." Pascaline's sadness

threatened to take her entire being. "Celeste won't be taught such foolishness. There has been a change in the nobility. Once, warriors protected the populace, now we..." A sob racked her body. "Is it because we are at a more peaceful time? But how can that be? France is always at war."

Praying that I might calm my sister, I pointed at a lad, perhaps thirteen, opening the blacksmith shop. A man, the smith, came around the corner with several bars of iron. "Do you think this village has been hit hard by war?"

"Why do you ask?"

"Because other than the statue, that's the first two men I've seen. And one's a boy." I nodded at a blacksmith and his apprentice. As the day went on, it turned out that my assessment was a bit more drastic than the truth. We saw other men working in their shops or out on the streets, but they were by far outnumbered by women and young children.

We passed a stone manor with darkened windows. It was not a new castle. Instead, thick walls surrounded heavy stone towers with slender arrow shafts that reached for the sky. Like the village, it looked like it hadn't changed for a century, perhaps two.

"Where is everyone?" I whispered.

"The building is in good repair. Someone obviously lives here."

"Maybe it's the witch who only appears at night," I teased my sister, hoping to bring a smile to her face.

A bubble of strangled laughter rose up her throat. Celeste, still deep in her mimicry, laughed, too, and clapped her hands.

Pascaline truly smiled.

The road split into a path leading into a small orchard. I kept watch. Pascaline slipped into the trees, snatched some ripe pears, and hid them in her skirt pockets.

Seeing no one, we hurried past a beehive along neat hedgerows to a wild forest, where we met the road again and entered a wood of ash and oak. In the shade of the trees, brown-capped mushrooms lined the road.

"I wish we had seen a pig eating them so we'd know if they were poison or not," I said sadly.

"As do I." Pascaline patted my shoulder.

The air grew colder as we traced the dirt path through the mossy grove to the ancient megaliths deep into the wood. An old stone foundation lay in ruins, but a clear pond was in walking distance.

"We could hang the ticking here and make a shelter," I suggested.

"Agreed. We need to see what we have before it gets dark."

Pascaline set Celeste on the ground with a few pieces of pear and built our camp. Once the child mashed the pears with her gums, she used the trees to lift herself and toddled a few steps. Following Air de Cour methodology, I created a song for Celeste and danced about her. She bounced and sang it with me with the sound of ba-ba-ba until she coughed. Pascaline busied herself with taking inventory.

The wind, blowing through the primeval forest, sounded like musical accompaniment to my voice. A bird squawked as it landed in a tree and nested down for the night. Deer grazed near the pond, amid moths flying low between the trees.

Drifting snowflakes fell.

Pascaline caught one on her tongue. "We will survive if perhaps we can buy some wax for our sheet." It was wonderful to finally hear a note of optimism in her voice.

Jakub

I investigated the three human heartbeats in the old stone ruins even before I heard the soft singing. As I drew closer, a baby's cry, and a raspy cough, preceded the sweet, frightened voice of a young mother: "I wish I knew what to do."

Another girlish voice said, "Maybe I can find the midwife the bakers spoke about. Stay here."

"In the snow?"

I called into the makeshift tent. "Hello? Who's there?"

I heard a hushing sound and slipped off my horse. "Pilgrims, are you seeking the midwife for the babe?"

A scrawny girl poked her head from the ticking. The knife in her unpracticed hand and the twisted scowl on her thin face could not hide a pretty complexion bestowed with a sprinkling of freckles on her nose.

"My sister's baby is sick," the girl said.

"Is the babe a child of a griselle?" I dismounted Castor.

"No! How dare you?" The petite shoeless girl stood her full height to stare me down, though I was taller than she.

My dead heart swelled. The girl reminded me of my late daughter not in looks but in spirit. Many girls sought Agata's care. Only a few reminded me of my late children.

"I dare because I can, girl. My wife, Countess de Banquier, often can help. But not all babes thrive—especially if they are born with a disease of Venus. I ask a second time. Whose child is this?"

"Mine. I'm a widow, not a griselle."

The older girl looked too young to be a widow, but many girls were married younger than she. The savage panic sounded in her frail body: a rapid heartbeat and rumbling stomach.

"Come, I shall take you to my wife. Fear not, I, Count de Banquier, serve this road and all who travel upon it."

Pascaline

I am not sure what to make of the strange knight in old-fashioned clothing. The count obviously is a descendant of the knight's statue in the center of town. Yet, his voice... or diction...is of a former time. Moreover, his skin has the same luminous quality as the tramps. Yet, I am too tired to be frightened. I need all that is left to fight, if necessary.

He glances at the cuff around Loretta's wrist, scrutinizing us. He assists us in dismantling our makeshift tent and collecting our meager belongings. I hope we have not shown too much wealth.

Like a knight of old, he takes my hand. "Please, Madame, allow me to assist you. Child, take your sister's babe for a moment. Don't fear, Mesdames, I'll lead Castor slow."

He lifts me onto his horse and hands me Celeste before boosting Loretta behind me. Removing his cloak, he covers Loretta's shoulders with it and ties her to my waist.

"Step gently, Castor," the count says to his horse after binding our meager possessions to the saddle.

"Do you believe this knight to be one of the fae?" Loretta whispers into my ear as we ride back toward the old stone keep.

"I believe we need the midwife," I reply. "And he knows where to go."

The strange man chuckles. He leads us into the old château's keep. Chickens cluck from inside their henhouse as the count lowers me and Loretta to the ground. The horse headed for its paddock followed by a few sheep. In a most gentlemanly fashion, the count offers his arms to help us cross the snow and moss-covered stones.

We traverse under boughs of spent lavender and other herbs hanging from the porch and into a large kitchen that looks practically medieval. Two woman servants perform their chores. They do not look alarmed upon seeing us arrive with the count.

"Madame," he calls. "I found these girls in need of your help."

"Girls?" Loretta mouths.

I ignore her in favor of feeling a pleasurable ache in my cheeks from the warm air of the kitchen. I want to remain in this moment forever.

A woman, somewhere in her thirties, comes around the corner. Her face is still unlined except one worry crease between her eyes, but her hands are used to hard work. Black hair peeks out of an old-fashioned French hood, and the cap and billiament are decorated with embroidered roses. Her soft woolen skirt is full, but unlike modern clothing, mostly gathered in the back. She wipes her hands on a heavy apron covered with the day's stains, looks lovingly at Celeste.

Under the glowing light of the candelabra, the count and countess's skin is pale as the dead gendarme we saw on the road. Again, I am reminded of the tramps, and shiver.

"Mesdames." He tips his hat to us, turns, and leaves.

I pinch my dry lips together. Loretta removes Helena's bracelet from her wrist. "This is the last of our family's fortune. Please, help my niece."

The countess's luminous face takes on a deep sadness as she waves it away. Metal burned the tramps, but hundreds of metal implements are in the kitchen so that's illogical.

"If not the cuff, we've pearls to pay you," I chance.

"I've never turned away a child in need. How may I serve you?"

"Thank you. My daughter's coughing," I say. "It began a few weeks ago and has worsened as the weather has gotten colder."

The countess listens to Celeste's chest. She shakes her head. "The babe has pneumonia. You must keep her warmer. Ought to keep yourselves warmer, too. I hear it in your lungs, Madame."

She gestures to Loretta and presses an ear against my chest. "Good. You are still healthy but malnourished."

"Why are you helping us?" I ask.

"I'm Agata the Midwife, Countess de Limousin," she says as if that answered the question. "Still giving milk?"

"No, my husband hired a nursemaid." I sob, but no tears fall.

"A nursemaid." The countess stokes the fire. "What has she been eating?"

"Goat and cow milk for the last six months."

"Any solid foods?"

"Bread soaked in milk, but she often spits it up," I say. "A little fruit when we can find it."

"And you, doves?"

"We eat whatever the baby doesn't eat."

"I'll find a wetnurse in the village—we've many women. Someone's always nursing." Agata rolls her loose sleeves and ties them back.

I note the strange way Agata didn't blink. She moves too thoughtfully and slowly about the kitchen. Her chest barely rises and falls as she moves a copper trough in front of a well pump and pushes the heavy handle.

Water flows into a large copper tub and into a smaller baby's bath

Metal isn't the problem. I must've dreamed Loretta hurt the tramps with metal. Perhaps they were shocked we fought back. Perhaps God protected us after all.

"Pray, Cook, any of tonight's stew left?" Agata asks.

"Yes, Madame," Cook replies.

"A cup each only. The older one, especially, hasn't been eating enough. I sense she's attempted to protect her daughter and sister from hunger. At midday, another cup. If they do not get sick, a full supper. The woman may need more time to acclimate to food again, but it wouldn't surprise me if the girl is well by morning."

The woman curtsies and leaves.

"I'm a woman of seventeen, Madame," Loretta offers.

Agata simply smiles. She boils a pot of water on the stove and adds it to the cold well water, slowly testing it to ensure its comfort.

Bowls of steaming meat and carrots in a heavy broth are brought to us.

"Eat, my lost lambs," Agata says.

If I were in a fairy story, it would be dangerous to eat it, but I am too hungry to deny myself. I watch Agata fuss over Celeste. I do not like this strange woman touching my child, but I cannot move to assist.

The baby is bathed in a shallow pan, road dirt scrubbed away with a sharp lemony-smelling soap. She hands Celeste the bar of soap to play with. Agata's eyes go over every inch of her tiny body, looking for parasites to be combed off. Celeste squirms as Agata rubs a lavender-smelling unguent into her chest. After she is wrapped in a linen swaddling and a wool blanket, one of the servants takes my child to a rocking chair and feeds her a bottle of goat's milk.

After we eat the stew, Agata bathes each of us in turn.

"Have you sold your bodies?"

I do not know why I believe lying is ill-advised, but I do. Perhaps the stories are true, and one cannot lie to the fae, even though the Fairfolk, pixies, and other spirits are myth. No one of substance believed in such things—except we met a band of loup-garous.

"Only our hair," I say. "I feared to mar our beauty with the pox; Loretta still hopes to attend court."

Loretta peeks at me. This is the first time I spoke of our identities since we met the loup-garou.

"Court?" Agata's eyes open a bit wider.

"I am Madame de Aubinet, but Loretta and I are also the daughters of Viscount de Fabron. Not that any of it matters now."

"Why doesn't it matter?" Agata asks.

"We're Huguenots."

"Yes, this king has a bee in his periwig about such things." Agata scrapes the dirt from under my fingernails. "Still, you must have acquaintances, Madame?"

"Our sister and her husband would not take us in," Loretta divulges. "We did not know our friend..."

My throat grows thick behind my trembling lips. "We thought he was our friend."

"Were you raped?"

I cannot believe the woman speaks so openly. I shake my head and explain our escape and how we found the rest of the family.

"Everywhere we looked, France abandoned us. We headed to the border but didn't know where to cross. To protect the girls, we ran from any men." Tears crest my eyes. "We heard about you from other women in town. That's why we didn't run from the count. Perhaps we could not run. I feel your trance upon me, but no matter what you must take from me, my child and sister will live."

"You have such a pretty way of speaking," Agata says. "I want nothing but to see Celeste grow and thrive."

Loretta

22nd of November

Cher Journal,

It's late, but I can barely believe our good fortune...finally! Everyone we've encountered in this town has been most gracious to us. The count and countess, especially, have shown more concern for our well-being than our own sister and brother-in-law. We've been fed, bathed, and rested as befits our station. I almost believe that I will get to make my debut someday.

After bathing us, Agata removed her apron to reveal a black gown with an Italian-influenced square neckline and jeweled partlet from a century before. I wondered if Agata knew no one dressed like that in Paris anymore. But, I must say, even a hundred-year-old gown is better than the torn and dirty dresses we've been wearing of late.

Agata led us up a set of stairs to a room overlooking the herb garden. A servant turned down a large bed and changed Celeste's diaper one last time. She gurgled with glee as Agata placed her in a basket set between two feather pillows.

"It's late. The water is fresh from our well. You needn't fear it. There is a garderobe in the corner." Agata rested her hand upon the babe's head. "Sleep, my lambs."

Celeste made a faint mewing sound and started to snore. She had not fallen asleep so quickly in months. As had become my habit, I kissed my sleeping niece After Pascaline fussed over her and tucked her in.

Weary, but worry-free for the first time since I left Andre's house, I slipped into the garderobe, knowing once I crawled into the soft bed, I might not leave it for months. Maybe I would leave it for another hot bath.

The toilet seat was clean; instead of waste, I smelled the lavender hung from the ceiling. Several clean rags were set out for our use.

I exited the garderobe and whispered, "They act the way nobles are supposed to act."

"Which is why I suppose I don't trust them," Pascaline whispered. "I feel perhaps we're being tested."

The bedding smelled laundered, as did the linen nightgowns Agata gave us. When I closed my eyes, I almost imagined I was at home. I yawned. "I can't keep my eyes open, Callette."

"Nor can I, and Celeste's asleep." Pascaline entered the garderobe.

Pascaline returned and climbed into bed. I snuggled to my sister's shoulder and considered what she had just said. "Maybe Agata wants something. It isn't silver or she wouldn't have turned down the bracelet."

"Agreed."

Jakub

"Are the girls settled?" I asked Agata as she entered our coffinroom.

She glided to her dressing table. Her companion, Suzetta, carefully loosened the lacing of her gown.

Her eyes were soft in a way I hadn't seen in over a century. "Yes, my love. I put them in the west room. They're noble-born girls, their father is dead, Pascaline is a widow, Loretta is a maiden. They've no protection and a babe to care for."

In the long years, I experienced a happy marriage and nurtured hearts so close it is hard to know where one's desires ended and the other's began. "Agata, you cannot keep them."

"Why? I miss having daughters," Agata said.

I sensed Suzetta's blood pressure rise, but she said

nothing as she assisted her lady escape layers of fabric.

I could not admit my own feelings but remembered the younger girl's bravery.

"Many girls come through those doors, but you've never made them your daughters," I said. "The château needs work. The king has summoned us. We need to sell more dye or raise taxes."

She frowned. "Please, Jakub, don't you miss holding a child in your arms, watching them grow into whomever God ordained?"

I sighed. I had known wars. I loved my human children as much as any father loved his children, but I had not been around to know them. I had known the eldest, Irina, best, though she had been her mother's daughter.

Agata clasped my hands. "What if they could help? Verily, Loretta wants to go to court. She's unknown."

"They're ill."

"In a day or two, Loretta will be back to health. I fear for Pascaline because I fear for Little Celeste."

"Is there hope?"

"Always, but Celeste is quite underweight."

I wasn't sure what to say. I knew precious little about infants other than they were fragile. "Very well."

My wife's slow, dead heartbeat quickened. "Thank you, Jakub." She leapt into my arms and kissed my lips sweetly. I whispered, "Take down your hair, Love."

Agata returned to her maid to prepare herself. "Won't it be a joy to have life in the house again? A baby brings joy. Loretta is young and full of light."

Suzetta, who combed out Agata's long black hair, huffed.

"But the lady's heart, if she's a lady, is full of sorrow."

Agata turned toward Suzetta. "I believe she's who she claims to be. She speaks as an educated woman. Ma chou, are you jealous?"

Suzetta's face grew red. "You barely know them."

"But I sense something."

"What have women like that ever done for anyone? Besides, they are Protestants. They hate everyone who isn't like them."

"If that is true, I'll kill them," Agata said. "Would it ease your mind if Jakub and I kissed you?"

Ienlisted a young gendarme, a local boy of eighteen of seemingly good health and spirit, to transport my letter to the king. Of course, if he broke the seal, he would know I had lied to the king. He would know my wife and I did not have two daughters, educated in a nearby convent, to debut.

Yet, I did not fear for I listened to my wife's good counsel. Besides, they were only girls, unimportant in every way to the laws of inheritance. Someone might question a son appearing, but no one would question daughters.

Chapter 12

Loretta

22nd of November continued

Cher Journal,

It is a strange thing to wake feeling warm after so many months of nights exposed to the elements.

Beside me, I heard no sound except Pascaline's snores. By the smell, Celeste needed a diaper change. I opened the bed curtains and slipped out of bed. The sun was high. It must be noon or later. Of course, it felt late when we arrived.

A stack of fresh ribboned diapers and infant gowns lay on the table by the bedside. Careful not to wake Pascaline, I took Celeste from the basket. Her mess soaked through her gown and swaddling blanket. Ick.

After I washed the baby and changed her into a fresh diaper, I blew on her tummy. She giggled and squealed, which resulted in a bout of coughing.

The bed curtains shifted. Pascaline called, "Lor?"

I bounced Celeste in my arms. "I changed the baby."

"Thank you." My sister yawned.

Celeste giggled again and reached for Pascaline as we drew closer. Pascaline rocked her, and Celeste fell asleep quickly. She slipped the child back into the basket.

I put on one of the velvet robes which were left on the dressing table. "Did you notice there aren't mirrors in this room?"

"Strange."

I opened the door. Though it was the middle of the day, the house seemed too quiet and dark. Thick curtains were drawn over the windows. No servants worked.

Outside, Agata's herbs moved in the breeze. Our torn travel gowns hung on the clothesline. Jakub's horse and a smaller white pony walked in the field beyond, along with several sheep that trotted behind them.

"Hello," I called down the hall.

No one answered.

I stepped into the hallway. "Hello?"

Nothing.

I turned around. "The whole house feels deserted."

Pascaline pulled the servant bell.

We wondered for many minutes if anyone would answer, but a woman wearing a nightdress and cap came in carrying a tray with two bowls of stew and a cup of milk.

"The countess says one cup of stew for midmeal, Mesdames," she said.

Though the woman's expression was content on the surface, I sensed she judged us. Perhaps she did not believe we were who we claimed to be. We introduced ourselves as we had last night.

"I'm Suzetta. Madame's maid and companion."

"Where is everyone?"

"Resting or working, I suppose," Suzetta said, now

visibly annoyed "Now, Countess told us to let you rest. We have a nanny goat for your daughter, Madame, and a woman is coming later in the evening. Her boy is nearly ready to wean."

The moment she looked at Celeste, the harshness in her manner waned.

"Until she's stronger, Madame doesn't want Celeste to breathe in the air from the kitchen. She doesn't want newborns to breathe Celeste's air either."

Suzetta fed Celeste the cup of milk and played peekaboo until we finished our stew. After she left, the house grew silent and still. It felt as if it was the wee hours of the morning rather than the afternoon.

Pascaline and I put Celeste between us on the bed and played with her until she was ready to nap again.

It was only as night approached the household came alive. Through the window, we saw the dairy wife's sons run bottles to the kitchen door. They spoke to someone, probably the cook.

Pascaline

Agata knocks on the door, holding two old-fashioned gowns. "Suzetta informed me both of you girls ate well without stomach upset. If it pleases you, you might have a full meal tonight. Or if you want to wait another day, I leave that decision to you."

"I thought this blue would look fetching against your eyes, Loretta, and the green highlights Pascaline's complexion and brings out those flecks of gold in her eyes."

Celeste gurgles and coos at Agata, but she ends up

coughing.

"Poor baby," Agata says. "Did the salve I put on her chest work at all?"

"She slept well," I say.

Agata rubs the ointment upon Celeste's chest again. Celeste makes a shrill scream, then laughs. This time, she is not the one who coughs. I do.

Agata pressed her hand to my forehead. "Poor dove, you better stay in bed. Loretta, have you been coughing at all?"

"No," Loretta says.

"May I brush your hair?" Agata asks us.

Her fingers rub a sweet-smelling oil into Loretta's hair before brushing it until it fell about her shoulders in ripples. She ties half of it back with a lavender ribbon.

I gasp. "That ribbon. I've heard it was a rare color."

Agata smiles. "The dye is one of our industries. I know you're a married woman, but I always like seeing my own daughters' hair flowing free. Should I put your hair up?"

"We heard the king prefers the English style," Loretta says.

"I hear he cares for fashion more than his people," Agata says.

"Unfortunately, that seems to be the case," I say cautiously. "It's strange. In some ways, France is thriving. In others, it's cold and wretched. Why are you doing this?"

"Doing what?" Agata gently braids my hair and twists it into a bun.

"Taking care of us."

"Because you sought me out, and I miss having daughters."

"But we didn't," I admit. "We walked in circles. I don't even know where we are."

"Forgive me. You were tired last night, and we're so rural we don't always stand on ceremony. Madame de Aubinet, Madame Loretta, you are the welcome guests in the home of the Count and Countess of Limousin. Enjoy my library and parlor. Or stroll in my herb garden if it pleases you. Parts of the wood can be dangerous, but if you wish to ride, ask my lord to escort you."

She touches Celeste in the same manner. "I feel no fever. The nurse ought to be here in an hour. I'll bring some broth."

Lying in bed coughing, I envy Loretta's good health. Our humours are obviously misaligned. Still, Celeste sleeps better than she has in months.

I have nearly fallen back to sleep when Agata escorts a woman with a small chubby boy into the room.

Agata sets blocks on the floor in front of the boy and introduces me to Charlotte, who calls me Madame Pascaline.

"We shall supplement goats' milk with Charlotte's milk so her son, and little Celeste will be milk kin. I hope you approve."

"Indeed, Countess. Thank you for your gracious kindness and thank you, Charlotte, for the care you will dote on Celeste."

Charlotte curtsies. I want to weep; I am elated to be a lady again.

Charlotte's face is tanned and careworn, but she appears to be in robust health. She gathers Celeste in her arms and moves to the rocking chair. To her son, she says, "Michael, look at Sweet Baby Celeste!"

"Baby," Michael repeats. He walks, not toddles, to play with the blocks.

"Is this your first child, Madame?" Charlotte asks.

"I miscarried before God brought us Celeste."

Charlotte nods. "Miscarriage is the sadness of all women."

I am surprised a peasant spoke openly, but better Charlotte's loyal service rather than betrayal from Jaqueline in times of trouble.

After Agata left the room, I ask, "Nurse Charlotte, is our countess all she seems?"

"More. She can't help it if she was..." Charlotte lowers her voice. "Bewitched."

"Bewitched?"

"The count and countess don't age, Madame. My mother was delivered by our countess, as was I. In my earliest memories, the count kept the road as he does now. That statue in the middle of town is our brave knight, Monsieur Jakub, Count de Banquier himself."

"How can that be possible?"

"'Tis said back in the olden days when knights were gallant and kind, the countess came to these lands as the count's wife. However, on the road, her great beauty charmed the Devil. He took her to Hell and set Lou Carcolh as guard. That's why our brave Monsieur and his gendarme hunted the beast, found the path into Hell, and rescued his beloved lady.

"Our countess, she's cleverer than all other ladies and most lords, perhaps even the king himself. She bade the count to 'bring me the shell.' She and the other women made it into a purple dye, which the king and lords wear to remind the Devil of their victory over him. Thus, the Devil left French shores. I hear he's in England or some such place. However, before he went, the Devil cursed them to outlive their children.

"She had children?"

"They died long before I was born, but the story says five. One died in infancy, but the other four lived on with healthy lives. The eldest was a midwife like her mother, the second was a soldier like his father, the third, a boy, entered the merchant's trade, and the fourth, a girl, swore to be an eternal virgin and rode into battle. 'Tis said the children were much beloved of their parents."

Though I do not quite believe the fantastical tale, I nod and thank the woman as Michael topples the block tower with a shriek.

"How old is your son?"

"Twenty months. I planned to ween him two months ago, but August was hot, and the grain withered. The good countess said a few more months won't hurt and will keep him chubby for the coming winter. She fears this winter will be as bad as the last."

"I fear it, too. My sister and I saw many starving as we walked."

After dinner, Loretta returns and speaks kindly to Charlotte. Loretta makes shadow puppets on the wall, which makes Michael clap and laugh.

After Jakub escorts Charlotte and her son home, we go to bed full and happy, until we wake to screaming.

I light a candle. Loretta sits beside me, a sheen of sweat reflecting the candlelight on her forehead and upper lip. Celeste, thankfully, remains asleep in the basket.

The scream dies.

Loretta slips out from the covers.

"What are you doing?" I whisper, every word followed by a wheeze.

"I shall discover what's happening." Loretta opens the door. Grunts, heavy breathing, and women's voices rise from below.

"Be careful." I quickly begin to gather our things if Loretta and I must climb out of another window.

Loretta

24th of November

Cher Journal,

What a fright to awaken to a hideous scream! I feared what I would find as I crept down the stairs, but I mustered all my courage and tiptoed toward the light spilling from the kitchen. I realized my stupidity when I peeked around the doorway and saw a woman, grasping a crucifix, sitting in the birthing chair.

Agata wiped sweat from the woman's brow. "A few more times, chou. You can do this, no pain. Let the pain go. God will protect you. The Holy Spirit will protect you. See the doves in the rafters. 'Tis an omen from God."

I did not see doves in the rafters. In fact, Agata's home is strangely free of stray birds and rats alike. I thought about Pascaline going through this alone in Andre's house and could hardly believe my sister survived it.

"Count your rosary...pray to the Holy Mother to intercede on your behalf."

The woman seemed to take comfort in Agata's words and counted her rosary until her next contraction.

Suzetta passed me in the doorway, holding a stack of linens. "Madame Loretta, it's late. You ought to be resting."

"Is there anything I can do to help?" I asked.

"Later perhaps. We can teach you if you're inclined. For now, be a good girl and take care of your sister and niece for us. We've other patients tonight."

I climbed the stairs to find Pascaline had packed all our things and stood clutching the basket in which Celeste slept.

"Everything is all right. It's a woman giving birth."

Pascaline let out a long breath and laughed. "Of course. I feel foolish now."

I slipped back under the warm covers and asked if her midwife told her stories to ease the pain."

"No, she told me I suffered because God punished all women with the pain of childbirth to atone for Eve's sins and to compel us to remember our place. She kept reminding me it's women's wickedness that makes us yearn for the forbidden."

When I told her the countess only spoke about God's love not sin, Pascaline sighed and said, "Countess de Banquier is obviously a learned healer and much beloved in her community. In fact, I don't think I have ever seen a noble so cherished. We must learn from her example."

I agreed and nestled into her shoulder but, still frightened by the scene below, I couldn't help but shudder. "Giving birth looked terrifying," I said. "So much blood and—"

"Yes, it's messy, ma chérie."

Pascaline admitted she was afraid, too, but afterward, when she held Celeste in her arms, she couldn't contain her happiness, even though Andre's family wasn't pleased that Celeste was a girl.

"He came into the room and held me, Lor. He didn't care. Celeste was his, and I felt safe for the first time in my marriage."

I felt a tear drip onto my forehead and praised Andre because I believed Pascaline needed to hear it, but I also hoped I was right. "Andre was a good man," I said, "and he loved you and Celeste with a full heart."

Pascaline's gaze took on a warmth I had not seen in weeks.

Chapter 13

Pascaline

I hold out my fingers hoping Celeste will take a few wobbly steps. "That's a good girl. Come to Maman." My child topples backwards and crawls to me. I pick her up and kiss her.

Loretta comes into the room, carrying a tray with two bowls of soup and a basket of Cook's fresh bread. She sets the soup on the table and closes the door. "What if the countess is a Dame Blanche rather than someone bewitched?"

"Why do you say that?" I ask.

"Because they are only awake at night."

"She is a spirit? Perhaps next you'll say she and her husband are loup-garou or lutin. Jakub patrols the roads at night. Wouldn't a wife submit to her husband's schedule, especially since their children are deceased."

"If she is a Dame Blanche, we must do whatever she says," Loretta says. "Dame Blanches are known for their whims."

I perk up at my sister's solemn tone. "What did she ask you to do?"

"Nothing. Well, Cook asked me to bring you dinner. The countess is busy with a mother downstairs and couldn't come up."

"Hardly a strange whim. Thank you for bringing dinner."

Loretta sits on the floor and reaches for Celeste. "Come to Auntie. Let Maman eat now."

I take a mouthful of warm lamb broth flavored with rosemary. "You're the best of all people, Loretta."

Celeste gingerly steps toward Loretta.

Loretta gives Celeste the cup of simple warmed broth, which she promptly puts to her mouth. She drinks quickly, but Loretta is cautious not to spill. If my child is always hungry, that must mean her humours are coming into alignment.

I take another sip. The warmth fills my stomach. "Remember saying Agata told stories? Perhaps it gives mothers comfort that their noble providers are enchanters or spirits or even bewitched. Then, they might love them instead of regular nobles, whom they hate."

Perhaps so," Loretta replies.

I finish my broth. It frightens me how quickly we have become used to living in this warm, clean room and eating this delicious food. What if we are cast out again? No matter what, we must prepare somehow, but how?

Icy rain pelts the windows. The clouds are dark and the wind rattles against panes of glass. Celeste pulls herself up using a nearby chair for leverage. I clap and put out my hands. Gripping a wooden chair, Celeste toddles toward my outstretched embrace.

"It's a small victory, but it's a victory," Agata says from the door, a deep pinch in her brow.

"Should we be moving on? I don't wish to take advantage of such hospitality."

Celeste says, "Maa…maa," and coughs phlegm and drool. I wipe it away.

"There's no going out tonight. Besides, where would you go?" Agata sits on the floor across from me and puts out her hands to Celeste, who cautiously takes a step toward Agata while hanging onto Loretta's arm.

"Where do the other girls go?" I ask. "The ones who have nowhere else to go."

Agata nods. "Those girls are taught a trade: spinning, weaving, running a dairy, among others."

"What about us?" I ask. "Will you help us find a trade?"

"Doves, you're educated in a trade which might be the answer to my prayers. To find us is a miracle. Jakub and I discussed sending you to Versailles to represent this family."

My mouth goes dry. "I heard the Devil took your children."

Loretta says, "I heard you're a Dame Blanche!" Agata laughs. "Truly now, girls, if you collect stories, listen to the one from the furriers afield. It tells how Jakub met a mighty horse on his road. The Devil bet him he could not tame it. Since it was a spirit, of course, Jakub couldn't tame it. The Devil tamed Jakub and bound him to his road. If he leaves it, he will surely die."

"You're teasing," I say.

"Indeed. When you've birthed half the county, you know all their stories," she says.

"What of Celeste?"

"Once the danger subsides, she might stay here to keep me company, and you could attend Court. Or perhaps we will all travel together if the king insists."

"My husband was a dissident," I whisper.

"You misunderstand. You won't go as Madame de Aubinet or Fabron, you will be the filles de Banquier."

"What if we're caught? The king would take your lands," I say. "And all of our heads."

"By your own words, your family is dead, few know you, and those who have seen you of late are unlikely to be at Versailles," Agata says.

Chapter 14

Loretta

9th of December

Cher Journal,

I am seriously considering Agata's offer. I ought to hate the king, but I want to go to Versailles and be surrounded by music and culture and life. I want to be warm and full and forgetful.

To that end, I decided to spend some time in the library today and was delighted to find an old harp in the corner. Several strings were broken, and the intact catgut disintegrated under my touch. Even the wood was soft under my fingers. Woodworm.

I glided to the wall covered in books—some old, some new. Journals written in Agata's flowing hand. Bibles written in several languages, Dante's *Divine Comedy*, Thomas More's *Utopia*, Robert Fabyan's *The New Chronicles of England and France*. There were several books on the occult in Romanian, English, and French. Another shelf held several books on courtly manners and languages published over the past few centuries.

I did not hear the silent footsteps as much as I sensed

the closeness. Jakub's deathly coldness overwhelmed my manners. I shouted, "Don't touch me!"

"I shall not touch you," Jakub said. "You may enjoy any book of Agata's library. She collects stories."

"I do like to read, but the harp drew me. I haven't played since we fled Paris, but it's my favorite instrument."

His eyes never left my face, and he never blinked. "I fear that harp played its last song decades ago. It was the instrument of a friend, long dead."

"Why do you watch me so intently, Count de Banquier?"

"Agata claims you wanted to debut, so you must be educated in courtly behavior."

My cheeks flushed as I certainly had not acted with politeness when he entered a room of his own house. "Yes."

"This house of sickness is no place for you—"

"Are we in danger here?" I asked, a little coquettishly.

He grimaced. "I kill only brigands, the occasional wolf, or mad dog. I kill deer, sheep, and cattle for our meals, but I never harm unfortunate girls who come to my wife in need."

I was counting the seconds until he would blink.

"What about tramps?" The words slipped out of my mouth.

"Tramps? What tramps?" His voice grew harsh, and I stepped back. He spoke more gently, "Loretta, you needn't fear me. Tell me what you witnessed."

"These strange tramps chased us into the forest. There was something bizarre about their voices, the way they did not blink, but it all happened so fast. You and your wife remind us of the tramps."

"Did they cross into my forest?"

"No, Count de Banquier."

"Good."

"But what of the Dragonnade?"

"They don't know you are here. However, if anyone comes for you, they will fall to my sword. My wife misses our children profoundly. Three noble-born girls—she fell in love with you immediately. You are under my protection for Agata's sake." Jakub sighed. "I was a good soldier, which means I didn't know my children as Agata knew them. However, this time, I shall do better. I know my daughters will represent this house's interest at Court."

Excitement filled my chest. My chance to debut. "Would you not rather have sons?"

"Daughters are just as fine, perhaps better, as they don't expect to inherit. Come, we must tell Agata what you told me."

Jakub offered his arm, but I did not take it. "You've nothing to fear from me," he repeated.

"Still, I should rather walk beside you."

"As you wish." He seemed neither annoyed nor put out in any way. We walked to the kitchen. Finding only Cook, we moved upstairs to the room Pascaline and I shared.

Behind the door, Celeste cried.

"Check your sister is dressed and announce my presence," he ordered, but not unkindly.

I did so.

Jakub kissed Agata's lips and told her not to worry. He ordered me to tell them of the tramps and Pascaline to add anything from her perspective. While he obviously expected us to tell him, he was not cruel.

Agata and Jakub listened quietly until we finished.

"Were they led by a woman?" Agata asked. "She might've been dressed as a nun?"

"No. Or at least I don't think so. There were a few women among them, but I didn't see any nuns," I said.

"But we were both in a panic," Pascaline added. "I thought my wedding ring stopped them. That Andre reached down from Heaven and stopped them." She sighed sadly. Agata wrapped her arms about Pascaline.

Jakub rose, bowed, and left.

Chapter 15

Jakub

Straw scattered across the cold ground when I opened the door to the barn. Dust and chaff lifted into the air under the animals' hooves and my footsteps. The stablehand, Jean-Victor, rose from his pallet. I asked the eighteen-year-old lad to gather three sheep. I hated wasting sheep on the horde, but it must be done. The world was cruel. Girls must be able to find their way to Agata.

"Purpose? Good Count?" he asked.

"To lure those who skulk in the night."

"Lesser animals?"

"Yes."

I went to the tack rack and saddled Castor.

"Have they come closer, Count de Banquier?"

"The two noble girls with the babe were attacked at the border."

"How did they escape?"

I could not explain the truth without giving away our weakness. "They carried salted beef, dropped it, and the monsters smelled the meat," I lied.

The lad unlatched the pin and shook a bag of grain to get the sheep's attention. When three animals exited, Jean-Victor leashed the animals together and drew them behind Castor. He wished me luck.

Frozen ground crunched under Castor's and the sheeps' hooves. Castor wanted to gallop but remained in a cantor so the sheep could keep up. I smelled winter in the air. Then old death. The dire slinking things were close. I did not spy them at first. If I find the horde on my land, I shall kill them all. Their pitiful innocence wouldn't save them this time.

The skulking creatures were at the border, taking shelter from the icy wind, but they had not crossed into my land.

Castor whinnied, and the sheep baah'ed as we approached. I dismounted Castor and untied the sheep. I cut the first sheep's throat and spilled the blood. It stumbled and, two steps later, its soul left its body.

Some slunk closer across the ground, but others walked upright. I noticed three new faces among those who walked. Grown undead men with calloused hands and in rotting clothing pushed weak vampires away and took the first bites of the still warm meat for themselves. Sister Sophie would never allow that.

I killed another sheep and threw it to the weaker vampires.

"Where's Sister Sophie?" I asked those nearest to me.

Between slurps and bites, one answered, "Gone to Paris."

"And David?"

A cackle erupted from one of the three men. "David finally learned the real joys of women."

Another vile man said, "After centuries under the yoke of that nun, he deserves it."

"Do you deny the treaty between our lines?" I asked.

"We ain't crossing into your lands, my Count," the man said. "The wood is the border. You're in our land. And we only let you 'cause the sheep."

I was vastly outnumbered, but these men were still peasants, untrained in the ways of battle and knighthood.

"Do you kill the women and girls who seek the midwife?" I asked.

"We don't know they seek the midwife."

Another man laughed and crept toward my horse. I threw a copper-edged blade. It struck true but did not smoke. He removed it with a pained shout. The wound closed.

He bared his fangs. "I'm not of Sister Sophie."

"So be it."

I unsheathed my silver-edged sword and chopped off his head in one movement.

His body moved, twitched, and smoked. The vampire must be descended from one of the Roman lines. The silver and copper cuff, the silver chain, and whatever other jewelry they had was what had stopped the vampires from hurting the girls. Less wealthy girls had not made it.

I picked up the head. "My horses are not to be touched. It's known."

Another man rushed me. I took his head as well and quickly dismembered his arms and legs from his torso.

"Who is your leader?" I asked the remaining vampires who sucked blood from the sheep.

The final able-bodied man lifted his head. "David." He sank his fangs back into the sheep's corpse.

"Who are these men?"

"Vampires we let walk with us."

I loathed the wearied, sickly choices of the horde.

"Do they hunt? Bring you food," I asked.

"No. Will you free us from them, Count de Banquier?"

"Indeed. Keep this final sheep for the men I have taken, but I better not hear that any girl seeking the midwife has been slain." I slaughtered the beast quickly so it did not know pain.

"Thank you, Sir Jakub, the valiant, fair, and wise."

I realized I had not seen their children among them as the weakest squirmed on the cold earth. The creatures crept to it and sucked out its blood before its body grew cold. I rode away from their supplications with pieces of vampire corpses twitching under the burlap. Agata and I would eat well.

Loretta

10th of December

Cher Journal,

Something appalling happened tonight, but we know the truth of our strange protectors and why they outlived their children.

It was the wee hours when I heard the horses naying. I peeked out the window and saw Jakub speaking to a stablehand. The countess and Cook ran outside with a bucket of water. A streak of blood stained his sword, and a bag of something horrible dripped red. Through the thick glass, I was sure I saw whatever was in the bag moving.

I listened.

"Sister Sophie has gone to Paris," Jakub told his wife as he cleaned himself. "David runs the troop now, but he barely has control.

These names meant nothing to me, but Jakub's next words made my heart go cold.

"I feared we might be overrun when we leave for court, so I seized pre-vengeance," Jakub said.

Agata and Jakub entered through the kitchen, and I quickly went downstairs. I followed them down a corridor and discovered a stairwell leading to utter darkness; I caught the sour whiff of mildew. Holding my candlestick aloft, I pressed my hand to the stone wall and descended.

The stone under my feet felt wobbly. Curiosity induced me to take another step. The light from the kitchen disappeared behind me as the stairs curved. The darkness manifested as a supreme icy presence, smothering my body from all sides. Though my nightgown and woolen slippers offered protection from the cold, goosebumps rose on my arms and legs.

I lost my orientation in the dark, but the wall was smooth, strong, and solid, so I continued into the depths.

The stairs ended, and I stumbled onto a stone floor.

The candlelight did not illuminate far enough in the distance, but Agata and Jakub crouched over the mutilated corpse of a tramp or perhaps more than one.

They looked toward candle's light, and I pressed against the cold stone wall.

"Loretta, come here, please," Agata said in a tone meant to be obeyed.

Though I wanted to run up the stairs and never know darkness again, I obeyed.

Before me, the tramps' body parts still twitched. Their mouths opened and closed. Their eyes blinked. A scream caught in my throat when a disembodied hand grabbed at my skirts.

I cried. "You...you are monsters!"

"Indeed." Jakub picked up the spare hand as calmly as if it was an apple that rolled away. "We're vampires."

Looking at the body parts, I whispered, "What are you...?"

"We'll eat them."

Agata walked beside me, leading me slowly up the stairs. "They broke a long treaty with my husband when they chased you. We learned they killed other girls trying to make their way to us. Such cruelty will end."

We climbed together until I could see the light from the kitchen. She kissed my cheek and released me.

"Go now, my sweet daughter, and speak to your sister. This is no place for you."

I dashed up the stairs to our bedroom, sweat dampening my gown.

My sister looked up from Celeste as I threw open the door.

"Don't let the heat out!"

Celeste was red-faced and snotty as her tummy had been upset tonight. As Agata suggested, Pascaline massaged lavender oil into Celeste's back.

"Pascaline, I discovered what they are!"

Celeste perked up at my arrival. She made noises with her lips.

"Who what are?"

"Agata and Jakub are vampires! They're cutting up the tramps, who are also vampires!

Still circling Celeste's tiny back with the oil, my sister gave me a pained stare. "And what, pray tell, are vampires?"

Sweaty hands flapping, I could not describe the horror. Mostly because I was glad Agata and Jakub ate the tramps. "I don't know, but Jakub hunted the tramps from the road. The tramps killed other girls. They...they are eating them!"

"Do you believe Celeste is in any danger?" Pascaline's voice was somewhere in between panic and disbelief.

"No. Agata wants to help her. All the babies..."

Pascaline scratched her cheek. "To call them vampires is the same as to call them the fae, is it not?"

I nodded. *Though I do not know if the fairy folk ate each other. Of course, I do not know if fairy folk did not eat each other either. Cher Journal, does anyone know this?*

"We met a pack of loup-garou; now we meet vampires. The world is big, Loretta. There's much we've to learn," Pascaline said. Celeste squirmed away from Pascaline's ministrations and reached for her pacifier.

I sniffed the piece of brandy-soaked linen stuffed with hardened animal fat before handing it to her. Celeste put it in her mouth and sucked on it.

Chapter 16

Pascaline

I do not understand how to soothe Celeste. She is clean; she ate two hours before. The baby's tears make her face red. I pat her back until she coughs up more phlegm onto my skirt and the floor. Some days, she seems as if she is on the mend, then she falls back with this tormenting cough. She doesn't even want a pacifier.

My child whimpers, clings to my neck, and rests a red cheek on my shoulder. I feel guilt for my annoyance deep in my heart, especially when Agata enters the room with some rags and a bucket.

"Mama," Celeste says.

I feel a surge of jealousy. "I'll clean it, I'm sorry."

"Nothing to be sorry for." Agata kneels to wipe up the mess. "Keep Celeste in comfort; I'll get this."

Watching a great lady do a task fit for a charwoman makes me want to weep. I am unworthy of such kindness. I am unsure what it means to be a vampire—other than they ate the tramps and live forever if the stories are to be trusted.

Agata meets my eyes as she takes a new rag to the wool of my skirt. "Do not feel sorrow. You're a wonderful mother, Pascaline."

I feel the pull of truth again. "But I'm not, Countess."

"You got two girls safely across France."

"I doubted myself the entire way…and I would've failed, if not for Loretta."

"But you still did it." She dabs my skirt. "Better we wash it. I don't want to spread illness to a mother."

She brings me a new outer skirt and unties the dirty one. I set Celeste on the ground to change into it.

"Mama. Mama. Mama," Celeste says to Agata.

"Do you think she knows me?" I ask.

"She knows you are her mother. That's all any babe needs to know. Right now, 'Mama' is her word for everything because she only knows one word."

Once my overskirt is tied around my waist, I wring my hands in worry. "Is that good?"

Agata brushes my cheek. "Babies grow at their own speed. Celeste still crawls, and I'd like to see her walk soon, but other than this lingering cough, she seems normal."

I sigh in relief.

Agata gives me a gentle embrace. "Priests oft say women understand mothering or children in some 'ingrained way,' but every first child's first steps are their mother's first steps. We don't know what we don't know."

"There's much I don't know. When Celeste cried, Andre rang for the nurse."

"Where is that nurse? She left you. Even in your ignorance, you didn't leave Celeste." Agata met my eyes again. "Two pretty sisters might have been adventuresses, but not with a baby in tow."

"It feels as if you know my heart."

"You and Loretta have good, kind, and loyal hearts."

I shake my head. "At times, I'm jealous of my sister's freedom."

"Every mother is."

Jakub knocks on the door.

"Mama!" Celeste crawls to him and lifts her arms.

"Why hello, Celeste." He picks her up and kisses her on the cheek. She tugs his thick beard.

"Fine grip," he says.

"I'm sorry," I cry.

"Whatever in the world for?" Jakub coos at my child and bounces her in his arms.

"Did you need anything, my love?" Agata asks.

"It can wait." Jakub set Celeste on the floor on her feet. My child gripped his fingers while she toddles around the room.

"Ma-Mama," she babbles all the while. She coughs a little more and keep babbling.

Celeste lets go of Jakub's fingers with one hand and points at the blocks. "Blah."

"Did she say a new word?" I ask.

"I think she did. The young lady knows what she wants." Jakub sits on the floor to play as Andre might have done if he lived.

Celeste picks up a block and hands it to Jakub. She sets another on the ground in front of him. She shows him another block and sets it on the first. She points at him. He sets the block in place. She brings him another block. She sets hers down and waits for him to set the last one. Celeste kicks over the tower and shrieks as if it were the funniest thing she ever saw.

The stacking begins anew.

Loretta

12th of December

Cher Journal,

Though I admit I am frightened that Jakub and Agata are vampires, they have acted in no way different than they ever were since we arrived. I feel we're mostly fitting in here. Pascaline joined us in a gentle dinner with several guests. Celeste spent some time playing today, which Agata said was a good sign. But there is always the threat of illness in a midwife's house.

"My heart's gladdened to see both ladies are well," Jakub remarked as two gendarmes assisted us with our chairs. I feared what we might be eating, but Cook had made a roasted lamb with a hearty sauce of savory onions and garlic. Roasted carrots were sweet and tender. Rich butter coated the bread.

Jakub explained Pascaline and I would travel to Versailles to represent the holding and family name at court. Pascaline and I waited to be questioned, but no one questioned it.

Pascaline pressed her fingers together. "What specific issues are affecting the holding that the crown might assist?"

We spoke about their needs and the rules of Versailles. The king's presence haunted us as if he were in the room. Then, we discussed my favorite subject: music. Pascaline boasted of my talents.

The mayor's wife invited us to play her harpsichord until

I was able to get my own. I excitedly accepted the invitation. Agata asked the mayor's wife if she might also assist us in the procurement of an instrument so I might practice.

However, our wonderful conversation was interrupted by the delivery bell. Suzetta hurried into the kitchens.

Agata finished her meal and quickly followed.

Of course, I peered after them and caught a glimpse of a crying woman in labor. She had a hacking cough, snot on her upper lip, and a wet sheen on her brow. Mud coated her bare feet.

Suzetta and Agata had a quick exchange before Agata dismissed her.

When I saw Suzetta returning to the dining room, I stepped aside, and she shut the door to the kitchen. To me, she said, "Child, don't haunt the door. Loathsome air infects the old and young alike."

Jakub rose to assist me to my seat while his gendarme seated Suzetta.

She turned to the count. "The countess is concerned that the house will become infectious. She's requested your help in assuring that no one enters the room."

Chapter 17

Jakub

Many in our community are ill from what Agata claimed is a disorder of the Phlegm Humour. Inopportunely, on my nightly ride, I heard someone coughing. I sensed the heartbeats of a single man and two horses. For caution's sake, I slowed Castor's pace and found a Royal Army tent and two hobbled horses grazing.

"Ho there. Who comes on my lands, soldier?" I asked.

The army tent opened. A man in half dress, a reddened nose, and a sword on his belt appeared. "Who comes to my camp?"

I raised my hand in greeting. "Count de Banquier. I heard a man camped. 'Tis but a mile ride from the house."

I felt the fever radiating from his body. "So close? Forgive me, Monsieur le Count, I thought I was farther afield." He sneezed. "I bring a message from the king."

The messenger handed me a summons for me and a letter of safe passage both emblazoned with the king's seal. He bent over in another attack of coughing.

I grabbed the blanket off his bunk and wrapped him in it. "Are you well enough to ride?"

He was not.

As I dare not expose my vampiric strength, I asked, "Might I stay with you tonight and summon a cart at first light?"

"I'll make it through the night on my own, but a cart in the morning would be a blessing," the messenger said with a bow.

I rode home, but it would not be good if the king's messenger died on my lands.

The stablehand, Jean-Victor, drove the cart to the camp. When the man arrived, he was even sicker from his night in the cold.

Agata assisted the messenger with his dirty cloak and wet boots. He could not stop coughing as she set him in a chair by the hall fire and brought him a chalice of warmed mulled wine. He sneezed, spraying human phlegm on our mantel.

Suzetta moved to clean it, but Agata told her, "Remain away and inform the girls of the visitor."

The messenger drank glass after glass of warmed wine until he fell asleep in a chair. Wheezing and congestion interrupted his snores.

"That does not sound good," Agata remarked. "I wish Celeste was stronger before such an ill visitor came to our door."

"We must give him every consideration. Host him as you would the king." I showed her the letter of safe passage and summons. The king must know of our deception."

"His humors are most maligned. Did you see the white on his tongue?" Agata tutted and took vinegar to every surface that might hold his phlegm.

We left him alone, and Suzetta approached. "I informed the girls. They are in their bed and will come down, if requested."

"Let our visitor rest," Agata said.

I showed Agata the king's summons. "The girls must be introduced to him on the morrow. The fact the messenger came alone proves he's at least half-spy, half-appraiser."

"Not of the girls!"

I embraced her. "Of the holding, my dear wife. There's no reason for him to doubt the girls' parentage when they cannot inherit the holding and title, but a king's spy is never a fortunate happenstance."

Loretta

15th of December

Cher Journal,

Pascaline and I dressed finely in Agata's out-of-date gowns. My dress was not as fitted as I would've liked, but the torso-length stomacher and woolen shawl covered my chest. Pascaline did the same, though she filled out her dress better than I did.

Agata spoke cautiously. Each word was planned. We were the legitimate daughters of the count and countess. Illness had kept Pascaline from debuting at court the previous years, but we planned to debut together in the spring.

The messenger bowed. "Court looks forward to seeing such beautiful ladies. Ahchoo!" It was a terrible sneeze, and the throat-clearing was not much better.

"To your wishes," Pascaline said.

We curtsied and asked polite questions about Versailles. I sang an old song.

Once the messenger grew tired, he returned to bed. Agata brought him hot-peppered milk. Pascaline went upstairs to change and check on the baby.

Jakub

Two days later, the well-rested messenger had regained his strength. The girls had behaved with grace and spoke in perfect dignity. He rode back to Versailles on a well-rested horse with a restored pack horse carrying his gear.

"Perhaps, that will please the sovereign."

To please myself, I went to play with Celeste.

Chapter 18

Pascaline

I encourage Celeste to eat with treats, but she wants none of it. She will not take Charlotte's breast for long. Agata gave me fatted broth to slip into her mouth by the spoonful, hoping for relief. Celeste wanders but does not play. She does not even want her favorite of all: Jakub.

She swallows some broth and spits up more. Celeste and I are both crying by the time she naps. Agata's only explanation is loathsome air and imbalanced humours.

Relieved, I move downstairs to the kitchen.

The pungent, fishy smell greets me as women scoop cups of golden fish oil from barrels into ceramic jars.

I overhear Agata say, "This will be a hard winter. The frost has come early. We ought to double the bread if we can. After the fish oils, let us prepare lemon vinegars. That should save most of the children."

I think, *Most of the children?*

But Loretta says, "What do you mean? You're the midwife."

"I lose mothers and children like all other midwives. People die, Loretta. If you wish to help me make the vinegar, Cook and I would enjoy the assistance," Agata says.

"These aren't potions," I say softly, entering the ice-cold kitchen.

"Dove, you mustn't listen to the townsfolk. These are honey and lemon, lemon vinegar, strawberries soaked in vinegar, and cod liver oil. Rosemary, garlic, lavender, chamomile, and salt can cure most things, but there are still many infections I cannot cure," Agata says sadly.

I press my hands onto the stone countertop. "And Celeste?"

"We cannot not know what God ordained; I'm sorry."

"I don't care what God ordained. He won't have Celeste!"

Agata and Suzetta cross themselves.

Loretta gives me a look of reproach. She mimics their gesture.

I bite the inside of my cheek in order not to say another word, and I cross myself. A noble is never to lose their temper or show their pain. "Forgive me, I will go pray."

These people have given us sanctuary. They committed treason by calling us daughters to a king's messenger. If caught, they face dishonor and death.

I hurry to the library, hoping to find something that might help. I can no longer pretend God gives the noble-born any special favor. For some reason, He allows ranks in the world. By chance, we were born into a rank. Once we were cast out, He did not look upon us. He also allows the death of thousands of innocents every day. Whatever slight chance Celeste has is in these walls.

I pore over death records. What I read seems beyond imaginable. Children of her county still die of both injury and illness, but Agata saves more mothers and children than she loses times a hundred, and the numbers of children she treats and who survive are unheard of in the rest of Europe. With a quick calculation, I realize with great sadness, she still loses about one in seventy mothers and one in twenty infants during delivery.

Yet, as I search through her remedy books, I find no witchcraft, just a caring and vigilant midwife. I return to the kitchen to help.

Loretta

17th of December

Cher Journal,

Pascaline and I assisted Agata in creating her vinegars when the younger scullery maid entered the kitchen door.

"Madame le Countess, a message of concern."

"Christine, what's it?" Agata asks.

"Jean-Victor is feeling poorly and hoped you might cool his fever."

"I'll go see him. Pascaline and Loretta, my loves, can you continue to assist Suzetta?"

We curtsied in response.

Agata packed a few bottles in a basket, put on her cloak, and rushed outside.

After our duties, Pascaline hurried upstairs to check on the baby.

After a few more errands with Suzetta, I joined her. My heart sank listening to the wails and coughs leaking through the door.

I found Pascaline massaging salve into Celeste's chest. She creates little crosses, while praying harder than I had ever seen her. That wild, terrified look in her eyes has returned.

Worse, I saw the same expression on many mothers' faces several more times this night as they brave the cold air for remedies. Everything is so unfair! We finally find respite after our horrendous journey and now Celeste is sick again.

Pascaline and the baby are crying. I am tired of listening to it. I want Celeste to laugh, toddle around, and play with Jakub. I want Pascaline to accompany me on the harpsichord when I sing, and I want her to smile again.

Pascaline

My sleep has been troubled by Celeste's coughing. I move to the window and feel the threat of winter. The world feels like there is no more magic—even in this place.

Outside, translucent moonlight wanders through the spent garden. The herbs have all been plucked; vinegars and smelly unguents have been made and delivered to help the ill.

A rattle sounds in my daughter's chest. "Celeste! She's not breathing," I scream.

Loretta jumps from bed and dashes into the hallway. "Celeste stopped breathing!" she shouts.

I force my daughter to stand. Too much heat radiates off her body. I strike her back as if I'm attempting to burp her. There is a gurgle and a wail. Sweet relief overcomes me, but I see the thrush on her tongue.

Agata races into the room with Suzetta close behind. She looks deep in Celeste's reddened face. "No pain."

Agata gives Celeste a cup of peppered milk, which forces the baby to cough even more. Eventually, the phlegm is dislodged. When it happens, her bowels loosen as well.

Celeste truly wails, high-pitched and terrible.

"Help her! I'll give the devil my soul if she lives," I cry, rocking my sweet daughter.

"I know," Agata says, taking the child to change her diaper. "But we both know that selling your soul will not help."

Once Celeste is in a fresh diaper, Agata puts her back into my arms. "The best medicine is to keep her warm and clean. To keep her apart from people with illnesses. Pray if you can."

"Bewitch her! Let her live forever like you!" I beg.

"I cannot, Pascaline. Do not ask me again to commit such a sin as transforming a babe."

"The legends of Agata are myths. Do you know how many children die each winter?" Suzetta says softly. "She does what she can, but syphilis, scarlet fever, pneumonia, and rubella all come to our village."

"What kind of God does this to children?" I cry.

"In the Bible, God basically tells Job to stop asking questions like that. He is God." Agata says.

"I'll become a nun if He wants."

"You cannot bargain with Him, Madame," Suzetta says.

"What is He good for?"

Suzetta crosses herself; Agata crosses her arms.

"I shall do everything I can."

"Andre risked his life so Celeste would live! I will not let her die." Holding my sweet child close, I lean on the headboard, weeping. My sister wraps her arms around me and weeps with us.

After Agata leaves, her exact words echo in my ears. *Do not ask me again to commit such a sin as transforming a babe.*

She won't change a child, but she knows how to transform someone. Little good does that knowledge do me.

Chapter 19

Loretta

22nd of December

Cher Journal,

The worst has come to pass. I don't know if Pascaline will survive it. I have cried myself out.

My sister's screams rousted me. I smelled the bile that left my sweet niece's body. I opened my eyes to see my sister forcing Celeste to wake. My niece's cheeks and hands were splotchy and purple.

Again, Agata came.

In a strange voice, she said, "Sleep, Pascaline. There is no comfort now but sleep."

Pascaline collapsed onto the bed; her eyes were wide and unseeing.

Agata and Suzetta adjusted my sister so she lay with her head on the pillow. Agata closed Pascaline's eyes and tucked her under the covers. "Rest with your sister, Loretta. She needs you."

"I can't."

"Come."

She took the basket holding my niece's limp body into the kitchen. She prepared the small bathtub, poured water on the body, and cleaned off the foulness.

Weeping, I re-dressed Celeste in a fresh gown.

Jakub entered the kitchen and stared at Celeste's little body. "Your sister will remember her child. I pray she remembers the playful moments more than the sickness. When she wakes, she will need your strength."

"I don't have any."

Agata kissed my cheek. "You do. More than you think."

Pascaline

I do not rise from bed. A hole in my chest beats where my heart should be. I ought to be sad, but I am not. I am furious, enraged.

Loretta holds me. I want to push her away, but I cannot free myself. I study Jesus's carved wooden face on the crucifix, which failed to protect Celeste from demons, unclean spirits, or foul air. I try to pray, as a good Catholic girl ought, but I have no words. I hate God. I hate the king.

I wonder why I fought to survive. Celeste is gone. *Does God hate me because we converted to Catholicism? Or because I was born Huguenot? Is this fate?*

"I want to die. It should've been me. If I were a better mother..." My voice cracks.

"Pascaline, you are a great mother. You never scolded Celeste. You never shouted even when she cried," Loretta soothes as she places a hand on my shoulder.

"But, sometimes, I thought about yelling. Sometimes, I

was jealous of your freedom. Sometimes…"

Jakub knocks on the door and enters with Agata.

He kneels and takes my hands in his. "Do you wish the coffin to be buried in the churchyard or family vault?"

"Why would you do this?" I whisper—a crack formed in the black empty hole.

"Because you're to be our daughters. We wish to give you whatever little comfort we can," Jakub says. "I believe the best wording for the funeral brass is: Celeste Beloved Daughter Born of Pascaline de Banquier and Andre de Aubinet. 1684-1685"

"Thank you," I say.

Jakub

Pascaline diligently rewashed Celeste's tiny body with lavender tinged water as if they were putting the child to bed. She dressed her in a lace christening gown. Careful no strings were caught between her toes or fingers, Agata wound a white shroud in preparation for burial.

The family priest anointed the child with oil as he said his last rites. Pascaline and Loretta placed a bed of rosemary and lavender into the casket. Her entire body shaking, Pascaline set the toddler into a tiny wooden casket and kissed her daughter one last time. Agata covered Celeste's face with the shroud.

The casket was closed. A wreath of rosemary and pine was set upon it.

I picked up the tiny coffin and carried it. It was not big enough to need more pallbearers. Two adult daughters might be needed, but I had enjoyed having a granddaughter. I had loved her. Yet, God took Celeste away as surely as He took Daniella as an infant and the rest of my children in their time. I hated Him for his continued negligence. Deep in my heart, I dreaded I might become attached to these two young women, and they, too, would die in their time. Loretta, especially, was so easy to love.

We moved the coffin into the château's chapel, where our family priest said a small private service. Pascaline wept horribly, sitting between Agata and Loretta.

"Soon, we shall cast open the doors," I whispered.

Agata crossed herself, took Pascaline by the arms, and looked deeply into her eyes. "Pascaline, forgive me this, but you must weep quieter in public. You're a noblewoman."

Under Agata's spell, the poor girl straightened. She took a deep breath and blew her nose. Agata wiped her face. Her eyes were still red from crying, but they were perfect crystal tears to match her ideal display of public sorrow.

The manor doors were opened.

Pascaline

My heart is missing as I behold the public mourners. The priest leads the family from the chapel to the grounds, where villagers hold white candles and follow us. Many women weep. The clanging church bells sound in my sorrow. Someone takes up a hymn. The rest join.

Loretta holds me up as Jakub opens the ancient iron door to the family vault. I step along the passageway, one hand on my sister's arm, one hand trailing cut stone walls.

Dust fills my nostrils. I do not want to leave my child in this cold, dark place, but I cannot make another strangled cry; I can only weep beautifully. Spider webs fill corners, and old funeral brasses dull with dust. My heart, wherever it might be, screams.

The priest opens the tomb. The tiny wooden coffin is slipped inside. I reach for my child a final time, but Agata and Loretta hold me close while the tomb closes. Celeste's funeral plaque is set in place. Her smile shines in the darkness. I try to scream as I reach for her, tugging away from Loretta. My body straightens; my will is Agata's.

We move above ground. The whole village is there. I cannot look at the well-wishers. I cannot look at Agata, Charlotte, Suzetta, or even Loretta. I can only hold my head high and see what is in front of me.

No one mentions my tears or even my child; they bless me and ask for intercession from the Virgin for my pain.

I am brought home, fed soup, undressed, bathed, and put to bed. I am told to SLEEP in Agata's commanding voice. I cannot stop sleep from coming, but before I lose consciousness, I see Loretta weeping. Her cheeks are red, and her nose is snotty. I still love her because she loves and mourns Celeste...and because she is all I have left in the world.

I wake. I cannot look at the bare spot between the pillows. I cannot endure to see where Celeste used to sleep. I escape the room. The stone corridor is so cold. I have no idea the time or even day, but cold light streams through the windows and Loretta is not in our room.

I hear harpsichord music. It is low and painful. Loretta is where the new harpsichord has been delivered. Celeste's death did not change the plan. There must be some way to find vengeance for my daughter and protect my sister.

I feel pulled. Agata. I know better than to fight it. I turn from the library and move to their private chamber down the hall.

Agata stands at the door.

"How long was I asleep?" I ask.

"You slept for a few days; you awoke briefly to care for your needs. We put you back to bed. How do you feel?"

"Angry," I say.

"Vengeance is God's." She beckons me inside.

I enter the antechamber but observe the room beyond. Curtains surround a large, ornately carved coffin. This is where the Count and Countess slept.

Agata wraps a shawl around my shoulders and leads me to the bench across from Jakub's chair.

"God says Vengeance is His, but my daughter is dead. My husband is dead. We looked upon the bodies of my father, mother, brother, his wife and children. I don't know how to live again. Only vengeance can satisfy me."

"Jakub may be the needle to lance the boil of your pain."

"Whose death can placate you?" Jakub asks.

"I want to kill the dragoon in my house if they are there... and perhaps my sister and husband. If they took us in, Celeste would've lived."

"Even at the cost of Loretta?" Jakub asks.

That question shakes me to my core. "I will protect her in all things."

"How would Loretta feel if you ordered your sister's death?"

"But she, too, was betrayed," I say.

"Be that as it may, would your sister's death make her lose trust in you?"

I am taken aback. I do not know the right answer.

"In eternity, we mustn't make choices that may have vast effects without knowledge and consideration," Jakub said.

"Jakub and I are your family now. 'Tis your father's duty to protect you and your sister," Agata says. What remained unspoken was that it was our duty to obey.

Agata smothers her will over mine, but as if my sadness has a life of its own, it presses back on her. Her will must not overtake me on this point.

"We must be mistresses of our own fate," I cry. "I'll not allow you to marry us away!"

Jakub strokes his beard. "What if I vow not to marry you without your permission?"

The words are so simple, my heart breaks again. "You'd do that for us?"

He takes my hands in his and presses them together. "Of course. However, you must take a vow not to kill or harm the king or any other untouchable courtier."

I shake my head. "No. I want to kill him. However, it would set the country in confusion….perhaps even lengthen the famine if the Dauphin is a weak leader."

"Dove, No one who did not have a direct hand in Celeste's expulsion may die."

My mind spins. "Just the dragoon, then?"

"I will kill only the ones garrisoned in your house…"

Jakub begins.

"No, make us strong like you, let us kill them and we'll save this holding."

"There is something else you must consider. No vampire or infected human can ever have children the natural way again. Our blood will poison your womb, and you will be unmarriable by human standards," Agata said.

"I still want to be like you," I said firmly.

Jakub met Agata's eyes. "They're to be your daughters."

Agata held my hands. "I have prayed upon this. I'll transform you, but Loretta must wait until spinsters age so you might be equals in eternity. If you truly love your sister, even in your sorrow, you understand she is not old enough to be like us. Eternity is known to drive the young insane."

"People, who kill, even soldiers, have been known to bury themselves into monasteries. Loretta must be kept safe from that."

I look at the floor. "I will never hurt my sister in any measure."

"Then let us speak to Loretta. We, four, shall come to an understanding and form a plan," Jakub says.

Chapter 20

Loretta

6th of January

Cher Journal,

Though no one felt like observing the holidays, we were forced to celebrate Christmas, New Year and Epiphany with the villagers. Now, the celebrations have concluded, and the village is quiet. Pascaline will die before the sunrise. I am afraid for my sister. And so jealous!

Pascaline

Moisture creeps up my back as I lay upon cold, thick snow and rest my head on the wet ground. I shiver.

Loretta kneels beside my prone figure and holds my hand. "I love you, Calette."

"And I love you. Five years and a few months isn't long."

Agata opens the lacing on my stomacher and unties my chemise, exposing my breast. She cuts open the flesh and drinks from my heart.

I know a thirst without end as blood is drawn from my body. My heart slows. My muscles stiffen and cramp as I grow colder.

Agata cuts open the skin over her heart and bids me to drink.

I gulp the salty, coppery liquid. My lips become sticky with it. I swallow again and again. I want more. I want all of it.

"She is ready," Agata says.

Seeing the blade that will kill me, I freeze.

Without a word, Jakub slices open the artery on my neck.

Time slows. I scream as a knot forms in my calf. I don't expect such physical agony in the change. My lungs flutter as I draw in my last breath as a human woman. My heart feels stationary, then shutters and beats harder. I hear cries of my people under a king who did not care if they lived or died. I want to save them all.

Far away, I see beyond Agata into a long bloodline. I see the dark pit of the vampire who created her and the Roman man beyond him, and another woman, and another man. An old song that my nurse once sang came into my memory. I feel as light as the girl I had once been.

Loretta sings the song in the darkness, leading me back to her. Jakub hums with her, though he is a beat behind. I sense the pressure of cold fingers as Agata gently washes blood away from my breasts and lips.

Agata taps my shoulders. "Come back, my daughter in blood. My named Firstborn, Pascaline de Banquier. Legitimate Daughter of Jakub Christian Banquier, Count of Limousin, and his wife, Countess Agata."

With Agata's hand in mine, I rise. I wobble on my feet. My muscles ache. Agata gives me another cup of her blood, and Jakub offers a cup of his.

My muscles tighten again. When I take my first unneeded breath, I am strong. Strong enough for my vengeance. I want to gallop like a colt. I want to feel wind in my hair. I identify Loretta's rapid heartbeat and pulse and am frightened of the wanton urge to taste the sweet, vital blood rushing through my sister's veins.

"Agata is correct, Loretta. Some changes are…strange."

"You've become strong, my daughter. Do you sense mental changes?"

I pinch my brow. "I don't think so, Maman. How do you control bloodlust? I feel…I feel…"

"A vampire's life is one of control, my daughter. It becomes habitual. Get a rabbit if you need more blood for the night. Loretta, remain in my room until your sister learns to control herself around humans."

"Why must I wait, Maman?" Loretta asks. "Please, change me now."

Agata pats her hand. "You must wait."

"The years no doubt seem long to you," Jakub says, "but in the centuries of your existence, these years are nothing."

The elder vampires speak in good sense to my sister. She trusts them; I do not.

"It isn't fair," Loretta says.

"None of that now, ma petite." Agata puts her arm around my sister's shoulder and draws her close. "Let us discuss gowns, ribbons, and other things you need to meet this fashionable King Louis."

I watch them go.

My heart weeps for Celeste, but my eyes are dry. Little

Celeste and I will never see each other again, but she will find her father, who loved her more than life. I will never go to Heaven, not because I am an immortal, but because I will be killing whoever I meet in my former Paris townhouse. In that I feel utter delight.

MARGRAVIATE OF BRANDENBURG
1686

A Pause

Gaius

Gaius Augustus Severus, styled Gaius Augustus Sören, lay in his granite crypt. Earth from the Carpathians, Rome, and Brandenburg surrounded him. A true ancient, he walked the Earth during the Roman Empire. The former Legatus of the Carpathian Mountains now went by the title of Präsidierender Bürgermeister and changed his name to match the names of Teutonic Princes.

A sense of discomfort, which he had not felt for a century, overcame him. He could tell when someone from his bloodline formed a newly born vampire. He felt the pull on his strength and the strength of his ancestors. He freely gave it; he doubted she would care if he didn't. It was not the first time a wild girl was reborn to a vampire's freedom.

Why now, and who had done it?

While he could simply rise, traverse the hall, and check, he did not feel like leaving his sarcophagus. The stone floor was cold and he did not want a quarrel with one of his trusted offspring if the accident had not happened in their home. Indeed, it must have been an accident.

Gaius's inner eye sought more information through blood. He checked his named Firstborn, Gunter Bach. Truly,

Gaius had no idea what Gunter's birth order was, as most of Gaius's elder once-human progeny were dead or betrayed him. Furthermore, Gaius's Firstborn had been a horse, but since Gunter needed a birth order for the census, Firstborn might as well be him. In return, Gunter had vowed not to transform anyone without telling him. Gunter kept that promise.

His grown children, the Second and Thirdborn, Leon and Sydella Bach-Sören, also kept their promises, and his other fledglings remained safely isolated with Leon and were too young to make offspring.

Gaius moved on to his ancient offspring. His former concubine, Phillipa, was still in the Carpathians. His other existing daughters were with her: except one.

He set his inner eye upon his most insufferable descendant: Agata, the creation of his creation, Nicheloa, his former brother-in-arms.

It was she, who created an exquisitely beautiful daughter from a young woman with deep copper hair and a splash of freckles upon her nose. He felt the newborn vampire's ache for vengeance more than blood.

Agata and Jakub were still in France. *Interesting. Why build a coven now? Is it the unrest in France? Does Agata know I recently transformed two vampires?*

Though Agata also created Jakub, Jakub was her husband as he had been in life. This newborn woman, Pascaline, would carry the title of Firstborn. Another girl was almost close enough to touch but stood in the shadows of life. She would be Agata's Secondborn. He could not see her yet, but he felt her in Agata and Pascaline's loving devotion. Jakub's emotional state was more complicated, but the centuries had not dulled his esteem for his wife.

Were the women lovers? Or something else. Gaius couldn't tell. He existed by information. He had to know.

A pretty young woman might be an asset if her rage could be harnessed. As a warrior, Jakub might know how, but Gaius doubted it. For the past century, muskets expanded. Weaponry would continue to evolve as swords did in the past. The French king served his vanity while Frederick William, Prince-Elector of Brandenburg and Duke of Prussia, focused on rebuilding his war-ravaged territories, but he also served his joy. Both rulers built standing armies.

The most ancient of vampires—seeing how the world turned—had formed a council of sorts. Gaius did not know what would come of any of it. He needed to be ready. He needed allies – even from former enemies – and one or both young ladies might be the key.

Fredrick William was a great leader and believed in business. Though he and France had been at odds, he might even pay for the trip if Gaius could think of an official reason to travel to Versailles.

Breaking the connection, Gaius rose from his crypt. The stone floor was as cold as he feared it might be. Quickly stepping in his leather house slippers, he wrapped himself in a long cloak. He crossed into the hall of chambers and knocked on Sydella's door. Behind the doors, her animals protested before she opened the door.

Looking like a wild nymph, her blonde hair was loose and, in her robe pocket sat a kitten while another rode in her arms.

Over her shoulder, his true Firstborn, Nix, peered at

Gaius. The horse's mane and tail were freshly combed and braided. A pang of jealousy brushed his heart, but not a bitter one. Over two thousand years old and with no vampiric horse companion to keep him company, Nix remained close to the former humans.

"Only two kittens survived," she told him sadly.

Sydella had been hand feeding a litter she had found trapped in a bag, in the river.

"I am sorry for the kittens, and forgive the ungodly hour, but I need you."

He knocked on Gunter's door, who answered with a curt, "What?"

"A daughter has been reborn. I want her."

Nix put his massive head over Gaius's shoulder and snorted. The old war horse had seen too many vampires born to be impressed with another.

"Agata made a daughter?" Sydella asked.

Her sea-blue eyes went a-gleam with delight. She never had met another female vampire. Though female servants milled about the castle, she only felt the capacity for companionship at court, with women of approximately equal status, which allowed for friendship.

"How did you know?" Gaius asked.

"Because you would've waited for a less ungodly hour if it was anyone else," she said.

Chapter 21

Pascaline

Flush with vampire and lamb's blood, I move into our room and open the wooden box where Loretta and I place our jewelry and pearls. I must know.

I hesitantly touch the gold ring. My fingertips do not burn.

I return it to my left hand, but as I am supposed to be unmarried, I slip it on my middle finger.

I touch the copper on Helena's cuff bracelet. The copper does not burn. I recall the searing flesh on the tramp's face, and ever so carefully brush a fingertip over the silver. My flesh tingles and sears red.

I wonder if silver burns Jakub.

Jakub

Pascaline's lips trembled as she entered my study. Her pale skin was broken by a strawberry flush on her cheekbones; her eyes were still moist from crying. Unlike every interaction before this moment, unlike she was taught, this day-old vampire showed no deference to me as a man, to my position, or even being the elder vampire.

Her breath sounded stilted in her chest. "Celeste's death was convenient for you," she said in a ragged whisper. Once the words left her bright red lips, her whole body shook.

"Is that what you think?" I asked.

"If this venture hurts Loretta in any manner, I shall bring down this house," she hissed.

I stood. Violence would not be to my benefit, so I did not use it, but I thought about ripping her poisoned tongue from her mouth.

Pascaline did not fall back as I would have expected. Her mind was overcome with too much festering grief to experience fear.

I motioned her closer. I opened a drawer and pulled out a large parchment envelope.

"Over the past months, I created these papers for you. Look...and you will understand why my grandchild's death was certainly not convenient and quite expensive."

Pascaline came around the desk. She looked at the three baptismal certificates, predated to days after each of their births as was proper.

"This is education paperwork for you and Loretta, signed by a Good Sister...and now Celeste's death certificate. I've dossiers for you both so you understand this family's history and the lovely convent where you spent your formative years."

Tears tinged with scarlet rolled down the girl's cheeks. "Oh, God, Count de Banquier, I'm sorry. I'm so sorry." Her nose started to run, and she covered her snotty face with her hands.

"Your words came from grief." I forced my voice to be

gentle. "From this moment on, I am your Papa, and Agata is your Maman. You and your sister are our legitimate daughters. I've the paperwork to prove it. You were baptized Catholic when you were babes. If anyone should come for you, you are under my protection. Understood?"

"Yes, Papa. From this moment on," she said softly.

I should have not allowed Agata to transform this daughter. She was mad.

I wished I could wipe my hands of the mess, which was Pascaline, and keep the bright little star of Loretta, but Pascaline had been to Versailles. I hated a weak position, but it was the position we were in.

Pascaline

Jakub flinches slightly when I call him Papa. He does not love me. In fact, Agata and Jakub both favor Loretta over me. They frequently hug her, call her endearing names and praise her musical abilities. I cannot blame them. I do not know how I might change it or even if I should. Favoritism will only make Loretta safer, and I shan't forget the paperwork that proves Papa loved Celeste. That has to be enough.

"If you want vengeance, you must be trained," Jakub says. "But promise me you will practice the harpsichord after each session."

"Yes, Papa."

He moves to his cabinet of weaponry, picks out two blades and waits while I enter the kitchen and drink deeply the blood of a newly slaughtered lamb. I cannot believe my pace as I follow Jakub down the wooded path outside the chateau. I wonder if this was the strength of men. No, I am stronger than any human man.

I leap over a fence without pause.

"Good show," Jakub cheers. He tosses me a sheathed blade. I catch it midair and feel the weight of the unfamiliar weapon.

"It's lighter than I expected."

"A good smith always considers the tradeoffs of weight and strength," he tells me.

I contemplate the fact that I am to be strong and learned in all things. I feel a guilty thrill I never thought possible after seeing my daughter in the grave.

But Celeste is beyond pain, and now, I can keep Loretta safe.

Loretta

10th of January

Cher Journal,

I miss Pascaline since her transformation. Now she is a vampire, we no longer share a room and only see each other at dinner or playing the harpsichord. I am always under an elder's watchful eye, though Pascaline has not tried to hurt me.

She is often with Jakub—no, I always must refer to him as Papa. It is too easy to make a mistake. In truth, though, I also called my first father, "papa" in private, "Lord Father in public." I find calling Jakub "papa" much easier. Is that strange?

He listens to my music each evening, claps politely and

only has kind words. He hesitantly called me "dove" today, as Agata does, but I could tell such things don't feel natural to him.

I closed my eyes as Maman gently combed my long, wavy locks and plaited my hair for bed.

"Tell me, dove, why you truly wish to go to court?" she asked.

"I shall be loyal to you, Maman."

"There's no doubt about that, but I want to know why you wish to go to court and become a vampire in the years to come. Pascaline wants vengeance, but what do you want?"

I looked at my pale hands, newly soft again as they were. "I don't want anything for myself."

"There must be something."

The pull of Agata's will lingered upon my mind, encouraging me to speak.

"I want to make music. That means I must go to Versailles." I spoke words I thought I would never admit. "Perhaps, I once wanted to know love, but since that's an impossibility, I'll settle for being the king's or perhaps a duke's mistress. For that, I must go where they are," I said.

Agata's brows rose to a point. The tiny creases around her eyes grew slightly deeper. "You are too young to be jaded."

"My parents were not happy, Maman. Nor my brothers. Helena was terrified of her husband. Andre was a good man, but Pascaline feared angering him."

"Yet, Pascaline mourns grievously."

"Yes, Pascaline loved Andre. It's killing her. But until we met you and Jakub, I don't think either of us knew the kind of love that might exist in marriages. I want you to know, you have nothing to fear from me. I've been trained in intrigue enough to know when I might twist or manipulate for the betterment of my family and my family's lands. As you are my family now, I do all this for you."

Agata laughed lightly. "And if you fell in love?"

"I'd give anything to feel real love like you feel for Papa," I said. "But there's no place in France for love anymore."

"You must be careful not to cause a scandal or catch syphilis, which would mar your beauty. If you become with child, you would not be turned until the child is grown."

"I've no interest in lying with a man unless it helps our family's standing."

"Jakub and I love you too much to ask you to do such a thing. Pascaline loves you even more than we."

I listened to Agata's gentle lecture but found it incredible a woman who existed in love for over several lifetimes might understand the world as it was. I made a silent vow. Agata and Jakub are innocents. Pascaline and I must protect them from the king and anyone else who would lay claim to their holding.

Chapter 22

Loretta

1st of March

Cher Journal,

We leave for Versailles tomorrow. I cannot wait for my debut!

Jakub

I entered a battle, I could not fight. I hated having no known enemy other than a king who loathed his nobles. Thus, I felt no disloyalty providing false paperwork proving the births of my daughters and nunnery records describing their education. Since they were just girls, it was plausible no one recognized them, even if any gendarme from my county happened to be on the king's private guard. So much was left to chance.

The girls were gracious and pretty, but that meant little. Both girls could play harpsichord and harp, but Loretta was an exceptional singer. It is said girls can be jealous with each other, but Pascaline accepts that her musical gifts are not as rare as Loretta's. She hopes to establish herself as a well-dressed lady in literary circles and attend Court, during the hours in which men work.

They kept details of their plan to themselves, though they openly believed they could raise money by selling dyed ribbons, barrels of dye, and even bolts of fabric, even though mauve and lavender colors had fallen out of fashion. I did not know if such things were possible, but Agata agreed with their assessment.

By making such spectacles of themselves, it was possible in Versailles, someone might recognize them but, in truth, I did not fear their past acquaintances. My estate paid for their upkeep and taxes. With the cost of gowns alone, why would anyone endanger their position and family budget by admitting knowing them?

There were other expenses, too. The family must arrive in a horse-drawn carriage, and I needed a man in livery. This was one of the established ways we might prove our nobility to Versailles.

Thankfully, my stablehand, Jean-Victor, drove our carriage from time to time, and I found livery that fit.

We were still on the right side of the equinox for the trip. Unlike Castor, carriage horses were not taught to work in the night outside the kept roads in town. They had to be rested as the world darkened lest they fell. Happily, this early in the season, there was plenty of fresh grass for the horses to graze upon.

Pascaline asked, "Do you need help, Papa? Now I'm strong; I might help you and Jean-Victor. Heading north, the driving bench will be mostly in the shade."

I had not expected such boldness from the girl who had

only become respectful once assured I had nothing to do with her daughter's death.

Hoping he would excuse me from answering, I asked Jean-Victor, "Would you mind if Madame Pascaline assists us on the road north?"

Jean-Victor did not excuse me. "If you say so, Monsieur le Count."

"Yes, please teach me. I want to help," she said.

"My countess?" I asked Agata.

"I give my permission, but be careful, ma chérie," Agata said. "Put on gloves and your woolens. Listen most attentively to your father and Jean-Victor."

Carefully covering her hands and wearing a wide-brimmed hat, Pascaline joined Jean-Victor on the driver's bench.

"Madame, horses are trained with commands, but roads, especially those in poor order, require a high degree of awareness. You must anticipate issues and support your horses when they become frightened. If any stumble, watch for lameness in the team."

The boy spoke kindly to Pascaline, who listened carefully and asked intelligent questions. More intelligent than I expected from a girl who'd only ridden inside a carriage.

I rode Castor in front of the carriage team. He was a good leader of the herd even if not the leader of the team.

The journey over my well-kept road was easy and took only two nights. Though the other ladies rode in the carriage, Pascaline remained with Jean-Victor. She was intimidated by the horses' stomping hooves at first, but she kept working and learned to groom the animals. Each day, her eyes brightened with inner confidence. For the first time, I bitterly noticed how much Pascaline's lively smile reminded me of Celeste's.

Once away from my county, we were hindered considerably by rain and the state of the roads. While my road was perfect, other counts apparently did not care to maintain theirs, and allowed holes to form in the winter. Some roads were even chained by their gendarme.

When the carriage inevitably became stuck in the mud, Pascaline jumped down and pushed it over a deep divot. She quickly checked the horses, speaking gently to them as she examined each hoof for lameness. She clambered back onto the driver's bench beside Jean-Victor, and we moved on until we were forced to stop again. Each time, Pascaline assisted in clearing fallen rocks, large branches, and other obstacles with nary a complaint, and I thanked Agata for giving her permission. Such a strange girl.

VERSAILLES
1686

Chapter 23

Loretta

9th of March

Cher Journal,

Crossing into the golden gates of Versailles felt like a dream. I had never seen such magnificence and splendor. Handsome guards stood tall in their livery. The first rooms were glorious, filled with magnificent murals and marble tile. A well-dressed usher escorted us to our assigned apartment.

My euphoria was short lived as the usher led us up the stairs of the north wing. The corridor smelled strongly of urine and smoke, making our rank and Papa's out-of-favor status obvious. The family was assigned a small one-room apartment on the second floor with a single large bed and one cabinet bed, that smelled of mildew, for our servants.

Over the dressing table, a large portrait of handsome King Louis XIV greeted us. We immediately opened the small window to give the room some fresh air. I couldn't believe this was considered a family apartment. It was fortuitous to have left Suzetta to midwife as there was simply no more room.

I never thought I would miss the coziness of Chateau de

Banquier or the opulence of Andre and Pascaline's apartment in Paris. I even missed my parents' house! I couldn't believe my ignorance about Versailles.

Jean-Victor concerned himself with our trunks. Maman lifted the bedding and set a layer of herbs between the sheets. She laid a line of salt around the room.

"We should get home as soon as possible," she said nervously. "I fear for your health in this crowded place...not to mention your sister's bloodlust." She mumbled the last part under her breath, but I heard her.

I did not say anything, because for me, there was no going home. I wanted the chance to sing and be assigned better accommodations for my talent.

I listened as Papa gave Jean-Victor instructions for our first meal. The young man left us with a bow.

Under Maman's watchful eye, Pascaline turned around so I could unlace her travel gown. Once she was unthreaded, she loosened me.

Maman quickly lay herbs under Jean-Victor's cotton mattress and wiped all the wood off his sleeping cabinet with her vinegars before we helped her change.

We were all outfitted in gowns when Jean-Victor brought in our first hot meal- a sliver of beef and green beans- in many days.

"I wasn't able to obtain any bread from the kitchen, Countess. I hope this will do." He bowed and went to his bed in the cupboard.

Pascaline

This moment will be catastrophic or triumphant. I trail arm in arm with Loretta behind our new parents. My embroidered satin slippers tread softly upon sparkling marble floors. The Hall of Mirrors is crowded with flickering candlelight and satin-clad bodies. The air is full of expensive perfumes and dusting powders, but it doesn't mask the human heartbeats, and intoxicating scent of blood.

Most wear paint. Maman, Papa, and I must wear paint to ensure we cast a reflection. Loretta made the correct choice by forgoing it and instead relying on her bare skin with a touch of rouge. She looks exceptionally pretty and youthful.

Loretta and I wear damask in demure shades of blue. Our stomachers are embroidered with swirling purple violets, blue forget-me-nots, and yellow daffodils surrounded by green leaves. Our hairstyles match, prim coils with a few curls framing our faces are pinned with early daffodils and a lavender ribbon. We are perfect, and the cool spring night feels perfect.

Some courtiers admire the thirty murals depicting Louis XIV's achievements, while others check their reflections or speak in gentle voices behind their fans. A four-piece quartet of violins plays soft music in the background. I notice how perfectly courtiers smile, but the smiles rarely go to their eyes; how they speak without saying exactly what they mean or committing to anything: how they laugh without joy.

Most are humans, but I sense loup-garou heartbeats—stronger than a human's with a more rapid pulse. I do not know all the loup-garou's gifts, but if they have the hearing of a wolf, I wonder if they hear my slower heartbeat. Thus, they must know vampires are in their midst.

We squeeze hands while we wait.

"The Count and Countess Limousin and their daughters!" the herald calls. The titles echo against the high ceilings.

We approach the king with precision steps. The herald says my name first as the elder. I step forward and curtsy. Loretta follows the same protocol.

Though my lips remain closed, I lie to the king — to France. I wish I do not enjoy the feeling of forbidden excitement. I never thought I would be capable of lying to an entire country, but if King Louis is France as he claims, then France abandoned me and my sister. France killed my child.

The king smiles. "Why, Count de Limousin, it seems like ages since We enjoyed your company. Yet, you and your wife seemed to haven't aged a day..."

I fear the king's excellent memory. Though outwardly I keep my composure as trained to do, I wonder if he recognizes me. The king speaks eloquently to Maman and refers to me and my sister as "Such lovely country roses," before dismissing us to our place.

We are forgotten publicly, but I do not doubt the king will be watching.

Loretta

9th of March continued

Cher Journal,

There is always music here and so much food. I am not sure how or what to say about that, because the rules for the populous do not seem to apply for the king's company. Pascaline seemed even more disturbed as if she was seeing it all for the first time. Of course, in a way, she is.

The king's table is laid in front of the fireplace every evening. Louis XIV sits with his back to the hearth. His seat is raised so he can see us all. Folding stools are placed for his chosen dinner guests. High-ranking ladies sit in the front row of the audience. Behind them we stand with other courtiers. We dare not miss the king's meal. It would be noticed, and we are low enough as it is.

Thus, after our grand debut, our family party followed the crowd to the king's antechamber and the Grand Couvert. I took one dancing step to the quartet's sound, which greeted us before we arrived.

We curtsied as a procession of officers from the Services for the King's Mouth brought in the first dish on the finest glimmering gold platter. My mouth watered at the sight of oysters. Bourgogne wine was poured for the king.

We curtsied again at the tureen of soup. The officer lifted the lid. A heavenly warm smell, which grew stronger as the soup was ladled into the king's golden bowl, wrapped the antechamber.

In the pause between courses, the officers brought in a magnificent bread loaf shaped like a pig. Soon after, an entire roasted boar appeared, carried by six uniformed men. My mouth watered at the overpowering, meaty smell. Pascaline looked as if she wanted to spill blood. Instead, we held our posture and curtsied as we ought—at an enormous salmon lying upon a block of salt, an impressive salad, a tub of roasted vegetables, and sundry, sweet-smelling nut puddings, and candied fruit.

The king finally rose from his chair. Only after every single person of higher rank than us left the antechamber, were we permitted to depart. Papa took hold of Maman's arm, and we all moved to our room.

It had been an amazing night, even though I was merely a spectator. Besides our room, the only disappointment, is Louis XIV is older than my first father and appears older than Papa. The sketches and portraits of him made him ageless. A dark wig, graciousness to the ladies and magnificent furs can't hide a wrinkled face. Papa sat in the room's only chair and lifted his feet on the bench. My sister and I undressed and did our best to fit in the bed. This close to Pascaline, I could see her veiled hunger and had second thoughts about closing my eyes.

Maman poured a sour-smelling draft that made my nose twitch from across the room.

"What's that?" Pascaline asked.

"Sleeping potion," Maman said.

"I don't want any."

I sensed the depths of power shifting behind Maman's dark eyes. "Jakub and I recognize the honor in you, but sleep is how we heal and function around humans. Do you want your Papa to attend Court in the morning?"

Pascaline took the cup. As she tilted her head back to take in the liquid, her hungry eyes stared directly at me.

Chapter 24

Pascaline

Loretta and I dress ourselves while Maman and Papa remain in the room. Most ladies are not seen until the afternoon, but the room still seems crowded. Strong and weak heartbeats mingle around the courtroom. Many men wear deep blue or red, but others wore pastel colors this season.

I pray men will like the color of Papa's dye in their damask and brocade justacorps and breeches. If we can catch the king's eye and bring the color into fashion, we will make so much money for Papa and tax money for the king; Louis XIV will forgive everything. Of course, that is only half the plan.

I bring a petition to the king's herald and await my turn.

Once called, I approach, careful not to waste the king's time but ensuring my steps are made with precision. I smile as I look at the man I loathe. I cannot show I hate him; I need to display love and adoration.

"Highness, many convents overflow with orphans and pregnant girls and women in need of care. The Bible tells us to care for orphans and widows. I prayed on these issues and ask the Court for more provisions for the destitute delivered through the convents. The convent where I was educated lost their two hives this winter, and I ask for monies to buy a new one."

The king looks at an elderly cardinal in dignified red robes.

"The generous lady speaks of things a lady cannot understand," said the cardinal. "Abbeys and convents have strict budgets to discourage tempting the women with luxuries. Besides, God places people in those positions in His wisdom."

"Does God not tell us He hears the mistreated widows and orphans? Does He not claim to hear their cry?" I say. "The people are taxed to their breaking point. They are only now able to bury their dead. They need bread and warmth."

"You step on dangerous territory, Madame Pascaline," the cardinal warns. "Would you deny the importance of Lent?"

I inwardly seethe but refuse even a hint of anger to appear on my face. Instead, I open my eyes wide and play innocent. "No, of course not. Forgive me, Cardinal. I only wish to help starving children. Traveling to Versailles, I saw many—"

The cardinal waves his fan lazily. "I do not deny your heart, but you know little of what you ask. Study it further, and you'll see your superiors know best. Remember Christ's words to his disciples in Mark 14:7, 'the poor will always be with us'."

The king's heartbeat remains unchanged. He will not press the issue. I wonder if I should continue to fight. I do not want to disappoint my new parents so early in our relationship. I hate my paralyzing fear.

"Next petition," the king says.

I curtsy and return to Loretta.

"You were amazing," she whispers.

"But I haven't changed anything," I whisper back, my hands trembling with rage.

Several more petitioners are denied. When the sun reaches its zenith, the king rises from his throne. As is routine, Court breaks for an hour.

The king and his guard approach.

He inclines his head toward us. "Madame Pascaline, we hear you're gifted in music, much more than one of your gender is expected. While I doubted the voracity of the statement, I witnessed your boldness of speech. You, a lady of such young years, have been here all of a day and already argued with a cardinal."

I blushed. "My sister and I've studied well, but Madame Loretta is the greater musician, Highness."

Loretta curtsies but does not answer as a lady would not boast.

The king smiles even wider. "Interesting."

Loretta and I curtsy again for good measure.

The king moves on.

A new danger emerges as two men in their prime sidle closer. They wear golden, moon-shaped medallions, and I remember the medallion on that loup-garou I saw in the forest. Their loup-garou hearts sound bolder and wilder than any human. I study the golden embroidery on their justacorps— phases of the moon and stars.

"Hello, Mesdames."

We both curtsy, but I step in front of my sister.

"Forgive me, have we been introduced?" I ask.

"No, but I must ask if you meant what you said?" one of

them says gruffly.

"Yes, but I've no power to alter anything. My words did not change anyone's heart."

"At least not yet..." The other's voice was smooth.

"What do you mean, Monsieur?"

"Our people also suffer; we could not even get an audience. You did, Madame."

"I shall do what the cardinal suggested and read more on this issue. Once I know more, I will bring forth another petition."

"Strange," the first man says.

"Very strange," His companion agrees.

Their eyes were on my face, my hands. I wonder if they knew what I am. *Mon Dieu, were these men from the forest? I should've looked more closely at their faces.*

"Strange for the loup-garou, perhaps." Loretta takes my arm in hers.

"You know us?" the gruff one asks.

Loretta turns us from the men without a curtsy or even a nod. Except for the king and our father, ladies of the court are never required to speak to men—especially men to whom we have not been formally introduced. The rudeness is theirs.

I love my sister.

Loretta

10th of March

Cher Journal,

Pascaline's amazing! I wish you could see her at court. She isn't afraid to speak her mind to human men or even the loup-garou. She told the king of my musical talents and by the time we returned to our quarters Jean-Victor handed me a note.

I opened it quickly and scanned its contents.

Maman opened the door. "Ma chéries, 'tis late. Let your papa rest."

Behind her, Papa had moved to the bed.

"It's the afternoon, Maman. Look at this note. I'm to play for the ladies on Sunday next."

"What a blessing. Court must have gone well?"

I giggled as Pascaline freshened my hair.

"It did! Ought I play one of my original songs?"

"As it pleases you," Pascaline said. "Just be careful."

"What do you mean?"

"I wonder what the king's game is. Or if it was the king at all. Those two men approached," Pascaline said. "I failed, Maman. A cardinal said I didn't understand budgets. Their eyelids fall upon the starving."

"But you were seen in your gowns. That is what matters," Maman said.

"I suppose," Pascaline sighed.

I wanted to comfort my sister, but I imagined playing the harpsichord for the whole court. After my song, when I would stand and curtsy, the applause would echo across the Hall of Mirrors, and we wouldn't have to sleep in this tiny room.

Chapter 25

Pascaline

I pace as Loretta sleeps soundly in the center of the bed. I ought to sleep as well, but daylight is coming. Even with Maman's potions, I find myself drowsy at the most inopportune times. Only blood keeps me going. I want more.

"I see your need," Maman says.

I wish I could see my reflection in order to know what my face is doing. I lean down and bite into her wrist. Her rich, metallic lifeforce flows into my mouth.

Her rhythmic, languid heartbeat soaks into my being, giving me her strength while it is weakening her. Scarlet visions dance in front of my eyes.

Her body goes limp; my fangs dig deeper. until I feel the pleasurable sensation that I dismembered her hand from the rest of her body.

Her heart skips a beat. "Enough, chérie."

I raise my head, lick my fangs and taste the blood on my lips. I look to see her hand is still attached.

Maman's eyes glint with amusement. "Go polish your teeth," she says in a raspy whisper.

I bring her a glass of water first. Though the mirror is useless, I go to the dressing table to polish my teeth.

Maman shakes Loretta awake.

"I ordered time in a practice room today, Lor," I tell my sister. We need time to ready you for your achievement.

Loretta stretches herself out of bed. "We shan't attend Court?"

I shake my head. "The cardinal's correct. I'll need to study the issue further and ensure my future petitions are accepted. But your victory or failure will come sooner. Let us prepare for it. How may I assist you?"

Loretta bites her lip. "If I write music on a slate, would you copy it on paper? Sometimes, I erase and need to go back. It becomes an awful mess."

"I shall help in any way that I can."

Loretta and I walk arm in arm across the grounds in our simpler dresses. We enter the library and find the door steward—a thin man with a pinched expression and curly white wig. I briefly wonder why a nobleman would ever choose to be a door steward and realize he had not chosen the job.

The steward opens one door for us. "We hear you shall be playing for the ladies this weekend?"

"Indeed." We know better than to make a fuss.

Loretta sits at the harpsichord and tests the keys.

Jean-Victor brings in a carafe of water and lemon as I requested and returns to our quarters to attend the needs of Papa and Maman.

We have plenty of chalk for Loretta's slate and I have all the paper, ink and quills I will need.

"I should think to play a song of love, but...what do I know of love?" Loretta says.

"Of all our adventures, now you're afraid?"

"Nervous. I don't want my song to be false."

"Your heart is full of love, friendship, and loyalty," I tell her.

Loretta plays a series of rising chords. Her bright, joyful personality returns with the complement.

Jakub

Agata thought it best to be seen early in the season. Therefore, I steeled myself to attend Court, though I found it dreadfully dull. Protecting our people should be the hallmark of nobility. Instead, I watched and listened to France's most powerful men yearning for more, pressing themselves toward the king, who surrounded himself with sycophants.

It felt as if hours passed while men pessimistically discussed, rather than tried to solve, problems in their counties—problems that could be easily rectified by giving men and boys jobs with proper wages to feed their families and providing protection for women and children from men who would abuse them. Build and provide for a strong gendarme, not to intimidate the poor, but to protect the populace and grain stores and keep the roads safe and in good order.

Though I could use my voice to force my will on these stupid people, I was quite clumsy at it. People would react, and it would be obvious I used my powers. Consequently, at best, I would be hung for witchcraft instead of tortured and killed in the rooms below the palace as many had been before me. I was a husband and a father, three women depended on me to behave as a modern noble ought.

I dared not reject an invitation to the Hunt. Though I had not been asked to go to war in many years, my prowess with weaponry was not forgotten. I killed a boar and gifted the dead creature to his highness for supper—a meal to which we were invited to watch but not partake in.

I missed my road, my village, my men, and Castor. But most of all, I missed Louis XII. He had been a great king, a warrior king. A king of the people.

Disgusted with the gluttony, overindulgence, and pointless inanity of Versailles, I found myself exceedingly resentful when Pascaline informed me she would be assisting Loretta with a song--of all things.

My clairvoyance sensed something undead approached. At least, that would be interesting.

Loretta

27th of March

Cher Journal,

More vampires have come. Moreover, Maman and Papa know them. I don't know what it means.

During the Grand Couvert, Papa shifted slightly so he might see about the room. He rested his hand on the small of Maman's back and whispered, "Gaius is here, my love, with two new offspring. Tall, blond, lovely creatures."

Maman frowned and looked out of the corner of her eyes. I saw the three vampires, not breathing human breaths, their luminescent skin betraying their death.

It was strange, though. We never met before, but I felt as

if I knew the shorter, black- haired one from a dream.

Mon Cher, I shall pause to describe them. All three died in their late twenties or early thirties leaving beautiful corpses, and though it is said seventeen is the bloom of youth, I am glad I am not yet a vampire.

Born to be a king, Gaius is not tall for a man, but his powerful, muscular form gives him a sense of authority. His broad shoulders and solid arms are accentuated by his justacorps. In fact, he is everything I thought King Louis would be rather than the older man he had become.

The other two—a man and woman—look so alike they might be twins, especially around their sparkling blue eyes, which holds the startling clarity of still water. The brother's pale hair was cropped close to his sculpted features. His is a more slender frame than Gaius, and taller. He has the same bearing as Papa, and I wonder if he, too, was a knight in a former age.

Though the woman is taller than the black-haired vampire, she isn't nearly as tall as her brother. She stands with inner confidence, perfect elegance and intelligence. She is the type of woman who could bring a king to his knees.

Cher Journal, I admit, I desire to be her.

Tonight, the lady wore a lovely rose gown, which set off the blush on her cheeks and I stared at her wondering who she was until the blond man turned to study me. His blue eyes filled with mirth. Yet, I suddenly feared mis-stepping and finding myself in his shadow because, even in this candlelit room, the man had the uncanny ability to remain in the shade.

He touched his sister's arm. She smiled at us over her rose-colored fan, as if to say, I see you, friends.

Pascaline gestured back with her fan.

We waited to see who might make the first move.

However, the vampires did not approach.

Chapter 26

Loretta

30th of March

Cher Journal,

Pascaline tried, and again failed, to bring a petition to help the poor. She also made contact with a young man who studied the spreading wheat famine. She claimed that winning the petition was not necessarily the goal, but only to be remembered, but she wants to win.

I wished I understood politics as Pascaline understood them. I try to listen, but I keep thinking of the old king's face. Regardless of his dashing chivalry toward the ladies, he was old. I can't believe I once wanted to be his mistress. I suppose I was naïve, and naïve girls think many foolish things. Worse, every time I believe I have outgrown my naiveté, something else happens reminds me of it.

I was relieved when Court was called for midday. My feet and knees were tired from prolonged standing. Walking provided some respite but different pain. I held my skirts to protect them from wet stone. Sunlight gleamed off the paths, damp from the rain and water leapt from the fountain of nymphs. If I become a vampire, I will never walk in the sun after a rain or watch the sunlight sparkling between stones.

I looked for a place to read my book about Psyche. Something was missing in my song. Something…

"Mademoiselle de Banquier?" A deep rich voice resonated behind me.

It belonged to a large man with a soft gaze in his brown eyes. Though he wore unfashionably flat shoes, he stood like one of the king's guards, straight and tall. I barely came up to his broad shoulders. Outwardly, the man was everything a man should be, except for a spiderweb of scars and burnt flesh on the side of his face which dipped into his collar and peeked out from his sleeve.

He wore his spiraling brown curls tied back with a black-silk ribbon. His red justacorps was embroidered with glittering golden thread, and his white lace sash was peerless. By his bearing, though, I guessed he was unused to wearing stays. Yet I did not think he was a pretender.

"Forgive me for being forward. I know we haven't been introduced, but I've a message from…my father to yours." Something about the way he said "father" chilled me. I knew he spoke of vampires.

"Yes, Monsieur, and you are?"

"My name is Charles Onfoy. My future father wishes to speak to your future father."

"I don't know what you're referring to." I stepped away. "I'm the daughter of Jakub Christian de Banquier, Count de Limousin."

"I also walk with the undead," Charles said softly. "Though I still live. I comprehend why your parents sleep during the hours of the sun and why you and your sister act as their representative. The king recognizes vampires, too. Be careful how you step, Madame Loretta."

I hid my mouth with my fan. "Who did you say your father is, Monsieur?"

"Gaius Sören, Bürgermeister, newly arrived in Versailles," he repeated. Fear deepened in his eyes when he said the name.

"I've never heard of this Sören, though my mother was created by a man named Nicheola created by a Gaius Severus."

"The same. Tell your father: Sören seeks him under Zeus tonight. You must not fail in this message. He set his eyes upon your family last night."

"I don't care what Monsieur Sören set his eyes upon, nor will my father," I said, "but I'll relay the message. Which Zeus?"

"Near the fountain of Apollo. Take care, Madame, we walk in dangerous times. Moreover—"

A loud boom resounded all around us.

Charles jumped. His hand moved to his belt and, finding no weapon, he stepped between me and assumed danger. Two small sailing ships were engulfed by a mock battle in the Grand Canal.

A sudden warmth spread across my body. Charles was a noble of the sword, like Papa. My heartbeat quickened; I wondered what it might feel like to touch his muscular arm. I opened my fan to conceal my blush for my sudden indecent thought.

The assembled nobles clapped and cheered. He pretended to do the same.

I fished a handkerchief from my skirt pocket so he might dab the sweat running from his brow.

"Forgive me, Madame. Normally when I hear things explode, people don't clap," he stammered as he wiped his face. I wanted to protect him from this sinful place.

He tried to return the handkerchief, but I waved it away. "Keep it; I've another in my pocket," I said.

I'd never felt a quiver in my stomach while speaking to a man before. If all women feel this way, it's no wonder why priests say women are lustful and not smart enough to make decisions for themselves.

My mind suddenly ran with tumbling thoughts about the mistaken beliefs which I held that I had never truly considered before. Perhaps I might write songs about it …if I could find a way to do so while still pleasing the king.

"Who keeps you company when your father sleeps?" he asked softly.

"That's none of your affair, Monsieur," I said firmly, though I did not want to end this conversation.

He bowed. "What I'm attempting to say is I also keep my own company when the Bach-Sörens sleep. I would be deeply honored if I might continue this conversation—even though I've no more business with your family." He bowed again. "May I walk with you?"

"I shall do nothing to bring a scandal onto my household."

"I'll not harm you or your reputation in any way," Charles said. "I swear it as a Frenchman, newly arrived in my homeland after many years abroad. I will swear upon my honor if you wish. I am the grandson of a knight, but I was a grenadier, with the rank of sergeant. I can summon my…

family's cadet if you wish for a chaperone."

The way he said family implied he did not think of Gaius Sören or anyone else as family. A spark of anger flittered across my heart, and I loathed myself for my earlier lust. *What if he had been part of a Dragonnade unit?*

Still, I did not want to end the conversation. "Did you serve domestically?"

"Abroad." He glanced around to ensure no one was too close. "I swear I only killed those on the battlefield."

I curtsied. "I walk the Grand Canal, and you may walk with me, Grenadier Sergeant."

Etiquette requires that one must always call a soldier by his rank, and Charles smiled the moment I did so. It was a true smile without lechery or pretense. Or at least I hope I read him correctly. We walked close enough to speak, but not so close someone would say we were acting scandalously. While everyone sought for a way closer to the king, no one paid much attention to an out of favor count's daughter and a grenadier sergeant. On Sunday, I might make them recognize me. At this moment, I was simply one of the many unimportant women of Versailles.

"Is it a fancy of mine or do you not love this Sören as I love my father?" I asked.

"Sören hasn't been a father to me," Charles said.

"Indeed, you don't know affection?"

"How can one know affection for one of them?" The pinch of his brow deepened. Anger made his scars more frightening.

"I love my parents dearly," I said quickly.

"You are blessed," he said.

"Shall you not become one of them?" I asked.

"I don't know if I want to live for eternity. My unit is gone. Gaius took my dreams of promotion. I've nothing."

Heat flushed on my cheeks, neck, and decolletage. "I apologize for asking questions which trouble you, Grenadier Sergeant."

"You cannot trouble me, Madame Loretta." He quickly changed the subject by inquiring about my book.

"It's the libretto for the new opera about Cupid and Psyche's great love. I was requested to play in the Peace Room for the ladies on Sunday." Feeling beyond bold, I asked, "Due to the time, my family shall probably not attend. Shall you?"

"Madame, I'm at my captors' convenience."

We turned off the path from the Grand Canal and passed the golden Enceladus Fountain, which was inspired by the giants who dared to climb Mount Olympus and attempt to dethrone the gods. Charles stared at the fountain. I wondered what thoughts swam behind his deep brown eyes.

Pascaline

I watch the other vampires watch us at the morning session, but they are not seen again in the afternoon. I quickly learn Bach-Sören Equīnus from Brandenburg bred the most magnificent hunting horses in the Holy Roman Empire. The family has brought a dozen to sell to the French Court with their prince-elector's permission to assist in bringing forth a needed peace between the courts. They spend afternoons in the stables.

I do not like that the scarred man approached my

unaccompanied sister. Papa will meet this Gaius at Zeus. Each day more courtiers will arrive. Perhaps more vampires. Who knew who else would come? I dare not wait a night longer. If I take my vengeance it needs to be tonight.

After the Grand Couvert, my sister and I stroll beside the Grand Canal, dazzled by the colorful gowns and chaotic movements of the crowd. The air is rich and fragrant with sweet flowers and perfume obscuring the smell of human flesh. I fondly remember my first time at Versailles. My eyes prickle with tears as a lady kisses her gentleman behind a fan. I can feel the heady excitement of new love within the innocent woman's chest. I remember how it felt the first time Andre kissed me.

I blink my eyes and return to the present, admiring the fretwork on a long wide skirt, then the dainty waist and slender neck that holds so much blood, moving past me. The woman turns as if she senses a predator behind her.

I blush prettily. "Forgive me if I stared. I was admiring all the embroidery on your gown."

She thanks me and compliments my auburn hair.

"Forgive me, is your seamstress a servant of your great house or is she in Paris?" I ask.

"Paris," the lady says.

I give her my card. "I will be most grateful if you would share the seamstress's address at your convenience."

Her pretty lips make an o as she looks at my card. I recognize the mercenary shine in her widening eyes, as she hopes to be acquainted with the daughter of a count—even if the Banquiers were out of favor.

"I should think the seamstress would also be grateful.

What a lovely shade of plum on your ribbon," the lady says.

"My own father's house holds the recipe for the color."

I introduce my sweet sister to the woman so I might learn her name. If anyone asks, a stranger will have evidence that she saw both daughters of Count de Banquier in Versailles.

We chat until the sky lights up with sparkling fire. The crowd claps, and I clap as well. It displays many colors within colors, heat and glorious light.

Loretta and I follow the crowd to the end of the garden where another great spectacle awaits us. I squeeze her hand.

"Good luck," she whispers.

I slip around the maze, searching for a quiet spot where I might sneak away to Paris.

Loretta

30th of March

Cher Journal,

I left Pascaline at the hedgerow. I wished with all my might I also could have vengeance. Celeste was my niece; I miss her, too. I especially miss how Maman and Papa doted over her. Papa especially often found his laughter with her, and he never laughs now.

"Come, 'tis late. You've a long day on the morrow," Maman said, close enough to my ear to make me nearly jump from my skin. I ought to have known the vampires would be watching us.

Jakub

G aius greeted me warmly with an embrace and a kiss on each cheek. "Your gracious lady did not come?"

"My lady has not forgiven you, Präsidierender Bürgermeister, is it?" I returned the embrace.

"Indeed. May I present Charles Onfoy, Grenadier Sergeant, once of the French Royal Army?"

I turned my eyes upon the taller man. His eyes met mine the way a fighting man did. A deep sadness resided there. I greeted him in the same embrace I shared with Gaius. His muscles felt like stone.

We, three, slowly moved to the Star Grove. Complex pathways and a meandering circular path merged at intervals, to form a pentagon around a shimmering pool filled with starlit water. A mountain shaped stone rose from the center. Few frequented this grove at night.

"Grenadier Sergeant, my daughter told me you walked with her and seemed to be a man of honor."

"Her kind words warm my heart," Charles said.

"However, I am not a girl, and I do not expect that your motives, or Gaius's, are honorable."

"I have never hurt anyone off the battlefield. Least of all, a lovely girl with a gentle heart. Is the lady your daughter?"

"Both girls are Agata's daughters. My Agata is the only woman for me."

"I don't believe you," he dared to say.

"Verily, I care not what you believe, human. However, treat my family with respect or I'll rip out your throat."

"Jakub, you speak rather warmly on this subject," Gaius said.

"I mean to be a devoted father this time," I said.

"To hear Agata say it, you were a devoted father the first time," Gaius said.

"My wife's love has always eclipsed her memory," I said. To Charles, I added, "The army came first to my shame."

"The army has also come first in my life," Charles said softly. "But it shan't anymore."

In his usual impatience, Gaius said, "Pascaline's rebirth surprised me; I must know why Agata expanded the bloodline."

I was somewhat relieved that the answer to his question might be the main reason for his presence but refused to show it.

"Let it be known that I owe you no explanation for anything that goes on in our family. But since the answer is simple, I will honor your request. Agata wanted daughters. The king required us in Versailles; debuting daughters allow Agata remain in the shadows." I sighed. I could not speak of Darling Celeste, though she was first in my mind.

"But why transform her?"

"The world isn't always kind to women. We gifted Pascaline with a vampire's strength to protect her and her sister, as she requested. I would keep our younger one closer if I could, but we believe she is worldly enough to remain out of most predicaments." I met Charles's eyes. "From your boldness this afternoon, may I expect you will ask her to walk again?"

"With your permission, Count."

I stared at the amphitheater. "Her mother and I shall consider it. I prefer the fresh air of my county and my horses rather than the city and palace. I don't know what to think about knights who play act, rather than battle for France.”

“I’m glad you agree this age leaves something to be desired,” Gaius said. “Though there has been animosity in the past, we must learn to be allies. The world is changing in many ways.”

I stroked my beard. “I see. I shall speak to Agata.”

“You may want to keep an eye on the elder girl; she left Versailles tonight,” Gaius said.

“I gave her a blade,” I said. “Tonight’s activity will temper her.”

“Or kill her?” Gaius asked, without waiting for a response. “Regardless, I sent my offspring to follow. She will not be killed.”

“Excellent, my Agata most surely would prefer she existed,” I said.

“And you?”

“She has a devoted heart, my daughter,” I said.

Gaius simply laughed, while Charles studied me.

Pascaline

From the darkness of my former garden, I squeeze Papa’s dagger as soldiers move in and out of my townhouse.

Someone is in my marital bed. Under my skin, my muscles twitch. Every roquille of blood in my veins boils, yearning for vengeance.

“Dear God, why did You forsake him?” I whisper. “Andre was a good man. We were content as could be expected. And if he had a mentor like Jakub...”

I know Andre is dead, but I pray the paper was wrong.

I scan for a sign of him. There is no sign of Andre: no scent of Andre's perfume caught in the breeze, no word spoken in his voice, no vision of his handsome profile in a window. A tiny voice in my heart whispers to creep inside and check every room and corner of the townhouse to find my husband, or his ghost, and steal him away. Burning tears rise to my eyes. "Andre is dead, and Celeste is dead. Focus! All that's left is retribution."

I open my corset and remove the lace covering my breasts. At the kitchen door, two foot soldiers in regimental gray and red suck down ale or possibly wine. One has thin gray hair protruding from his cap. The other is younger with brown hair. I decide to kill the elder man first.

"Need company, boys?" I draw closer and raise my skirt to show a bit of ankle.

"This one ain't right in the head. She's mad to come here!" When the older man speaks, I observe his missing incisors. Pity excites my rage.

"Still has what counts." The younger man removes his hat.

Snapping open his pants, the older man lunges at me. I bite into his hand, grab his arm, and swing him into the rose bush, which cracks under his weight.

The younger man stands with his mouth and pants ajar. I swipe fingernails across his face, ripping into the flesh. He screams.

I pause as blood leaks from his once-perfect face. The part of me who is the vampire fills with desire; I ache to lick his face. But no. Not yet. Vengeance first.

Digging my fangs deep, I rip open his throat and swallow

the blood that rises into my mouth. He will never scream again. I allow myself one more mouthful of blood and the flap of skin that follows it.

I kill the elder man caught in the roses with a slash across his neck.

Pain erupts through my shoulder as a bayonet pierces me from behind. I gasp. Adrenaline rushes through my body, as does an all-consuming pain. I allow myself to fall, hoping the blade escapes my flesh.

Once free, I immediately heal. I turn and rip the rifle from my next victim's hands. I shove the bayonet in the heart of my attacker. I pull it from the wound to allow the blood to flow freely...and stab him again. I, indeed, have become an angel of death.

Leaving the rifle behind, I regain my hold on the dagger. Another young soldier swings his rifle. I laugh and dodge. On his upstroke, I stab him, knock him to the ground, and pounce. I force his chin upward, exposing his throat. My fangs puncture his flesh. His screams falter in the night air. As his life force runs down my throat, I muse how easy men were to kill.

"What in the hell? Help!" another cries.

I look at the retreating form. My muscles tingle as I tackle him to the floor. Lifting my knife, I stab him in the back and roll him over to slice open his stomach. Blood and intestines spill through shredded flesh and French livery. After I slash his throat, he finally sputters and dies on the cobblestone ground.

I enter my former home with a vague notion I should be concerned about my ignorance of how many men make a squadron. However, I feel only apathy because I am indifferent to my death. I care about nothing but blood and vengeance.

Voices come from Andres's private study. I enter the room. A man and a possible rent-boy or young soldier are in an embrace. Before they know what happened, I use their closeness to kill them both.

When I climb the stairs to my bedroom, Andre's former valet, Paul, presses a regimental uniform.

"Madame…" His breath catches in his throat. His eyes are full of terror.

"Was it you?"

"I'm just a valet, Madame!"

My first thought is Paul should be whipped for collusion. But I do not have a whip. In the cold place where my heart formerly resided, I know he only did what he had to do to protect his life. Still, I drag my blade across his neck and taste his blood as it pours out of him and onto me.

I drop him onto the floor and enter the bedchamber where a man—most likely the commanding officer by the discarded uniform—enjoys a woman, wearing my old court wig, in my marital bed.

"Are you his woman?" I cry. "His mistress?"

The man removes himself from the woman and scrambles out of bed. "Who are you?" He grabs my hair. "Who sent you?" He slaps me.

He will be sorry that he sees only a bleeding woman. He doesn't understand I'm death.

"You killed my husband," I scream. "My Andre! My Celeste!" I close the narrow space between my body and the man and slice open his throat.

The woman watches and screams. "La Dame Blanche! Dame Blanche!"

I am full of righteousness, but death empties my soul. Andre and I will never make love again. Celeste will never laugh again. My only hope is that they are together in Heaven.

"Don't kill me, Dame Blanche!"

"Get out." I yank her off my bed and shove her into the hall. The woman runs, still screaming, "The ghost of Madame de Aubinet has returned for vengeance."

Tears trail down my cheeks, as I wonder what I should take. The fine rugs and ticking are soiled with bootprints and blood. Ruined. The baby's crib is bent and broken.

I look in the wardrobe. My old wigs were damaged; my best silks and jewels had come with me and lost to who knows where.

I reenter Andre's study and remove a crooked painting to expose the hidden safe. The door had already been forced open. I see Andre's green velvet waistcoat on the floor and slip it into the bodice of my bloody gown.

Men's voices echo from the street. Coming closer. I must fight or flee. On my way out, I steal a discarded cloak from the dead boy, who is about my size, and realize this house is no longer my home, and there is nothing left to take.

I open the garden window, climb through the bushes, and slip into the tiny fountain. Strings and blobs of red gore slide into the water as I wash off a lion's share of blood.

Madame la Marquise de Aubinet is dead.

Pascaline, Fille de Banquier is undead.

Chapter 27

Pascaline

Standing in bloody water, I sense the approach of vampires, and raise my dagger. The two tall, blond vampires appear, dragging behind them, the woman who had been in my bed.

"Lower your dagger. You've nothing to fear from us. I'm called Sydella Bach-Sören. My brother is Gunter Bach. We were sent by our progenitor, Gaius Sören, to protect you."

Gunter rushes into the house.

Sydella continues to grip the woman's arm as she speaks to me in perfect French. "If you mean to have vengeance, little sister, do it smartly," she advises. "At least, you ensured you were seen at the festivities. Now, watch as I use my power to make sure this woman won't identify you."

I stand dripping in the fountain as Sydella forces her will upon the terrified woman. She repeatedly commands her to remember that drunken soldiers are to blame for setting the fire that Gunter is presumably setting to the house as she speaks. And no, there was no vengeful ghost, just another prostitute, escaping the callous hands of the soldiers.

It seems surprisingly easy to do given the woman's fear. I wondered who I might befuddle.

She releases the stupefied woman, who runs away, screaming, "Fire! The garrison is on fire!"

Sydella turns back to me. "Your rebirth drew us to Versailles. We certainly would not allow you to meet Final Death." She steps toward me and rips the stolen cloak and my outer dress from my body.

Shocked by the action, I drop Andre's velvet waistcoat in the bloody water. I snatch it up as she gently covers me with a non-descript woolen travel cloak.

As she assists me out of the fountain, I ask, "Do all of us feel when a vampire is reborn?"

"No, the progenitor feels only when our bloodline expands. The Countess de Banquier and her husband are Gaius's descendants and so are you and I." Gunter and Gaius raised me as they raise their horses. Now I'm Rittmeister."

"Ritt...Ride...you're a knight?" I ask the tall, beautiful blonde.

"The age of knights is over. In modern parlance, I am Captain of Horses."

I am pleased warrior men would give such an important job to a woman. Sydella must have incredible strength in both character and muscle.

She throws my dress and soldier's cloak through the open door into the house. The fire begins to spread, flames licking at the windows.

Gunter drags a burnt body into the fountain and tosses it into the bloody water.

"I carry you?" His voice is clipped and thickly accented. He mimes holding a baby and running.

"I can run."

Gunter grips my hand tightly. We run from the once splendid house I shared with my husband. Overwhelmed by memories of Andre, both good and bad, I weep. Even crying, I easily keep pace.

Gunter and Sydella bring me to their lovely quarters in the West Hall. I hear a healthy heartbeat and feel a strange draft drifting from under the door.

"Whose heartbeat do I hear?" I ask.

"Though originally from France, Benoit Lécuyer is Gunter's cadet. He is, but thirteen. Too young to transform."

Sydella scolds most mildly. "And you're young, Liebchen, and ought not to make such scenes. And never use your vampiric gifts in Court."

"What's the relationship between you and the sergeant," I ask.

"Outwardly, my bodyguard and inwardly my charge," she said. "As the cadet is to Gunter."

"I assume you know that he approached my sister."

"Yes, that was for the best. She might not have listened to Benoit. We studied Charles's character closely and hope to transform him. He's a man of honor and dignity."

Gunter counts the money he collected from the soldier. He tries to press a sum into my hands, but I refuse.

Gunter grumbles in a foreign language.

I do not know what he said, but I understand his tone, and I try to explain. "I only wanted Andre's waistcoat. He loved it, and I loved how it once felt on my cheek as I leaned into his chest. I will bury it with our daughter."

"I should've known Agata would transform a romantic, strong-headed girl." Gaius appears at the doorway along with

Charles. "Jakub claims Agata only wanted daughters of all things."

"We seek a way to protect the count's holding," I say cautiously.

"Will you be in Court tomorrow?"

"No. I attend a lady's literary salon to bring the dye back in fashion."

"For the love of a thousand Gods," Gaius mutters.

"You sell horses to find your way, why is this any different?" I say.

"You know us?"

"I listen to rumors, Präsidierender Bürgermeister. Is that a self-aggrandizing title?"

Gaius laughs. "How much like Agata you are."

Sydella kisses my cheeks. "May God's luck smile upon you, Pascaline."

I must take control of this. I might be the youngest vampire in the room, but I outrank everyone here—even if I am only the daughter of a count. "May I, Mademoiselle, claim our kinship?" I ask.

Sydella claps her hands together. "Indeed, you should."

Her eyes are bright and shining. I feel a slight regret to have asked my question with a mercenary intent.

"But you ought to know I model horses, while I allow men to believe I'm not training them in good form. A lady such as you may not want to associate with me."

"You've nothing to fear in that regard. Papa won't understand why one lady might associate with one and not the other, and Maman won't care. For as long as I have this family's sworn vow Loretta shall be safe from you and yours, I shall call you my kinswoman and friend."

"Of course, Madame Pascaline. We've no reason to harm Loretta," Gaius says. He bowed and whispered, "I pray your mother told you not to use your voice too often."

"Both my parents fear the past. And Sydella told me the same."

Praying the vampires never find a reason to harm Loretta, I cross the path to the north wing with a deepening emptiness in my chest. Vengeance has not healed me. It is cold; as cold as Celeste's grave.

Loretta

30th of March or perhaps the 1st of April

Cher Journal,

I was awakened so late, and now I cannot sleep. What a relief to see that Pascaline has returned unharmed. I don't want to think about what she has done, but if she can know happiness again, I will be happy as well.

I did not know why Maman held my arm tightly. Pascaline must have had her fill of blood. But of course, I bow to her greater knowledge of such things.

"Is it finished?" Papa growls from the dressing table chair.

Pascaline nods. "Yes, Papa."

"You'll not harm another soul while we're in Versailles?"

"Papa, I..."

"Swear it." He glances at me.

"I swear by God, I shan't harm another soul while we're in Versailles."

"Even if they stand in your way," he adds.

"Agreed." Shifting the subject, Pascaline says, "I met the three vampires tonight."

"What did you think?" Maman asks, her arm on mine.

"I like Sydella. Gunter seemed more subdued, but Gaius is a little too used to his position. He tried to flatter me. And Charles...I don't think he likes vampires much."

I immediately turned my attention to the subject of the man I'd met on my walk.

"My own observations support that theory," I say.

Papa ran his fingers through his beard. "I learned tonight that Charles was a prisoner of war."

Papa went on, "He mentors a young cadet, whose life is his reason not to escape or disobey. I don't know if he's a younger brother, cousin, or even his son, but the boy's life obviously means something to the man."

"The cadet was sleeping when I met the family," Pascaline said. "His heartbeat sounded healthy. They said he was thirteen." Pascaline's eyes lingered on me.

"Is Charles old enough to have a son that age?" I asked.

"Might be," Maman said. "How much are we outnumbered?"

"In this party, three vampires to three vampires. Gaius came to us as equals," Papa said.

"Though in a stronger position," Maman said firmly. "With a grenadier and a cadet."

"Would you expect less?"

She shook her head.

"The three vampires includes Gaius, his named Firstborn, Gunter Bach, his named Thirdborn, Sydella Bach-

Sören, who carries the names of both men as she was once a foundling, a war orphan," Papa said.

"She isn't a concubine?" Maman asked.

"No. She's the Captain of Horses!" I say excitedly.

"Indeed. Originally the men bred warhorses, but as the nobility changed, they requested permission from their prince to sell gelded hunting horses to France. Only Brandenburg and their allies can own warhorses. No one owns their stallions or mares except them," Papa said.

"Gaius's Secondborn?"

"Another foundling, Leon, also bears the name Bach-Sören. He remains in Brandenburg with two young vampires—I checked." Papa sighed. "Gaius does not believe in coincidences. He thinks we sensed whatever he is doing and decided to create children."

"Hmm. Even if he has taken in war orphans, I don't believe Gaius has changed," Maman said.

"You're right. That sergeant is not a happy man," Papa said.

"Can we help them?" I asked.

"Not unless we wish to fail here," Papa said. "Gaius said the men who are eaten are without honor."

Maman harrumphed. "What does Gaius know about honor?"

"The sergeant agreed with him. He has seen war upon war."

Pascaline stared at Maman, but she turned toward Papa. Something was unsaid in her expression. Her mouth opened and her lips curled, exposing her fangs. Her delicate hands became claw-like as if she readied to strike.

Maman lay back. "Go on, Pascaline, I see your need. Afterwards, Jakub shall give you another sleeping potion, so you're ready for tomorrow."

Pascaline bit into Maman's wrist and sucked in her blood.

My body broke out in gooseflesh as she lifted her head and met my eyes. I did not dare move. I had no doubt my sister loved me, but something cold intensified her horrifying expression.

Pascaline licked her fangs to ensure every drop went down her throat. Perhaps I was wrong to plead to be a vampire early.

Chapter 28

Pascaline

Though I am to model the embroidered purple fabric on my gown and take orders for the dye, I am welcomed gladly to the ladies' literary salon.

A young woman, Catherine d'Eliot, rises to recite a poem by Marie d'Cheance, a false name if I ever heard one. The poem considers how hearts break over a memory, even one long forgotten, at the slightest suggestion.

Remembering Andre, I sense something false in the recital. At first, I think it might not be the girl's memory but perhaps her mother's or father's. As the poem goes on, I wonder if her experiences were not romantic love but love of a dead relation. I understand that pain well enough.

The girl curtsies to gentle applause and sits beside her mother. Though not traditionally beautiful by French standards, her mother is striking. She has dark, smoldering eyes and lovely posture. Catherine is a bit plain now, but if she follows her mother, at thirty, perhaps even older, she will turn heads in a way she does not at eighteen. The observation makes me question if I made a mistake, stopping my appearance at twenty-two. Sydella and Maman are beautiful in a way I will never be.

The ladies read and discuss a book about the joys of pastoral love. During the discussion, I ache to feel Andre's arms about me again. I wonder about the other vampires' secrets, if these noble, well-bred women had ever killed anyone and drunk their blood.

The hostess serves watered-sweet wine and a soft cheese tart. I sip the wine and decline the tart. I purchase the book of poems and the novel that will be discussed next week, and I move toward Catherine and her mother.

"Excuse me, Madame and Mademoiselle d'Eliot?"

They turn toward me. "Yes?"

"I am Pascaline, the elder daughter of Count and Countess de Banquier. I listened to the poem most intently. You recited it beautifully."

Catherine nods in a pleasant manner, curtsies, and thanks me.

Her mother's mouth twists into a slight frown but quickly eases into a gentle smile. As I knew she would, her mother had encouraged Catherine to speak to me. A courtier always reaches for the light of our Sun King.

"Do you think, my friends, the poet was inspired by the love of a sister or brother lost to them?" I ask.

The girl's face breaks out in a pleased smile. I had been wrong about her looks. Nerves had made her plain. When she smiles, she lights up the entire salon.

"Yes, the poem was about my brother. He died when I was seven."

I press my hand to my heart and tilt my head. Both are practiced movements, but I desire to convey I feel their shared pain. "My condolences to you both. My sister and I also lost brothers. Such a deep sadness." I lower my voice. "Pray, may I ask why the poem seemed framed within a romantic context?"

Catherine whispers, "Because no one wants to hear my sadness for my brother or Maman's sadness for her son."

I nod with empathy and change the subject.

"Madame, I should hope you and your daughter enjoy the entertainment at Versailles. After morning Mass, my sister plays harpsichord for the ladies. I approached you because I believe Mademoiselle shares artistic qualities in common with my sister. Loretta writes songs."

I feel Catherine's heart pounding faster and temper my bloodlust by biting my tongue. The girl is young and of gentle temperament; her blood will be sweeter than the glass of wine in my hand. Catherine turns to her mother, who studies me briefly as her court smile falters. I hope I am not showing my fangs.

"Catherine's true focus is her career. We seek for her a husband this season," Madame d'Eliot says.

"Of course, marriage is the career of all women," I say, hiding my actual thoughts. Catherine, young as Loretta, looks ill at ease.

"Does your sister have a chaperone?" Madame d'Eliot asks. "Or just your driver?"

"We don't have an attendant, but often find it agreeable to gather a small group of ladies with either Count de Banquier..." I use the lie the Bach-Sörens themselves told. "Or Mademoiselle Bach-Sören's escort beside us. We're slight relations."

The mother stiffens again.

"Do you know the Bach-Sörens?" I ask.

"Only by reputation. It's said they don't resemble each other as siblings ought, and one is as big as an ox."

"Oh, dear. Their mother, a widow, remarried. Her first husband was from the Italian Peninsula, and her second was Dutch. The eldest brother is the son of the first, the younger ones from the second. The large man within the party is not a relation, but Sydella's escort ordered by our king, one of France's mightiest grenadiers, Sergeant Onfoy..." I continue the complete fabrication, hoping it was true enough. "No man dares bother us when Sergeant Onfoy is around, but we mustn't stare at his scars or speak with cruelty as he can be sensitive, though he'd never admit it." I ensure my timing was perfect in my pause. "Heavens, in case you heard, there's a fifth. Cadet Lécuyer runs errands for the diplomatic party. They also have two manservants. The family speaks to them so kindly one might assume they are also brothers."

She considers my story. "No seed is spread with more fervor than a rumor in Versailles." Madame d'Eliot finally bestows her brilliant true smile upon me.

We converge in our quarters. I show Papa the receipts for ribbons sold. Maman sits in the bed. "Good work, child." she says, sinking into the pillows and closing her eyes. Her paler than usual face signals the need for blood.

"Papa, what are you doing?" I ask, as I see him untie his cravat.

He kicks off his shoes. "Sitting with my wife."

"But the Grand Couvert?"

"I'm not wasting any more evenings watching the king

gorge as we starve," Papa says.

"You must."

"I hate leaving my county," he mutters, stretching his toes.

"Your absence will be noted!"

Papa looks at me. His voice is firm. "Pascaline, I shall not be dictated to by my daughter. Prepare yourselves so I might spend time with my wife."

Is it hate in my chest? Yes, hatred of my weakness. No one listens to me: not a cardinal, king, or even the man who claims to be my father. I freshen my dress, wishing I did not need Papa's, or any man's permission, to speak. No matter what priests said about women's sinful nature, I have no interest in sin—even in this palace where sin is normalized behavior.

"Hopefully, Loretta and my presence will be enough to not insult the king," I snap.

There must be a correct strategy, but what is it?

Everyone claws their way to the king; he ensures it. Papa will not. This hubris might kill us all. Papa believes he will out-exist this king. Though he might, it will not be a comfortable existence if he and Maman are thrust into poverty or tortured before the king dies!

My heart feels as if it descended into the depths of my own sore feet. *If I could openly protect my sister, I would teach her how to defend herself. We would not need men—at all.*

Loretta and I file into the king's apartment with perfect court expressions. I watch the first course, oysters, enter on a large silver platter, as I wonder how I will protect my family.

Maman grows weaker every day, giving us her blood. More importantly, I must secure Loretta's future. *Why can I not unsee what I've seen?*

Life—or whatever this was—would be much easier if I could forget. My heart fills with something worse than apathy. It is the knowledge the world is an unfair place. No matter what I do, I can never change it alone, even if I exist thousands of years. I need a community to work with me.

Gaius and Gunter sit on either side of Sydella at the king's table, eating meat fresh from the hunt. Charles is in the crowd with the cadet.

Seeing them together, I doubt Benoit is his natural child. Other than brown hair, they do not resemble each other. Behind Charles is a scrawny translucent girl of seven or eight with her hand on his justacorps. Candlelight leaks through the ghost. No one else seems to see the child skitter up his back and whisper in his ear. He bows at the next course, his hands pressing her legs close to his chest as a counterbalance. He knows she is there.

As if now that I know how to see ghosts, I see other ghosts lining the walls. Most stare at the king, their expressions filled with agony. Some sit in chairs the living or undead sit in. Some mingle through the crowd.

"Do you see that?" I turn my fan toward Charles.

"Sergeant Onfoy?" Loretta whispers back.

"No, the ghost."

"What ghost?"

I look at my sister and remember she is not like me. "Never mind. Vampires sometimes see strange things."

Loretta squeezes my hand.

Though the child's ghost sits on Charles's shoulders, tying and untying the black ribbon binding his shoulder length hair, I pretend the king's dinner is the most exciting thing I have ever seen. Like all the other courtiers, we smile and curtsy at each dish as required, when the officers of His Highness's Mouth bring in the giant peacock-shaped cake but lament the fact that we do not get to taste it.

The ghostly child bounces down and the officers carrying the cake walk right through her. She climbs on the king's table, looks into the eyes of the peacock and whispers to it. Perhaps to a child it seems a giant toy? Charles does not react to her incorrigible manners, probably because he assumes no one but he can see her.

Agata says breads and cakes give vampires digestive issues, which explains why vampires at the king's table do not touch the magnificent cake. Nor do any of the ghosts, I notice.

Loretta, however, can still eat cake, and I will ensure she will. Somehow.

Chapter 29

Loretta

7th of April

Cher Journal,

I've much to tell you. One week before Easter was the day I made my mark on Versailles! I shall start at the beginning. Pascaline did well yesterday at the literary circle. Small orders came in overnight. They stopped at midnight for the Sabbath. Maman and Papa were pleased. I could not pay attention at Mass as I was so excited. As we made our way to the Peace Room, only my full skirts hid the tremble of my knees. To remain calm, I told myself I only play an ingenue.

I curtsied to Madame de Maintenon and other greater nobles in the magnificently appointed Peace Room. Though I feared falling, I stepped across shining parquet floors with a practiced smile upon my face. My blue satin glimmered in the sunlight spilling through the windows. My gown was not as elaborate as many, but it fitted with perfection, and the stomacher, embellished with lavender ribbons and ruffles, was stunning. The trim work is what Papa and Maman needed people to see.

Still, I longed to touch the lovely, embroidered taffetas and shimmering silks with abundant bows, opulent lace, and sparkling gemstones. Most women and men dripped with ornamentation. Not I. For my musical debut, I wore a string of my Maman's pearls braided into my thick strawberry-blonde curls and a jaunty purple ribbon tied at my throat.

"The song I shall play is an original piece about the betrayal and forgiveness between Cupid and Psyche." I carefully modulated the tone in my voice to sound clear and innocent. Even if Madame de Maintenon was not the queen, it was an open secret she became Louis XIV's wife over the winter. I would treat her as queen in all but name as other nobles did.

I sat on the padded stool. Excited to touch the splendid two-manual harpsichord, I gave Madame de

Maintenon one more nod before pressing the first chord.

The tempo started soft and slow as Cupid fell in love with Psyche's beauty. It's important that my music projects true emotion, so I flooded my heart with sadness for my late mother and niece. Using the second panel of keys, I deepened the instrument's notes and forced feelings of the betrayal I still felt from France into the music. I repeated the chords to produce a deep, irregular rhythm that reflected Cupid's feelings about Psyche's betrayal.

I moved up an octave and changed the tempo as the song moved into the ideals of romantic reconciliation. As I played, the entire Peace Room was forgotten. Only after I played the last note would I know how my performance was accepted. And I found I did not care, for I loved the song I played. When the final chord resonated over the crowd, I rose and curtsied to mild applause.

"Your mastery of the harpsichord is a triumph for one so young," Madame de Maintenon said.

The clapping, while still polite, grew a touch louder. My heart soared. Perhaps I cared in that I wanted to do well.

"Thank you, Madame de Maintenon." I curtsied again and backed toward a group of lesser noble ladies. Several of the women quietly congratulated me. A pretty opera singer—a common girl and new favorite of the king—and her accompanist stepped toward the harpsichord and prepared to perform.

I found my sister in the shadows. She touched my hand and kissed my cheeks. Her deep brown eyes showed her pride in me, but her deathly white skin looked more like a statue than a living woman. Like me, she wore her auburn curls in the English style, but hers were twisted with a purple ribbon, which matched the ruffle on her gown and sleeve ties.

We stood quietly listening to several other opening acts and applauded politely when each had finished. As the official concert began, I glanced around the room. The grand murals, gilded plasters, and shining bronzes disappeared when I spotted Grenadier Sergeant Charles Onfoy standing tall in the crowd of men on the far side of the room. I liked the steady way Charles's soft brown eyes looked upon the court without coyness or pretense.

He wore court fashions rather than his regimental uniform, but the modest blue justacorps did not hide the muscles in his burly frame. White paint did not cover the fact his face had been enameled by the sun and badly scarred from battles I imagined there must be scars on his right shoulder, chest, and arm connecting the visible scars on the right side of his face and hand. Though his clothes were of fine quality and brown hair neat, he wore no medallions to tell of his valor. He did not even wear a cross or a wig.

Beside him, the cadet, Benoit Lécuyer stood in the Präsidierender Bürgermeister's livery. He was slender in the way of many growing youths. Charles patted his shoulder and whispered something to him, and the boy chuckled softly. The interaction made my heart flutter harder.

My skin flushed, blooming with desire. He was nearly a decade older and a warrior, but I was a woman of marriageable age and walked with the undead, as he did.

I flicked my fan in his direction and asked my sister, "Do you find the grenadier sergeant handsome?"

Pascaline smiled gently and whispered, "Yes, I'd say he's handsome."

I wondered how I would catch his eye, but he looked right at us as if he knew we spoke about him. Feeling reckless, I touched the tip of my fan with my index finger. (I wish to speak to you.)

Charles blushed and glanced down with a smile.

Benoit looked from Charles to us and said something I could not hear.

When Charles raised his head again, I opened my fan and moved it to my left hand. (Come and talk to me.) I opened my fan part way to show four spokes. (At 4 o'clock) An hour after the concert was due to end.

Charles made an imperceptible nod.

Pascaline's cold hand touched my arm to regain my focus. She sent her own message. (I shall be watching you.)

Charles did not hold a fan. He gave a serious nod to my sister. We both understood. Even if we did not see her, I would always be protected by a vampire chaperone.

Benoit did not have a fan either. Instead, he pointed at his eye and then Charles.

Pascaline stifled a giggle behind her fan. "You've two chaperones," she whispered.

Pascaline and I left the Peace Room arm-in-arm. The path to the north wing was reasonably safe from the sun between our parasol and the shadow of the palace.

Maman and Papa awaited us.

Their lead face paint applied over their vampiric complexion looked dull in the darkness, but Versailles had many mirrors. Soon, they would leave the sanctuary of our room for Evening Mass.

"How did it go?" Maman asked in a whisper.

Though a lady should not raise her voice, especially in Versailles where we were obliged to follow strict etiquette and protocol, I could not contain myself. I squealed, "Madame de Maintenon called my playing a triumph!"

Maman embraced me and pressed her finger to my lips. "Congratulations. Remember, a noblewoman must always control her emotions."

Pascaline added, "Her playing was wonderful. Better than the court musician, to be sure! I think she might've outsung the opera singer if she had the chance."

My cheeks flushed under my sister's praise.

Papa gently touched my hand. "You mustn't wallow in the sin of pride within these walls. Once we're home again, you may crow as loud as you wish."

"Sergeant Onfoy came. We shall walk at four."

I looked into Papa's face, waiting for my next warning, but it was Maman who spoke.

"Do not forget, daughter, he's under an enemy's command," she said.

"And a soldier most certainly has had women before," Papa added.

"Now, go into the sun, my lovely girl, before all you have is night. But be wary. Not all gentlemanly men are gentle." Careful not to smear my face paint, Maman kissed my cheek, pressed a book into my hand, and gently pushed me out.

I heard Pascaline sobbing as the door locked behind me.

I scratched on the door frame to be let back in.

Vampires have excellent hearing, but they did not answer. Something must have happened that they didn't want me to know, but what?

I put my ear to the door and heard soothing words from Maman, but I could not stand at the door too long without notice. I took my book and strolled to the magnificent gardens. I hoped Charles would come.

Feeling the idle breeze and watching the sun dance across the spray of the fountain, I felt alive. Though I hated to admit it, part of me was glad they spared me the darkness of Pascaline's tears and rage. Besides, if I was a vampire now, Charles might not have wanted to walk with me.

Charles and Benoit approached and bowed. "I've no ear for music, but you play beautifully, Madame de Banquier."

"Thank you, Grenadier Sergeant Onfoy," I said softly.

"May I present Cadet Benoit Lécuyer, our chaperone from my family."

"A pleasure to meet you, Cadet Lécuyer. My chaperone watches from the nearby shadows."

I ached to know how it would feel to kiss Charles, though he was not what Versailles calls fashionably handsome.

"Is something wrong, Madame?"

"Only my parents reminded me that you..." I trailed off.

"Work for the Bach-Sören Family. I shan't forget, nor should you. What are you reading today?"

I looked at the book in my hand—the third part of L'Astrée, written by Honoré d'Urfé. It's a novel of pastoral love surrounding short stories." I wondered if Maman shoved this particular book in my hand by accident, or on purpose.

"Would you read some to us?"

"As you wish."

We sought a quiet bench. A gentleman and lady stopped us to congratulate me as we arrived. I did not know their names but thanked them kindly.

The man rudely muttered something about Beauty and the Beast as they walked away. The woman giggled, Benoit clenched his fists, and Charles seemingly did not care.

"I can't imagine how they could find such a brave man ugly," I said softly.

"Undeniably, the sergeant is brave," Benoit agreed.

"Are you brothers, may I ask?"

"No. We met at the prison camp," Benoit said. "After an—"

"Ben!" Charles interrupted, "Madame Loretta, I could live a long time not being reminded of that God-forsaken place—especially on such a lovely spring day. I'd enjoy hearing more of your book, if you please."

With every word I read from my book, my skin grew hot, and my blood raced with desire. I wanted to fling my braids free and press my lips to his. This is what my song, my music, needed—to know love—to be kissed!

Yet, Charles made no move toward my person. He sat quietly, listening to the story until the king and his entourage approached. I stood quickly, smoothed my gown, and affixed a smile upon my face. I placed the book in my offhand, held my fan in my right, and moved my feet into first position. I curtsied low as Charles and Benoit bowed.

The king paused. His wig's dark curls fell toward me. Courtiers whispered as they surrounded us. The king did not acknowledge Charles or Benoit as he normally did not bother with low-ranking men.

"Madame de Banquier, I hoped we should meet again. Unfortunately, my schedule did not allow me to hear you play," Louis XIV said.

"You flatter me, Highness."

"It is said you're often found reading, Madame, and your sister enters Paris for a literary salon."

"I'm blessed to be born in such a time as this. I seek history and myths for my next songs, Highness."

"Indeed. Do you sing?"

I had the feeling he knew the answer. Still, I answered in the affirmative.

"I should like to hear you."

"Thank you, Highness." I curtsied again.

"Does your sister play?" the king asked.

"Yes, but she's unwell, Highness."

"She seems to have the delicate constitution of your mother, but I would hear her play, perhaps as your accompaniment."

I couldn't say no, so I curtsied. I held my breath—a sudden spark of inspiration. "Highness, forgive me for the boon. I realize..."

The king's eyes narrowed.

"Pascaline would love to accompany me. She wishes to serve, Highness. The problem is my sister's eyes. The Hall of

Mirrors is bright in the afternoon sun."

"Only young ladies would think the simplest of requests is a boon. Go to the Chamberlain and request curtains to be hung. There will be many singers on Easter."

"Thank you, Highness. You honor us with your kindness." I curtsied again.

"You honor me with visions of your beauty."

He and his entourage walked away, talking about the growing wheat famine, a subject in which I had no learning. Charles seemed to understand, for anger appeared in his browline. I studied Benoit. He was as ignorant as I.

A few ladies paused to whisper, smile, and giggle. "You're mightily blessed to catch the king's eye." They followed the entourage. Several more men walked past. Then, a man with a dour expression stared. I gasped. I had not seen the youngest of my elder brothers since he left for his studies. Gabriel had not been hanging from the tree in front of the chateau.

Though he was a year younger than Pascaline, he looked older. I would think him a man of thirty rather than a man of twenty-one. He might not have stood in the way of the Dragonnades. He might have seen it coming and converted.

He sneered as he passed by. I shivered.

"Frightened, Madame?"

Unsure of what to tell Charles and Benoit, I said, "Not of singing, Sergeant. I can never be afraid to sing."

"I suppose such a valued member of court on the rise..."

"Please, come and see me," I said quickly. "Both of you."

"If you wish it," Charles said. "And if Gaius gives us leave."

"I'm sure he will," I said excitedly.

"You, Madame, don't know Gaius. He has his whims," Charles said.

"Most men have whims, but I still think he will, Sergeant," I said.

Charles and Benoit escorted me to my family's apartment, where a sea of flowers greeted us. Pure white lilies and roses, of cheery yellow or pink, perfumed the hall.

"They're all so beautiful," I whispered.

Charles frowned. "All these are for you, Madame Loretta?"

Papa swung open the door. His fangs bared. "Your mother took Pascaline to the chapel so you and I might talk about your admirers. Excuse us, gentlemen."

"Papa, I—" I felt embarrassed and ashamed, in front of Charles and Benoit. I dared not say a word as the men took their leave, and Papa ushered me into the tiny apartment overfilled with more flowers.

Papa pointed out five small boxes. "Open them," he ordered.

I did as I was told, finding a piece of jewelry in each one. How pretty they sparkled in the dim light. I wanted to feel the gems draped upon my throat. "Oh my!" I started to say as I turned to Papa. My heart sank.

"Pascaline informed us—and your mother agrees—the flowers are nothing, but if anyone asks, I've forbidden you to keep gifts of higher value. You must not give these men the wrong idea."

Angrily, I thought, Why is it my fault if men sent gifts? But I dutifully said, "Yes, Papa," and I tried not to sulk.

"You shine brighter than these jewels," he said, "but a lady's reputation is easily lost and hard to regain with my standing. You must be cautious. Now dress for services; I shall return the jewels."

Snatching up the five boxes, he strode out of the tiny room so I could freshen my ribbons and cover my hair.

By the time Papa returned and escorted me to Mass, I regained my composure.

Holding his arm, I asked, "What do you think of Sergeant Onfoy?"

"I remind you, Gaius is not to be trifled with. Therefore, I can only assume the sergeant is also dangerous."

"He's kind to Benoit."

"Do you know why?"

"No. But I learned they are not relations."

Papa frowned. "That might mean many things, Loretta."

"What do you mean?"

"Ask your mother."

I slid into the pew with Maman and Pascaline. I briefly remembered Pascaline sobbing and wanted to ask her about it, but it was not a good time to talk. Instead, I allowed my heart to beat for Charles Onfoy throughout the sermon and prayers. He did not seem dangerous—at least not to me. Besides, ultimately, Pascaline and I need a worthy male ally for our plan to work. I hope it will be him.

Chapter 30

Loretta

8th of April

Cher Journal,

My sister and I crowded together on the bench in front of the harpsichord in the practice room. She flinched as I touched her cool hand. I don't think vengeance helped Pascaline.

"Do you feel you might play without weeping if I sing a love song?"

"Of course, Ma tigresse. My heart is stone now."

"Don't say that. I know you love me."

She touched my cheek. "I do, and I pray you never feel as I do. Tell me of your song."

"It's the beginning and end of Madea's love for Jason."

Fearing what my sister might think, I showed her the music I had written for the performance. She scanned the notes, humming the melody quietly as she read.

She embraced me about my shoulders. "Loretta, that's truly avant-garde but may not be what the king wishes to hear."

"I care for your heart not his."

"You're too much the adventuress!" she teased. It was wonderful to see her in such good humor.

"Should we begin?"

"And a taskmaster." She shifted to the center of the harpsichord bench.

I imagined the concert; I imagined my modest curtsy under thunderous applause.

Pascaline was out of practice. However, she played the practice harpsichord for hours, relearning what was lost. Once she remastered the instrument, I wanted Pascaline to push the instrument further. I yearned for the harpsichord to touch even the most hardened courtier's soul, but it did not seem to be made for such a thing. I needed something else. An instrument that could build sound like a harp could.

Frustrated, I turned to my sister. "What if we fail?"

Pascaline hugged me about the shoulders. "You won't. You're a marvelous singer, and you created a spectacular song. I'll not fail you."

"Big sisters must say things like that," I said.

"Doesn't make it less true, my tigresse," Pascaline replied brightly.

My heart lifted as a deep, manly voice said, "I seek Mesdames de Banquier."

The door to the music room did not open.

Pascaline's smile widened. She went to the door and told the steward, "The sergeant may enter."

I quickly smoothed my simple braid and dress, trying to brush away chalk dust that marred the wool. I wished I had dressed for court.

"Welcome, Grenadier Sergeant Onfoy. Come in," Pascaline said.

Charles bowed. "What little I heard sounded

magnificent."

Pascaline and I curtsied in thanks. Pascaline continued to study Charles, who endearingly stammered and looked about the room. "As my charges rest at this hour and Benoit is with his tutor, I find myself without an occupation." He gestured at our empty pitcher. May I assist with your good work and have this refilled?"

"That would be most kind, Grenadier Sergeant Onfoy," I said.

"Yes, thank you," Pascaline said.

He bowed to us and the door steward. Pascaline gave me a knowing smile. Her eyes followed him down the hall before the steward closed the door. "Are you in love?" she whispered.

"I don't know," I said. "Perhaps Charles is my muse?"

She squeezed my hand. "Well, whatever you feel, put it into your song."

I considered my emotions. "I certainly feel giddy whenever he's nearby. Is that normal when I barely know the man?"

"Enjoy the feeling while it lasts. But I must say, his battle experience makes him seem older, perhaps too old for you."

"Andre was ten years older than you. There's no difference." I hated how petulant I sounded. I quickly added, "I wonder how much older Jason was than Madea." Then I realized I was only burying myself deeper in a hole of my own making.

I turned to the slate, wondering, if my feelings were musical notes, what would they be?

I transcribed the answers and hummed the tune I wrote.

Pascaline tilted her head. "May I suggest something?"

"Of course."

Pascaline sat on the harpsichord bench and played complementary arching bridges to the harmony. We tried the stanzas together.

I clapped my hands. "We're getting closer, but I need more sound."

"Forgive me if this is overstepping, but what if I add my voice an octave lower during the chorus."

"Now who's the adventuress?" I teased.

Pascaline blushed and smiled as I had not seen her smile since Celeste left us. It was almost as if music was healing her.

We worked for another half an hour until the steward opened the door for Charles, holding a carafe of sparkling water with a lemon floating happily on top.

Though he seemed not to wish to intrude, his presence filled me with exciting, hopeful feelings I should not have for a man who was not my betrothed or husband. Pascaline gave me a knowing smile and offered him a glass of water and a seat. She returned to her task of copying the slate to paper.

I tried to pummel the harpsichord keys into deference to my wild heart.

As soon as Pascaline finished copying the slate, I looked it over. I erased the slate and scribbled more notes. Amazed by the emotions swirling inside me, I sipped my water until I gulped it in truly an unladylike manner.

I set down the glass and smiled at Charles. "I think this is better."

He stood and refilled it. He was like Papa- a brave knight—even if the time for such things was over. He quested for water in the castle kitchens and brought it to me because he perceived we needed it.

Full of giddiness, I approached and accepted the refilled glass. Wanting to say more than thank you, I ached to tell him every strange thought in my head. Instead, I forced myself to return to my music.

It was no use. Even my music couldn't quiet the thoughts in my head. I found myself thinking about what it might feel like to be held in his muscular arms. Obsessed with the thought of pressing my lips against his, I imagined his big hands caressing me sweetly. Activities an unmarried lady would dare not speak of, held court in my brain. I relished these romantic secrets in private. As long as Charles did not know, it couldn't be a sin.

Cher Journal,

When Charles escorted us back to our quarters, Maman and Papa were out. Another necklace had been sent to the apartment. Charles frowned as soon as he saw it on the small dressing table. Pascaline quickly plucked up the card and read it. Her deathly skin paled further.

"I shall return it," I offered, before she even said a word.

"Indeed," Pascaline said. "It's imperative we return it as soon as possible. The so-called-gentleman put words not fit for your eyes. Or Papa's."

"May I return it for you?" Charles asked Pascaline.

Her hand trembled as she handed it to him.

"May I?" he inclined his head toward me.

"Yes."

He flipped open the card.

"Your sister would not understand this?" he asked Pascaline.

"No."

I felt a surge of anger. They treated me as if I were a child, and for the first time in my life, I was jealous of the way a man looked at my sister with concern.

"But you do?"

Pascaline appeared as if she might cry. "Not exactly, I understand that... That whole line is frightening if it means what I think. And Papa might duel him or do something equally stupid. He's terribly old-fashioned."

"I spend most of my time standing near Sydella so men's actions don't force her to expose her vampire's strength. You, gracious lady, ought to take her example in this."

Pascaline nodded.

"Good. Promise me you won't go near this man. The way this note is written...I don't think it was for either of you to see."

"Who would it be for?" I asked.

"Papa?" Pascaline half-asked, half-answered. "He wanted a duel?"

"We cannot know. Either way, this person is dangerous."

I interlaced my fingers with Pascaline. "Will you be in trouble?"

"Trouble? I might threaten the man a little but, on my honor, I won't physically hurt him. With your permission, might I introduce you to my elder brother tonight in the salon?"

"Another vampire?" I asked.

"No. My eldest human brother, Henri Onfoy."

"I did not realize you were from the Honorable Onfoy family," Pascaline said. I had no idea who that was, but obviously a courtier.

"We're only a petite noble family, and our title was lost after our grandfather had to plow his own lands or see his children starve. But you might find it suitable to have an acquaintance at the morning session, especially if you debate with any more cardinals."

Pascaline acquiesced.

Once Charles left, Pascaline began to tremble.

"Did you understand the note?"

"Not the words exactly, no, but it described making you his alone before the king has his chance."

"What else?" I pressed. "Tell me."

"Tying you up and choking your voice away? If Andre were here, he'd have said the same thing Charles did. We must stay away from that foul man."

"Do you think Charles...?" I could barely say the words. How could I? I don't believe in love.

"He's fond of you, at least. We'll learn more of his character as time goes on."

Pascaline

Gamblers crowd the Grand Salon, but we stand in a quiet corner as Charles introduces us to his brother, Henri, and Henri's friend, Isaac Langlais, the count in whose county the Onfoy estate resided. I had seen them both before. The men room together with two other men in the north wing. Charles seems slightly annoyed with the younger man's presence, as our ranks make the introductions more complicated. I am annoyed that even as a vampire I am a weakling but see the wisdom in having many friends and acquaintances.

The men bow. Their manners are perfect: kindly interested but not overbearing. Though they both carry walking sticks for fashion, they amble with a balletic refinement.

We curtsy in response, but I do not trust them enough to downturn my eyes.

I do not know how being acquainted with Henri Onfoy will protect us; however, like Charles, he is a tall, imposing man. He has less sun damage about his eyes and no visible scars, but his waistline is thicker, and the deeper pinch on his brow signals he spent his time at Versailles rather than the army. Since Henri wears a wig, I am not sure if his hair is still brown or streaked with gray, but I see the resemblance to Charles.

As we interact, I learn that Isaac Langlais is a man of twenty-three and still grieves the loss of his father. The family lost his father's court appointment five years earlier, as the elder count became senile. The young count hopes to reclaim it. Isaac Langlais has not brought forth a petition of any type, but he listens.

"Are you married, Monsieur Onfoy?" I ask.

"Widowed, Madame," Henri says sadly.

"Childbirth?" The question slips before I can stop it.

"Yes." Henri gives me a quick nod.

I remember to cross myself.

He changes the subject without a large veer. "Count

Langlais seeks a wife this season. His need is greater than mine."

I do not feel pressure in his statement. Yet, of course, there is. I fear Charles tried to trick us in some way, yet my heart tells me he has not. I hate feeling as if I were out of control and out of time. I wonder why men felt the need to be central to our lives.

"Is it true the Bach-Sörens are distant relations?" Isaac asks.

"Indeed. On the maternal side," I say.

"The sister is quite handsome," he says.

"Indeed, Cousin Sydella is pretty," Loretta says without missing a beat.

"I spoke with the eldest brother, but he looks higher for his sister's future," Isaac says with marked sadness.

I note with interest that my sister is not the only one in this conversation deep in an infatuation.

"How troubled you must be," I say. "Do you like to ride? Mademoiselle Sydella is a great rider."

"No, Madame, I don't." His voice becomes soft. "You cannot know what bridal gift the brother requested."

"What kind of bridal gift?" Loretta asks.

"He claims I must buy her a horse – and not just any horse, but one of theirs - and give her leave to ride at will. In addition, a horse for all future children. I have no great holding to keep a stable or a hunting ground in which she might ride. My land must be fruitful."

"Have your holdings struggled with the wheat famine?" I ask.

Isaac looks taken aback. "Indeed, Madame."

"Oh...forgive me" I play innocent. "I worry about the famine. Too much, Count de Banquier claims."

Isaac says a few comforting words and shifts the subject back to Sydella.

We listen quietly, carefully chancing nothing that might be construed as encouragement to the young man. Isaac Langlais is an impoverished count, a nobody. Yet, he was obviously watching Sydella. We might be able to use him for something.

The lie I told Catherine's mother is correct. Henri is imposing due to his height, but Charles's very presence conveys a menace that a woman cannot show if I am to raise House de Banquier's standing.

I wish I did not see Loretta's deep infatuation, perhaps love for the man. Perhaps I fear he will take her from me.

Chapter 31

Loretta

12th of April

Cher Journal

Pascaline and I drank hot lemon and boiled spring water all week. Afterward, we polished our teeth with paste and frayed twigs. We practiced until we found the sound I wanted. We are ready. We will be perfection.

Yet, in dreamy moments, I fancied to ask Pascaline what it felt like when Andre used to hold her. Yet, I did not want to see my sister sad, so I did not. I dared not ask Maman, though I heard her and Papa in the deep hours of night from time to time. Their love was not sinful or ruinous, no matter what priests said.

I could not believe love would be ruinous with Charles. Yet, I remember the pain in Isaac's eyes as he spoke of Sydella. I don't feel pain when I think of Charles, only delight.

Jakub

My resting wife's eyes were closed. Her skin looked dry and flaky, as if she turned to ash. Instead of the normal languid heartbeat, I was used to hearing, her heart sounded like a frightened rabbit. A low rumbling echoed within her body. The daily feeding of Pascaline and me was taking its toll.

I needed to get her home. Agata had always been the strongest, and able to control her bloodlust, even with prolonged exposure to two humans in our small room. She needed fresh blood before someone unknown called.

I found a rat in the stairwell. I quickly broke its neck. I brought it to her and cut its throat with a knife.

I opened her mouth and poured gore down her throat.

Her eyes fluttered open. "Hello, my love."

I kissed her lips. "I need to find you more blood."

"See if the kitchen has any blood sausage."

"As you wish."

I knocked on Jean-Victor's cabinet. "The countess wants blood sausage; see if any is available?"

"Indeed, Monsieur le Count." The lad scurried out.

Agata and I embraced, and she leaned against me. "How are our daughters?"

"Acting immodestly. Loretta bemoans the lack of a harp; Pascaline presses me to allow Loretta to give a real concert. In good news, our tax bill this year will be high."

She clapped her hands together. "So, the girls are doing well."

"Extremely. I will need to send for more dye. Pascaline claims you must be seen this Sunday, both for the girls' song and the Easter celebrations."

"I shall be ready," she said sleepily.

Pascaline

I should rest because I will play Loretta's song after morning Mass. Instead, I wander the dusky garden. I stare at the candlelit windows and the inhabitants moving about. Most people are rather boring. Husbands, wives, and their children bed down for the night. Same with same gender courtiers who room together. A few argue, but most live quietly and make the best of their situations.

I miss Andre so badly on nights such as these. I want a man's touch, but my husband is gone. Worse, I ache for blood, but I promised I would not kill any courtier. Papa and Maman are drinking from rats. I dare not take Maman's blood tonight. I find a rabbit nibbling on blades of grass. I leap upon it and break its neck. Hiding in the bushes, I suck it dry. Refreshed, I feel like I might sleep. We need a sustainable source of blood. The other vampires must be getting blood from somewhere.

Chapter 32

Jakub

Loretta and Pascaline's dresses were blue, edged in purple. My sweet wife wore mauve damask, which set off her black hair. Our kinswoman, Sydella, in her womanly finery, joined Agata. I gladly noticed a few young women wore lavender ribbons in their hair or on sleeve ties or lacing.

Gaius and Charles joined me. "With Pascaline's sharp wit and Loretta's musical ambition, they may succeed here if the elder can control her bloodlust," Gaius said.

I inclined my head at the ancient vampire. "That is our hope."

The women approached the harpsichord.

Gaius pointed at Charles's left eye—and I sensed vampiric blood there. Infected—Charles would turn when Death found him. I saw a glimmering about the man's feet—a ghost of a child. There were many ghosts in the castle and everywhere else in France, but this one seemed attached to him. As Gaius and Charles did not introduce her, I ignored the presence.

The women curtsied before Louis XIV, his secret wife, greater nobles, and honored guests.

"This original piece, Highness, is the story of Jason and

Medea's great ruinous love," Loretta said.

"You dare write music as well?" Louis XIV said.

Loretta smiled sweetly.

Pascaline's smile was not so sweet. "We dare to exist, or what's the point, Highness? One as brave as you understands this well."

With every word, a knife entered my heart. *Why must Agata's daughter take such risks!*

Thankfully, the king appeared amused.

With perfect languid movements, Pascaline backed to the harpsichord. Loretta took her place beside it.

Though I heard the women practicing, I was shocked at the discordant harmony of the three voices: Loretta's, Pascaline's, and the harpsichord. Loretta's excitement exposed her girlish heart, untempered by experience. Her lavish soprano, young and light, reached new notes I felt in my undead heart. At our feet, the ghost child danced. Weaving in and out of the audience or going through courtiers' legs.

In unison, Pascaline warned of coming ruin. The elder girl sang slower in her heartbreak as if she had experienced a sadness no man could comprehend. She sang of the guilt of deceased children. Under Pascaline's fingers, the harpsichord had a voice of its own, deep like a reverberating heartbeat. The languid notes resonated in the air. Yet, it joined together in an unimaginable way.

Standing beside Gaius and Charles, I needed to collect my emotion of pride. More necklaces, more flowers, more attention would come.

Beside me, Charles wiped a tear away with Loretta's handkerchief, edged in red thread. I felt faint when I witnessed his immodest expression toward Loretta. She might have any man she wanted—a dashing knight, a handsome prince, a well-healed duke, even the king would not deny her. If I had not made such a foolish vow, I might win the king's favor with two lovely daughters' hands in marriage. Of course, that's why Pascaline insisted on the pledge.

The music ended. Three voices dropped away. The last notes were those of Loretta's hopeful soprano. Unexpected, Pascaline sang a final low note, and her voice moved through the octave to match Loretta, who held her note. Doubled sopranos rose once more, denoting hope of true love.

The king smiled and gently clapped; the women curtsied to the crowd.

"Bring harm to either girl, and I will end you. Twice if I must," I whispered, without turning my head.

"Fear not, Count, the scars on my face will grow repulsive, and our blossoming acquaintance shall end," Charles said sadly.

"My men are above pining," Gaius warned.

Another man approached. He asked for Pascaline's company as if I were a pimp rather than a father. The ghost child scrambled toward Charles and wrapped her arms about his leg.

Before I could open my mouth at the untoward and dishonorable man, Charles stepped forward. "My charge is kin to this honorable family."

He destabilized the conversation without giving anything away.

"But of course." The man stepped away.

I felt close to Charles in a way I had not felt since I was an officer in Moldavia. I could see why Gaius wanted him for his legion and why Loretta's affection was well-established. Certainly, this child, ghost or not, had regard for him. She climbed on his back and rode on his shoulder.

If this man asked to court my daughter, I would give permission.

Chapter 33

Loretta

16th of April

Cher Journal,

Our latest song was marvel. I still wish to find a greater sound than the harpsichord, but I'm happy with the instrument's performance under Pascaline's skilled hands. She played perfectly. The king applauded, but we still are in the north wing. And we have another problem...

Pascaline

The spring sun shines brightly above us, but Loretta and I walk covered with veiled hats and parasols. Gabriel approaches. My brother looks sickly. I wonder how wrinkles could develop on the brow of a twenty-one-year-old man?

One word echoes in my brain. *Torture.* Gabriel was tortured.

"What a strange thing, Madame Pascaline. I have three sisters and the middle one certainly resembles you and the younger Madame Loretta. Truly uncanny."

"Madame Loretta, I heard you play; you play so much

like my beloved sister once did. Quite beautiful."

Beloved.

We were never beloved by our brothers or first papa. We were ignored and struck if we spoke out of turn to any of them. Our lives were surrounded by women. Our first-maman, our nurse, governess, maids, and our sister. It seems a lifetime ago. It is a lifetime—Celeste's lifetime.

"How interesting, Viscount de Fabron." I ensure my voice is steady. "Excuse us."

"I might expose you," Gabriel hisses to our back.

"You wouldn't. It would hurt you, too," I whisper.

His emotions drift toward me and engulf my heart. The error in his heartbeat thuds against me, inflaming my bloodlust.

"You were once such a kindhearted boy," I whisper.

"I matured and came to understand discernment."

"With a boot on your neck?" I ask.

"More than a boot, Madame. You'd do well to remember the king accepts no dissenters or non-conformists. Nor will I, least of all by women." Gabriel steps closer. "I need money."

I step back and push Loretta behind me. There must be some escape. My mind spins. The dark thoughts swirl. I know one way to deal with Gabriel. *One permanent way.* I refuse. I want to scream, sob, and rip out my hair. I do not.

Perhaps if I can make him an ally, he won't harm Loretta.

"Madame Pascaline!" Sydella and Maman walk arm in arm.

"Excuse us, please," I whisper.

"For now, Madame," he says.

I doubt Gabriel is frightened of women, but Charles and Papa loom behind Sydella and Maman. Though swords are out of fashion, Papa always wears his rapier.

Charles bows his head, "Mesdames, it seems you wish to speak; may I speak with Loretta if you don't need me."

"You should!" I say brightly, hiding the distress squeezing my chest.

Papa and Maman return to chapel for the evening Mass. I take Sydella's soft cool arm.

Loretta

Cher Journal,

My emotions churned, but I did not want to think of Gabriel or the ruin he represented. I asked Charles if he might like to walk about the Grand Canal. Charles put his arm out. When I took it I felt safe.

I pressed him to tell me about the battles he had seen.

He abridged his words, but he did tell me. Strangely, they were not the stories of valor I had heard from other men, but of messy chaos, of bombs, grenades, dirty wounds, amputated limbs, scars, and above all, trusting other men.

"Forgive me if such recollections hurt you, Grenadier Sergeant."

"I doubt you could hurt me, Madame. Those mock battles hurt me." He pointed at the canal where two more miniature ships broadsided each other.

If he might love me for my frivolity, I might love him.

Charles's voice changed to the bark of a man used to ordering other men. I saw the real him. "Now, tell me who that man was?"

My lips trembled.

"Don't cry. If he hurt you in any way, I'll kill him."

"No. Nothing like that. I swear it's not."

We passed a trellis filled with white flowers that trembled in the afternoon breeze.

Charles glanced over my shoulder. We were alone. Papa would be angry if he knew I was alone with a man.

"If it ever came to escaping some danger, would you go to Brandenburg?"

"Brandenburg? With your peop—"

He interrupted me. "They're not my people. At best, they're my employers."

"I can't leave Pascaline! We've...been through much together. It would be a sin."

"Very well. But I expect your sister to halt all behavior unbecoming of a lady. She must be a Godly woman again."

I bit the inside of my cheek. Pascaline is Godly. However, we need a male ally due to the stupid laws of the day. I signaled with my fan I understood.

"Don't be saddened, Madame. That came out harsher than I meant. I have great respect for your sister, but I've seen young vampires in Brandenburg—they are frightening, unpredictable things."

"Grenadier Sergeant, I'm sometimes frightened of Pascaline, but I also know she'll never hurt me, or you, or Cadet Lécuyer. Or anyone who is good."

Pascaline

Sydella and I wander the gardens in view of our charges. I enjoy the touch of her arm on mine. I never felt this giddy way for a woman before, but I imagine what her golden hair might feel like across my bare chest, or how her fingers might feel running down my neck.

"Love might be blossoming between them." Sydella gestures her fan at Loretta and Charles. "He treasures that little handkerchief your sister gave him."

"Would your family be parted from him?"

"If he would join your family or Loretta joins ours, my dear, there's no parting. Many allyships begin with matrimony," Sydella says.

I nod.

"Who is the man who frightened you?"

I met her eyes.

She shrugged. "Loretta is still quite young and does not hide her emotions as well as you."

"Viscount Gabriel Fabron."

"This Fabron wears the look of a tortured man. Will you need our assistance?"

"Not yet. But tell me, who is the man who has saddened your eyes?"

"Viscount Bernard. He struck one of my beautiful horses yesterday."

"Allow me to beat him in courtly conduct tomorrow, then," I said.

"If you would, I'd be grateful. My brothers don't want

me to do anything that may shame the family. As it was, Gaius and I quarreled after I tossed Bernard from the stables, and Gunter was on his side! Unbecoming of a lady," she snorted. "It's unbecoming of a gentleman to strike what is holy, and horses are always holy."

There was no fear within Sydella's words. She was not afraid of her brothers. She simply was annoyed by a family quarrel. I wonder what it would be like to not fear men.

I clasped her hands. "Are the women of Brandenburg as free as you?"

"In Brandenburg, I exist as a brother and have full rights in my share of the business. There are some differences, but most women have the same problems as the ones here. But I've heard England's giving women land of their own, to travel to America. They need wives."

I press my left fang with my tongue. "England's coverture and inheritance laws would apply?"

"I'd assume so."

"I must research them."

Chapter 34

Loretta

18th of April

Cher Journal,

I made a new friend today. It's so wonderful to have a friend my own age...

Pascaline

Though selling dye to make a huge tax payment is important, by the end of the season, Loretta and I plan to be so popular Papa never has to attend Court again. Moreover, Loretta and I must be surrounded by true friends and allies, something that shall never happen if I keep arguing with every cruel petition that crosses the king's throne. And there are many. Still, I promised Sydella I would break down Count Bernard. And I did.

During the recess between the morning and afternoon sessions, I am happy to see Catherine and her mother slowly approaching.

We do not practice. Instead, Loretta sings an old favorite song. Catherine reads a poem about the smell of wheatgrass and the promise of a good summer. She beams when we applaud. Her smile is even more beautiful when she isn't pretending she did not write the poem. "You should play, Calette" Loretta says.

"Oh, Lor," I say to my sister. To the others, "I enjoy playing, but I don't have the inspiration to write my own music or poetry."

"It would be a quiet forest if only nightingales sang," Loretta says.

I take my turn at the harpsichord and play a few chords of a soft, sad song I learned as a child.

"Maman and I heard you speak today about the plight of peasants," Catherine says, when the performances turned to conversation.

"Yes. Unfortunately, what I'm most passionate about is not in a lady's sphere of influence."

"Still, Madame Pascaline, you're an excellent speaker," Madame d'Eliot says.

"The way you did not back from that silly viscount was amazing. I would've been petrified," Catherine declares.

"I was scared," I say. "Mostly of saying something ill-advised, overstepping, and upsetting our most gracious king. I studied the issues well; I hope well enough."

"It's hard to believe the nobility ignores the wheat famine when children are starving," Catherine said, agreeing with the sentiment I had made to the court.

Madame d'Eliot adds with the utmost caution. "When I was your age, I read Marie de Gournay. She believed all women should be educated, and I insisted Catherine have an education in Latin and Greek. I only pray it isn't her undoing now."

"Our maman claims a lady must have the ability to keep conversation, and the right man will love her more," Loretta says.

"Hopefully, the right man will be the one my father chooses," Catherine says with a deep sadness Loretta and I understood too well.

"He has one in mind?"

Catherine's eyes fill with tears.

Loretta takes Catherine's hands. "Please, don't cry."

"Monsieur d'Eliot has many opinions about what is important in a husband," Madame d'Eliot says. "In many ways they are correct..."

Catherine cries, "Papa wants badly for me to marry into a title. He wants his grandson to be someone!"

Watching Loretta comfort Catherine, I feel ill. Catherine and Loretta are both eighteen. The king and Church claim it is a woman's duty to marry and bear children, and society would fall apart if man and woman did not become one.

Loretta holds Catherine until she wipes her eyes. I give her a quick embrace. Her mother's eyes show her embarrassment by the outburst. Concerned that Madame d'Eliot might shoo Catherine out of the door, I quickly ask the girl if she would like to play a game. "Rhyming in a round, perhaps?"

Fortunately, Catherine calms and Madame d'Eliot thanks us for our graciousness. Soon, we, four, are laughing. Of course, with her interest in poetry, Catherine thrashes us all in the game.

Once alone, Loretta fidgets by fingering notes on the

harpsichord. Her face is caught in serious apprehension she had hidden from Catherine and her mother. "I like Charles better than any other man I ever met, and I long to kiss him… but hearing Catherine, I'm unsure if I'm ready to marry."

She noodled the keys. "Papa would think me wicked if I wanted Charles to escort me to the ball, perhaps even kiss him someday, without knowing for sure if I wanted to marry him?"

"Unfortunately, Lor, men, even Papa, would say that's wicked."

"What do you say? Am I a fallen woman?"

"Because you want to attend a ball? Of course not. It seems to me that you cannot know you favor him or even know if he is the man you wish for as a husband if you're not well-acquainted."

Loretta

18th of April, continued

Cher Journal,

I wish I was as confident as Pascaline in knowing what's right and wrong.

Charles, Benoit, and I walked along the garden. A few women said hello to me and complimented my dress. As proper, I always admired them in return. Charles and Benoit inclined their heads at their introductions. The ladies curtsied and immediately moved on.

"We ought to stay near this hedge for the shade," I said.

"As you like it." Looking at the expanse of rich green, Charles said softly, "Do you know why a lawn is so perilous?"

"Why?"

"Grass is full of blades."

Benoit snorted, and I giggled briefly before setting my court smile. "I like it when you joke."

"I shall endeavor to do so. Would it please you if I told a riddle?"

I nodded.

Charles glanced at the blue sky and recited: "It's said, from the back, I am drab, but from the front, I can stab. My breast beats with ferocity and I feed my wife so she may defend our house with grandiosity."

"Hm, say more," I pleaded.

"We wear our colors proudly and sing sweet words quite loudly...do you know me?"

"You are...a...robin redbreast?" I asked softly.

"That I am."

I enjoyed the way Charles's soft brown eyes were full of me.

"Madame, how did you know it so fast?" Benoit said.

"The good sergeant looked to the sky," I replied. "So, surely it must be something he'd find there."

Charles blushed. "Actually, I looked to the sky trying to ensure the riddle was suitable for a lady, but I must compliment you for your observation skills. Tell me, why do you write so many love songs?"

"When unsure how or what to play, I think of Pascaline's sisterly friendship. She's my heart's companion. Though, once, I felt the stirrings of love in my heart."

Charles smothered a frown with a court smile.

I had said the wrong thing. He must not feel what I feel.

Cher Journal, Of course, he would not feel it. He is a

soldier, a noble of the sword, and I only sing songs.

I spied two men drunkenly snicker as they urged each other forward. The smell of wine grew stronger at their approach.

"Excuse me, Madame de Banquier. We spoke to your father today," one said.

A drunken giggle erupted from the other's mouth.

I averted my eyes. Etiquette-wise, a lady was not required to answer a gentleman's greeting. However, I did not want to displease Charles by showing rudeness. I glanced over my shoulder at the hedge behind me. The men either did not notice my discomfort or care.

Charles straightened his back and placed my arm in Benoit's before putting himself between us and them. "How strange. Her father told me nothing of men speaking to my charge's young cousin without a proper introduction."

They backed away as one threw a curse upon the ground.

"Thank you. Escort me home if you desire, but please don't leave." I dabbed my eyes. "They are not gone."

"Why would we leave?" His face was simply open as if this sort of thing always happened. "As your father permits me to walk with you, I certainly would not betray his trust by leaving you alone," Charles said.

"Thank you." Feeling heedless, I squeezed his left hand. "You won my heart."

Charles jerked back. "You're too young to understand what you say," he said softly. "Any gentleman would step in front of a lady in peril."

I did not want to hear those words, because they were not true and if Charles wanted to protect me, I wanted it to be because he thought I am a wonderful.

Andre stepped into death for Celeste and Pascaline, because he loved them.

"Thank you for your honor, Sergeant." Pascaline carefully opened her parasol before stepping away from the shade. I made a terrible misjudgment if my vampire chaperone felt she needed to step in.

I straightened my back. "Forgive my imprudence."

I Pascaline pulled me deeper into the hedge's shadow and took a handkerchief. As she dabbed my eyes and blotted my brow, I plucked a stray leaf from her hair.

Andre might have, but most would not.

Pascaline turned back toward Charles. "If you hadn't handled the men, I would've had to do something with two wine-soaked bodies, so thank you."

"One must be careful. I don't think even the hungriest young vampire could eat two men in one sitting, gracious lady," Charles whispered.

Pascaline met his eyes. "Especially when one doesn't have the kitchen staff to prepare them?"

Benoit snickered. I stifled a giggle and hid my lips behind my fan. I made a mistake, but neither Charles, Benoit, or Pascaline seemed angry with me.

Chapter 35

Pascaline

Though I wish to kill those two young men who approached Loretta in the garden, my revenge on Viscount Bernard is not finished, and I need a few gulps of blood to satiate me. I cannot take more from Maman. I found him in the Salon and sent him a note spritzed with rose perfume.

It's a warm night, meet me in the garden.

Laughing, I pretend to drink too much wine and kiss him as he approaches. He grabs my wrist roughly and pulls me toward the north wing.

Instead, I pull him into the darkness of the garden, still laughing. He laughs with me. I kiss his neck, his wrist, push off his justacorps, and loosen his shirt. Aroused by the musk of his skin, my fangs expand, and I bite down—hard.

A tingle of warmth begins in my throat and spreads as blood transfers into my mouth. Feeling carried away by euphoria found in healthy blood, I am still careful not to lose control. I cannot allow Viscount Bernard to die at the hands of a vampire; I need him weakened.

He is too drunk to fight my voice as I press my will over his.

"You won't strike anyone again, especially an innocent," I order him.

He nods.

"You enjoyed this night immensely, but you will never be able to describe it, or me, with any eloquence," I say.

He nods again.

"Now, go to your bed and sleep peacefully till morning."

He does. I sit on a quiet bench and allow myself to dwell on the ecstasy of fresh blood in my belly.

Chapter 36

Pascaline

I duck under a spider web that stretches across the stable door and step on the hay-covered floor. The dusty smell of straw tickles my nose. Each large stall holds a beautiful animal, but I catch the glimmer of Sydella's blonde braid in the moonlight.

I overhear Isaac Langlais say, "Will you attend the ball, Mademoiselle?"

Though a few stable hands work around them, Sydella checks her horses for injury or fatigue. I notice how gentle her calloused hands are with each animal. She is such a strong horsewoman that all the horses in the stables press toward her. Charles remains close but does not intercede on her behalf. His mission confuses me.

"I-I..." Sydella stumbles over her words for a moment.

"Perhaps, I could be your escort," Isaac says.

"My brothers will not allow it. If the Grenadier Sergeant doesn't attend me, Monsieur Bach shall."

"It seems to me—" he huffs.

"Pray, Enough, Monsieur." Sydella continues to brush the horse. "My brothers will never allow me to marry you. I beg you to find someone else."

"Mademoiselle Sydella," I say, as I step out of the shadows.

We kiss each other's cheeks. Something strange and unexpected grows in my heart. I feel a simple infatuation. She's lovely, tall, and gentle with all of God's creatures. Yet as dangerous as a viper. How could one not be infatuated with such a marvelous woman? No wonder why every man in Versailles wants to court her.

I turn to the young count and curtsy. "Count Langlais."

Rebuffed, Isaac inclines his head and presses his way out of the stables.

"Thankfully, Count Langlais isn't a violent man; he simply cannot understand why I can never marry him. His mind is caught in the loop of duty and childish expectations." She sighs. "He watches me too closely."

A sliver of light cuts through the darkness of my mind. "When you're done here, walk with me?"

"My escort must accompany us."

"Indeed, he shall, for I need him."

I turn to face Charles and smile. "Sergeant, I'm glad you're here. I've got an idea that might strike twice with one stone, and it would be most kind of you if you would help it come to fruition.

Charles crosses his arms. "What stone and why?"

"I need an escort for the ball of la Fête du Muguet."

"It's cruel to play with a man's heart," Sydella says.

"Pray, let me finish," I say. "Catherine d'Eliot fears her father will marry her to an older man. Her father doesn't need money. He wants a title in the family. I believe that Isaac Langlais might be the perfect groom. Young, handsome, soft spoken and needs a large dowry."

"Who's Catherine d'Eliot?" Charles asks.

"A girl I met at the Paris literary salon."

"What might Langlais offer? He can't buy her a horse for a bridal gift," Sydella says.

"Catherine writes poetry but fears her future husband won't let her continue. What if Langlais allows her to write?"

"Will he?" Charles asks.

"I mean to find out. Fear not, Sydella. Catherine d'Eliot is not the only girl whose father seeks a husband this season. Langlais will be my escort and, together, I will find the right bride and his eyes will be removed from you."

"In the meantime, Grenadier Sergeant, my sister hopes for your arm at the ball if you're not engaged with Sydella. She has the loveliest violet dress and hoped you might wear this ribbon in your hair rather than your normal black one."

"I dare say, Grenadier Sergeant, a lady deems you a knight," Sydella says.

"Viscount Bernard is rumored to be in his bed with a wasting disease. Too much black bile in his humours, his doctor said. Not enough blood," I say.

"Madame Pascaline, I did not hear that," Charles says. "You both ought to take care!"

"I always take care, and I give you the same advice," I say.

"Excuse me, Count Langlais, Madame Pascaline hoped to speak with you," Charles says.

Isaac hides his handkerchief as he turns and bows. His

eyes are red. Cupid shot a festering arrow into his heart, and his head has no good sense to fight it.

"Madame."

"Tell me, Count Langlais, do you have the pleasure to escort anyone to the ball?" I ask.

"No, Madame, I've no sisters or betrothed," he says bitterly.

I wait for a moment as my question sinks in. Suddenly, he smiles. "If you're not so engaged, would you accept my company?"

"That would be most gracious of you, Count Langlais."

I feel a strange warmth about my plan. This emotion drives away my icy sorrow. I want Sydella happy. I want Catherine to be happy. If Isaac is suitable for Catherine, he will be happy, too.

"I've many friends and acquaintances if Madame Loretta requires an escort," he says.

"Good Count, my sister's escort shall be a man of your holding." I gesture to Charles with my fan.

Isaac looks shocked. "Truly, Madame? But he is so... Of course, I suppose many young ladies find a man of the Royal Army exciting company."

"My sister is taken with Sergeant Onfoy; Monsieur Onfoy won't be upset, will he?"

"I cannot see why, Madame."

"If Monsieur Onfoy doesn't have a lady to escort, I can ask a lady from my literary salon." I mention to see if he is scandalized by such an activity.

"You attend a literary salon?"

"Yes, every Saturday with the King's and my father's

permission."

By his response, he is not appalled. "No wonder Saturdays are so quiet," Isaac jests.

"I hope I've never offended you too," I say with mock sweetness.

"Not at all. I found your words regarding the poor profoundly beautiful. It's almost as if you experienced such things."

"Many poor sought refuge at the convent where I was educated," I say softly.

I send a letter to Catherine but do not receive a response. As dusk purples the sky, I go to her family's townhouse in the village of Versailles. To build a luxurious house in the village, Monsieur d'Eliot must seek a court appointment. There is only a tiny garden surrounding it without a place to hide, so I must be quick. Calling on the strength I'd acquired on the journey that led me to the Banquiers, I climb the fence and listen for her.

Catherine weeps.

I scale the wall and knock on her window. "Catherine, let me in."

Though we are on the second story, she does not seem surprised I am there. She opens the window immediately.

"Forgive me for not answering your letter, but he's an old man," she cries before she remembers her manners and greets me warmly.

I return her curtsy with an embrace. I do not need an explanation. "What's his rank?"

"Baron. At least as old as Papa."

"Has anything been announced?" I ask.

"Not yet."

"So, time is of the essence. Do you wish to be married?"

"Of course."

"There's a man of my acquaintance who is twenty-three. He's handsome and seemingly of gentle spirit, but he needs a wealthy girl to run his impoverished holding."

"His holding? He has a title?"

"Are you acquainted with Count Langlais?"

She shakes her head. "A count? Truly?"

"I don't know if he would let you continue your literary career. Shall I find out?"

Catherine clenches her eyes shut. Her heart races. I push a fingernail into my palm and move closer to the open window to keep my bloodlust in check.

"Come to the ball tomorrow night, and I shall introduce you."

She opens her eyes; they are bright. "This sounds like a *romans heroques!*" She bites her lip. "But Papa?"

"I shall send a note insisting you come. Or my mother can send the invitation if that's better."

She hugs herself. "I can't imagine Papa would deny your mother."

"Be of good cheer." I quickly embrace my friend and escape before the temptation of her blood becomes too strong.

Chapter 37

Loretta

1st of May

Cher Journal,

Tonight will be a night of adventure! Pascaline has a plan to help Catherine and I will be able to hold Charles's muscular arm as long as I wish without anyone saying anything about it... Even the thought of my fingers touching his justacorps is exciting!

Pascaline

We pause in the hallway waiting for the herald's call. Maman holds Papa's arm and enters the room, Loretta and I behind them. Everything is proper. The Hall of Mirrors looks like a dream festooned with garlands of flowers.

Standing beside Isaac Langlais, I feel his insides buzzing. I want to bite him; instead, I enjoy watching the dazzling silk dresses and justacorps around me. All the ladies wear lily of the valley as is tradition, pinned to gowns or worn in the hair. Behind me, Loretta's and Catherine's hearts beat with quick excitement and the promise of the night's undertaking. Her mother is an innocent in all this, and I pray her husband has a gentle temper.

Isaac and I both stare at Sydella's pretty pink lips, almost the same shade as her rose-colored gown. Her clear blue eyes look as if she is full of laughter. I wish my fingertips lay on her forearm. However, that is not the plan. Charles bows to Jakub and gives his arm to Loretta. She looks up at him as if she is in the most wonderful fantasy.

We watch Madame Royale and her escort perfectly dance the first dance. The music changes, signaling visiting royalty and royal offspring to join the merriment.

The intricate dance continues. The song changes again. Other couples are allowed to join in the first minuet. Isaac's court smile is as restrained as the elaborate dance steps.

Isaac and I dance at arm's length of each other. We slowly step into each correct position, ensuring we never look scandalously into each other's faces. The conversation is polite, if a little dull. Loretta and Charles dance together beautifully. His lips move as he counts to ensure he is in step with Loretta. It must have been some time since he had danced a minuet. Still, Loretta's invitation is all the encouragement he needs. I see the infatuation written in her bright eyes. I wonder who else notices.

On the sidelines, Catherine stands between Maman and her mother. Isaac watches Sydella dance with Gunter.

With my persuasive gifts, I whisper, "My kinswoman is not for you, Count Langlais."

His eyes do not divert from her, though he tilts his head and touches his ear as if my voice pained him. "I can make her brothers understand," he whispers.

I have him.

I drop my persuasive voice and say firmly, "My kinsman won't accept you as a husband to my kinswoman. I speak as her and your friend. If you keep following her, her brothers may take offense."

His eyes fall to his feet, and he misses a step. "I have not meant to offend."

"My kinswoman mentioned you wanted a wife you can trust to manage your estate while you attend Court. It seems you need a modest girl whose father would accept a title for an exceptional dowry. I may know such a girl."

He titled his head to the side as if weighing his choices. "She doesn't have a noble title, but she has good breeding and a gentle temper."

"Who?"

"Catherine d'Eliot. Have you been introduced?"

"No, Madame."

"After the dance, will you escort me to my mother? She and the d'Eliots are acquainted."

As the music ends, Isaac accepts my hand upon his arm. We walk together with my fingers just touching his arm as we ought. With my fan, I gesture in Catherine's direction.

"She's rather plain. Not like Mademoiselle Bach-Sören at all."

"She's not yet nineteen." I peer into Isaac's face, intent on reading his expression. "You look to Mademoiselle Bach-Sören because of her wealth. Her beauty is simply another benefit. Let us not pretend otherwise. But, Good Count, you can never make her happy. Will you not wish for your wife's happiness?"

"I would not dare to wish for it, but I would make my wife happy if it were in my power."

Careful not even a hint of my persuasive gifts should leave my mouth, I say, "It isn't in your power to make my kinswoman happy. However, our young friend might be the happiest of brides if you looked kindly upon her."

"How so?

"What if you married a soft-spoken, sweet-natured, modest girl who loved books and was happiest when surrounded by books?"

Isaac frowns. "Books? I don't have time for such a hobby; I must serve his most majestic king."

I press on. "Count Langlais, should you not allow her to follow her literary aspirations?"

"I suppose that would be satisfactory, but my wife must never write under her married rank or her maiden name."

"No, no, of course not. As I said, Catherine d'Eliot is a modest girl who would make a kindly wife if you understood her love of poetry and written word. It is said her father has made himself quite a fortune."

"I do want a kindly, modest wife."

"And it is said that your grandfather once had a magnificent library. Perhaps I might introduce you tomorrow night? She'll be at my sister's table in the Grand Salon. You may find her more beautiful than at first glance," I say, deciding to wait on the introduction.

Loretta

2nd of May

Cher Journal,

As planned, Sydella, Catherine, Pascaline, and I arrived early enough to gather at a small table. We played Belle, Flux, et Trente-et-Un with the stakes a sou for each hand. The Grand Salon was the house of acquisitiveness. No one coveted a pot of just four of the lowest coin in the Realm. Charles and Benoit did not even sit as they would not lower themselves to a woman's game and etiquette did not allow them a seat at a table if they did not play.

The night was still young when Isaac Langlais came to my table.

Pascaline stood and welcomed him as if she were his equal, rather than allow our escorts speak. He bowed low, addressing us in order of rank, starting with Pascaline and me ending with Sydella and then a nod to Charles and Benoit. He waited as Pascaline introduced him to Catherine, who smiled brightly. I witnessed a love song in the making: A shy girl with a beautiful smile, a handsome count with soft brown eyes.

"You're gambling?" Isaac asked with a touch of concern.

"Fear not, Count Langlais, we only play for sou and ribbons," I said brightly, gesturing at the three dishes.

"What's the point of that?"

"So, this table remains all ladies," Sydella said. "Even our escorts don't bother to join, but you may if you wish."

Isaac nodded to Charles and Benoit. "I came to meet Mademoiselle Catherine, but I shall sit."

He put a sou in each of the three pots. While I dealt the cards extra slowly, Isaac said to Catherine, "I understand you enjoy reading."

"I adore *romans heroques* and poetry." She blushed prettily.

"It's my understanding you wish to follow Mademoiselle de Scuddery's example."

Catherine answered truthfully as Pascaline had said she ought. "My father seeks a good match for me this season. I pray my future husband allows such things."

Isaac asked her if she was ready to run a household.

"My mother has taught me well in such things, Count Langlais," Catherine said.

"I should think, Mademoiselle, if your father finds a worthier match, perhaps a nom de plume would assist you in your literary endeavors."

"I use one anyway; my mother insisted upon it."

Though the cards were dealt, no one turned theirs over as we watched the more exciting game unfold.

Isaac's eyes widened, and a hint of respect grew. "You're published?"

"Only a small book of poems, Count Langlais."

"What an achievement for someone so young."

I studied his expression of respectful avarice. He did not mind the extra money a literary wife might bring. I smiled at my sister. Pascaline had been right. *This is a love song!*

"Alas. My wife would never see the far-flung places in romance novels. Most years, she would not even see Versailles. I don't know if my modest means could win your heart, but the estate has a large library. I seek a bride who will be happy in my château because that and my title are what I can offer. It's all I have."

"If I were to remain at the château, might I continue to write my stories and poetry?"

"As you will, as long as you write under a pseudonym. My family's name and title ought not to be associated with such things."

"If God blesses the union with children, might they remain with me at the château, perhaps with a tutor until of age?"

He fiddled with his hand. "As it pleases you."

We slowly turned over our cards; Pascaline won the Belle round with a jack high.

I dealt the Flux round.

Catherine glanced at me. I could see she was at a loss for words in the negotiation.

I mouthed, "Salon."

She turned back to Isaac. "Even so, might I host a lady's literary salon? I visit one in Versailles."

"You may host any noble or gentle lady whom you like," he said, perhaps somewhat gruffly. "As long as you keep things within the household budget."

Catherine had the highest flush and took the second basket. "My maman taught me well."

I dealt the cards for the final round. The count looked deep in Catherine's eyes. Her cheeks grew rosy as she exchanged cards to make thirty-one. Though we were careful not to make it obvious, not a lady played against her or him.

Catherine got to twenty-nine and Isaac folded.

"I shall speak to your father. If he is agreeable, we will

petition the king." He bowed and left.

Catherine's eyes shined brightly.

"You were right!" she said breathlessly to Pascaline. "How did you know?"

"He seeks a wife, ma chérie. I told him about our friendship; he seemed interested."

"But I'm the least beautiful woman at this table."

"Don't say such things," Sydella said. "Your curls are thick and shiny. Your eyes smolder under your thick lashes, and your smile is sweet. Men like those attributes. Tell her, Grenadier Sergeant."

Charles looked like a lost little deer. My heart ached to know all aspects of him. Why did I fear being his bride? I don't fear it, but I don't want to leave Versailles.

Benoit jumped in. "Forgive the Sergeant. That's what fifteen years in the army does to a man. You have a pretty smile and a nice complexion...and I'm impressed with your negotiation skills. Any man here would be lucky to find you."

Catherine giggled. "Thank you, Cadet. Grenadier Sergeant, may I ask if you think Monsieur Onfoy will approve of me?"

The lost deer expression disappeared. The Charles who was used to ordering men about returned. "Any man would be blessed for you to concede to be his wife. Why care what Monsieur Onfoy thinks?" Charles asked a bit too sharply.

"Everyone knows Count Langlais is quite attached to your honorable brother," she said. "I want him to approve."

"Monsieur Onfoy shall be happy as long as the bride is in good health and kindly to his friend," Charles said.

"I'll treat him kindly, I promise," she said. "He's

everything I ever dreamt of. I won't even gamble again, not even for sou, if it pains him."

Charles sighed. "Don't upset yourself. Unless he's an idiot, the count knows this is simply a place and you're using the rules of it to your advantage. Even if he is an idiot about the game, Monsieur Onfoy won't be."

Pascaline's advice was more practical. "Now, use your own money to further your literary career, but ensure household accounts grow through wise management and every year, he will grow to love you more."

"What if I make a mistake?"

"You will, of course. So will the count. Now is the time to be bold. In the next week or two, I see much happening."

An hour later, Catherine's mother hurried to our table. With gentle mannerisms, she accepted my invitation to sit at our table.

"Catherine, is it true you spoke to Count Langlais tonight?"

"Yes, Maman."

"He spoke to your father, most directly. He claims he wants to make you a countess," she said.

"That seemed to be his intention," Catherine said. "But I couldn't dare hope it was true."

"I introduced them; I hope you don't mind. He's a fine young man, the count over the Onfoy's small holding and a close friend of theirs." Pascaline gestured toward Charles. "Who, of course, is acquainted with the Bach-Sörens," Pascaline gestured toward Sydella, "which is how we know each other."

"My prayers are answered. You're most generous,

Mesdames. I've been terribly afraid for Catherine in the palace."

"We understand Madame, our mother, and Sydella's brothers fear for us constantly," I said.

"Even you, Madame Loretta?"

"Versailles may eventually lose interest in my songs, Madame d'Eliot."

She squeezed my hands. "If such a ghastly thing should occur, I would give you my patronage gladly."

"I thank you most kindly, Madame d'Eliot."

Madame d'Eliot thanked Charles and Benoit for keeping our small party safe.

Charles inclined his head. "It's my honor to serve the ladies."

Cher Journal, I'm sure he lied. He doesn't think this assignment is worthy of his skills. Perhaps it's a lack of grenades.

Chapter 38

Pascaline

The June sun is achingly bright; the hall is crowded. I only realize the two loup-garous had not been there when they return to Versailles. They seek the king's attention. Again, their petition is not heard. They speak in quiet urgency to each other.

Feeling emboldened by my recent success, I approach. "Excuse me, but my name is Pascaline de Banquier."

"We know," the gruff one says rather insolently.

"I fear I was rude to you before. Messieurs, what petition did you want to bring to the king?"

Golden eyes bore into me. For a moment, I think they will not answer.

Charles approaches, carrying the ghost on his shoulders. She peeks from behind his head.

"The lady asked a question, Monsieur le Viscount." His voice is slightly threatening.

My sister's infatuation is certainly a useful figure. I can see why he fascinated her so.

"I am Honoré Tellier, Viscount. This is Doctor Alliard. We seek to procure medical supplies for the Hotel Les Invalides," the gentleman says.

"May I visit you there? I go to Paris on Saturdays."

"It's no place for you, Madame," Honoré says.

"Of that, I'm sure. However, the cardinal always claims I haven't witnessed the terrors."

"Madame, I've been there," Charles says softly. "These men are right. It's no place for you."

"Nevertheless, I must go. I also ask to see your budget, Monsieur so I may discern where I might assist you."

The doctor looks at Charles. "Is this a jest?"

I answer before Charles dares answer for me. "No, Monsieur le Viscount, Monsieur le Doctor. I want to help those who are suffering. Count de Banquier is a soldier; he will approve charity to soldiers."

Honoré's face is a mask of loathing. To Charles, he says, "Same price as before if the lady means to come and see the horrors."

He and his companion turn away.

"What do you mean price?" I ask.

Honoré turns. "We need blankets for the hospital."

"I'll tell my father. What kind of blankets? Wool? Maman has many sheep. I'm sure I can get wool."

Honoré looks to Charles.

He sighs and pinches his nose. "If you bring blankets of any type, the charitable act distinguishes you from other vampires who simply use the hospital to procure blood. I'll handle any money to keep your hands clean."

"But how much is it?"

"A Louis."

Sydella, Charles, and I arrive at Hotel Les Invalides. I awaken to the sound of a baby crying in the arms of a woman who clutches the child to her chest. Tears slip down her hollow cheeks as she disappears in the twisting streets of Paris. I wonder if her beloved husband, father, or brother is somewhere in the building or if she is alone in the world.

I say a quick prayer for her and her baby's safety. Sydella's manservant carries in the crate of promised blankets. I am unsure what I expect inside Les Invalides, but it is far worse than any imagining. Coughing, wheezing, cries of pain, and things crashing are the melody of this place. War has twisted and broken their bodies. Loathsome air and foulness have entered many of them.

"So many are sick..." I whisper.

"Are you well, Madame?" Charles whispers.

"Frightened."

"Do you want to take my arm?" Sydella asks.

"Please. I didn't know..." I take a gasping breath. "What war does to bodies."

She pats my hand. "It isn't like any story you may've heard."

Honoré Tellier approaches in a dull gray woolen coat, sprinkled with many men's blood and gore. He hardly seems the same man I met at Versailles. He smells as if he was touched by death, but his eyes blink, his lungs expand and retract, and his heartbeat has a strong, powerful rhythm.

"I brought blankets, Viscount Tellier," I say quickly. "My father hopes they help in your good cause."

"Yes. The men are wrapped in the blankets they die in, or they need to be burned to keep the lice and other diseases down." Honoré's voice has a low timber, but his hands express wildly.

I try to hide my attraction to his blood-soaked fingernails with a quick nod.

"I wish the king's advisors would deign to lower themselves enough to visit this place," Honoré says, "to see what their wars wrought. Hell, or even follow a Dragonnade unit to see what they have done in the name of the church."

I shudder.

"Be careful, Monsieur. Your mind may be benevolent, but your king disallows such thoughts," Sydella says. "You cannot take the risk."

I find my voice. "Risks? Is that why your petitions are not heard? Have you angered the king?" I ask.

I wonder if he is the wolfman who spoke to me without clothes? If so, does he recognize me?

Honoré studies me. "I moved a population of loup-garou across France's borders. They'll join the Germanic city-states or sail to America. More travel to my estate, and my men will move them, too. I wonder why a pretty girl like you doesn't believe in the lie."

I step backward. "What lie?"

"Keep your thoughts in your own head, Monsieur," Charles growls.

"I simply wonder why you aren't afraid of arguing with a cardinal about the lie we tell ourselves."

"What lie?"

"That the nobility is set in our positions by God, which is why we are safe there. Because, most assuredly, peasants do not love us. They love their frivolous king but look at us with fury. We're the personification of their taxes and loss of their sons. They will kill us all eventually," Honoré says.

"That's dangerous talk," Sydella says.

"It's a dangerous world," Honoré retorts.

I do not understand the looks between Honoré and Sydella. I must regain some control of my fear, so I focus on business. "How may I assist you in your good work? Pray, what supplies do you need?"

"What we truly need is more turpentine and honey. Of course, if you follow that corridor, you will find what you need."

He places his hand out; Charles pays him two Louis d'or.

Charles stops at the door of the stairwell. I follow Sydella inside, where a scrawny boy sweeps fouled dust into the air and beyond. Bodies of fallen soldiers lie on slabs. I did not want to touch the recently dead.

"The dead no longer needed their life force, but they can protect the living." Sydella lays her hand on a body, opening its milky eyes. "This one's still warm. Try it."

Seeing the truth in her words, I expand my fangs and drink in the vitality. As I do not fear hurting them, I swallow until my bloodlust completely fades. I feel glorious and wonder if Maman came here, would it heal her?

A woman in a long black habit enters the room. Sydella and the nun speak briefly. The nun's fangs expand into a corpse, blood coats her mouth. I draw closer. Blackened purification mars the edges of exposed skin. "Are you Sister Sophie?"

"And you are?"

"Pascaline, the elder daughter of Count and Countess de

Limousin. Your people…"

"Madame, I've been ousted, and my people splintered."

"But why?"

"They were no longer willing to care for the weaker children, and they broke the accord. Your father kept the fear of God in the Horde, but they no longer believe. Alas, the world changes. The ancients tell me it is to be expected."

"What children?" I asked.

She meets my eyes, first with spiteful animosity, and then it dulls. "You don't know about the children? Your parents most surely do."

"I do not."

"My children are vampires too weak to care for themselves and half-mad with desires they do not understand. I tried to save them. Instead, I cursed them to this plane of existence, forever in want."

"May I assist them?"

Her eyes stop blinking. "Your father wouldn't approve." She licks her lips. "But your skin and hair are so lovely. Your blood should be so healthy…give them your vigor."

Sophie grabs my hair. I jerk back. With a strength and speed, I do not expect, she punctures my neck. I feel a connection I have not known before. For a moment, I see her how she was before the plague. Young as I am, perhaps even younger. Every family sacrificed a child to the church.

In her family, it had been her. I see her children, not as the creeping things she protects, but how they were. In glorious rapture, I do not want the moment to end, but Sydella rips her away from me.

The women shout at each other. Their noise brings in

the men. I do not understand why everyone is so angry. I did not mind.

Charles forces my mouth open. "Drink."

"I want to help the children."

"We know, drink." Honoré drains a corpse into my throat. The blood is not warm anymore, but I drink it.

Chapter 39

Loretta

16th of June

Cher Journal,

Papa went hunting again with the king's party. Charles had been invited as Sydella's escort, and Papa wants "a good look at the man to know his character". Maman is sleeping, slowly turning to ash.

Pascaline wants to study an issue, something she saw at Hotel des Invalides. Though she mentioned we can purchase blood for Maman, she had been unnervingly reticent about her experience until we were alone in the library.

"Sydella and Charles are cross as I fell into duplicity on Saturday," she whispered. "I didn't want to worry Papa without discussing it with you."

I asked what happened, and she said she met Sister Sophie, who warned her that the horde has fragmented, like the tramps, and are dangerous, in great need or both. She wants to help the hospital and said something about needing honey and turpentine while I worked on my next song.

As the sun beat down, the library grew muggy. I left my sister to study and took a book to the cooling side of the

Fountain of Apollo. In one of the garden's most lovely places, the statue of the golden god burst forth from the water ready for his daily flight.

"Why, Madame Loretta, don't you look as beautiful as the sunlight?" a strange man said.

I stepped back as he reached for my hand, as we had never been formally introduced. Imposter.

He loomed over me, and his gentle words became whispers of a different type. I backed away and excused myself with a curtsy. "I must meet with my father."

I hurried toward the library, realizing how alone I was.

Fear quickened my steps. The gravel path seemed longer than before. I sought another woman, a group of people who might protect me, but found no one. I heard laughter from somewhere. Were people laughing at my distress? I didn't dare scream or cry. That simply was not done.

I was closer to the castle's main wing, but the library seemed far away. Time slowed.

Thinking I headed for the library, somehow, I got turned around in the garden. I had to keep moving through a dark and horrid grove or the man would be upon me. Louis XIV was gallant toward women; he could not be angry if I begged for his protection until I found Papa.

Branches and underbrush grew thicker. With panniers widening my skirt, I turned to the side to pass. Sweat, tears, and face paint stung my eyes. I could barely see a few feet ahead as darkness was closing in. It was impossible to know what could be waiting.

I pulled myself through two elm trees and saw Apollo in the flesh astride a massive black horse with fangs.

My eyes deceived me. It was Sydella's brother, Gunter.

Knees trembling, I clung to a tree. Gunter looked as if he wanted to consume me, yet he made no move against me. He smiled; his fangs exposed as he dismounted.

I tried to step back but was caught by the underbrush. "My father...will be looking for me..."

Gunter fished out a handkerchief and handed it to me. He freed me from the sticks as Nix advanced on my pursuer. In hesitant French, he said, "Charles has his official duties, Gaius ordered me to watch you. Come, Nix is a terribly messy eater." He put out his hand.

"Swear on your honor, I'll be unharmed," I cried.

Gunter stepped back and held out his sword. "May this break if I tell a falsehood: I shall bring you to our quarters and acquire you a good meal. Fear not. Benoit's there, Gaius may be. We also have two servants. We won't be alone."

He sheathed his sword and picked me up. He carried me as if my heavy skirts and I weighed nothing.

The lech screamed.

I looked toward the horse and hid my face, but I saw the murder.

"Nix likes warm food. Men who would harm a girl is a favored meal. But neither of us could harm you, our soon-to-be kinswoman."

"How..." I had many questions, but none were appropriate to speak to a man who was not my father.

The lech's screams echoed for a long time. Nix finished his meal and bounded behind us. Gunter carried me to his apartment—the lovely type I dreamed of being assigned at Versailles.

Benoit jumped to his feet. "Madame, have you been hurt?"

Gaius ordered his servants to bring me water to freshen myself and a fine dinner. "The child must need cake because she is young and human. Benoit shan't be disappointed, I'm sure."

I could not stop wondering if all this was staged, but Gaius's younger manservant brought me fresh water as the manservant brought boiled carrots with rum-soaked raisins, greens, lovely roasted minnows, a side of beef, and a small cake with pretty sugar scrollwork and sweet berries from the kitchens. Benoit filled his plate with appealing things; I politely took a smaller portion.

Gunter spoke kindly, in that gentle way he had with his sister. Gaius rose to wipe the blood from Nix's fangs; the giant horse's feet pranced about us. Benoit seemed happy for the company. I was a little too afraid to pet him, but I offered him a piece of meat which he took. I almost felt comfortable with my hosts—until Sydella and Charles entered the apartment.

Gunter smiled at Charles. "Please, sit. Due to our guest, we ordered an extra fine dinner."

"Why are you here?" I hated how ragged Charles's voice sounded.

I explained what happened, hoping he believed me.

Benoit handed Charles a plate.

"Nix ripped out the throat of some lech who tried to rape your paramour," Gunter said with an evil glee. "Loretta's young. She needs comfort in such a time."

"My God, were you ruined?"

I drew back in my chair and shivered. "No."

Sydella placed an arm on me. "Fear not, Loretta. He doesn't mean that."

Nix nudged me with his snout, but I could not move with Charles's furious eyes upon me. He did mean "ruined" in both meanings of the word.

Nix, finding me unresponsive, nudged Sydella instead. Sydella patted his head.

"I'm sorry, I'm too scared to pet him—even though I'm told he's kindly," I cried.

"It's hard to believe a knight's daughter fears horses," Gunter said.

"Where was your sister?" Charles shouted. "Probably not remaining out of trouble as we warned her."

I felt small, frightened that he might strike. I hated this feeling, especially regarding Charles. I wanted him to love me and speak sweetly. A big tear rolled down my cheek. My lips trembled. "She's at the library, studying something for the hospital. I was writing another song. I cannot afford not to write new music every week."

My nose filled up and dripped as I wept.

"What in hell is wrong with you?" Sydella snarled at Charles.

Then, she focused on me, rubbing my arms and rocking me all the while encouraging me to eat. "You'll please everyone if you enjoy a fine meal."

After a few sniffs, I did so.

Too soon, Gaius entered with Maman, Papa, and Pascaline.

Maman rushed across the room and embraced me. Her face looked so ashen in the greater light of the day. "Were you hurt?”

"No, Maman, the Bach-Sören's are perfect hosts," I said. "I was frightened."

Again, I wondered if the scene was staged for my parent's benefit. By their eyes, they considered the same.

Gaius simply pressed the conversation as he wished: "Allow me to formally introduce my new Firstborn, Gunter Bach. I should think he's a man who you would call friend. And we must speak."

"Could you not have sent a missive?" Maman asked.

"For you to ignore, Countess?" Gunter said.

She glanced at the fan in her hand. "I see your insight. Please speak, I shall listen."

Gaius pressed his fingertips together and offered seats to my family. "France emerged as Europe's greatest military power, but Louis hungers to impose his will on the entire continent. He even looks to Asia for allies."

"His Highness desires to create defendable boundaries along France's northern and eastern borders," Papa said.

"Those borders keep expanding," Gaius said. "There's much anti-French talk in the Holy Roman Empire."

"Talks don't always lead to war," Papa said.

"Yet, France is not disbanding its standing army between wars. His highness's opponents recognize the need to resist and thus do not disband their armies either," Gunter said. "The Holy Roman Empire will not tolerate further expansion. There's talk of the need for an allegiance between other countries."

"Spain already turned against France," Sydella added.

Pascaline watched quietly, but I did not understand the

conversation. Since when had Spain turned against us?

"You must see it is essential to become allies," Gaius said.

"I do," Maman said. "As much as I find your company repugnant, you were kind to my younger daughter and speak with wisdom."

Maman's eyes fell upon Sydella. Then Gunter.

"I swear I'm not the man I was," Gaius said.

"That's yet to be seen. My husband and elder daughter will speak in my stead."

Maman turned to Charles. She opened her dark eyes wide and spoke in a low, soft voice that pressed Charles to lean toward her. "You watch my younger daughter closely. What's your purpose here?"

Charles began with an argument: "What type of lady asks such questions?"

"The type who looks after her child's welfare."

"She's not..."

Agata put her hand up. Even in her weakened state, Charles gasped as if she took his voice away.

"Pascaline has become mine. In a few years, Loretta will be. I feed and clothe them. I give them love. They return my affection. In every way that matters, those girls are my daughters. Answer my question, Sergeant, or I will rip the knowledge I seek from your mind as painfully as Gaius once did to me."

"I work for the Bach-Sörens."

"To what end?"

"I want freedom and promotion so I might marry a lady...Loretta...if her father allows it."

My heart did an excited flip. He loves me?

"Have you known women?"

He clenched his lips shut, then a torrent of words spilled out. "I visited the camp followers now and again. I... Gaius keeps a mistress for me. A poor noble widow."

My heart sank. He has a mistress?

"Hmm. Any signs of the diseases of Venus?" Maman asked.

"I-I... only lice...in the army. Not here."

"And your mother and father?"

"My father is dead. My mother is a Godly woman and runs our family estate in my brother's stead. Your daughters are acquainted with my brother, Henri."

Papa and Maman glanced at each other. "Do you expect an inheritance?"

"No. I'm the fourth son, but there's only land, no monies."

Agata smiled. "Pascaline is as lovely."

"But Pascaline isn't whom I love."

He does feel what I feel!

Maman said, "Good. You're dismissed."

"You've improved exceptionally in the past century," Gaius said.

"I often use my gift to ease birthing pains," Maman said.

"You still midwife? At your young age, you learned so much control of your bloodlust you assist with that bloody mess?"

"Agata is a midwife," Jakub said proudly.

"I know it means nothing, Agata, but I'm proud to have such a progeny."

She lifted her head to study him. "That must be nice for you. I still feel the impotent rage and fear I felt when you threatened me. However, my feelings do not matter in this. You speak a truth our king refuses to hear in his vanity. My beloveds and I must have options. So must yours."

"You ought to have been a queen."

"I ought to have been the wife of Jakub, which is exactly what I am." She looked over the half-eaten meal. "You set a fine table for my daughter; I appreciate that."

Before I left with my family, I took one more look at Charles.

Chapter 40

Pascaline

I bring a petition to the herald.

"Why, Madame de Banquier, another petition? Here I thought we were to have a quiet summer," he says.

"We shall see, Monsieur," I say with enough tartness to grab the king's attention.

I do not know if these people will be for or against my proposal. Even when quiet, there is a din of close heartbeats. I am constantly elbowed and jostled as women attempted to gain a more intimate glimpse of the king and catch his eye. At least my skirts are wide enough my legs have room to move.

I quietly wait my turn with the other ladies until the herald calls, "Madame Pascaline de Banquier."

Ensuring my mannerisms are perfect, I step toward the king, who sits with a pleasant expression on his face.

"Highness, the shortages at the Hotel des Invalides have recently come to my attention. With ongoing wars, they need more medicine, particularly honey, which is spread on wounds and combats rotten skin."

"You have seen this?" The king asked.

"Yes, Grenadier Sergeant Onfoy, Mademoiselle Bach-Sören, and I visited the excellent sergeant's brother-in-arms, who fell at Luxembourg." I move to my point: "Sovereign, you may recall my father gifted an apiary to the convent where I was educated. I wondered if small proceeds, perhaps but two percent, from that apiary's harvest might be sent to the Hotel des Invalides rather than in France's general fund. We spoke to a brilliant doctor, Viscount Tellier, who would stretch the funds well. Moreover, even the paltry sum of fifty d'Louis would offer so many of your soldiers needed comforts. I brought a list of items Viscount Tellier needs and costs to procure such items, Sovereign."

The courtroom is silent as I set the list upon the tray of the king's messenger. I curtsy.

The messenger brings the list to the king, who scans it. With a quick wave of his hand, another man—whom I did not know—rises from a backless chair. By his seat, he must be a duke or marquis.

The king and this man speak softly for a time.

Then, the king turns back. "This seems to be in order. Have the budget of Hotel de Invalides raised another fifty as the lady requests and a five percent harvest of the convent's honey go directly to the Hotel de Invalides. Of course, France hopes we may persuade you to sing, Madame Pascaline."

I wish to jump up and down. I assisted the loup-garou in a meaningful way. In doing so, I created another ally for Papa, one who knew how to escape France if it came to it. In truth, I like Honoré Tellier. He had not been angry when I gave Sister Sophie my blood. He only cautioned me to use the gifts God bestowed upon me more prudently.

I curtsy. "Yes, Highness." I understand a bargain had been made. I back into my spot with Sydella and Loretta.

Several other petitions are heard. The herald proclaimed, "A petition from Count Langlais who requests permission to marry."

My heart leaps with sheer joy.

Isaac, Henri, Catherine, and Monsieur d'Eliot approach the king. The men bow, and Catherine curtsies. Catherine has a pretty little smile as she gently holds her father's arm, but her heart pounds with intensity of a woman in love.

"My liege, I met Monsieur d'Eliot, a man of upstanding dignity in the trade of wheat and corn," Isaac said. "I beg your permission to wed his daughter, Mademoiselle Catherine, whom I have come to admire greatly throughout this season."

Isaac gestures at Henri. "The past two weeks, my friend, Monsieur Onfoy, has been our chaperone. He can attest to her good character."

"Monsieur d'Eliot, you consent to this match?" the king asks with a bored air.

"I do, Highness."

"Let it be done on Sunday next. Next petition."

Isaac's heart pounds because he came to Versailles to find a bride and found one. Perhaps not the one he thought he wanted but certainly one who suited him and what he had to offer. Catherine's eyes sparkle as she peeks toward her handsome young count. Yet, she curtsies politely and says nothing.

The men back away and return to their place. Catherine returns to her place with her mother, where the women quickly embrace. The only man frowning is an older man, most likely the baron Catherine did not want. I watch him closely. If he was angry, I might have taken his blood, but he is not. More than anything, he seems annoyed, but there are many parents seeking husbands for their daughters every summer in Versailles.

Catherine's heart flutters in excitement to marry a handsome young man. All Isaac must do is be kind and keep his word about the writing. Catherine will give him the world if she can. Her knight-in-shining velvet rescued her from a terrible fate—the fate of not being a writer.

Heat spreads into my fingers, up my arms. It mingles with the warmth in my heart. Today, I made the world better for wounded soldiers and a young couple for whom I wish the best.

"Why do you smile?" Sydella says beside me.

"I simply wish to ensure all people are happy," I say.

Sydella returns my smile. I feel myself swimming in her blue eyes. Loretta squeezes my hand. Charles makes a distrustful harumph sound in his throat.

"There isn't much hope for happiness, but we wish you well in your endeavor," Gunter says.

"You're much too intelligent to make such wishes," Gaius says. I'm not sure if that last comment is directed at me or Gunter.

Court breaks for midday. Gabriel corners me and Loretta. I press my sister toward Sydella and Charles. Though she glances back, my acquaintances keep moving her to the garden.

He inclines his head sharply. Gabriel clutches his crucifix hard; it scratches the skin between his fingers. I do not fight him as he takes my arm, fearing my greater strength might kill my brother. He leads me to a quieter place.

"Since you cannot stop making a fool of yourself, Madame, I shall find you a husband to keep you away from the palace," he whispers. His voice is low and dangerous. He sounds much like our first father. "How dare you go to such a place as Hotel des Invalides!"

My earlier warmth goes cold. "Gabriel, I'm accomplishing good works here." My thoughts race as I try to plan. I whisper, "No one shall speak a word against you."

The coldness in his smile makes me tremble. He wants to get us away from Versailles. His way.

"Leave us be. We'll let you be. Please," I beg.

"You'll obey me as the Good Book says a sister ought. I command you and Loretta to marry the men I say or I shall tell the king of your deception. I'll have Count de Banquier in the dungeon by morning."

Avarice dances in his eyes.

"Why would you do this?"

"A man approached your protector for your hand in marriage or just a night with you. The fool turned him away. I'm not a fool."

"You've a wife; would you do this to her?" I ask Gabriel, who has changed utterly into a morally broken man.

He grabs my arm, tightly squeezing. "Madame de Fabron will remain out of this."

"Does she know what you plan?"

"She'll never know, the foolish little hare-brained creature, she is. Understand?"

I know what he wants me to say. I answer, "Yes."

Gabriel releases me; I hurry to my friends. Children race through the garden, playing a game of their own devices.

What beautiful little creatures, children are. Their little suits and dresses are muslin rather than satin for easy cleaning. Behind them, a governess watches as she holds the hand of a tot who pauses to pick flowers.

I salivate. I think of my Celeste playing with blocks. Hunger vanishes. My parasol, wig, hat, and the rest block the terrifying sun, but I cannot stop shaking. I find my friends in one of the many shaded areas.

I study Charles, who stands beside the bench where Sydella and Loretta speak. The easiest thing to do was ask the king for permission to marry Loretta to Charles. But that will destroy what they are building and our relationship with Papa.

I send a quick signal to Loretta: *Discuss this later.*

I turn to Gaius and Gunter. "Will you walk with me?"

"Need that man dead?" Gaius licks his fangs. "He's broken but healthy."

"No, I have questions."

"Such as?"

"In your long years, have you found any way to bring back the dead?" I ask.

"Not if they're dead more than a few minutes, no," Gaius said.

"Maman claimed she couldn't have changed my daughter, not even to save her, or Celeste would've gone mad. I connected to the Good Sister. I saw her children. Are they mad?"

"We don't know. In the old Empire, I changed my entire unit, boys as young as Benoit. However, they all died."

"How?"

"I filled their heads with stories of valor. They sacrificed themselves to the needs of the unit. We ate them willingly and set their bones on plinths. Thus, other boys gave themselves to us gladly. This is why my army does not allow boys to march." Gaius paused. "Watching you, Madame, I don't know if you lived enough life to exist as a vampire. What were you thinking with that accursed nun?"

"I know Sydella and Charles were angry—"

"Are angry," Gunter corrected. "That was beyond foolish."

"Yes, but I wished to help the children. Besides, I'm filled with ponderances and grievances."

"What type of ponderances?"

"Was there any path I might've taken that would have ensured my Celeste's survival?"

"No path could ensure that, Pascaline. Children die each day."

"But why?"

"There's evil in the world. Your God and most of mine don't care about the lives of individual children. Mine are known hedonists; your God has a better image."

"But I fear what I might do to Loretta or another innocent. Each night, I fear it."

Gaius presses my hands together in his. I am shocked by the intimacy within the interaction. "We love our younger siblings too. We made mistakes when they were children, but we chose not to take their blood. Not ever."

I pinch my eyes shut. "Is Charles Onfoy a good man?"

"Yes."

"Who is the ghost child I've seen on his shoulder?"

"She's a child who died and did not move on. She will

eventually, most do," Gaius says.

How little information he gives. "Will you let him go with Loretta if their love grows stronger?"

"If it serves our purpose," Gaius says.

"What's your purpose?"

"In regard to your family, I want to rebind and strengthen the broken bloodline. I thought it was clear."

"You speak plainly for Versailles."

"We speak plainly because invention is not valuable in this conversation."

"Interesting," I say.

"Speaking of matrimony, will you marry me?" Gaius asks. "You would be so valuable to my army."

"I've never been to war."

"You know the courts. We want you to shine, yet you dim your own gifts here. Fredrick William would deny you nothing."

"I won't leave Loretta. With the prince-elect's austerity measures, I cannot imagine her music will be welcomed."

"What about Gunter? Or my Secondborn, Leon. Both men are used to having an independent sister."

"We won't put binds upon your person," Gunter says. "And we won't own your body. We want you to seduce kings and princes for us."

"And the matrimonial regime laws in Brandenburg?"

"Are the similar to those in France."

"Until that changes, the next time I marry; I marry for love."

"An imprudent reason to marry, but I suppose you must know the sorrow as well as the joy of such a union," Gaius said.

I studied Gaius. "I do miss the touch..."

He steps backward. "Gunter or I cannot touch you or take you for our army without marriage. Agata and Jakub are dreadfully set in their time."

Loretta

16th of June

Cher Journal,

Every time, Gabriel approaches, I get more frightened. Charles gets more angry. He doesn't know what I keep from him. He only knows I am keeping something from him.

At the day's end, I did not want to leave the safety of the group, I felt annoyed by Versailles's whispering fans, laughter, tapping of canes, shuffle of slippered feet, and swishing long trains.

When we were finally alone, I whispered to Pascaline, "What did Gabriel want?"

Pascaline's expression became vacant as she glared at a portrait of King Louis XIV staring down at us.

"Gabriel wants to marry us away from Versailles. He did not tell me who, but he obviously believes he'll acquire money for the unions."

My thoughts went blank. I could see a terrible fate in store. "What should we do?"

"Would you marry Charles?"

"Why?"

"If you're married to Charles, you can't be married to

someone else," Pascaline said. "I believe Papa would approve."

"What if I'm not ready to leave Versailles?" I spoke carefully.

"Would Charles take you to Chateau Onfoy?"

I wrung my hands. "Brandenburg. But he knows I shan't leave without you…and he entertains a mistress! I know most men have them, but…"

Pascaline pressed her hands to my shoulders. "We'll come up with a different plan."

I wiped my eyes. "What are you thinking?"

"I'll ensure your happiness without destroying another's. We must be watchful next week."

I agreed.

Pascaline

My former brother hounds Loretta's steps. He is always near, watching. A word may cost Jakub his chateau. We will be sent to the dungeons. I must put Loretta somewhere safe, somewhere Gabriel cannot touch her.

In the night, I dress in a maid's clothing and steal my way out of Versailles. I seek various opera houses. Men, both wealthy bourgeoisie and poorer noblemen, pursue young ballerinas and opera singers. Loretta needs protection and the operas will not provide it.

Do I trust Jakub and Agata? As parents, yes, as courtiers, no. I will watch my brother.

After midnight, my brother's carriage leaves the palace grounds.

I follow.

The carriage and driver are known to three sets of street wardens and guards on the path from Versailles. He is let through without much effort.

His carriage stops in front of a boarding house on a cheap, dark street. Gabriel moves through the final chains into a dark alley. His coachmen go to the stables to receive care for the horses. The two men smoke and complain about rich men.

In darkness, no one sees me scale the wall. The private room Gabriel keeps for his mistress is cheap and holds two old beds and a table with four chairs. There are not even curtains on the windows. The room's only decoration is a crucifix. At least, the chamber pot is ceramic, clean, and in good condition.

In gaudy, old fashions and a dirty wig, the woman greets my brother.

She kisses his cheek, and then his lips.

He passes her some candles. True wealth for a woman of her class. If she is willing to do with half-light, she can probably eat for a month on such a high-quality gift. Whether or not she is a prostitute, I cannot say, but the mistress, like many others, has found temporary protection in catching a nobleman's eye. She seems kindly. She makes him a cup of chamomile.

She rubs his feet and asks how his day was. Thankfully, there does not seem to be children.

I observe the other windows, the boarding house has

a single chambermaid who scrubs the floor. I scale to street level and slip past street guards to return to Versailles and watch the gates to see when Gabriel returns. I can blackmail Gabriel with adultery, but that will not be to my benefit. While illegal, only women are ever punished for it.

Chapter 41

Loretta

7th of July

Cher Journal,

I plucked the first notes on the borrowed harp. I loved the control of depth of sound as I transferred my soul's music through my fingers. I wanted to hear the song the way it sounded in my heart rather than being controlled by the volume of a harpsichord.

Charles's tall stature over other men made my body yearn for him. I wondered if Charles could feel my pounding heart as I plucked the strings. I wanted to share the feeling. My harp rang my heart's commands to Charles: Though I'm excited by the knowledge you love me, I need you to show me your heart. I must know if my trust is founded.

I turned my head with a practiced movement and saw Gabriel watching us again. His steady gaze upon my person instilled a deep fright. The song I played could no longer contain my feelings.

I slipped away from the music I had prepared and pulled a new tempo. I moved my fingers faster in an untried rhythm and, finding it pleasant, raised it an octave, so the audience would never know it was not originally part of my song. I felt powerful and avant-garde, experimenting in the middle of a performance in front of the king.

I doubled the chords with my own voice.

When I looked again, I saw Charles standing beside Gaius.

In truth, I wished I might ask Pascaline if this is how it felt with Andre, but I couldn't ask her. I would ask Maman if this is what her body felt for Papa, but then they would know my lustful heart. They might not want me to be their daughter anymore if something wanton was taking control of me.

Sydella whispered in Pascaline's ear.

Pascaline smiled prettily, the way she used to smile when she looked at Andre. My sister touched the other woman's arm. Would Sydella take Pascaline from me, too? I felt a bitter, sinking jealousy of the woman. I wished I knew Charles as Sydella knew him.

I looked back at Gabriel who stared. No doubt, anyone would misconstrue his gaze for infatuation, like other men.

Putting every emotion into my final verse, I finished my song. This was a dangerous game. The longer it went on, the more likely Pascaline and my secret will come out.

Pascaline

Knowing Papa is not up to date with fan language, I slip beside him and whisper in his ear. "I know it's not my providence, Papa, but we must do something about that man: Gabriel Fabron, Viscount."

Papa stares at me with hate in his eyes. "He's not dead?"

"I gathered information these past nights. Apparently, he was at university where he was converted before the sacking. As our other brothers are dead, he was allowed to step into the role. But Château de Fabron is still in shambles. The Fabrons are wealthy enough with long term investments but are short on capital. We might need to pay him something. I will find some way..."

He gently squeezes my hand. "There's much you don't know. However, my child, you needn't worry. From my observation, Onfoy is worthy of Loretta."

"It's a good plan as long as he's willing to have a long engagement," I say with caution.

"Why a long engagement?"

"Might Onfoy's connection to her be a case of courtly love? Sydella claims he is a man who might be a knight, if born in a different century," I say.

Papa runs his fingers through his beard. "Little wonder, I found the man's company agreeable."

"And I don't believe Loretta is ready to leave Versailles."

"Ordering her papa is a bad habit for a woman, even a vampire woman, to become accustomed. Loretta will leave when the family leaves at the end of the season," Papa says with a finality I do not like and Loretta will not accept.

Chapter 42

Pascaline

I feel as if I am always running, unaware of how much time we have before Gabriel spills our secret to someone. Perhaps I can extend it, so I begin to sing more often. Soon enough, there is another gift at our door. I hide the gifted necklace from Maman and Papa.

Though Papa will be quite upset if he knew, I send the giver a short note. He awaits me with a bottle of wine. I take a sip and give him the rest. Soon, he is drunk.

I look deep into his eyes and whisper, "You and I had a wonderful time."

"We did?"

"Of course, we did. You're an excellent lover, but you won't have me again. You're too much the gentleman to harm a sweet girl by speaking of our rendezvous. This night was a dream and, whenever you think of it, you will smile. Dwell in the knowledge this moment is all the sweeter because it's ephemeral."

Once he agrees to my terms, I walk the man to his room and tuck him into his bed. I send Gabriel a message to meet me.

As the setting might lead back to my not-lover, which

might lead to me, I pry the gems from their setting and wait.

Gabriel arrives, and I press the jewels into his hand. "These were from a gift."

He sneers. "It'll cost more than this to rebuild a chateau."

He will want more. I am not sure what to do or how to answer. "I have nothing else."

"De Banquier sells dye."

"It's paying taxes!"

I step back as my brother's hand flies. He looks shocked to have missed my cheek.

I race to our quarters and wait until the sun rises, fearing to close my eyes.

Loretta

10th of July

Cher Journal,

My sister's eyes looked puffy when I woke. I wondered what she accomplished in the night. She signaled that we would wait to speak until Papa left for Court. Pascaline freshened her hair and face, then helped me with my rituals.

"I was thinking, Lor, what if we seek second strings for a chance to play for the king," she whispered, her expression wild.

I ached to sing to violins. I chewed on the inside of my cheek and glanced at Maman who slept deeply. "Papa won't like that."

"Do you care?"

"I do wonder how I would sound accompanied by

professional musicians," I said.

"Let's find out. What would you like to sing?"

Fretting at the adventure Pascaline and I were undertaking, I held my sister's arm as we moved into the Grand Salon. The second violinist raised his eyes as we approached, stood, and bowed toward us.

I was unsure what to say to a man.

Without intrigue or enchantments, Pascaline asked, "Would you, and perhaps, others in the second quartet, like to accompany my sister on Sunday? I cannot pay much, but we have these ribbons." She showed the man four perfectly dyed purple ribbons of the highest quality.

"In front of the king?" he asked.

"It's only a concert for the ladies, there's no guarantee you shall play for the king, though he has been there most Sundays."

"You brought music?"

My hand trembled as I handed him a copy.

The man scanned the sheet music. He tapped his finger with the melody. "Composer?"

"Loretta de Banquier," Pascaline gestured toward me.

"We practice tomorrow at eleven," I said, firmly.

He smiled lightly. "I'll do it and ask the others."

We curtsied, and as we hurried away, I thought it prudent to remind my sister that Papa shall kill me if he discovers I was alone in a practice room with four men."

"No, he won't. Besides, ma chérie, I shall be there," Pascaline said.

Wonderful, isn't it, Cher Journal? He'll kill us both.

Pascaline

In the gardens, three young women wearing violet lacing approach. One looks vaguely familiar from the literary circle. Though at first glance, they seem young and free; their pulses are fast and frightened.

"We heard you assisted Catherine d'Eliot," the eldest whispers. "How much will you need to help us find husbands before our father chooses someone?"

I muse if I could make some money as a matchmaker, I might pay Gabriel to leave us be, but unfortunately most young ladies do not handle money or have control over their dowries. Whatever small pittance these girls might offer me it would not be enough to rebuild Château de Fabron. My better bet was to ensure these girls begged their fathers for violet dresses to prove their wealth which would confirm Papa's continued protection and agreeable temperament as Loretta and I began to defy his moral code and build larger spectacles.

"I will, but I shan't break relationships or betrothals. I simply ensure introductions are made. What are you looking for?"

Listening to the young ladies' concerns I contemplate how even if I exist for centuries, there are still only twenty-four hours in a day. I wonder how Maman and Papa deal with it.

Chapter 43

Loretta

11th of July

Cher Journal,

I'm so happy to report our first rehearsal with the quartet went wonderfully!

Pascaline returned to our quarters to sleep the sleep of the dead. I hoped to see Charles, but my downfall approached. Gabriel's feather fan quivered slowly in front of him. However, courtly behavior did not hide the tendons in his neck. Face paint and wigs did not favor his looks, nor did his sneer. His voice was barely over a hiss.

"Do you mean to keep up this charade, Madame?"

"I don't know what you mean, Monsieur."

Without warning, his fan handle struck my arm. My former brother blurred in front of me as my eyes filled with tears. I gulped in breaths so they would not fall down my cheeks from the sharp pain.

"Don't mock me, Madame. You'll find me a vicious enemy. I checked to ensure you are not under the king's protection."

"I have no interest in doing anything to you. I simply

want to sing."

"Madame Loretta, your last performance was wonderful," a woman's voice called.

Gabriel withdrew a few steps as Gunter drew near. Gunter and Sydella were covered in paint, wigs, parasols, and heavy robes, but did not obscure Gunter's sword, openly displayed on his belt.

Gabriel left without a bow.

Holding my right arm, I allowed Sydella's embrace.

Gunter walked behind us as she led me to a quieter place in the garden.

"Why did your former brother strike you?" she whispered.

My eyes opened wide.

Sydella kissed my cheeks. "We exist by information," she added. "I must say, that was rather ill-advised of him."

"I don't think he wants sisters, but since we're here, he wants us as assets."

"How do you plan to proceed?"

"I should fear him if he was my protector."

"You're a good reader of character.

Unfortunately, his mistress also suffers his ill whims," Gunter said.

"She does?"

"Why does that surprise you?"

"I heard once from a certain lady; the wife receives the worst of the nobleman while the mistress enjoys the spoils – especially in a place like this."

Sydella shrugged. "I enjoyed my years as a wife, even if it did not last."

"Now, tell your papa what Fabron said to you. You haven't much time left," Sydella said.

I found Papa and Jean-Victor sitting in our room, going over receipts. Maman and Pascaline lay on the bed. "Gabriel has become more persistent. And Sydella said I must tell you."

Papa put his quill back in the inkwell. Jean-Victor slipped into his cupboard bed. He did not want to know our secrets.

"We return to Chateau de Banquier in a month," Papa said.

"It's only July. There's a great excitement coming in September with the ambassadors from Siam," I said.

My mouth went dry when Papa's clasped his fan handle, but he only used the fan as a fan. "I won't leave my daughter without protection in this din of inequity, and your mother cannot keep up with our needs."

"But, Papa, you—"

"Versailles is dangerous! We shall return home at the end of the month."

Pascaline rose and sat on the edge of the bed across from him. "But, Papa, surely you understand the military advantages of an allyship between Siam and France, even better than we do."

"Your mother and I will discuss it," he grumbled.

Chapter 44

Pascaline

I am glad not to be singing so I can observe. Loretta's song begins with her singing without accompaniment. The second-string musicians take their places dressed in royal blue and gold. Loretta does not turn or react as four instruments harmonize with her lovely soprano and the violins climb to match her vocals. The vibrating strings echo off the mirrors that surround us. The effect works as I imagined. It feels satisfying to think I might have some aptitude for effects, even if Loretta is the more talented in music.

I watch Gabriel's eyes fill with desire, not for Loretta's flesh, but for her potential as a prized bride who could elevate him financially. Beside me, my parents clap and nod as people congratulate them for Loretta's success, but Papa's eyes are on me. I do not want to return to our quarters to answer his questions.

I hate this fear.

"Why were violins playing?" Papa eyes me sharply.

"I negotiated—

Maman grips my arm. "What did you offer?"

"The chance to perform in front of the king and the ribbons they wore in their hair. We all fear the king's schedule might be mercurial.”

“Pascaline, we would not have Loretta acting in an immodest manner,” Maman says.

“Singing isn’t immodest, even for nobility. The king performed in ballets.”

“Granted, if it was truly just for the ladies, but men are watching and sending gifts,” she says.

“We send them back.”

“Loretta feels affection for Sergeant Onfoy,” Maman says. “It wouldn’t do to break his heart.”

“Loretta’s a modest girl, and Sergeant Onfoy’s a man of integrity. She has done nothing wrong.”

Maman turns to Papa. “I do not understand this century or this place, but if Loretta loves this man and wants to marry him, we ought to encourage it. She is too young to be so jaded.”

Images of Loretta trapped in a marriage to a worthy but loveless man runs through my mind. “Perhaps we should encourage her to sing.”

Maman’s brow wrinkles as she studies me.

Papa glances at Maman before meeting my eyes. “To what end?” he asks.

I am close to overstepping. Dangling from a thread of truth, I say, “The time she has in the sunlight is short enough.”

“Oh?”

“If Loretta is too young to join us in death, then she is also too young for marriage. Onfoy is a decade older. He went to war at thirteen and will be twenty-eight next month.”

“You are mere months into undeath,” Maman says.

“I fear not eternity but these early years in a marriage. Fear of one’s husband kills the love one feels toward him—”

"It is not your providence to meddle. I'll speak to Onfoy and instruct him in what will be expected of him if he is to be my daughter's husband," Papa says.

I should let Papa have the last word. Yet, frightening rage and self-loathing squeeze my heart. "I only wish to ensure my sister's happiness and continuation of your holding."

Gaius is correct Papa and Maman are set in their ways. I take a chain from one of our pendants. I pray Maman doesn't notice its missing. Fearing I might be caught unaccompanied by prying eyes leaving Versailles which might bring scandal to my house, I rush into Paris proper. I wait until Gabriel leaves his mistress's apartment, but before his coachman sees him, I block his path.

The pinch on his brow deepens. "It's not safe for you to be alone, Pascaline."

"I must speak to you where we will not be overheard. Allow Loretta to be free. I give you this."

I hold out a gold chain. Like a greedy child, he snatches it from my hand. I feel our difference in height as my brother looms over me. I want to perceive the boy I once knew in this man, but all I could see was the terrible influence he might have over Loretta.

"You will do as I say," Gabriel growls. "Or I will ruin you both, as well as your protectors."

If I cannot persuade Gabriel to leave us be, I will sin, in the most depraved and wicked sense of all.

"All I ask is for you to let us be! We found a way on our own. We ask for nothing and would not take anything from you or your son." Remaining composed, I keep my voice soft. "You would destroy the family's name and honor if it was discovered what happened to your two sisters. Leave Loretta alone. Let her sing."

"No."

I try a gamble and pray for a long engagement. "I will marry who you will, but Loretta loves Charles Onfoy."

"The ugly scarred one?"

"A man of honor and kindness in his heart."

"The Onfoys have no title and little money."

"How have you become so jaded?"

I do not fight him as he ignores my question and grabs my neck. "Loretta will marry whom I tell her to marry. So will you. Perhaps you won't be as prized as Loretta, but you're beautiful."

"I won't."

I do not fight as he presses his fingertips into the back of my neck.

"If Count de Banquier is too much a fool to sell your beauty, then I will. Or are you paying to keep Loretta intact?"

The last statement is a barb to puzzle me, but I answer nonetheless. "Jakub de Banquier is a knight! He is everything you should wish to be!"

Gabriel's sneer uglies his face further. His fingertips dig deeper. My fangs expand. Before I expose my strength or hurt him, I hurry away, confounded by the dreadful change in my brother.

Chapter 45

Loretta

13th of July

Cher Journal,

Papa is vexed. I had plans to walk with Charles, but he informed us we will stay in for the entire day. Once we were working, Pascaline snuck away. She promised to tell me what's going on when she gets back.

Jakub

Loretta slowly picked her ribbons for the day. She giggled brightly and whispered something about "Charles" to her sister.

Not Grenadier Sergeant Onfoy, but Charles.

No matter what Pascaline said about a long engagement, Loretta was not dressing for Court, but for courting.

I put my hand on her shoulder. "My sweet child, thanks to your good works, the family sold enough barrels to please the king, but you're pressing the bounds of modesty. You've walked with Sergeant Onfoy many times."

"I enjoy his company."

"Loretta," I took her hands in mine. "I find him honorable. Our kin from Brandenburg have only said kind words. So, I must speak to your grenadier sergeant."

"But, Papa," Loretta said, "I'm not ready to marry."

"I've been lenient with your music, even with those violins. However, for your reputation, I must speak to Sergeant Onfoy. Where and when are you to meet him?"

Loretta ran to the bed and took Agata's hand. "Maman, please...Papa will listen to you. I'm not ready to leave Versailles."

Agata raised her head. Flakes of grayed skin fell like dust on her pillow. "Your papa is a man to be trusted to always do what's best."

"But this isn't best," Pascaline interjected. "Transform Charles if you want a warrior son, but it shouldn't have anything to do with Loretta. She should be encouraged to sing."

"I do not need daughters who act in a presumptuous and reckless manner."

"Jakub!" Maman cried. "Don't say such things."

A knock on the door interrupted us. Sensing Gaius's presence, I opened it.

"If you mean to give Onfoy a career and your daughter, then he's yours," Gaius said.

"You would give us such a boon?"

He shrugged. "It has been my greatest wish to ally myself to you."

"I don't want to marry him for your allyship," Loretta cried.

"You don't love him?" Gaius asked.

"Of course, I love him...he's perfect!"

"Child, what's the difficulty?"

"I don't want to marry him for evil reasons or intrigues, just for love!" Tears dripped down Loretta's cheeks. "And I'm not ready for the responsibility of being a wife."

"There is, in fact, no problem," Gaius said. "Really, Jakub, benevolence will halt this quarrel. Your daughter's simply frightened. Did you not bring your earth? I find spreading earth on my hands calms me when I travel."

Gaius turned away.

"Hardly one to speak of benevolence," Agata said.

I found Charles in the gardens. He looked surprised to see me, but showed the respect accorded to a man of my rank.

"Each night and day, my dislike for this place grows," I explained. "Yet, I find you to be a man after my own heart. I will consider it a blessing if you agree to teach my men the ways of battle in this century."

"Gaius..."

I raised my hand. "Allies have long been won with marriages."

Charles stiffened and he contemplated what he wanted to say before he asked, "You'll accept me as a suitor for Loretta?"

"I'm not so blind to the world. A grenadier sergeant is not an acceptable husband for a count's daughter. If you accept this position, you'll be made a lieutenant in the Royal Army. Further promotions are up to your skill."

"Gaius offered me…I hoped to earn…" he stammered. "Soldiers don't respect officers on purchased commissions!"

"A gendarme unit is not the Royal Army. You're from a lesser noble family. Allow us to help each other."

"I'll be without honor!"

"Your honor is not your rank. It is your actions and what's in your heart. Moreover, I wouldn't have Benoit presume he may question your orders."

Charles tugged on his jacket sleeve. "Benoit?"

"Of course, he shall come as a cadet. In my quiet realm, there's much for him to learn. Agata sees your fear regarding his well-being."

"You listen to your wife in such matters?"

"Indeed. And you'll put Loretta's happiness above all other goals. I care not for the law. If ever comes a night you strike her, the day follows when you meet misfortune."

"A father's wish for his daughter does not surpass a husband's rule over his wife," Charles said.

I smiled serenely. "I speak not as a father. I order you as the lord of the lands you will serve. Loretta will exist in contentment and felicity. I existed in a married state for nearly two centuries and never found reason to strike my wife, but in this world, a lady's happiness is directly influenced by her husband's temper and his actions toward her. Loretta's happiness, Sergeant, will bring my own wife's happiness."

Charles almost snapped regrettable words. Instead, I watched as he forced himself calm.

I pressed my hands together, lacing my fingers. "I give you my blessings to marry my daughter if she'll be loved even when she is tired or her heart is full of sorrow."

Charles's heartbeat quickened in his anxiety. "I will always love her."

"I have no doubt Loretta will cleave to her husband, but she isn't to be separated from us. If you and she leave Agata and me—you must never part her and her sister."

"The implication is I shall keep my wife and her sister?"

"Only if you take Loretta away from Agata. Otherwise, I shall provide for Pascaline as is my duty."

"Is the lady not in want of a husband?" Charles asked.

"Of course, but it may take time. However, it is our wish that neither know poverty again."

Charles harrumphed. "They have never felt the stain of poverty."

"You make many assumptions, son. Some false. Consider my terms with wisdom; I believe you will find I am fair."

"Beyond fair," Charles said.

I moved down the path. I needed to petition the king as soon as possible so I could leave this vile palace.

Pascaline

The vastness of the rage churning in my heart frightens me. Papa had promised not to marry us without our permission, yet he and Charles speak about Loretta's future without Loretta present. Moreover, in September ambassadors from Siam are coming. While this is a military allyship, we may impress them with the dye if enough pretty girls dress in shades of mauve, lavender, or plum.

Charles sits beside the fountain of the Enceladus to gaze upon the titan's suffering. Papa's words seemed to trouble him. At first, I think it is concern for Loretta or Benoit; I learn better when I hear him mutter, "What is being a lieutenant to a rural count when I might one day lead Gaius's infantry."

Gaius plays both sides. Interesting.

I hide deeper into the brush as Henri approaches. Charles stands and the brothers embrace.

Henri wastes no time with amenities. "I appreciate what you did for Count Langlais, but you've been seen walking with the younger de Banquier girl among the gardens several times."

"Yes. Her father and my charge are distant cousins."

"I am aware, but that does not explain why today Monsieur le Count sought you a promotion. Is it true he wishes you to lead his gendarme?"

"As a sergeant, I often acted as an instructor. I believe I could serve him and his men well, but as we have no title, I must be a lieutenant."

"You mean to accept this position?" Henri asks.

"If the king allows it, yes. I might enjoy being in-country. This promotion doesn't make you happy?"

"Of course, it makes me happy, but you may wish to tread carefully. It is said the younger de Banquier girl took your hand and claimed you won her heart."

I ought to have cautioned Loretta more severely about taking such risks, especially if she is not sure if she wants to marry this man.

"De Banquier is a respectable man and leads a respectable family. The poor child got frightened and felt faint," Charles says.

Charles is an extremely out-of-practice liar. Henri

narrows his eyes and presses his lips together until they form a tight line.

"I was only assisting her."

"Of course, I don't believe your actions to be untoward to a lady. However, the king has taken notice of Filles de Banquier, which means so has everyone else. Take the situation if it is offered, but remember your actions reflect on House Onfoy. Don't be a fool. There are whispers about that family and their strange habits."

"No doubt there are whispers about every family," Charles says.

Hearing enough, I leave my hiding place and ask with my enchanting voice, "What type of whispers, Monsieur Onfoy?"

Henri turns, bows, and tips his hat to me. Charles spins around. His hand moves to the knife on his belt.

"That the Countess sleeps all day and only attends church," Henri replies.

It is easy to bewitch humans. I simply must be careful to avoid getting caught. But Charles knows what I am about to do, and he does not stop me.

I whisper, my voice as ethereal as the breeze, "But the countess has been ill. A woman's illness."

"A woman's illness," Henri repeats.

"She prays for deliverance."

"Prays for deliverance," Henri repeats.

"That's why it took us so long to debut. We worry about our maman so much.

"Onfoy is a name of honor and dignity. We're pleased you call us friends."

Henri agrees.

"Now, remember."

He snaps out of his daze.

"Monsieur Onfoy, are you ill?" I inquire. I wave my fan as I try to cool him.

"No, Madame, just the afternoon sun in my eyes. I did not see you approach."

We speak a few more gentle words until Henri departs.

"You're following me?" Charles asks. "Why?"

"Sydella tells me your heart's true, and you're worthy of my sister's affection. However, my sister is but eighteen. It is my duty to ensure she is properly married to one who will make her happy to face the night for eternity. Why do you hesitate to take my father's offer?"

"Because a field marshal in Gaius's legion can provide for your sister better than a lieutenant."

"Where? In Gaius's castle? Among the soldiers? You ought to ask Sydella or Gunter what it was like for a young lady in that place..."

The line on his brow deepens. "Loretta wouldn't be alone. She'll have Sydella...and you...if you would come."

"You'd provide for a wife and her sister?" I ask nervously.

"If that made Loretta content in Brandenburg, I would provide for you until we could find you a proper husband."

I do not want to go to Gaius. In Brandenburg, it will be harder not to marry him. He is the type of man who always wins because he plays all sides. "What if Loretta was made for Versailles? You've heard her sing this season. Surely, your heart has been touched?"

"It has, but this is a place of soul rot and exquisite

horrors."

"Is Gaius's castle different?"

He looks over my shoulder at the fountain. "Very different."

"Tell me, were you happy there? What did you see? Is it a place for Loretta to sing?"

Charles turns away.

My mind moves quickly. I realize how to save them. I also know it is a bad idea. I grab his sleeve. "Because Papa's house is so innocent, it is a dream. I cannot allow malevolence to fall upon it. If you help us protect it…"

Charles keeps his voice low. "It is not in your providence to protect your father's house. You're not—"

I sigh. "A knight? A man? That I know better than you. That's why I want you to come. Papa's men will never follow me, even if I were to try to lead them into this age.

"However, I know Versailles and I understand illusions. Gaius isn't nearly as benevolent as he wants to appear. Loretta loves you, but she's not ready for marriage."

"That's hardly your decision. You take many liberties," Charles snaps. "Leave me be or I shall revoke my offer to provide for my bride's sister."

I leave him with his deliberations to focus upon my own.

Loretta

Cher Journal,

Pascaline spoke to Maman, and Papa at length tonight. She insisted it could only be good that we stay for the emissaries from Siam. She discussed the business benefits to France from the relationship and asked Papa to explain the military advantages as he saw them. They are to arrive on the first of September. By the end of the discussion, Pascaline had gained us another six weeks in Versailles.

Chapter 46

Loretta

14th of August

Cher Journal,

I don't know what happened tonight, but Benoit was thrust into our apartment early this evening. Pascaline ran out. Hours later, Charles appeared with blood under his nails and smeared on the edges of his temples. Papa went into the hallway to help him wash and discuss what happened. I was dressed in a simple, modest gown and had taken off my night cap, so Maman freshened my hair before she let me out.

"Sergeant, my maman gives her regards," I said with a curtsy.

He bowed. "I pray for the good countess's continued health."

Not touching Charles, we strolled down the corridor to the gardens below. Benoit walked behind us, and I did not doubt Papa was close by.

"I love you, Loretta. I don't know what is to happen, but I need you."

"My family needs me in Versailles," I said cautiously.

"A woman goes where her husband wills," he said.

My heart sank. Charles had spoken words to bind me. To bind my music.

Benoit's breath hitched behind me.

I trembled, but I said with as much firmness as I could, "A human woman, perhaps, but I intend to be a vampire."

Rage filled his eyes. "Why does my heart belong to such a hard-headed woman? Heretic."

I refused to cry. Instead, I smiled politely. "I attend Mass each Sunday, Sergeant Onfoy, but I haven't seen you there. Maman and Papa say there's no submission except to the greater love. I'll follow you when you know more than I, but I won't marry a fool who believes he knows everything."

A flush reddened his cheeks. He looked away from me to Benoit and back to me. His jawline was tense as he stared at the ground in rage. For a moment, no one spoke. Then, he broke the silence. "A life or undead existence costs more money than you understand. My estate is struggling. Your family is struggling. I might be a field marshal with Gaius, but your father can only hire me to lead his own gendarme! Do you know what a field marshal makes?"

I shook my head. "I don't, however, no matter what the gain, I should not wish for unending war, Sergeant. Nor should you."

"What do you know about it?" He snapped.

"I may never have stepped on the battlefield, but I've seen the soil crushed and the populace ravaged under a lumbering army. War is a vicious, merciless thing that feeds only itself."

With those words, Charles's rage disappeared.

"Who are you?" he asked.

With all my heart, I longed to tell him my true identity. Surely not in Versailles, where the walls have ears, and every window might be a pair of eyes. Definitely not where Gabriel might hear me.

Instead, I said, "I'm simply Loretta. I represent my family to the best of my ability in Versailles. I love music. Only you know if I'm worthy of your regard."

"I must know if you are one of Gaius's tricks. I no longer trust my senses," he said.

I untied a lavender ribbon from the end of my braid. "Gaius uses who and what he will, but my heart is yours, Charles. I've loved you since we walked among the daffodils. I look to the day we can marry and be joined in eternal love, but my family needs me in Versailles—as will you—if you take Papa's opportunity. I pray you forgive me, but we must wait to marry."

I tied my ribbon around his upper arm as if he were my gallant knight. My heart stopped as I felt his bicep under my fingertips. That magical feeling was short-lived.

"Loretta," Papa hissed. "Come."

"Goodnight," I said to Charles and Benoit.

Papa sneered as he led me away. "You'll marry him."

"I want to marry him. However, I'm not ready to marry him yet, and we fail if you don't have a representative at Versailles."

"Enough!" Papa shouted.

I cringed but obediently returned with him to our room. I don't exactly know why I hesitate to marry Charles; I only know something inside me tells me it's not yet time.

Jakub

The tiny window was open, allowing for a slight breeze into the stuffy room, but I wanted to escape. I did not know what I should do with either of the wayward women who were my charges. In some ways, they were quite learned, educated ladies; in some ways, simple, foolhardy girls.

Loretta had the good sense to stop arguing after I shouted. She went to bed.

After tucking Loretta in, my sweet Agata poured over Suzetta's letters from home, carefully dictating housekeeping directions to me since her hands had become arthritic from lack of blood.

"Were our human children so defiant?" I asked.

"Of course, they were," Agata said.

Chapter 47

Loretta

17th of August

Cher Journal,

I am furious and frightened. I don't know what to do, and my so-called parents won't listen. They don't care about the plans we made. They think our small successes will protect us forever, but they won't. It is not enough to sell a little dye here and there; we must sell enough dye to be important to the king's budget. And we—or Maman—won't be safe without a worthy male ally to put in place as heir to the County Limousin and the Banquier's holding.

Pascaline asked me to remain at court after nightfall, to have a private talk in the garden. The waning crescent moon made for a good stargazing party, which was a good excuse to be out of our chamber. Pretending our mission was merely a protracted stroll, we traversed the many paths, arm in arm. The wind loosened strands of hair from her bun. I am sure my hair also looked a mess. My mind was on a dark truth, which I did not want to believe. Jakub lied when he said daughters were as pleasing as sons.

I was eager to hear what my sister had to say. Perhaps she had thought of a way to convince Papa and Maman to see the folly of their outdated ideas. When we reached our destination, my eyes adjusted to the darkness of the torch-lit garden and when I looked around, felt relieved to see we were alone. Still Pascaline spoke in hushed tones.

"Do you enjoy Sergeant Onfoy's company?"

"You know I do."

"Perhaps, you should marry him," Pascaline whispered.

I recoiled at yet another betrayal. Would my own sister join forces with the others who insist I marry and leave Versailles?

She must've seen the disappointment in my eyes.

"Damn me!" she cried. "I put you in danger. I ought to have known better than to trust a pair of homebody vampires." She pressed her icy hand onto my shoulder. "As I see it, you have two options: You enjoy Charles's company, that's more than many marriages—"

"But what if he takes me away?" I asked in a small voice.

"He accepted Papa's offer."

"Which means he, and I, will live in Limousin. But he's a soldier and traveled most of Europe. What if he gets bored and doesn't want to stay with Papa?"

My sister's lips trembled. Bloody tears glittered in the torchlight. "That's his right. He'll be your husband; according to the law you and he will be as one. I'm sorry."

The security of the holding paled in comparison to my dream of singing in Versailles.

I clenched my fists. "So, we simply fail? Charles might protect the holding from some invader, but he can't sell the dye—and if Papa were to do it, we'd be homeless again! The ambassadors of Siam come next month."

"I agree with everything you say." Pascaline stared at the damp grass, biting her lip.

"You said I had two options. What were you thinking? Tell me."

"Yes, there is another option, Lor, but it's bad. I'll love you no matter what you do, but you might lose Papa's love. Maybe, even Charles."

She crushed me in a hug, then abruptly let me go. "No. This is a bad idea. You know love. Do you know how rare that is? We need to figure out some way to make Maman and Papa understand.

"I will do anything to stay in Versailles."

Pascaline cupped my face. "We know the King's character and you're a favorite."

"He's a lech," I whispered. "And he allowed the Dragonnades."

"Even so, he's the only man who can protect you from everyone else—including vampires, loup-garous, probably even pixies." She gave me a wavering smile.

"They barely accept my singing. If I gave myself to the king, the sin would be unforgivable to a knight and his lady. Charles won't forgive me either. Why are there different rules for different people!"

"You know the answer." She carefully plucked Helena's bracelet out of her pocket. "Take it and you'll be safe from marriage until the king tires you. Strike Papa or any vampire who comes for you."

"What about you?"

My sister simply smiled and clasped the filigreed sparkling bracelet upon my wrist. I heard her fingertips sizzle.

"What if they beat you?"

"They won't," she lied and kissed my brow. "One of us must escort Maman and Papa to their holding, ma chérie. As long as I can obtain blood, I'm only three nights away, four at most. Keep all our jewelry to bribe messengers if needed."

A dark hollow fear filled me. "What if I get pregnant?"

"Maman told me no vampire or infected has ever made a child. That vampire blood poisons the womb...ought I infect you? Or do you think you will want a child someday?"

"I mean to be a vampire someday."

She bit her finger. Scarlet rose from the wound.

Without question, I opened my mouth. She set her bloody finger on my tongue, and I swallowed the salty metallic liquid.

Pascaline

My heart trembles. Loretta and I choose our words carefully as we write the message to the king. No matter what his foibles, Louis XIV is a clever man, never to be underestimated. We wait on a bench near the library. Though the king is gallant, and sure to respond, I am surprised he answers and summons us the same night.

We curtsy to Louis XIV, who limps slightly.

"Highness, we request a boon," I say.

He turns to his guard. "Remain here."

They bow as they accept the command, and the king gestures toward a nearby fountain. "I'm busy, but a request from you is always interesting." Camouflaged by the sound of water, Louis XIV says, "I know what your family hides along with your Brandenburg cousins."

Neither I nor Loretta respond.

"Perhaps," he continues, "you might make it so the king, set here by God, might also never die."

I cannot pretend I am surprised. The king loves himself above all others. "I'm sorry, Highness, but you would die a king and be reborn into our family—just as I was. The best we can offer is to be the count's son, but you can inherit the holding, and we'd have an elder brother. I promise we'll be good sisters."

The king's eyes narrow as he studies us, but his voice remains smooth. "But who will inherit France?

"The Dauphin, of course."

The king eyes me. "I must consider this carefully. Why offer such a gift?"

"Because no matter what may come, today, you're the only man who can protect Loretta and allow her to sing."

"Sing?"

Loretta explains. "I'm not ready to be a bride, yet our father wants me to marry.".

"Sergeant Onfoy? Is it his scars? I could deny the marriage."

"No, Highness, I love him, but I ache to make music. I must sing."

"She needs time to be young, Highness," I add. "The world's not ready for the change in traditions or law, but a sovereign can make a dispensation. We ask nothing against God's law. I studied the issue in the library. If you truly wish to be Jakub's son, once reborn, you can inherit the holding from him. You're an excellent administrator, and we don't doubt you will lead the holding well and care for the countess as your mother.

I pause perfectly. "However, if you don't wish to be Jakub's son, we ask you make dispensation so if Jakub and Agata have no son, Loretta's future son shall retain the holding."

I glanced at Loretta, praying she did not flinch. I hadn't completely planned out our strategy, but it would buy time. And even if the vampires were angry about our sins, they would never dare harm Loretta.

"What do you want for yourself?" he asks.

"Only for Loretta to be safe in a well-appointed apartment, well-fed, and happy. She'll also need a maid," I add, "so she may spend the next years focused on her music. We've been attending to each other's needs as my father only brought a manservant and driver. I beg for this, so I may serve you in my best capacity."

"Which is?"

"Serving our father's holding and bringing charity to those who need it. You will see how much my charity will be quickly turned into goods and funds that bring in taxes—"

The king's laugh cut me off. "How can I say no to such an arrangement, Madame Pascaline? Madame Loretta, I shall send for your things."

I squeeze my sister, knowing it might be the final time I embrace her. Loretta follows Louis XIV into the darkness so she may live in the sun.

Jakub

Charles scratched on my door. "Gunter told me."

"Told you what?" I asked.

"Loretta has gone to the king."

"She has?" I hid my rage. Considering Agata and Gaius's fragile allyship, I said, "But I'll still transform you as planned, if that is your wish. Where's Benoit?"

"Asleep in our quarters."

The room felt tiny as I sat with Charles, awaiting explanation from my errant daughters. Charles is everything a man could want in a son. Why are women so irrational?

Pascaline crept into the room; her face fell into a frown. He rose to his feet.

"Why is my betrothed with the king!" Charles growled.

She did not retreat. "Loretta isn't ready to marry."

He squeezed his hands into two massive fists. "You're lucky you aren't a man," he growled.

"Only the king can protect Loretta. So, yes, I placed her with the king. If Loretta isn't old enough to be a vampire, she certainly isn't old enough to marry one."

"You're ruined. Everything you touch dies," I said. These words would linger between us. Perhaps for centuries, unless I rid myself of Pascaline. The king must return Loretta to me. I'll have the better daughter and a good son-in-law to train my men.

Pascaline retreated to the far corner of the room and covered her face with her hands.

"Jakub, my love," Agata rose, ash falling from her body.

"Do not speak the words of the Devil. They lead to actions of the Devil. 'Tis our girls' work that makes our county thrive.

"Charles, while you have every right to feel betrayed, you must acknowledge that their good works freed you and your cadet. Return to your room. I shall deal with my daughters."

From the chair, I studied Agata in her weakness. She did not hate Pascaline. Charles must have realized it, too.

Indeed, Agata caressed the girl by the shoulders and put her to bed.

"I must say goodbye to our rebellious daughter. I need your blood, Pascaline," Agata said.

Pascaline nodded.

Agata bit into the girl's throat to retake the blood that she had given. We needed to escape Versailles. The lack of fresh blood and feeding from each other made us all weaker.

Once Pascaline slept, Agata's skin glowed with the energy of youth. She approached my chair and pushed back my clothes.

"Are you strong enough?"

"To put you in a better mood? Yes." She pressed her lips against mine. "Besides, all the children are sleeping."

"Having children again has been quite a change."

She sat on my lap and expanded her fangs. "Indeed, but not everything need change." Agata kissed me hard and dug her pearly fangs deep into the flesh of my tongue.

Chapter 48

Loretta

18th of August

Cher Journal

It is after midnight and the king left me without affection, but said, he would see me when he was less busy.

Nervous and lonely, I sit on my cushioned settle to write down all my thoughts. Why did Pascaline ask for dispensation after she poisoned my womb? Perhaps only a few drops of vampire blood wears off, and I'll need more someday? Perhaps it doesn't matter. Pascaline must have a plan.

My rooms are lovely: a well-appointed parlor with two high-back settles which make a comfortable nook in front of the fireplace where an old portrait of the king stares down at me. Behind two lovely glass doors is my bedroom along with my private garderobe and a cupboard bed for my future servant.

Wait...someone is tapping on the window...

Cher Journal,

Gaius and Maman were just here. Wearing Helena's bracelet, I hurried to let them in through the window before I thought to strike.

"Here she is, Countess. Safe and sound." Gaius easily lifted Maman inside and climbed in after her. To me, he inclined his head. "What a charming apartment for a young lady."

Maman scowled, her fangs were stained, and her skin looked healthy. She had taken blood from somewhere. I feared for my sister.

I tried to make polite conversation. "The king said my maid shall come tomorrow."

Wringing my hands, I asked, "Did you hurt Calette?"

Maman stood perfectly straight; chin held high. "I took her blood so I might see you. Do you not love Charles? Your father hired him, bought him a promotion, all for you. You threw it back in his face. He's so angry, I asked Gaius to find you."

"I love Charles, but I cannot marry him yet. I'm not ready to be a wife. I need to sing."

"Back in my day..." Maman muttered and shoved a basket of her remedies into my hands.

Gaius laughed. "You've finally become as interesting as your sister. If your parents decide you are too shameful, I will always give you and Pascaline an occupation whether or not you marry Charles."

Maman gave Gaius a look of such contempt I might've laughed, but I knew better. "Well, daughter, if you mean to stay, let's clean any bad spirits from this place. Only God knows which sinner used this room last."

Gaius asked what he ought to do.

"With your greater strength, please wipe the walls and ceilings with this cleaner. Allow no insect to escape."

He bowed and took the chore gladly, crawling up the wall, sponge in hand. She and I wiped down the wood with her vinegars and placed herbs in my bed, the maid's cupboard, and in the cushions of the settle.

Once my apartment was freshened, Maman kissed me. Gaius assisted her out the window. He's a strange man. I don't understand his motives. Perhaps after I become a vampire, I will.

Pascaline

I wake at the normal time, yet I cannot forget Maman's whispered words after she took my blood: *If you do not behave properly, you'll be forced to sleep until we leave.*

I hate to be frightened of Maman.

With the belief we betrayed them and the shame they incurred by our actions. Maman and Papa use the impending cold weather as an excuse to travel back to their county.

"We must stay for the ambassadors of Siam," I remind them.

Papa barely speaks to me. However, he concedes. "Charles and I understand the military advantages. There is little doubt France needs the military support of King Narai."

The entire French Court knew when the emissaries would arrive. Everything is scheduled. After their ship docked, the papers claimed even the poorest peasants went to see our friends from the East.

Loretta

18th of August

Cher Journal,

I slept better than I thought I might. An efficient, soft-spoken older woman named Josephine came to my door as my personal maid. She dressed me and combed and styled my hair perfectly. I hope we will be friendly to one another. I already miss Pascaline and Maman's affection.

Chapter 49

Pascaline

Court is packed with the excitement of the visiting emissaries. We dress well in pink taffeta and lavender velvet, so do all our friends and customers that we made over the summer. Gaius, Gunter, and Sydella find us in the excitement. Loretta looks at Charles shyly but does not move to touch him as she might have once done.

"How is your new situation?" Gaius asks Loretta.

"The king has been feeling unwell," Loretta says. "We simply talk of music, and he reminisces about his ballets."

"You're still untouched?" Gaius asked.

She blushes and ducks behind her fan. I know, for she told me as much.

The room silences as the three emissaries of King Narai of Siam, Kosa Pan, Ok-luang Kanlaya Ratchamaitri, and Ok-khun Si Wisan Wacha, enter. Surrounded by knights and the king's guard, the ambassadors wear striking, pointed hats and exotic silk clothing. Their jackets are cut looser and have less ornamentation than the ones French courtiers wore.

They kneel and bend even lower until their foreheads gently touch the polished marble floor. They raise their eyes and gaze upon the king. I wonder what they think of the king and the French people.

Pan speaks of an eternal alliance between France and Siam. I am enraptured by the man's smooth delivery and gentle voice, as was all Versailles. They present many gifts: gold, tortoise shells, fabrics, carpets, porcelain, lacquered furniture, and two silver cannons. After delivering a letter enclosed in a beautiful machine, the ambassadors withdraw.

The king invites them to visit his apartments and gardens. And he offers Loretta's voice as entertainment.

Loretta kisses my cheek and silently follows the men. I pray she is safe, but I cannot protect her anymore. I dab my eyes with my handkerchief.

Loretta

1st of September

Cher Journal,

I was glad to see my family. Pascaline looked paler, but healthy. It was exciting to play my harp for the ambassadors. They only speak quietly and respectfully to Louis, but they complimented me through him. I have begun to plan my next small concert for the ladies. I wonder what type of stories the ambassadors enjoy.

At this point, they seem to like all things French!

5th of September

Cher Journal,

The ambassadors are ordering vast amounts of French products to be shipped to the Siamese Court: mirrors, French cannons, carpets, globes, telescopes, glasses, clocks, and most importantly, velvets some of which are dyed with our dye!

Navigating Versailles on my own, I find it harder to know what to sing. Is that strange? With Louis's permission, I visited my parents' quarters. Pascaline was joyous and asked me all sort of questions. Maman looked a little ill, but she was on her feet. As my parents conceded it was good, we stayed, though Papa's narrowed eyes claimed I was a terrible girl.

He announced, "I shall transform Charles after Sunday Mass, and we shall set off a few days later. I'll be glad to leave the corruption behind."

I wonder if he meant that I am the corruption.

Chapter 50

Loretta

16th of September

Cher Journal,

Tonight, Charles will die. I spent Mass praying he will come back.

Gaius and Sydella approached me after my concert. I speak to Pascaline each day at Court, but soon, they will be leaving.

Sydella whispered, "You should come to say goodbye."

I spent the rest of the day wondering if I should, but in the end, I went.

Pascaline embraced me. Charles frowned.

His eyes were filled with hurt. "I did not know if you would come to my transformation."

"I wanted to say goodbye for now. I hope you understand."

"I understand enough to know you thought you must stay," Charles said gruffly.

"Will you be well?"

"I still have a new job, a promotion, and your family ensured Benoit was assigned to remain with me, I can thank you for that. But this room is no place for young humans."

Benoit and I left the room without argument.

"Will he forgive me?" I asked.

Benoit studied me carefully but did not speak against me as he might have done.

For a moment, he looked as if he might say a cruelty. Instead, he kept his voice soft. "I don't know, probably. Lieutenant Onfoy and I both understand this agreement is the reason we escaped Brandenburg. Maybe they offered him something he didn't want to turn down, but I never wanted to go back there, so thank you."

Relieved, I went to get my new harp—a gift from the king.

Pascaline

Sydella and I leisurely stroll to the village. We find a soldier blubbering and smelling like cheap wine. His knuckles are bruised, and he has a black eye.

We smile at each other and approach him.

"Bad night?" Sydella says.

"Good now." He touches his manhood.

With his eyes on Sydella, I plunge my fangs into his jugular, flooding my mouth with abundant, vigorous, drunken blood. I gulp the first warm mouthful, then the second. Living blood is glorious, especially when I do not want vengeance, only substance.

The man screams, but Sydella takes her turn and presses him into the wall. We do not let go until he weakens.

Sydella's pulse races beside mine. We are so close. She

is so beautiful with blood on her lips and the faint trace of her light blue veins under her rosy cheeks. She turns. I meet her blue eyes. I can drown in them.

"I want to kiss you," I whisper.

She pulls me close. I feel the quickly fading warmth of the soldier's blood inside her. I rise to my toes and kiss her lips, tasting the man's blood on her sweet flesh.

"Charles will need him," she whispers. "After the transformation..."

"Indeed. After..."

"No matter what happens tonight, I still must travel to Brandenburg," she says.

"I know." I pinch my eyes shut at the pain that floods my heart.

"You could attend me?" she asks.

"I cannot leave my sister until she's safe."

"I cannot leave my herd or my share in the business," she says.

I understand. So does she.

We lift the dead body and put his arm over our shoulders as if we are carrying a drunken man to bed.

Gaius blesses Charles and kisses his cheeks. Gunter, Sydella, Agata, and I embrace him in turn. So the men do not stain their clothing, Papa and Charles strip to their breeches. Scars run down his right side from the burns, and his back bore several scars from a lashing. I shiver. I hate I caused the man pain. I tell myself if he's wise, the pain will be temporary.

Charles relaxes on a thin pallet. He does not tremble as Maman prays over him.

Maman presses his brow with her cool hand. "Fear not, my soon-to-be son."

Papa sits over Charles and sinks his fangs into Charles's wrist. He drinks in his blood until Charles's skin mottles. Papa stabs himself in the chest. The dark blood spilling from Papa's heart flows into Charles's mouth. He gulps the blood.

Flush with vampire blood, he lies back on the pallet.

From outside, I hear Loretta's soft playing and her voice, along with Benoit's under the window, singing the old medieval song, Le Bouvier.

Papa stabs through Charles's scars to the carotid artery. He clamps his mouth onto the wound.

Sydella and I move to the cabinet to bring in the body. Next, Loretta sings J'aims San Penser Laidure. Gunter fed Papa and Gaius fed Charles. I feel a connection to the bloodline in our souls. This is why Gunter said the possible human relationship did not matter. Charles is still angry with Loretta and me. I pray someday Charles will forgive us, marry Loretta, and love me like a sister-in-law.

Sydella and I bring the dead body to the center of the room. We set the corpse in front of Charles and open his uniform.

Without hesitation, Charles kneels before the mass of dead flesh. He takes the knife from Papa and rips through the dead man's sternum, breaking his bones. He digs out the heart.

I am glad he is no longer a grenadier sergeant but a vampire. A man of Jakub's holding.

I lick my lips as Charles brings the thick, fibrous muscle to his mouth. He bites into it; warm blood spills down his chin. He takes another bite before the blood hits the ground.

Beside him, all of us vampires feast on the corpse until all that is left is bloody bones.

Papa follows Charles to his room, Agata brings Benoit into ours, Gaius and Gunter return to theirs, and Sydella and I walk through the garden. Though it will cause me heartache when she is gone, I crush my lips against hers. We make love on a pile of damp leaves under the moonlight.

Chapter 51

Jakub

I was relieved to be on my way from that foul palace of decadence, though I never spoke those words lest they get back to Louis XIV. Standing before our luggage, I told Pascaline, "I do not need your assistance and expect you to ride in the carriage with your mother."

"I suppose now you've a son, you don't need a daughter," she whispered.

"Not one who does not honor her parents," I replied.

She said nothing else. For four long days and nights, she quietly obeyed.

Charles, Benoit, and Jean-Victor rode atop the carriage and took turns driving while I rode Castor. The lads seemed to enjoy each other's company. Jean-Victor was older, but Benoit outranked him by birth and status, so there was blessed little competition between them. While Charles and Benoit had limited experience handling carriage horses, they were happy to assist without complaint. The ghost girl remained close to Charles, occasionally leaning upon him or crawling on his lap, but she never spoke or spooked the horses.

The smoothness of my road and the smell of my forests greeted me.

"How beautiful this place is," Charles murmured.

Our village came to welcome us. Agata greeted many of them. She touched their hands and faces and asked about their little ones. She claimed many successes in Versailles and excused Loretta for having remained to sing for the King.

No one contradicted her. Finally, we let the ladies and the luggage off in front of the chateau. Jean-Victor took the carriage to the stables. He was gentle with the horses, kindly and loving, as he checked their feet and muscles.

I showed my new son and his cadet the barracks. It was a small building, but serviceable for our needs. "Most men live in town; occasionally, we house some of the boys here. Mothers don't always give them the freedom to train. Overworry."

Charles was careful to remain a step behind my stride. Benoit behind him as we surveyed the men at arms - most of whom had other vocations within my village.

"I wish I could capture such a lush green place with a poem," Charles said softly. "I had not imagined such prosperity among the populace. Everything Loretta told me about this place was true. No wonder she loves it.

"Of course, that means we must fear the lax softness of the county as much as any pleasure garden," he added.

As a sergeant, he led men and boys on the battlefield, but much of his time between battles was spent keeping morale and discipline.

I probed Charles about an expected dowry if he did not get his first choice in a bride.

He grimaced. "I suppose it is for the best we join as a family."

Benoit opened his mouth but closed it and looked at his feet.

"Indeed, it is."

We stepped into the sparring ground where twenty men between thirteen and forty stood tall. My eldest man sat tall, as he was twenty years older than the oldest who stood.

"This is your new commander, Lieutenant from House of Onfoy and his cadet, Benoit Lécuyer. Lieutenant Onfoy has seen nearly fifteen years in service to the Crown against the Dutch, Spain, and our other current enemies. He is the grandson of a knight and a man of honor in his own right. Follow him as you follow me."

My two sergeants explained the three major threats to the county.

A man stepped forward. "Count de Banquier, what of those who creep in the night?"

"Have they crossed into our lands?"

"No. But they slide closer and retreat."

"As if trying to tempt you across the border?" Charles asked.

"Yes, Lieutenant."

"We shall ride the road tonight and see for myself. It may be that once I am seen, the enemy will retreat. I'm gladdened to be home," I told them.

Charles and Benoit moved from an introduction to drilling the men. They were patient, well-spoken, and gave clear direction as they explained strategies they had seen on the battlefield. The men and boys moved in formation.

I saw Charles in an even more favorable light.

At dinner, we walked through the garden toward the château. Other than bees buzzing in the apiary, it was magical and quiet. I had missed this place so much.

My happiness faltered as Charles, Benoit, and I entered Agata's hall. Pascaline was singing a crib song as she helped Agata. I was at a loss. She seemed one step ahead of me. Perhaps she was even ahead of her mother, but even after two hundred years of marriage, it was hard to tell what was behind those quiet, dark eyes of my Agata.

"Charles is everything I hoped our human sons grew into," I told my wife.

"He is the binding tie with Gaius," she said. To Charles, she asked, "How are you settling in? Do you need any extra blankets?"

"Everything is comfortable. Thank you, Countess."

Pascaline came into the room and with perfect manners and waited for Charles to assist her with her seat. He did so.

While fare was simpler than at Versailles, it was more delicious. Agata pressed another pork chop onto Benoit's plate and patted his shoulder. "Eat, eat!"

"Thank you, Countess." He ate with a lad's appetite, which pleased her.

"He is verily a great cadet," I told Charles.

"He is. I thank you for keeping him by my side," Charles said.

Between the courses, I turned to Pascaline. "I'm saddened it is no longer the age of knights, but I gave my word of honor. "One of my daughters will marry Lieutenant Onfoy."

She stiffened. I was glad to see her speechless.

"You're pretty and have good qualities, even if you're not my first choice," Charles said.

Pascaline replied. To me, "I'll never marry Lieutenant Onfoy." To Charles, "I'll never love you the way Loretta does, and I shall never hurt her."

"If she loves me, why didn't she marry me?" Charles said.

"When did you ask her," the girl said tartly. I kept my anger in check, but I wanted to slap her.

Agata took Charles's arm. "Lieutenant, my daughters may've made a grave mistake, but they aren't malicious. I hope you might look beyond this embarrassment and find Loretta loves you after all. Pascaline seems to think that is the case. She is a good judge of character."

"Your daughters will ruin us," I snapped.

Agata laughed. "Strange, my love. According to the receipts, they saved us. Is the king not happy with you and this holding for the first time in decades?"

"Whether he marries Loretta or another, Charles is your lieutenant and will teach your men well."

"You forgive them?" Charles asked.

"They've done nothing I need to forgive. You and their papa, however, must look into your hearts and decide for yourselves."

"Is it my scars?" Charles asked.

Pascaline shook her head. "We do not fear your scars, Lieutenant. Only what you might do. You're a vampire, a decade Loretta's senior, and my sister is still human. How do you not see the danger?"

I studied the girl. She seemed to sincerely believe she had helped her sister.

"You've such kindly affection for Benoit, Lieutenant. I'll be sure to tell Loretta," Pascaline said.

"He's my cadet, Madame. I've no affection for him, nor he for me. We have a duty to each other."

"You might say my duty is to protect my sister, but I also feel affection."

"Why ruin her happiness?" I asked.

"We ruined nothing if Charles is the man of her dreams."

Charles threw up his hands. "You're the most exasperating conversationalist I ever met! No decency or shame!"

She smiled innocently. "You ought to be glad I refused to marry you."

My insides twisted, enraged at the girl and her sister for despoiling my good name.

Charles laughed. "I'm most glad!"

My cheeks flushed. "Why can't you be more like Sydella? That woman knows how to talk to men, how to be modest..."

"Sydella was taught to protect herself. Will you teach me and Loretta these things?"

I grabbed Pascaline's elbow and wrenched it to force her to walk into the chapel. "Pray on your sins!" I bellowed before shutting her inside.

Through the door, Pascaline did not pray for her sins. She prayed, "Mother Mary, keep Loretta safe. Hold my sweet Celeste in your arms."

I faced Agata's most disapproving look.

"There was no reason to become parents again if you're not willing to know our children as well as the Lord's prayer."

"That was not why we turned them!" I knew I stepped into a trap.

"It seems to me, my love, Pascaline proved she was right to fear what a vampire might do to a human girl."

"Go and order her to pray on her sins!"

"Very well, but you know how I feel about fighting at my table." Agata went into the chapel.

Charles, Benoit, and Suzetta quickly began to eat again as if the ugliness had not occurred.

Pascaline

I kneel at the altar. I should have never agreed to be a daughter. If I had been wise, I would have claimed another relation like second cousin once removed. But Jakub would have never given Celeste a grave in the family vault. *Use your brain, Pascaline,* I tell myself.

I know what I must do, but my parents' tempers grow thin. Especially Papa's. The critical thing is Loretta is safe; Celeste is beyond pain. All they can do is kill me.

Maman enters. She touches the holy water, makes the sign of the cross, genuflects toward the alter and sits beside me. "Why must you quarrel so, Pascaline?"

"Forgive me, Maman. I love being your daughter and appreciate everything you have done for us, but this cannot stand."

"Sleep. Come at it with a clear mind," she says. "Though Jakub built me a utopia, the moment it expanded, everyone had their own ideas on how to run it."

I chuckle. "I won't try to rule your utopia but allow me to protect it because we're not safe yet. The men don't see. It's not a battle as they know it, but I swear we still are yours."

Maman embraces me tightly. "I know."

I sit in the chapel and stare up at the statue of Mary. *If I had money of my own, what would I do?* I do not have an answer. There are wild women who run away from brutish husbands and scandalize their families. I might do that too; except I could never be happy as an adventuress.

But then what?

I love Maman. Though I am angry, I do like Papa, and Charles and Loretta's love will grow if we do not hamper it. I liked Charles just fine in Versailles, which means I will like him here—if I can figure out how to reach him.

Chapter 52

Loretta

20th of September

Cher Journal

Many with court appointments overwinter in Versailles, but Court seems empty without Pascaline. The noise level dropped over the course of days. I miss Pascaline, Celeste, my second set of parents, my first family, and Charles. I remind myself no one in Versailles can know about my love though I might imagine what the touch of Charles will feel like.

I consider what new song might please the sovereign. I know what I want to sing about, but the king only tolerates artistic visions which complemented his own. I don't feel Louis's type of music in my soul. He's not a god or even put on his throne by God, though that is what he and the Church enforced.

I crossed myself as had become my habit and said a little prayer for Celeste. I'm not sure if my heart is truly Catholic. Papa once said, I have the paperwork proving I am, so I am.

Jakub

Our next family meal was the same. With her hair in a simple plait and plain dress, Pascaline seemed younger than Loretta. Yet, I could not help but wonder if this was a disguise. She rejoiced in needling me with her foul questions and evil heart.

"Papa, now I prayed upon my sins; may I train alongside the men?" Pascaline asked.

"Certainly not."

"But I want to learn to be like Sydella. I heard the men discussing those who creep in the night. What if—"

"Assist your mother as your providence dictates," I said.

"Very well, Papa." Pascaline turned to Charles and Benoit. "Lieutenant, Cadet, would after supper be the appropriate time for questions?"

Charles frowned.

Agata smiled and patted Charles's wrist. "It seems better that Pascaline asks questions outside of your training hours. I have no stomach for conversations about war at my table. When you walk the garden, might I trouble you to bring in lavender and rosemary?"

"Yes, Maman/Countess," Pascaline and both young men said in unison.

I bowed my head and said nothing.

I looked out the window over the kitchen garden to observe and listen to them.

Benoit offered his hand to Pascaline as they stepped outside. He slowed his pace for the girl. After a few steps,

Charles also slowed his pace so Pascaline might walk between them. The shimmering little ghost skipped ahead.

"In that line formation you drilled today, what exactly were you aiming for?" she asked.

"The enemy in front of our muskets," Charles said, annoyed.

"How much leeway does a foot soldier have?" Pascaline asked.

"None. They're put in a line and told what to do," Charles said.

"If they break formation?"

"They're whipped or shot, Madame," Benoit said.

"Even if they're making moves to win the battle?"

"A foot soldier doesn't know what moves to make...and there are rules of engagement to consider," Benoit said.

"Thank you, Cadet. How do I learn the rules of engagement?"

Charles froze. "There are books in your family library, no doubt."

"But what I need to know is what happens if an order countermands another order?"

"Madame, in the Royal Army, ultimately, we answer to the king. The king tells his generals what he wants, the generals strategize, and down the commands go. Orders never contradict orders," Benoit said.

Except I once was a knight of France and, before that, one of The Brave of Moldavia. Orders were counteracting and contradicting. Charles had been a grenadier sergeant; he would know it, too. All that mattered was the battle was won.

"So, if a soldier sacrificed something for the greater

good?"

"You ask about sacrifice when you sacrificed my rights as a husband?" Charles roared.

Benoit pulled Pascaline away from the other man, but the girl just shook her head. Innocence disappeared from her eyes. "God above, men are dull. We went to Versailles for a reason. That reason has not changed."

Charles looked at Agata's herbs. "Which one of these damned plants does the countess want?"

Pascaline knelt, cut the lavender, and laid it gently in her basket.

"Women go to Versailles to be adored, find husbands, and play cruel, silly games," Charles snapped.

"Is that all you see? Women go to Versailles to represent their families' interests. We, too, ultimately answer to the king."

"You only think of your twisted intrigues!" Charles still shouted.

"I thought you were a grenadier, but you're still an unthinking foot soldier. Shoot at what's in front of you; never wonder why." Pascaline snarled back.

"We all take orders from the count. If you continue to disobey your father, not even your mother can protect you," Benoit said.

"We're loyal to the count," Charles said.

She sighed. It was not the sigh of a defeated woman but one who was thinking. "So am I."

She harvested the rosemary stems. "I will love the count forever for the kindness he showed Celeste. He didn't get upset when she spit up all over his beard and church velvets. Not a day goes by that I don't remember her gripping his fingers when she learned to walk. So, it is not a game—not how you mean it—and it isn't over yet. Maybe Papa forgot, maybe you didn't even know it. But we won't win by shooting dumbly at a line."

"I shan't listen to another word." Charles grabbed her elbow and walked faster than he ought to walk with a lady. Benoit clutched the herbs she had collected and followed.

The little ghost girl appeared. "You're hurting!" She grabbed Charles's leg and hung on to him. He loosened his grip on Pascaline. Still, Benoit and Charles escorted the lady to her mother and left.

Though I do not like Pascaline's words, I cannot pretend I am not affected. I have no weapons to fight my enemy, only two women who claim they are my daughters.

I grabbed a bottle of Agata's summer wine and found the men in their quarters. The little ghost girl was on a small pallet in the corner. They stood as I entered, but I raised the bottle. "Wine?"

"As you please, my Count," Charles said.

I sat heavily at Charles's table and asked if they minded if I smoked. I took out my pipe.

Benoit found glasses and hurried to pour the wine. He glanced at the pallet. The little girl disappeared, but I sensed she was still there.

"Forgive me how I spoke to the lady, and I regret taking her arm as I did."

The child was suddenly beside me. I felt her icy ether reach into me as she stared without blinking. I felt her death.

"Greta, what have I told you?" Charles pointed at the

pendulum clock.

"I'm supposed to be asleep when the little hand is on the eight?"

"That's a good girl," he said.

"Don't hurt 'em." Greta floated to her pallet.

"She has limited knowledge of army discipline," Charles said.

Benoit followed her and lifted the blankets. She disappeared under them.

I smiled, impressed with the boy. "I've never known a human who can see ghosts."

Benoit lit my pipe. "I can't, but I can see the movement of the blankets and the direction you and the lieutenant look, my count. Also, the lieutenant talks to her when he thinks no one is listening."

Perhaps his quick wit was why Charles kept him safe at the prison camp. He rolled Charles a cigarette and one for himself.

"A man cannot be expected not to cry in pain when someone twists the blade in his heart, but the lady's words gave me much to consider," I said.

"Was there truth in them?" Benoit asked.

I pinched the space between my eyes. "She believes her words are true."

Charles regarded the boy through the haze. "Of course, it changes nothing. Our job is to teach the gendarme modern fighting techniques."

"Then, what happens?" Benoit asked.

Charles gestured at me. "We go where the count commands. That's the job. In many regards, it's no different than the army."

"Cleaner quarters and much better food," Benoit offered.

"Much better," Charles agreed.

"Do you wish to be a vampire, Ben?" I asked.

"I'm not sure. The changes I have seen in the lieutenant worry me," he said. "I don't want to be starving and make sausages out of people like the vampires in Brandenburg."

This was the first time either the lieutenant or cadet had spoken about what they had seen at the prison camp. I wanted to press for more information, but Charles spoke first.

"What changes?"

"You pace and grind your teeth more. You just lost your temper at a lady. And you haven't told a single joke or a riddle or even a pun since you transformed," Benoit said.

"I don't feel like joking, but don't worry, I'm sure I shall again." Charles looked at his cigarette. "It all goes up in smoke anyway."

Benoit groaned. From her pallet, Greta giggled.

"You asked for a joke; you didn't ask for a good one," Charles said.

Charles had lied to Pascaline, or was simply unaware of it, but I was sure he had great affection for Benoit...and the little ghost, too.

Chapter 53

Pascaline

Autumn storm clouds are tinged with daylight as I press the last of the lavender into drying paper. I inhale the perfume of the flowers and dream of Versailles: the dancing, singing, and passions. I miss it. To brighten my mood, I remember how I helped several young women find kindly husbands simply by ensuring the right introductions were made at the right time. I was able to give charity to several organizations without the help of my "father," but the king alone.

Jakub is angry enough to kill me. I shudder at the fear the château might have an oubliette...and if I am tossed in, I will not die.

"Loretta's safe and that's what matters," I whisper.

I pray my plan will protect Loretta. I ache to hear my daughter's laughter. I desire my husband's or Sydella's touch. I pinch my eyes against the tears.

I hear a girl's faraway laughter.

Charles's loud soldier's footsteps approach. He is also strong enough to throw me in a dark cell. A lump catches in my throat.

His ghost floats behind him.

I do not want to hear his roar again, but I cannot leave this occupation. Maman is my only friend now; I do not want to face her wrath by leaving a job undone.

He bows. "Madame Pascaline."

I incline my head. "Lieutenant." I wonder what the etiquette was with ghosts. Charles never introduces her.

"It's best Loretta isn't here," he says gruffly. "Last night, I wouldn't have been able to control my bloodlust... If she was my wife... I cannot pretend I'm not wounded, but I understand why you did what you did."

"Is anyone injured?" I ask.

"My pride. Gunter and Jakub assisted me."

"Do you need more blood?"

"I'm fine now."

I place the top board on the press. "How close is Gunter?"

"I'm unsure; I can find people, but my gifts are still... awkward. He's watching for certain. He's close."

I set the first blocks on my press. "My gifts are also undeveloped; I fear getting caught."

"Yet you enchanted my brother."

"Since I wasn't trying to hurt him, I figured you'd let me."

Charles places the last two blocks. "How did you know about the intensity of my bloodlust?"

"Because I felt it since my turning."

"You don't act like it."

"I cannot wallow in it. Maman told me it doesn't get easier, but the bloodlust becomes habitual."

"You still call the Countess, Maman, even here?"

"The intrigue can never end. Loretta is too dear to risk."

Charles frowns. I hold my ground though I want to scurry away.

"Loretta's safe exactly where you placed her. You ought not to have such fears."

I put my hands on my hips. "You ought not to tell me what to do."

"Must you be contrary?"

"Am I supposed to forget you're angry when you're the stronger, armed with a sword, when the sunlight is but over that hedge?"

"A man of my rank wears a sword, but it's a gentleman's duty…"

I tremble. I do not want to show any emotion, but it spills out of me. "You've an occupation. I'm not allowed to have one other than courtier, adventuress, or worse. I spent the season ensuring you have a job and Papa has a holding, yet, I must listen to you and Papa discuss who gets saddled with my upkeep in eternity."

"You might get married."

"I wouldn't be so cruel to marry until my heart mends."

"You loved Andre de Aubinet?"

"When I remember his kindness, I love Andre as my husband and Celeste's father and even the hero he was, but there are times I hate him, too. It's my deepest wish Loretta only has reason to love you. Both of you. But you're certainly not helping."

"I apologize for making you the target of my wrath. I ought not to have said such things to a lady." Charles inclines his head.

"Thank you," I say quietly.

He stands there, watching me, so I ask, "Do you like your rooms here?"

"They're quite comfortable."

"Is Benoit contented?"

"Madame, I shall tell him you thought of his wellbeing. Any man is happy to know a lady considers such things."

I gesture at the ghost. "And your child?"

"You can see me?" The girl's ghostly glow peers from behind Charles.

"Greta needs very little, but I made a pallet near the fireplace."

"Hello, Greta." I kneel to meet her eye. "Is Charles your papa?"

Greta shakes her head.

"She was the unit laundress," Charles says.

"But I can't do clothes anymore," she whispers sadly.

"Why didn't you go to Heaven?" I ask, wondering if Celeste wanders somewhere alone.

"Dunno. After the cannonball went through the wall, I was with other dead people, lots of dead people. Some were bad. I heard Charles..." she giggles as she tries out the name. I wonder if this is the first time she called him - or any adult - by their given name. "...praying, so I found him. There were toys in the castle, but I couldn't pick them up. Also, the horses are nice and Sydella, but I don't know about your Papa."

"Papa's a good man," I say though I do not know if I believe it either. "Greta, since you've been here, have you seen a baby ghost?"

She shook her head.

"Did your child have a burial?" Charles asks.

"Yes."

"Though Gaius isn't an expert on ghosts, his understanding is ghosts get lost if they weren't buried or there weren't prayers or tears to help them go wherever they're going. Whether we call it Heaven, Valhalla, Elysian Plains, or Asphodel, it doesn't matter."

"No funeral?"

Greta shrugs. "Armies keep moving."

I embrace the ghost. "I'm so sorry." I feel my soul being pulled toward death. I find myself wondering if I can be with Celeste.

"Can I play with the blocks in your room?" she whispers.

"Of course! In fact, I'll have them sent to your room," I whisper back.

"But you mustn't leave a mess. A lieutenant's room must remain tidy," Charles told her.

I gesture at the press. "Will you want some of these drawer papers to keep the winter mustiness away from your trunks?"

Charles chuckles. "As it pleases you and the countess."

"Did I say something funny?"

"Madame, you don't understand the path Benoit and I've traveled these last years. We've lived at a prison camp, a vampire's castle, Versailles, and now here. In all that time, sweet lady, no one has asked about our desires in the slightest. We were given both food and comforts depending on the location. We stole or gambled for the rest."

As I listen to Charles's explanation, I consider how we also stole to survive. I wonder if Charles would forgive Loretta if he knew.

"Sydella, Gunter, and Gaius tell you what you need and turn every action in their favor. Even your father does it to a certain extent. It makes one insecure about trusting anyone."

My tears come unbidden.

"Now, we are in this beautiful, innocent place that time forgot. It's enough for a fairy story, then a nymph, in terrible mourning, asks me if I want drawer papers of all things. It feels like a joke."

Loretta

23rd of September

Cher Journal,

According to the newspapers and rumors from several men, the king's previous mistresses had influence. If so, I'm unsure how to get it. I listen quietly, not speaking or bringing petitions, though I wonder if I should.

This morning, I spied Henri watching me.

At recess, knowing he would find me, I walked in the quickly fading garden. The air turned so cold and damp, it slipped through my woolen dress, past my skin and sinew until it nestled into my bones. I considered how I spent the previous autumn homeless and afraid. Now, I am a favored lady of Versailles—one of the king's unofficial mistresses.

"Why are you here, Madame Loretta?" Henri asked me.

"I am under the king's protection until my father returns," I replied.

"To what end?"

"Same as you, to please our sovereign."

His frown deepened the crowsfeet around his eyes.

"And my brother?"

"Pascaline claims he and his cadet made fast friends with our carriage man, Jean-Victor, who is also a member of the gendarme."

"We heard many strange noises coming from your rooms, not to mention such comings and goings, before your family set off," Henri said.

I tried to change the subject. "I've a post allowance. My sister and I write messages. If you wish to send word, I'm sure it will help your brother's heart to receive a letter from you."

Henri's eyes narrowed. "What's your game?"

I told a half-truth, "There's no game except to make music."

"Music?"

"I labor upon a short opera. Do you overwinter, Monsieur?"

"This year I must. Count Langlais is honeymooning. There's much to rebuild."

I felt Henri's hidden rage at my and his own insignificance. I wondered if it was Pascaline's vampire blood now within me.

"Is Countess Langlais happy?" I asked.

Henri shifted his weight too quickly, out of courtly step. I stepped back.

"The countess is a dutiful woman and attends to what God, the king, and her husband deems appropriate, Madame."

"I hope she's happy. I miss her terribly."

Henri made the same grumpy sound in his throat Charles sometimes made, but it was terrifying how large he seemed. I could not stop seeing visions of Pascaline being knocked into the gravel when she sought work.

"May I assist you in some way?" I asked.

"Not that I can see." He wanted to say more. He did not. He was too experienced a courtier.

"My father's men arrive with a dye shipment in a few weeks; perhaps your brother will be among them. I shall send word if he is."

He thanked me and stepped back into position.

I curtsied and walked away.

I quietly reminded myself that Henri was a gentleman, beneath me in rank, and I was under the king's protection. His hands wouldn't strike, till, I worried about Henri's tongue.

Gabriel blocked my way. The dark circles under his eye and ashen skin spoke of illness, but his deep scowl frightened me. "Walk with me."

Not seeing a way out, I did.

"You'll marry the man I name, and you won't speak to Henri Onfoy or any man without my permission again."

"I'm the mistress of the king," I said.

"Unofficially. I expect you to save every gem he gives you. When he loses interest in you, you'll be more worthy."

"He gave me a harp."

"Learn the ways of love and acquire diamonds."

"Gabriel."

"You owe me your obedience. Do as I say, or I'll have every person in Château de Banquier tried as heretics. Perhaps witches. Do you know what is in the lower rooms of the palace? What foul deeds have been done there?"

I stepped backwards. "But they're Catholic, I swear."

"I'd hate to see boots bruise my sisters' necks." Gabriel

gestured to a balding man, who might have once been dashing, but now his gold-edged justacorps looked too small and wrinkles set his face in a sneer.

"He is the man you will marry. You will play harpsichord in his home and bear his children and never step foot in Versailles again."

"If I…?"

"You won't tell the king anything unless you want Count de Banquier to lose his holdings." Gabriel smirked. He thought he had me.

"What is my groom paying you?"

"Enough to repair the château."

"What if the king does not lose interest in me?"

Gabriel cackled. "Do you have any concept of how many girls have slept with the king only to be sent away when he tires of them? Of course, you don't. Enjoy it, Madame, your time will be short."

The clock rang out. "We must return, Monsieur," I whispered.

"Indeed," Gabriel said.

I kept my face behind my fan so no one could see my distress. If Pascaline was beside me, she would say, "Put that fear into your music, my tigresse."

Refusing to cry, I thought about the myths that described the way I felt. I found few, as fear was considered beneath the nobility. Yet as I looked over the court, I could not help but notice that the palace was a decadent monument to fear. Louis's fear of the nobility, their fear of him. We were surrounded by splendidly dressed guards and spies. Everyone pursued a way to the king. Girls younger than me sought to usurp my position. For what gain? I wanted freedom to make music, but what did they want?

I thought of Papa and the king, Charles and Henri, Gabriel, Gaius, and all the men who tried to decide my fate, and would have, if not for Pascaline. Not one of them asked what I wanted - not even Charles.

A new thought popped into my head: Perhaps, Charles isn't ready for marriage either. His life was the army. If we married now, he wouldn't have time to grow from the grenadier sergeant to Lieutenant Onfoy.

I saw Gunter standing in the shadows, watching. I inclined my head but feared to speak.

"Madame, Nix and I travel to your father's house tonight," he said.

"May I give you a letter for Pascaline? Perhaps some sheet music?"

"Indeed. I shall meet you before the Grand Couvert. Fear not, Madame, you chose your protector well." He glanced toward the throne. "The men's words are words, nothing more."

I curtsied and went to my room to write to Pascaline.

Chapter 54

Pascaline

In the kitchen, a woman grunts in labor. I cannot remain in my room as I hate the woman for no reason other than I miss Celeste and ache to hold her in my arms. I walk to the graveyard and enter the family mausoleum. I sit beside her grave marker on the bare stone and study the likeness. If I'd only been a better mother, she would be alive.

"Madame Pascaline?" Benoit calls from outside.

"Yes?"

"You received letters," he says.

Andre? I almost breathe in his name as I climb the steps. Then, I stop—and I remember. "Loretta?" I blink away tears as I take the letter.

"Yes."

I thank him and turn away to open it. My sadness morphs into terror.

Most of Loretta's letters contain news of Versailles. However, this time I find a song that makes no sense unless a code. Twelve notes, five flats, five sharps, plus the whole notes, half notes, quarter notes, and a few stars and hearts.

I hurry into the library and noodle my fingers against the harpsichord as I study it. It does not take me long to decode it.

Gabriel still demands that we marry whomever he chooses, as a way to rebuild the château. I don't know what to do. Return to Versailles.

I jump to my feet and find Jakub sitting with Charles and Benoit. No, even if he does not care for me, I must never forget he is Papa.

Furious, I must ask permission; I say as sweetly as possible, "Papa, Loretta sent me a message. She needs me. Please allow me to return to Versailles."

I show him the letter and decoded music.

"The king's whore…"

"How dare you?" I scream. "Never call my sister such a name again."

He stares. So does Charles and Benoit.

His voice drips with loathing. "You'll not raise your voice again."

I should not have embarrassed him, especially before the other men. I run upstairs dress in my woolen travel gown, gloves, and a wide-brimmed hat. I move into Jakub's study and find a blade. I touch it; it needs to be sharpened, but its point can kill a human with enough force.

I climb out of the window. It will take me at least three days to get to Versailles. Perhaps longer to Paris. I pray to find Gabriel visiting the same mistress.

In the evening breeze, someone undead watches me. If it is Maman or Papa or Charles, I will surely be brought back home, but no one approaches.

Loretta

1st of October

Cher Journal,

I don't know what to do.

I remain quiet unless it's time to sing. Not feeling my music, I sing old favorites. Anytime tears threaten, I consider the messages behind the myths. I scrutinize Gabriel as he goes about his day, hoping to find some way to escape fate. I miss being surrounded by women who are not in competition for the king's favor. I'm not even sure I can trust Josephine to keep my secrets.

I pray for Pascaline to come.

3rd of October

Cher Journal,

I'm so scared I cannot sleep. Lying in bed, listening to Josephine snore behind the screen, I thought of the great Huntress Atalanta, and instantly felt my inspiration return. It wouldn't matter at all of the audience didn't understand it, or even if they booed.

I jumped from my bed and tripped over my slippers.

"Madame?" Josephine asked with a yawn.

"I want to write a concerto about Atalanta!"

"At this hour?"

"Just a few notes, I promise."

I scribbled a few ideas at my desk and tucked them into

my pocket. I bade Josephine to bring a letter to the king's apartment. Though Louis might be asleep, his guard would not be.

My Gracious and Royal Highness,

Would it displease you if I went to the music room rather than attend Court for a time? I have become quite inspired.

M. Loretta of Banquier

Josephine returned; I asked to be dressed so I might be ready when the king called.

Papa's rule stopped applying to me the moment, he thought I seduced our king. Josephine would be my chaperone, but I was no longer afraid of what Papa would do to me for discussing and rehearsing my music with men. And no man would dare touch the unofficial mistress of the king.

I was still frightened Papa might punish Pascaline for my sins, but according to her letters, Papa only growled, never bit. It was the perfect time for a spectacle of purple fabrics— over the winter, cloth could be dyed and gowns could be made. Next season, it would be the color—enough women would be wearing it at the beginning of the season that everyone would want it by the end. Most importantly, Papa and Charles would understand what we accomplish. We are the knights of this age, not them.

The king's messenger brought me to him on his normal waking hour. Men bustled about his room, preparing him for his day.

Louis XIV was reading a parchment. He did not bother to look up. "Madame, how wonderful to hear that you have been blessed with renewed inspiration. Any hints?"

"Atalanta, Highness."

His eyes alighted upon me, now with interest.

"Highness, if my idea works as my mind sees it now, it might be a bit of a spectacle with lovely costumes in every shade of purple to help sell the dye."

"All the better!"

If you approve, I will write Venus's song for Pascaline's range, unless you wish to appear."

"How droll. Write the part for your sister." He inclined his head and dismissed me.

Josephine entered the practice room with me. As she was uneducated, she could not help me write my songs, but she kept my water pitcher and inkwell filled.

Standing at my slate I said to Josephine, though truly speaking to myself, "I shall begin my concerto with a call for remembrance to Atalanta. The girl was abandoned by her father, who wanted a son, so the poor thing was raised by a bear sow."

"Yes, Madame," Josephine said.

I felt a little tear in the corner of my eye when I wrote "father" and "cello" on the slate, because I would need the celloist to play in a deep, disapproving tone. "There must be a quarrel between them."

"Yes, Madame."

Writing this concerto is exhilarating. I will not fear seeing Gabriel, Henri, vampires, or anyone else.

I have found music again.

Chapter 55

Pascaline

Though I yearn to go to Versailles, my presence will not help. If Gabriel is willing to threaten the king's mistress, he is in a more dire situation than I understood. Hiding from sight, I eat a multitude of rats in the alleyways and wait for my brother to meet with his mistress.

My prey comes into view. He climbs the stairs to the upper alley where his mistress resides. I press myself flat against the wall and grip his heel. With all my might, I pull him down the stairs. He cries as his head strikes the pitted and cracked stone steps. He lies prone, his body erratically twitching as his blood spills.

Deep with hunger, my fangs expand behind my lips. I dive upon him.

"You're mad!" He pushes me off and lifts his cane.

He hits me with it, once, across my side. I ignore the pain and rip into his shoulder. My fangs pierce through velvet and linen and into flesh. His heartbeat echoes throughout my body, and his screams surround me. I cover his mouth.

As with other victims, I feel most alive when I eat their flesh. Using my greater strength, I pull him down to the river. His body grows limp and heavy in my arms. I bite him again, this time on the neck, and enjoy the ripping of his skin. I savor the salty liquid on my tongue. The meaty flavor and taste of his blood makes me momentarily forget he is my brother.

I remember and release the body, letting it fall into the river. I watch it splash into the dark, foul-smelling water. I hate wasting the meat, but if his body is found, it must not look like vampires killed him. I pray an animal or fish will consume parts of the body. Perhaps a few nibbles from an otter, carp, or sturgeon will hide my crime.

My brother's blood covers my hands, and I dunk them into the Seine. I am the worst type of sinner. I once was an ordinary woman. Ordinary mother. Now, I am a vampire. Yet, even the luscious taste of Gabriel's blood could not make me forget I once cuddled with him.

Bloody tears stream down my cheeks, but Loretta is safe...for now.

I walk away, in a mental fog. I do not know if I want this for Loretta. I do not want her to know what I did, but she will know in the morning.

I will most assuredly be cast out. Perhaps that's for the best.

I wonder about the Viscountess Fabron. I must chance Gabriel's wife still does not know our connection. I cannot imagine Gabriel speaking to her about his ungentlemanly plot against his sisters. I can only pray he did not. Our nephew will never know us. After what I have done, that will be for the best as well.

I raise my head to view Gunter's silent approach, with the hot burn of blood in my eyes. Straightening my posture, I meet his gaze.

"Killing is a permanent solution for an impermanent problem, Liebchen. We kill too much, and we will be caught," Gunter says. "And you wasted his meat."

"He is my brother; I couldn't eat him."

"I sincerely doubt that."

I bite my lip. "I was tempted, but better the body be found nibbled upon by fish. Perhaps they'll think he got drunk and fell into the water."

"Or blame someone else. When nobles die, peasants burn."

"I did not consider that." I look at the cobblestones.

"Pray, allow me to teach you as I escort you to Limousin."

"I want to learn," I whisper and remember Jakub's knife. I had not even used it. "What will you require?"

"Do you trust anyone?" He put out his hand.

I take it. "Loretta."

He grins wide enough for me to see his fangs. "And she, you, for good reason."

Gunter and I ride Nix into the night and throughout the next day. We are protected by dark storm clouds, but always stay ahead of the rain. There could be little doubt Gunter or Nix control the storm, but neither makes outward movements.

As the sun rises, I weep bitterly for what I have done. Then I cry for Celeste. Gunter allows me to cry without a harsh word. Leaning against Gunter, I wish Sydella was with us. I dream of how her touch felt on my skin. I want to feel anything now, but sorrow.

Once I am calm, Gunter instructs me kindly. "Metaphorically, your victim became a ghoul. In his failed attempt to glue together some semblance of a life, he lost something vital that made him a person. We need not lose it, too."

"But how would I have kept Loretta safe?"

"If I was in your shoes, I would have gotten Gabriel sent on to America on some sort of court-appointed journey where he will be away—and if he dares criticize the mission or try to return, he would die by the king's hand. Your hands would be clean."

"How did you learn all this?" I ask.

"Though I appear twenty-seven, I'm one hundred and sixty years older than you—much closer to Jakub and Agata's age than yours."

Nix brays.

"Nix must think us both quite naïve given his longevity," I say.

Nix whinnies and nods his head.

"He is brilliant and has taught me much."

"Such as?"

"Patience, especially with the children."

"Oh?" I say, trying not to sound too interested.

"Of course, if Nix could talk, he would tell you Sydella never misbehaved."

"But did she?" I say.

Nix tosses his head.

"No. Sydella's only crime was ours. She grew beautiful, and we instructed her to hide herself away being her walled garden. Even so, boys climbed the walls. One killed her cat -

the friendliest little thing. Nix ripped his arm off.

"We insisted Sydella be married for all the trouble we thought she caused."

"Did she comply?"

"In a manner of speaking. She ran away and married a farmer." He laughed. "She and her man were happy for a time. We let her be."

"What happened to him?"

"Unfortunately, she was unable to bear children. The marriage was annulled. With nowhere else to go, she returned to us. Perhaps that is why I've such sympathy for your and Loretta's plight. Though, again, there were better options, such as an elopement in Brandenburg."

"But that would've forced Jakub's hand."

"We have contingencies."

Something malicious deepens his grin. Gunter carries the same malignity I see hidden in Gaius. Once again, I am glad I did not marry into the family, though I do not regret my time with Sydella.

"What is your ultimate goal?"

"Today I shall ensure that House de Banquier does not fall. Tomorrow, who knows?"

We stop at the edge of the holding where Papa's gendarme watches the border. Charles gives me a sharp look.

In a harsh tone, he snaps, "Those who creep in the night are on the move, and you disappear for several days. Do you desire your mother to cry?"

Gunter frowns. "I shall bring the lady to her mother but let us not pretend you or Jakub could not always find her if you wished, Charles."

The few men gasp for Gunter's informality. Gunter and Charles gaze at each other and signal a furious understanding without speaking.

Benoit clears his throat. "We're glad to see you safe, Madame."

Charles extends his hand. "Show me the blade you took," he says, no longer scolding.

I pull it from my skirt and pass it to him.

He presses the point and the long edge into his hand. When he does not bleed, he raises his eyebrows and smirks. "A knife like this is pointless!"

A pun! He does not hate me.

"Have it sharpened and returned to the lady." He barks at one of his men, who rushes to see it done.

He takes Gunter and me aside. "Did you see Loretta?"

"No. It would be too dangerous to be seen at Versailles, but the problem is..." My voice cracks. "Solved...gone."

I crumple into tears again. Nix put his head over my shoulder.

"Why did you not inform me of the danger?"

"I tried." I sob.

Gunter's voice is no more than a hiss. "You soil your good name by speaking of Agata's tears, while you or Jakub might have ensured the girl's safety. You allowed your untrained sister to face a devil alone. Young vampires make mistakes, but Nix and I won't always be around to clean up your and Jakub's mess."

Charles finds a handkerchief to wipe my eyes, but the tears keep on flowing while I silently berate myself. Who am I? I will never be a real warrior like Sydella or Charles. I have no heart for medicine like Maman. I will never sing like Loretta. I've been a horrible mother...and now, I have killed my own brother.

"Why are you still crying?" Charles asked.

I wish my voice was not so small. "Am I still a person?"

Nix stamped his foot. He rested his head on my shoulder than gave Charles a very pointed look. I petted his mane.

Charles sighed. "Everyone cries after their first bad battle," he says. "Or they get black out drunk. I'm glad you chose the former. Tears will be easier to explain."

Thankfully, I stop weeping when we arrive at the chateau.

"What have you done?" Jakub's low hiss is full of loathing.

I ensure my voice remains steady. "I protected Loretta so she can continue to represent Chateau de Banquier's interests."

"Charles and I followed the bloodline and watched you kill your own brother," Papa shouts.

I want to ask why they ask me questions when they already know the answers, especially after what Gunter had said. "I tried to talk to him, but he wouldn't listen. I even gave him a few jewels, but he wanted more." My voice cracks. I cover my face with my hands before the tears restart. I cannot allow any more weakness or no one of this house will respect me.

"How can we trust a woman who would kill her own brother?" Maman says. "Must I make you sleep forever?"

I stand at my full height, which admittedly is not that impressive beside warriors. "I'll do whatever is necessary to keep Loretta safe, even if I'm bound for hell."

Gunter pipes up, "If it is Hell or Brandenburg, consider Brandenburg."

I give him a crisp nod. "I shall." I will not show anymore distrust by announcing I would not leave my sister behind. No doubt he knows it and so do the rest of the vampires.

"Gaius will take her?" Papa runs his fingers through his beard.

"Gaius will marry her to rebuild the bloodline, especially since the other marriage has been delayed. Our interest in the girl is even more piqued than it was and if you only are going to squander this treasure..."

I cannot breathe. Papa's expression reveals how much he wants to get rid of me.

"You cannot consider such a match," Maman says to Papa.

"I agree," Charles says. "No matter what Pascaline's crime. You don't know what I've seen."

"Fear not, Maman, I shan't marry Gaius. The benevolence in his personhood does not balance with the wickedness," I say.

"You claim to judge a vampire who has existed before Christ?" Gunter asks.

"Not at all. I only judge if a man will be a good husband or not. Gaius will not be a good husband nor can he give me what I desire," I say. "No matter how much Papa wants to get rid of me, the king's mistress will beg for my presence at Versailles. I am a lady of the court, and the king will not accept the match."

Gunter laughs. He embraces me. "I foolishly thought I must protect you. Even I've been blind. Be well." He takes his leave, still laughing.

"You're an evil woman," Papa says. "And I won't look upon you. I cannot cast you out, but I do not want to see you at my table."

Chapter 56

Loretta

8th of October

Cher Journal

Today was a magnificent day, and my concerto is coming together.

Waving my finger to music only I could hear, I said to Josephine, "I must show the Caledonian hunt. To show my muse's impressiveness—on her own—without her suitors."

"Then, the quarrel between her and her father. Then..." I trailed off.

"Did Hippomenes have to find the apples?" Josephine asked.

"I'm not sure, my friend, but this story is a tribute to Atalanta, not her suitors."

I fell into my music and worked as long as I dared. It would not do to be late for the Grand Couvert. Josephine and I quickly cleaned my clutter in the practice room with just enough time to be dressed properly I sat in my appropriate, assigned seat, sampling delicacies from the sea and the hunt.

After taking a bite of a particularly delicious pate, I considered how as the king's unofficial mistress, I certainly ate richer foods than I had at Maman's table. Everyone around me spoke kindly to me. Atalanta's aria, in which she cries to the Olympians for her freedom, was never far from my mind. Papa shall hate my concerto.

As the first course was served, I sought Gabriel in the crowd. He was not there.

By the fourth course, I heard the gossip. Viscountess de Fabron had called both the Versailles and Paris gendarme to search for her husband.

Chapter 57

Loretta

11th of October

Cher Journal,

Gabriel is still missing! Court is abuzz with the wicked aspects of the story.

In the dailies, the news is there is no news. All that was known was Viscount de Fabron visited his mistress in Paris proper, as a weekly habit. The mistress lived in a dark, raised alley that was chained after nightfall. The carriage man always let the viscount off on the main road so he did not have to pay to unchain the alley. The viscount always returned in an hour or two at most. When he did not return, the carriage man waited until morning. He informed the Paris gendarme.

They searched each house near the alley. He had not been seen. Blood was found on the stairs and the cobblestones next to the river. The mistress was a poor seamstress with an ailing mother and no father. Gabriel brought her candles and food each week. She had no reason to harm him.

The gendarme's theory was he must have tripped on slick stairs, cracked his head, and fell into the river. Or he was assaulted in the darkness. However, no one requested a ransom or had any information.

Still, I don't feel safer. If Gabriel is dead, I regret it sorely, as I did not want anyone to die.

I questioned Gunter on his absence. In response, he said, "I brought you a small barrel of dye. I know a seamstress and dyer in Paris proper who needs some work. What do you want for costumes?"

Though I could not leave the palace without the king's permission, I was able to send for the seamstress.

I wonder why Pascaline did not come to see me, or even respond to my missive.

14th of October

Cher Journal,

Tonight, I played a small part of my concerto, Songs of Atalanta, for the king. Louis grew nostalgic about the ballets he had written and performed in his youth. His stories are a bit self-aggrandizing, but who am I to say anything? I made a complete spectacle of myself all season.

Bizarrely, I am not sure how I feel about him now. My lover is both generous and apathetic. The way he sets his eyes on someone who displeases him is terrifying. Yet, he truly seems to love his secret wife and both his legitimate and legitimized children and grandchildren, even if he could not be completely faithful.

I am simply here to remind him of youth, it seems.

Most of the time, when he summons me, we don't make love. He wants me to sing songs. Sometimes I fear my place in Versailles. Yet, when I ask if I displeased him, he simply laughs. "A gentle girl like you is never a displeasure."

I copied the concerto for Pascaline and sent it to her so she might learn her part.

Pascaline

I miss you. Come to Versailles. I wrote the dual part of "Venus and Hippomenes" just for you!

Josephine is nice, but she is little more an escort and maid, not a friend.

I listen but do not understand what some men say. Forgive me for not representing this family well and spending more time in Court as I have almost finished my concerto. Look at the finished "Song of Venus" and explain how we'll sell a million barrels of dye!

All my love,
Loretta

Pascaline

I open the package of sheet music. I hurry to the harpsichord and scan the music Loretta wrote for my optimal range. I imagine how it might sound and quietly sing it. My heart fills with joy. This part is a gift beyond anything I might imagine. I begin to play. Dreaming of how our voices racing with violins and harpsichord and each other would sound. It has all the hallmarks of a masterwork. I wonder how I would get permission to go to Versailles after what I have done.

Papa enters the library. "What's that you are playing?"

He is not as angry as he has been.

I curtsey to him as due his station.

He is even less angry.

"Lor..."

He turns around and walks out. I consider if it is better if I let him go or chase after him.

I find Maman and show her the letter.

Maman shakes her head. "Why do you two not understand how much you hurt your father? The dye has never mattered to him."

"But, Maman, we..."

"Until you are to be trusted, you cannot be in Versailles without an escort. Tell her to find someone else."

I eat lunch and go to my room as was expected of me.

Loretta is an amazing composer and a wonderful sister. Yet, I cannot disobey our parents. It would disturb the image of our family that we built at Versailles. Maman and Papa have never seen our vision. They choose not to see it.

Chapter 58

Loretta

18th of October

Cher Journal

Today, the king received word that my father's livery was spotted. I asked for permission to meet them. He allowed it.

My heart ached to only see Benoit and Jean-Victor with the cart, still I waved as they pulled up.

Benoit kissed my gloved hand. Jean-Victor bowed.

"I cannot say how pleased I am to see you both. How goes it at the holding?" I asked.

"Madame Pascaline takes risks, Madame Loretta," Benoit said sadly.

"It's my fault. I should've never let her drive the cart," Jean-Victor said. "Now, the count is angry with her all the time. She isn't allowed to eat at the table."

"Jean-Victor, my friend, don't fret. The countess is the brightest woman in the world. She'll smooth it over, I'm sure," I said.

That seemed to satisfy him. Benoit began the direction of the unloading with the palace footmen. He handed me a tube of sheet music wrapped in waxed paper.

"Madame, your lady sister sends her compliments on your music. She said it was a masterwork and hoped she might play Venus, but your father forbade her to travel. She's not coming…she suggested a few other singers for you. She also sent funds for the violinists."

"Oh no!" I cried, but quickly regained my manners. How fares the lieutenant?"

"He's the greatest of all commanders," Jean-Victor said. "I don't think the rest of the lads ever knew as much as we learned this month."

It struck me oddly that Jean-Victor's referred to himself as a lad. We were the same age, but I was a woman, and the king's mistress. Worse, if I wasn't the king's mistress, I would be Charles's wife. All of this made me wish to weep.

"If I wrote the lieutenant a letter, do you think he'll read it?"

"He'll read it," Benoit said. "But he's still heartbroken."

"I miss him," I said. "How long will you stay?"

"We must turn around before the roads get worse," Jean-Victor said. "Soon, they may be impassable without the Count or Madame Pascaline to assist us. See, even I forget she's not to drive anymore. Madame Pascaline was the best aid I ever had on any trip. She even smiled as she cleared rocks."

I felt a pang in my heart when he said my sister's name. "I'll have a room and hot meals readied for you, and I'll have letters for my family before you set out in the morning."

19th of October

Cher Journal,

Last night, the king and I shared my bed. I hate not knowing whether I am pleasing him or not.

"You seem in good spirits," the king said.

"I heard from my sister, Highness, but she cannot attend me."

The king frowned.

"Should I bring you the letter? There's nothing I believe you would find distasteful."

He glanced over it.

My Dearest Sister,

I wish I was still with you in Versailles. I wake and miss you. I reach for Celeste. Of course, she is not there. I cannot help Maman with her patients. Their pain echoes into me.

Bad news. Papa refuses me permission to travel this late in the season on the chance that the carriage gets stuck in the weather.

I find Lieutenant Onfoy more honorable by the day. He leads Papa's gendarme with efficiency and, dare I say, love for his men. I have shown him Celeste's grave. He and Maman come with me in the evenings to visit her.

I wonder how Madame de Fabron fares in

her sorrow. Are you acquainted with her? Send me more news. I cannot wait until spring.

All my love, Pascaline

"Who is Celeste?"

"Pascaline's daughter, my Liege."

"So, the rumor was correct? She debuted late to hide a bastard?"

Heat rose behind my eyes. I don't dare answer with a lie. He was too observant. "Celeste died from pneumonia after a bout of scarlet fever."

The king's finger brushed my cheek. "Tears?"

"Celeste was just a babe, Sire, and a happy one. The entire family mourns."

The king frowned.

I did not move. I feared the danger if I displeased him. He returned the letter. "And you trust her with this Onfoy?"

"Of course, Sire. We're sisters," I said.

"Sisters have fought over men before."

"If you knew Pascaline, you would know she'd give her life to save mine."

"She plans to give me immortality, then?"

"She offered it, so she must," I said. "Will you accept this gift?"

He rose from the bed and took a delicate step into his slippers. "A hard decision. I've been a king and don't know if I wish to live as a lowly count. Play me a song, a light song to help me think."

I moved to my lap harp and plucked out one of Louis's favorites.

Chapter 59

Loretta

22nd of October

Cher Journal,

I struggle to find the right young lady to sing the dual part of Venus and Hippomenes. Most are being pressed to audition by their parents, but there was one young lady whose voice was without equal. Unfortunately, she was a tactless commoner.

She raised her voice in operatic acrobatics, which were not on the page, as she sang for Venus. These gymnastics added nothing, only lengthened my music.

This would not do—my concerto only had so much time before the court musician would begin his concert. While he was happy enough to assist me in my musical endeavors, as it would please the king, I knew better than to step on his toes. I wish I knew what to say to discourage such behavior while encouraging the girl's gifts.

The court musician, however, was used to being in charge. He tapped his baton. "Mademoiselle, the story is of Atalanta, not of Hippomenes. Your song follows her tempo."

"Even during Venus?" her mother asked.

"Begging your pardon, but Venus is the smallest role," I said.

The court musician did not bother to answer the singer's mother. "The concerto is perfection, Mademoiselle, it would not do to lengthen it."

The young singer's cheeks reddened. "If I cannot sing how I want, I don't want this part. Dropping one's outer dress..."

"Then, I'll find another Venus. Goodbye," the court musician said.

I was dazed he spoke so plainly.

The girl also seemed shocked. Then, she wept, perfect tears. Fake tears.

The court musician patted her hands and walked her to the door. She pulled herself away from him and flounced out. Her mother curtsied at us, and then followed.

"Young common singers are more trouble than they are worth," he said with a huff. "Are you sure you cannot persuade your sister to come?"

"I'll try once more," I told him.

Pascaline

In the shade of Maman's Garden, I watch the men drill in the fields below. Singing Loretta's *Songs of Atalanta*, I mimic the men's movements to achieve realism in my male role. I pause as they shift from infantry drills to those of the light cavalry.

Papa mourns the old heavy cavalry, already falling out of favor, as musket balls could pierce most of the armor available. Yet, he understands the need to change with regard to battle.

Though I've been told that soldiers are whipped, Charles does not beat the boys, nor have them beaten when they misbehave; he sends them to work in the stables or fields: mucking stables, turning fallow fields with manure, carrying women with newborns home, or transporting unmarried women to a new mistress to teach them a trade. Charles never shouts unless he needs to be heard over the chaos of the drill itself.

Boys train as hard as full-grown men, but Papa and Charles agree on was the importance of hearty ration, which was the primary strategy for training the strongest grenadiers in the current Royal Army and the strongest men and horses in the cavalries of the past.

I practice loading and unloading a musket alone. I drill aiming, but I dare not fire lest they know what I am doing. I pray I will remember the steps if the time comes. I practice the blade work that Papa had shown me when he was at least fond of me.

This cannot hold for long, so I must learn what I can now.

Maman calls me to lunch since Papa will eat with his men. "You received a letter," she said.

Happily, I open it and read it aloud to Maman.

Calette,

I miss you. Please, come to Versailles and stay with me. I cannot trust anyone but you—

Maman shook her head. "I will not argue with your papa over a concerto. Nor should you. If Loretta is as safe as you say, you need to let her succeed or fail on her own."

"But, Maman, do you not see that her success is our success?"

"No concerto can mean that much." And she gave me a look that let me know this conversation was over.

Chapter 60

Loretta

25th of October

Cher Journal,

I am so frustrated! I've yet to find our Venus/Hippomenes. Every girl who tries out is hopelessly not ready, tries to outdo me, expands Venus's role, or even splits the parts. They question and, of course, do not know that the costume change in front of the audience will sell dye to the wives and daughters of the nobility. Moreover, we cannot stop rehearsals.

The two violins and viola race with my voice. The viola sings out Hippomenes' song, but the two violins are playing too slow. Why do they not see my vision!

Trying to speak as simply as the court musician spoke, I told both violinists, "I wrote this song in a staccato. This is a race after all."

"How do you think you'll keep up, you're just a woman."

The court musician broke in, "So was Atalanta."

"Touché." The violinist said. "But this pace can't be kept! This song is fifteen minutes."

"Are you saying you can't keep the pace," I asked.

The man stood and stepped closer to me. "If you weren't the mistress of the king—"

"You'd what? Tell my father that I am pushing you too hard. This is nothing. Do you know how hard my father pushes his men?"

The court musician tapped his pedestal with the baton. "That's the problem, Monsieur le Count did not have sons, so he pushed his girls beyond any feminine endurance. Still, the song is a race, so race with the lady's voice."

We begin the footrace song again.

As Atalanta, I keen: I must win, I will never be happy a Roman wife, confined within the walls of a home. I need the forests, the mountains...

Hippomenes raises the first golden apple, and the music and the footrace pause. Timing is crucial. I cry out: "Why can't I look away? Why must I have that apple?"

The violins begin again with my voice. The viola's echoing tone always a step behind my soprano. Two more times Hippomenes raises golden apples to pause the music. Hippomenes wins!

My aria moves from plaintive to angry to sorrowful for making such a horrible agreement with my father. I sing in lament to the cello:

Now, I am owned by another man because a foolish vow I made to you. Did you ever love me? You who abandoned me and only sought me once I was famous...

The cello dies as the viola tries to convince me that Hippomenes loves me.

The music is not enough. The part must be sung. I did not want to hire another opera singer.

Chapter 61

Loretta

1st of November

Cher Journal,

My concerto is so close to perfection but I need Pascaline.

Papa's livery was due to arrive today. It seemed like it took years going by. I hurried to the delivery gate to speak to Benoit, or perhaps Charles, flying past the side eyes from the gendarmes who worked with him. No one dared speak against me. Still, I wished Jean-Victor had accompanied them. Jean-Victor was always polite to me.

"Our house shall make so much money, selling dyes and fabrics," I said, loud enough that Papa's men heard me. "I must show you the costumes, and I pray that you will assist Papa in accepting orders..."

"Orders?" Benoit asked.

I might have him, now I must seem polite to Papa's lower ranking men. I smile toward them. "But first, allow me to offer our gendarmes a hot meal and clean bed in the barracks before you set off again."

The men become considerably more enthusiastic about

my company. Benoit dismissed them to their lodging.

I took Benoit's arm and led him to my apartment. We left the front door open and, of course, Josephine was my chaperone as was one of the king's guards.

"What do you mean you'll have many orders?"

I showed him the sketches of the costumes I had sent to the seamstress.

My Atalanta hunting tunic was a shimmery lavender fabric, but the three-part costume that Pascaline would wear was especially daring.

"You expect Pascaline to drop layers of fabric? Count de Banquier won't like that!"

"Well, yes, first, she will be a musician, then the Goddess Venus, and then for the race, Hippomenes."

"I don't know if she will make it."

"She must! Who else can I trust to sing it if not my sister?"

"Your sister is your constant admirer, but there are hundreds of singers in Versailles and Paris."

"But I need Pascaline. Tell her, and tell Maman!"

"Your father rules the county and his daughters. Wayward as you both may be."

"My papa is a fine man and a great warrior, but we are selling the dye that keeps the county and holding safe. Papa doesn't see it as work. This doesn't make Papa a bad man or even a bad leader. Everyone, even the king, has blind spots."

Benoit scratched his chin. "I'll talk to the lieutenant. He'll know what to say to the Count."

"Thank you!"

When accepting my mission, he kissed my hand. I wished I might embrace him. However, I would not put him in danger by doing something so ill-advised. Instead, I passed him the finished concerto and several letters for my family.

Benoit was just about to leave when my doorframe became filled with the large form of Henri Onfoy.

"Excuse me, you are Lieutenant Onfoy's cadet. Are you not?"

"Indeed, Monsieur. Cadet Lécuyer at your service."

"Would you please deliver this to my brother on your return trip?"

"Indeed, Monsieur." Benoit bowed.

Henri looked in my direction. "Madame." And left.

Pascaline

Charles enters the garden as I practice reloading a musket. I quickly throw the weapon under the bench, but I have been caught.

Charles chuckles. "Madame Pascaline, a lady of your intelligence must realize I know how many muskets are in the armory. I might have worried, but you aren't shooting, just practicing the loading and unloading."

I nod.

"I should like your opinion on this letter from Henri, as it involves someone close to your heart."

I take the letter.

Charles,

Mother says she is glad you are in the country, and simply put, she is full of wishes of love for you. However, I pray you reconsider your employment for this strange family. While Monsieur le Count is honorable as you say, the young lady of our joint acquaintance is devoted to music. She apparently asked the king's permission to spend all day in the company of court musicians. It is said she was heard speaking to musicians as if she were a common woman. Though her maid escorts her there, the company certainly is not appropriate for a young lady. If the young lady falls, their house may be despoiled and may take you and our good name with them.

Consider your and our position wisely.

Henri

I frown. "Are you reconsidering your position?"

"No. In fact, it seems to me that one should speak to court musicians if one is making music for the court. She has a chaperone after all—if the maid is respectable?"

I smile. "In her letters, Loretta has been diligent in reporting that Josephine is indeed respectable and efficient in her duties."

"Then, I am glad we are of one mind."

"Are we?"

"You've been acting mostly in obedience to your parents, so we must be."

Chapter 62

Loretta

3rd of November

Cher Journal,

At dinner, I was shocked to see my eldest sister in the crowd, her skin drawn and pale. The dark circles under Helena's eyes showed the hardship of her journey. She only had a single gendarme to attend her. All through the meal, I wondered why she would travel to Versailles this late in the autumn.

In perfect protocol, she bowed at each course, which would feed our king and his company. She waited until the meal ended before she slipped closer.

I held my breath. I regretted the death of Gabriel and feared what Pascaline might do to Helena if she knew our sister was at the palace.

"You look beautiful, Madame Loretta. Versailles has treated you well," Helena said.

"Your dress is pretty," I replied. Established etiquette concluded, I curtsied and turned away.

"Madame…"

I did not give her a chance to say my former name.

"Madame, forgive me, but I retire early."

"Wait! I don't know who else to turn to. You have your youth and your voice and used it to find a protector... I heard Pascaline was here..." Tears filled my sister's eyes. "Matchmaking. I need a matchmaker."

I took her arm to draw her closer. "How did you hear this?"

"Gossip and society pages. They held your picture and claimed you're rising in the king's estimation. I heard from young Countess Langlais that two friends introduced her to her husband. Please...I'm desperate."

"Very well, Madame Durrant. For whom do you need a matchmaker?"

She whispered, "Camile-Marie."

My voice caught in my throat. "She's but thirteen?"

"Georges Benefiel came to the Durrant estate after you escaped him, believing you were there. He has a mind to take a virgin bride. A most assured virgin..."

I pinched my eyes shut. "I'll send word to my sister, but I don't know what she'll do. Illness took Celeste away, and you'll find Pascaline quite changed."

Pascaline

Another letter came unexpectedly. I crack open the wax seal, happy to see Loretta's hand. I am less excited by the contents:

Helena has come to court in dire straits. Return to Versailles as soon as possible. Tell Papa no one else understands the role or anything you think will work. As I've been without you, I've realized how out of touch Maman and

Papa actually are...

To calm myself, I noodle pretend keys on the dressing table.

All I must do is make it to Versailles. I will go, but it is still best if I have Papa's permission.

"Get to Versailles," Gaius says. I jump by the unexpected voice and survey the room. I am alone.

"Loretta is in more danger than you know," he says. "If you are not there, her soft heart will put her in danger."

I find Papa.

"Loretta requests me to appear at Versailles and sing for the ladies," I say. "And I keep hearing Gaius telling me to go."

"I won't let you shame this household again," Jakub grumbles. "And I know Helena Durrant has returned to Versailles. Gaius informed me of the danger."

"Will you help?"

"No."

"Benoit delivers fabric and dye. I might travel with him."

"It is not desirable a lady travel without a carriage," Papa says gruffly.

"I shall run!"

"If you leave this house again, I will treat you as all others who creep in the night," Jakub says.

Chapter 63

Pascaline

This is such a bad idea. I do not want to be exiled, or worse, die again. I want to sing, dance, and exist. I want to see beyond this age of sorrow. I want to know love again—and, this time, my choice of love—whenever I find it.

I hurry to the cart where Benoit ties the dye barrels to the front supporting beam.

"Cadet, please, help me? Take me to Versailles."

"No. I'll be in trouble, and you'll be in more," he says, tying a smaller, lightweight barrel, most likely his clothing or personal supplies. He covers the barrels with a quilted tarp. It will easily block the sun. Men stand by for orders to stack the barrels filled with dyed damask and velvet. They tie them down and cover them with oilcloth.

"But Loretta needs me."

"The lieutenant has always taken care of me; I can't betray him." He dismissively waves a hand. "The count will duel a man who harms his daughter's honor."

I hate the tears in my eyes. "Dueling is illegal."

Benoit's face does not change. "At most, he'll get a fine. She's the king's mistress after all."

"I'm sorry, tell Papa I'm sorry, and tell Maman I love

her."

"Madame!" Benoit cries as I run past the barracks. I stop. For Loretta's sake, I must tell Charles. He isn't in his quarters. I enter and wait quietly. On Charles's desk lies a diary. I do not open it. There is no information I could not pry from Benoit or Greta. Instead, I set my head on the table and take deep breaths to quiet my trembling. Greta creeps toward me. I pull her on my lap and feel the quietness of the grave in her lost soul.

I will undoubtedly be hurled from this small Eden, but that does not mean Charles and Loretta also must be cast out. Moreover, for my vow and memory of Celeste and Greta, I will protect it. Whatever Gaius wants, it isn't a concerto.

"Pascaline?" Charles asks.

I jump up, set Greta on the floor, and pull the scroll of music over my shoulder.

"Loretta and I have found a new way to sell dye and solve our problems."

"With your father's permission?" Charles asks.

"No..."

He slams his hand on the desk. The diary bounces, but a piece of paper floats to the floor. I pick it up.

Dancing white fingers across the harpsichord...

Sounds from your pink lips...

I am never bored....

Giddy like a drunken man...

I meet his eyes. "It's a poem!"

"Please, don't read that."

I set the poem on top of the diary and clap my hands together. "Charles, you write poetry? How wonderful! Does Loretta know?"

His frown grows deeper. "The count won't take any more insolence. You'll be chastened. He may kill you!"

I nod slowly. "I must take that risk. Gaius told me I must go, or Loretta will be in danger." I point to the poem. "May I show Loretta this?"

"No," he snaps. "What's wrong with you? Get your head off the moon!"

"My head is right here. I'm sorry we're on different sides. If you don't want me to show Loretta your poems, you ought to show her."

"It's not even good," Charles says.

"Perhaps, but there's promise. I knew you still loved Loretta!"

"I never denied I love her," he huffs.

"Loretta always says the world would be a quiet place if only nightingales sang. She'll love your effort to create something beautiful, whether or not you are proficient. Besides, we're vampires. You've centuries to get better."

"I hope you survive to read the next draft," Charles says.

"Me, too."

He grabs my arm. "If you force me to fire, I won't miss."

I yank myself free. Gripping Loretta's music, I run. Charles will tell Jakub, and they will come. I need to get to Versailles first.

Chapter 64

Pascaline

They believe me evil. I cannot help believing the same. Perhaps I do not deserve to exist forever or know love again.

I don't want to be an adventuress, but somehow that's what I've become. My heart wrenches with sadness, and my feet feel heavy. Yet, I keep running, my braid slapping against my back.

I have no home. I might go on to Brandenburg. Or England. Or America. I might wander forever alone with the knowledge Jakub and Charles can always find me in the bloodline if they wish. Oddly, I feel strangely relaxed in the acceptance of my fate.

I stop near midday to rest when shadows are short. I am still undead.

Jakub

"Jakub, don't," my dear Agata cried.

My heart ached for my wife, but that girl would cause the downfall of this great house. I worked too hard for this holding. If a woman of my household arrived in Versailles without escort, making a scene, we would be exposed. And if another Fabron died...then what?

"If I can bring her home, I will," I lied. "However, we must increase our efforts to school her about the repercussions of reveling in senseless violence. I shouldn't have to remind you, as she has hurt you, most of all." I kissed my wife and left.

"You claim her violence is senseless," Agata cried after me, "but nothing she does is senseless."

I walked to the stables, comforted in the knowledge Agata's gifts were those of domination rather than clairvoyance. She would not witness me kill her daughter.

Charles and I saddled our horses. "Are you ready to fight this monster?"

"No," he said sadly. "But I will."

Loretta

7th of November

Cher Journal,

Something is going on. A plot that I don't understand.

Gunter knocked on my door and entered. "You sent for your sister?"

"Yes."

"Good, I have something I need doing, which might weaken me, and I may need to feed."

"Does it matter if I'm infected?"

"Who infected you?"

"Pascaline."

Gunter smiled. "Reason?"

"To ensure I didn't get pregnant."

He laughed. "Sydella always knew you were both worthy of our and Agata's devotion."

Gunter sat in my chair and listened to the whispers of Gaius and Leon, who watched everything and gave orders. "I'll cast clouds over your sister so she might prove her worth to either Jakub or perhaps Honoré Tellier. Either way, she won't be forced into Brandenburg."

Beside him, I played my lap harp. Gunter relaxed on my upholstered bench and closed his eyes. The tension left his shoulders.

"Deine Musik hilft mir, Frauline. Bon...bon...gut..." Gunter's words shifted between languages. I was thrilled that my music could relieve his tension.

Soon, he focused his eyes upon a spot on the ceiling, waving his hand as if pushing away an invisible force.

Pascaline

In the forest where I hide from the sun, heavy, dark clouds move overhead. I cannot see beyond the storm. *A vampiric storm?* Hoping the cloud cover remains thick, I dash north. I follow when the clouds turn toward an old château.

In sunlight, three men, a priest, and his armed escort by their uniforms, ride under the church's flag. They approach a group of ragged refugees. The refugees begin to scatter and flee as they attack! The terrified screams of women and children echo over the fields as they move, too slowly, for the men on horses. Some cannot run, but crawl or writhe, pulling themselves along through the mud.

Mon Dieu! A child vampire is stomped into the ground by one of their horses. The men do not even slow. The priest snatches a child from the crowd and chains him. The undead child struggles until he is viciously struck quiet.

Charles had mentioned that those who creep in the night were on the move. I wonder if these people are seeking shelter from a noble house who might assist them.

Thunder cracks over the sky and resonates over the plain. This is where the storm wanted me to be.

"I hear you, Gaius!" I shout, and though my legs are heavy and sore, I gird my skirts, kick off my slippers, and hide my sister's music in a tree.

"Hold on, Loretta. I hope I'm right."

It begins to rain. In front of the château, a man drops his clothes and turns into a tawny wolf. *Honoré?* I ought to have known Honoré Tellier is foolish enough to help the horde. He races across the field toward the horses. Another wolf, a woman, goes to assist one of the many broken children crushed into the earth.

A horseman raises his musket and points it toward Honoré.

How I wish I could fly.

Jakub

Though the air's movement was warm and slow, the horses whinnied, and sheep scattered nervously at the sound of thunder rolling over the frozen fields.

Charles pointed out Pascaline under cloud cover, racing toward three men on horseback. The wind whipped her auburn locks.

A vampire-woman chased after the horses. "He's my child!" she screamed. "Let him go!"

The wolf-woman blocked the horses to protect a young walking dead from being trampled, nearly being trampled herself.

"Look there, they have stolen a child. Are they taking it to the king or a bishop?" I shouted. Whatever their ultimate purpose, this could not be good for House de Banquier's future and certainly not House de Tellier's present.

"What's your will?" Charles shouted over a rumble of thunder.

"I'm still a knight, by God. These people need assistance." I rode past the cowering women and children. "We will kill our monster after we save them."

Pascaline

Fat raindrops fall. I pump my legs, dashing through the icy mud, fully aware I am revealing my strength to other vampires, the horde, the loup-garous, and the king's men. With my dagger in hand, I leap upon the man aiming for Honoré. My opponent and I are both thrown from the bucking horse and tumble to the ground.

My blade blossoms red as I cut his throat.

Bon Dieu, I'm killing men of the church or the Royal Army or who knows who else. I don't know if this is right! But I can leave no survivors to tell the story or all these people will die. Honoré and his wife (or whoever the wolf-woman is) will go to prison and likely tortured. And Jakub won't ever forgive the scandal.

The man screams and dies in front of me, blood spraying. "I'm sorry, but I can't allow you to kill children."

Honoré's other enemies turn.

A musket ball hits my leg.

Blood oozes from the wound, but I rush the second man head-on, barreling into him as he shouts blasphemous prayers. *Hah!* He thinks Jesus's name could save him while he tries to keep hold of a wounded vampire child? I go for his leg. The undead child falls to the ground.

A silver cross is pressed to my throat. My flesh bubbles and blisters as I scream and roll off him.

"God curses you!"

Bon Dieu, how my skin burns. It does not matter; Loretta will still love me. I do not know if Sydella would ever want to kiss me again. I hope so.

Another silver cross presses into my cheek. I smell the smoke as the skin blisters and cracks. A large pair of hands grip my shoulders and press my face into the mud.

I roll over and stab at him. He dodges the blade, removing his weight from me. Using all my celerity, I charge. I bite into his neck, splitting the flesh and sucking the blood. With a burning desire to scratch my cheek and throat as the skin heals, I remain clamped onto my enemy's throat.

I turn in time to see Honoré hurling his furry body into our final enemy. By the time I let go of my opponent, the last man was dead. Honoré moved to assist the child I sought to save.

To my horror, Jakub and Charles cross the field, making their way toward me. It is Charles who loads his musket and aims at me. Time stops. Looking down the barrel, I prepare to meet final death.

Loretta

7th of November continued

Cher Journal,

I write as Gunter stares at the ceiling. His lips move as if in prayer. "Come on, girl, you saved them, now run. We still need you."

Pascaline

I hold my ground as Jakub and Charles approach me.

The clouds are shifting. The other vampires will expect me to stay under the storm, rather than risk the sunlight. Running is futile. Jakub may be my enemy, but I must get through to him. If I don't, Loretta, and even Charles, is in danger. A loyal and true knight would not fear two men who could not possibly be beaten in armed combat. *I must be courageous; I must be a knight.*

I grip Jakub's old dagger and a blade I take from a horseman. Knowing I did not have either man's reach, I rest in the knowledge that, even if I fall today, Loretta will be safe with the king.

"I won't let you hurt them," I shout as Jakub steps closer. "This splinter of the horde are innocents."

Behind me, cracking and popping fills the air as Honoré Tellier turns back into a man. I don't look toward his nakedness since, no doubt, I'll be blamed for that, too.

Jakub

Surveying the chaotic scene in front of me, the naked wolf-man trying to assist a vampiric child, blood trickling down Agata's daughter's leg, and the burns on her face and neck, I ordered, "Put down your blades, Pascaline."

"So you can kill me more easily?"

"There is no easier, and you cannot defeat me in single armed combat. And certainly, you cannot best us both. You must yield."

She lifted her chin to look at Charles, her lips quivered. "This is why I can't rely on a gentleman's duty. The music hanging on the tree is for Loretta. Make sure she gets it. I swear to all that is holy, if you ever lay a hand on her, I'll come back to haunt you, and I won't be a nice ghost."

The clouds were circling. Light from the sun touched the ground inches from Pascaline. She did not retreat—though she only wore a traveling gown.

"Why must you do this?" I asked, genuinely trying to understand how a young woman could have such strong aspirations.

The wind blows fiercely around her. "Because no one stands for the horde, or even for me and Loretta, unless they can use us. You stand only for you, which is why, eventually, your house will fall. We are not the only ally Gaius courts. I cannot believe I've been so blind to the fact that Charles is with you because Gaius willed it so."

"The horde isn't worthy of Gaius..." I began. "Certainly not worthy of your protection."

"Who among us is worthy? Besides, you were the one who stupidly kept the horde weak when they might have been a strong ally."

"She is so interesting," Gaius whispered through the bloodline. "Put your pride aside, Jakub. Pascaline is correct and will die before she yields. Remind you of anyone?"

"But what if the horde overpowers us. What then?" My question was to Gaius, but Pascaline answered.

"In truth, I don" know how much longer the nobility can survive, but it will be longer if you make allies closer to the ground. At least, we won't be caught unaware."

"Right again," Gaius whispered in my head. "It would do you more well than harm to spare her."

I needed time to ponder. And I wanted Gaius out of my head.

"With muskets, there is no need for a fighting class," Charles murmured.

I remembered the sins of my past. Did I not grow into a wise and fair man?

"Throw down your blades, Pascaline, and I will be merciful."

"Allow me to go to Versailles?" Her voice warbled. "I know you don't believe me but I-I don't want to hurt people."

"Absolutely not, but I'll return you to your mother. She can get the ball out of your leg."

"Forgive me, Papa." She turned to run.

Charles placed a well-aimed shot in her unwounded leg.

She screamed. Blood sprayed out of the small hole and gushed down her leg.

My son was an excellent shot. There could be no doubt he aimed for the artery and hit it. If Pascaline was human, she would be dead within seconds. As a vampire, blood loss merely ensured a loss of consciousness, which would make it easier to bring her home to Agata...or find some irons and a dark hole to bury her in, whatever I decided.

Charles reloaded and kept his musket trained on her.

She did not look away as I raised my sword. She did not scream or beg. She stared. Destroying this silly little monster would surely be a sin.

"You're the most head-strong girl! Oh, I should tie you to that tree. I should let you burn, but I won't. You shan't die today."

Fighting consciousness, she tried to rise. Failing, she drew her knife but did not point it at us. Tears streaming, she wept as she sliced into her own flesh and dug out the musket ball. As the hole enlarged, I saw shards of shattered bone in the wound. *Damn good shot.* Blood soaked into the earth. It was astounding that, with so much blood loss, she succeeded in digging out the second ball from her other leg.

She picked up the blood-covered lead balls and shards of bone. "Do I save these for our guns?" she asked, rolling them toward us.

One hit Charles's boot. Wounded men with battle-lust in their blood have done strange things while in pain. I supposed this girl was no different.

Bloody sweat covered her broken skin. I noted, with some nostalgia, how innocent Pascaline looked, and it reminded me she had been only twenty-two when she became one of us. Still, she had been married and widowed, and suffered the death of the child that she bore. Now, she has murdered her brother to ensure her sister continued to walk among the great beauties of Versailles. All that, in the course of twenty-two years, plus one.

Pascaline fainted as her bones automatically shifted back into place.

The vampiric child shrieked. Tellier held onto him more tightly. Beyond, other vampiric children came closer, attempting to reach for Pascaline for her blood, so rich and powerful, it would heal them all.

Charles stepped closer to ensure she was not eaten. When she awoke, she scurried out of my grasp like a trapped tiny rabbit, and scrambled toward the naked wolf-man, Viscount Tellier. The vampiric child grabbed her hair. She tugged herself away and turned back to me.

"Papa, tell Charles he is wrong about Loretta. I made a deal...I-I..."

Watching her fight delirium, I forgot my antagonism. "You need rest."

She laughed, too manically for my liking. "Don't you remember the story of poor Louisa? I couldn't...can't...let the king keep my sister like her. So many cages..."

"Who is Louisa?" Charles asked.

"Have you not studied our king? No cage...no shame... no dying in a convent. Loretta is free," Pascaline said.

Charles looked at me. "Is it possible Loretta is still a virgin?"

"Don't be an idiot," Tellier interjected. I truly wished he

would put on some clothing.

I glared at Charles. "Does it matter? Pascaline is confused with pain, but I can attest to many attempts to protect her younger sister. More than we will ever know." I surprised myself by coming to Pascaline's defense.

Pascaline dragged herself up and tried to walk. With a loud crack, the weakened bone in her leg, rebroke. She stumbled into the mud and, weeping through gritted teeth, she dragged herself to the closest dead body and fed. Her lips became as red as the stains on her skirts and her wounds reclosed immediately.

Several undead children writhed closer.

Still weeping, Pascaline rose and took a hesitant step. This time, the bone held. She limped past us, away from the vampiric children.

The closest child groaned and cried, no doubt upset his easy undead prey had risen. The rest turned toward the dead bodies Pascaline left behind.

"Where are you going?" I asked.

"Versailles." She ungirded her skirt. "I must reach Loretta. I've been requested to sing."

Tellier collected the things she dropped and handed them to me. "The lady needs more blood. Take her to Versailles. Or I shall."

Pascaline

The clouds remain above us as I ride with Charles on his horse. I wish I was stronger. I wish I had not been shot twice, burned, and succumbed to pain. My legs throb, and my limbs can't stop shaking. After I was shot, never, in all of eternity, would I have guessed I'd escape final death and be on my way to Versailles—with Charles and Papa as escorts.

Riding beside us, Papa asks, "You knew violence was coming between us. Do you think, daughter, you have precognition?"

I lean into Charles's back. My vision spins from the light filtering through the clouds. "No. I just follow my intuition."

"How do you know you do not have precognition if you still work on instinct?"

"Because I'm not seeing a future. Only the present and patterns of behavior."

I drift in and out for a moment, and then shake myself awake.

"You'll heal faster if you sleep," Papa suggests.

"I can't sleep."

"Why?"

"Because you and Charles might bury me undead or worse."

"Why do you think I would do that?" Charles spat.

"Did you not just shoot me?"

"Yes, and I am sorry for it." He sighs. "But I needed to stop you from running! And you're the one who wanted to join the gendarme. I told you what would happen if you continued to disobey the count's orders."

"You did, but you also never let me officially join. Besides, we have much to discuss."

"Such as?"

"My, and your, future within House de Banquier."

"Is your heart so broken you'll never be a wife again?"

Charles asks. "My brother will have you."

"Then, your brother would be a fool and your house would fall when he dies. No, he needs a bride who is a proven mother. The real question is, would your brother be gentle with a child who is not his?"

"How would I know that?" Charles snaps.

Underneath us, our horse balks slightly and makes a low whinny before recovering his pace.

"It's alright, boy," I whisper. "Don't mind his tone."

Charles sighs. "Why do you ask?"

"You mustn't think me so wicked I'd leave my sister-in-law and nephew in the cold. I still weep for my crime, but I did it for good purpose. Now, I must ensure my brother is replaced for their security. A widow has no rights to her husband's estate, and the boy is still only an infant."

"Are you meaning to say my brother would marry your sister-in-law?"

"The Dowager Viscountess Fabron offers an untouched dowry and a good head on her shoulders. Loretta has sent me reports. Moreover, I witnessed he was kind to Isaac Langlais," I offered. "And he is ten years your senior. Was he kind to you or was he a bully?"

"I suppose he was kind, but I haven't known him since I went to war. Last season at Versailles, I saw him more than I ever have..." Charles paused.

"You think like Gaius," Papa says softly. "No wonder he wants you."

"Perhaps I do, but I can't stop thinking of things Gunter said after I murdered Gabriel."

"What was that?"

"He talked about losing what is vital to making us people. I fear I lost that when Celeste died. I don't want to become like Gabriel, but maybe I already am. Maybe that's why you can't love me like you love Loretta and Celeste. So, if it pleases you, make some paperwork claiming I went to a convent. I'll leave after I finish my obligations to Loretta, and I'll disappear on my way."

"Pascaline!" Papa said.

"What do you expect to happen then?" Charles snapped.

"I don't know, I'll be an adventuress. I'm well-aware you can always find me, but I trust once I'm gone, you won't."

Papa turns in his saddle to study me. "I don't know if I can love you. It doesn't matter. Agata loves you."

"So, you will resent me for eternity? This is not a good plan."

Charles sighs and shakes his head. "Pascaline may think like Gaius, but she isn't like him at all. Half of my memories of working for Gaius feel like a garish nightmare. There were dozens of contingency plans—"

"I have dozens of contingency plans," I said.

"Regardless, if it helps you stay, I cannot resent you any longer. You were right to call me a dumb foot solider shooting at a wall."

"I don't think I called you dumb."

"Whatever you said, whatever your sins, mine are greater. I know it will be a long time until I regain your and Loretta's trust, but I'm willing to wait. As you say, we have time."

"You don't know all I've done."

"Perhaps not, but I know you were scared, and you faced

hell to ensure Loretta's dreams come true; I never did."

"But—"

"Before you argue, I'll make one more point. Not even one of our brave and mighty kin chanced to speak to Greta, much less hug her, and give her toys. They can see ghosts as easily as you. She was nobody in life. Nobody in death." He wiped his nose with his sleeve. "But you speak to her, and when you see she requires comfort, you comfort her. That fact alone should've told me everything I needed to know about the person you are."

"I forgive you for shooting me. You did not know all the terrors I have seen, just as I do not know yours, but if I am to stay, we must tell Loretta and Maman as soon as possible about this quarrel."

"What? Why?"

I enjoyed the men's fear, ever so slightly. After all, Maman's and Loretta's fury was the only vengeance I would receive for my trouble. "I don't want anything I might hold over your head. You'll hate me, and unlike the sword of Damocles', when the sword falls, it's implausible that it would only hurt the intended party."

"Who else would it hurt?" Charles asks. "Loretta?"

"Loretta is simply the most precious to me. But Maman, Greta, Benoit, the sweet beast we ride upon, even Papa and Castor. Perhaps all the men you teach and who respect you mightily... Ought I go on?"

Chapter 65

Loretta

7th of November

Cher Journal,

Pascaline has come! With Charles and Papa—and they don't hate me...or her.

Pascaline

I study Helena sitting in Loretta's private apartment. She appears sad, but she also looks healthy enough.

Rage vibrates in my throat. "You shouldn't have come here."

"I came for my daughter's welfare," Helena says.

"When you cared not for my daughter! Celeste died of pneumonia. Be glad I don't destroy you. I'll never look on you again."

Loretta takes my hand. "Pascaline, please listen. This has..."

Helena went to her knees. "I apologize for my cowardice. I thought the bracelet would be enough that you might find shelter in your time of need."

I don't reply.

Loretta presses our sister to speak.

"My husband has made a terrible match for Camile-Marie with Georges Benefiel. We're too low to even request the match to be blessed by the king. I heard you were protecting brides…finding them good men."

"She's only thirteen," I whisper.

"Georges Benefiel contacted us after you escaped him and—"

"You let my child suffer," I say from the part of me who hates the fragility of being a woman who has no rights to the future of her children.

"Please, I beg of you, no matter what has happened between us, don't let my child suffer even an hour with an old and infected husband."

"Why did you not bring your child to Versailles and beg protection from the king?" I ask.

"Camile-Marie has been locked away. I don't know what to do."

I turn to Charles. "I must kill again."

"I see that," he says.

"Will you stop me?"

"No. But I fear that with every death you are more likely to be caught. More likely to bring ruin onto your house and your younger sister."

"I agree. Remain here, and if we are betrayed, kill Helena." Tears spring to my eyes, and I cover my face with my hands to hide the tinge of scarlet. Why must I exist in such turmoil?

"Pascaline, you cannot threaten and cry!" Charles

instructs. "You lose your credibility."

He glances over my head at Helena. "Fear not, Madame Durrant, I kill only on the battlefield."

"I wish I could kill Benefiel," Loretta whispers.

"No, you do not," I say, tempted to use my bewitching voice. I do not. I love Loretta too much. Tears still trickle down my face, but I force my voice calm. "You and I shall speak of payment later. It might be your husband's life, and then you will walk France alone and discarded. I haven't decided." I march out the door with the terrible knowledge I cannot blame Helena for Celeste's death. I can only blame God—and one cannot openly blame Him in this country. It is treason.

Loretta

8th of November

Cher Journal,

I don't think Helena believed me today when I warned her that Pascaline was mightily changed.

"What will she want? Do you really think she would take my life?" she asked in a shaky voice. "Jean-Pierre's life?"

"I've no idea," I said, truthfully. "Lieutenant Onfoy?"

"Nor I."

Papa strode into my apartment.

"The boys arrived safely with the cart. Why did you not stop her?" Papa snarled at Charles, not caring Helena could see his fangs.

I grabbed my father's hands. "Why can't you understand what we're trying to accomplish?"

"It's not a woman's place to decide what battles are virtuous, young lady. We already had to chastise your sister, and I would not have a repeat of that terrible action."

So, Pascaline reached Charles but not Papa's heart.

"Papa, this is Madame Durrant, Helena Fabron Durrant."

Papa acknowledged her with a, "Madame." However, he simply did not care she was in the room. Helena was merely a woman, rarely at court, in every way unimportant.

"Papa, look at this map. I shall show you what we've accomplished." I tugged my father's arm to the map of the lands under the king's control. "We've made you allies—including Madame Durrant!"

"And Honoré Tellier," Charles mumbled. "Pascaline is a friend for life of the loup-garou."

"Please see." I pressed my hand to Papa's holding. "Here is Limousin. Pascaline has made you an ally through marriage, here."

I point to three smaller holdings as well. The women are our friends, and they will ensure none of us is alone. This is what Pascaline and I've been building! If the Viscountess Fabron marries Charles's brother—"

"Why did you not explain all this?" Papa growled.

I refused to shrink from his fangs. "We tried, you refused to listen. You only see sin in this place, but there's also goodness. Even our sister, Helena, who we once thought betrayed us, has become an ally for what Pascaline means to accomplish right now."

Cher Journal, I realized then though Pascaline might wish to kill Helena and Jean-Pierre, she would not. Helena could not be an ally if she was walking France alone in poverty and few men would marry a widow with eight children under the age of thirteen. They were more valuable to us alive.

"I see," Jakub said. "If she betrayed you once…"

Charles pressed his hand on Papa's shoulder. "As the old joke claims: When the Adversary is at your door, what type of steps do you take?"

Papa did not answer.

Charles revealed the punchline. "Big ones."

I giggled. I couldn't help myself.

Cher Journal, oh, how I yearned to kiss Charles! But alas, I did not kiss him because I am the king's mistress until I am ready to leave Versailles.

Chapter 66

Pascaline

I creep toward the palace walls. Nix clip clops on the stones and snorts.

"Will you let me ride?" I ask the vampire horse.

The giant steed bows his head. I clamber on his back. He grunts, snorts, and paws the ground. His short black coat feels like the softest velvet.

Nix rears up and races into the night. I lean into him as he jumps over a hedgerow. I wish Sydella was beside me for her equestrian knowledge. The wind blows my hair about my face and chills my hands. Unlike a living horse, Nix does not fear darkness or any other obstacles in his path.

We reach Benefiel's holding in hours. If I ran, it would have taken me days. Of course, Nix was a young strong horse of ten years when he was reborn, and undeath made him even stronger.

Though I cannot talk to him in horse, Nix knows to find an unguarded section of wall and jumps over it.

He let me down beside a tall wall outside the château. I climb it, looking down once. The mighty beast nestles in the leaves as I creep onto Benefiel's ground.

Scaling the wall to the inner keep, I find one window

lit by candlelight. No woman wants to be married to such an old man. Certainly not a thirteen-year-old girl. Though I can rescue Camile-Marie if I do not destroy the original sinner, another girl will know her fate. In most likelihood, the girl will not have a vampire aunt to save her.

I slip through the open window and steal into the man's bedroom where he lay. Legendary snores blow the strands of white hair spurting through his upper lip and down his jawbone. His face is even more wrinkled in sleep.

I desire to bite him and take in his blood, but I am wiser now, and I do not. I want to bash his head in with the walking stick he tapped against the floor so many months ago. I don't. I will not leave a mark or spill blood on his ticking. I want vengeance for how he treated Loretta and me, yet vengeance would be as cold as it had always been.

I search his dressing table for a means to his demise. An old man must have several medicines and medicinal plants. I dump pennyroyal elixir into his mouth. He chokes briefly but swallows. His pulse races faster, and he opens his eyes, but I stand in darkness, and he doesn't see me.

Next, I feed him a sweet tasting belladonna berry and realize that he is fully awake. I use my powers to order him to swallow...another and another, until he consumes five berries.

His eyes start to weave about as if he sees more than one of me in the room.

"Rise and sit at your dressing table."

On quivering legs, the man did so. A quicksilver pot is on his dressing table. I mix it with water until it's drinkable and bring it to his lips. The first sip spurts out of his mouth.

Drink, I whisper with my mind. *Drink.*

He drinks it.

Groaning, he clutches his chest and stomach. I watch as his body convulses. His eyes widen and pupils dilate. He stops breathing.

I push a few bottles over and spill the contents across the dressing table. He does not have a mark upon him that would expose this attack as the work of a vampire. I pray it will look as if he had confused his medications or suffered a heart attack.

I wash my hands and return to Nix. He carries me deep into the wood, where we wait for daylight to pass. He stares at a chubby red squirrel, and when it dares come close to see if we have food, he eats it. I could not blame him. I, too, hunger. I suppose hunger is the consequence of a peaceful murder. I crawl onto the expanse of Nix's muscular body and fall asleep. He nestles me once as the sun comes close and we shift our position. Under a deep canopy of trees, we fall asleep again and wait for nightfall.

We awaken just before dusk. I wonder aloud. "Kinsman, how many battles you must have seen."

He nays and scratches his foot.

"And many missions of mercy?"

He nays again and nods his giant head.

I comb and plait his mane because Sydella once told me he liked it. He does seem to enjoy the attention. The sun sinks lower, and once set, we move on.

Pockets of snow cover the grass and frozen mud. The wind blows, like a living entity, over fields and through forests. It howls equally between the hovels of peasants and the great châteaux of the rich. But those in châteaux have fires warming their homes.

At Abby de Amelia, freshly scrubbed walls do not hide the broken, caved-in roof on the north building or the newly expanded cemetery with dozens of insignificant grave markers. Their orchard is bare and filled with diseased trees. This is how Helena will repay me. She will be so relieved.

I climb the tower, which houses noble-born girls, and find Camile-Marie's room. Even sleeping, the girl in the bed had tried to make herself as small as possible. Her elbows press into her sides. Her pallid skin is covered in the sweat of a nightmare.

"Awake, Camile-Marie."

Her blue eyes flutter open. My sisters' eyes. Helena whom I loathed and Loretta whom I loved. But Camile-Marie is an innocent girl. Even in my fury, I can choose to love her.

Camile-Marie tightens her grip on the covers. "Who are you?"

I am surprised she does not know me, but she had been seven or eight when we last met—and it was only for a break in travel. Had we even spoken, other than niceties? I cannot remember.

"I've been sent by Madame Durrant. I'll take you to Versailles."

She shakes her head. "Papa'll be angry if I leave. I'm to marry Georges Benefiel—"

"Do you wish to marry him?"

"I must."

"Why?"

She becomes smaller still. "Because I was told I must."

"I can place you somewhere where your Papa cannot

touch you, whether or not you marry Georges Benefiel. Do you want to come to Versailles and meet the king?"

"Yes!" Her eyes brighten. "How will we get down?"

"I need you to dress warmly, then be brave and hang on."

"Is this a dream?"

"Perhaps, is it a good dream to be rescued?"

She whispers, "It is."

The girl holds onto my neck as I climb down. She whimpers and grips me closer. As a human woman I was afraid, but as a vampire, the wall is a thrill.

We reach the ground, and I lower her from my shoulders. I take her hand, and we walk through the darkness to Nix.

Camile-Marie steps back, but the giant beast bows.

"He likes to be stroked on the mane."

The girl reaches out and touches his soft velvet coat. "Are you of the fae?"

"Something like that."

Nix sets off, faster than before. Camile-Marie screams as we leap over stone walls.

"Don't be frightened," I say.

She smiles at me. "You're of the fae. I knew it!"

At Versailles, Nix carries us directly into Gunter's quarters where Charles and Papa await.

"You found the girl untouched?" Papa asks.

"Thankfully, yes. She was sequestered in an old convent." I whisper when I tell him I poisoned Benefiel so the child would not hear. "I hope, Papa, you see I'm making strides with my anger."

Gunter tucks the child into a bed. Nix pushes him

away and lies beside her. I cannot help but smile. Nix misses sleeping with Sydella.

Rebuffed, Gunter says, "Fine, but you don't get to keep this one."

Nix snorts.

Gunter sends word to Helena, who comes quickly.

She peeks into the room and sees her daughter. "Am I a...widow?"

"No. I shan't let your children suffer the financial loss of their father, but I've considered how you will repay me."

Helena pales.

I laugh, giddy from my success. "Like the good Catholic women we are, you and I shall ask for the rebuilding of Abbey de Amelia in order that it may continue to do its good works. We shall make a petition to the king in the morning."

"The Abbey?"

"Yes. One roof is collapsed, among other things. Ready yourself to argue with a cardinal and agree with everything I say."

"Madame, 'tis late. Nix won't stop you from sleeping with your daughter, but he does tend to hog the bed," Gunter says, no doubt to lighten the tone.

I'm secretly satisfied that Helena does not appear to have released her tension. She answers most seriously, "The papers claim the Bach-Sörens train the greatest horses, but I had no idea they were trained to sleep in their beds."

"Most sleep in stables, but the horses have their own personalities," Gunter says. "Nix imagines himself a great silly dog who loves children, women, and others who don't throw grenades or shoot at us."

Helena does not laugh or even crack a smile. I know why. She has disobeyed her husband. Jean-Pierre might come to Versailles, beat her or their daughter in the middle of court, and not a single person would say a word against him. He could marry Camile-Marie away again and there was not a single thing she could do to stop him.

Gunter must realize this, too. "You and your child have my protection if you need it. I won't be leaving France for a year or two."

"Thank you."

"Still, I believe the less you speak about what you've seen tonight, the better. Pascaline has become my and Charles's sister, not yours. And we mean to have Loretta when she's old enough."

He bows, exits, and enters his own room. I turn to my former sister. "Don't worry, I'll come up with something to placate your husband's temper."

Chapter 67

Pascaline

I quietly wait my turn with the other ladies until the herald calls, "Madame Pascaline de Banquier and Madame Durrant."

I hear a few groans as I step toward the king, who sits with a pleasant expression on his face.

Confidence spreads through me.

"My Liege, Madame Durrant has brought forth to my attention the many shortages at Abbey de Amelia. This year alone, they buried seventeen nuns and thirty-nine children."

"Another abbey, Madame?" the cardinal asks.

Helena barely glances at the king as I gesture toward her.

In a small voice, she states, "My child, Camile-Marie, was educated there and spoke of the need for the restoration of the old nunnery's infirmary, one that assists many, many children."

The cardinal steps toward Helena. "The nuns take a vow to live with poverty."

She bows her head against the argument.

It does not matter; all I want is a witness to my statements. I present the rebuttal.

"Of course, they do," I say. "Which is why they don't have money to fix the roof. The abbey pays virtually no taxes because they have no assets, so we wish to raise funds, not only for their roof, but for an apiary, apples, oranges, and lemon trees."

"Nuns don't need—"

"Forgive me, Cardinal, I wasn't finished. Though the nuns may benefit, I believe fixing the roof of an Abbey ought to be done for the children living inside the building. Forgive me for mentioning, Highness, that these assets will not only bring health to the poor children, but harvests from an apiary. Oranges, apples, and lemons can be taxed, Highness. My own good mother, Countess de Limousin, understands this well and harvests fruits to make medicines from her own trees. I promise you, she will teach the nuns if they don't have the knowledge. If the church cannot afford the expense of a broken roof, we shall raise funds to protect your subjects within, but we need your leave, Highness."

I gesture to the cardinal. "Now, I am finished."

Louis XIV handles my polite gall with an extended lack of expression. Helena's wide eyes continue to stare at the floor as the entire room goes silent.

Finally, he smiles, magnanimously. "The ladies have made an excellent case. I shall send monies to have the roof fixed and to purchase the needed saplings. Next petitioner."

Helena and I curtsy and take our place among the women. I feel my heart warm from the success—and the knowledge I might trust both of my sisters again.

Chapter 68

Pascaline

I do not like coming into the King Louis's second antechamber alone. The gilded woodwork, plaster, and marble make the king's chambers cold. Normally, there would be courtiers and servants about, but even the king's guards remain in their rooms. I take care my footsteps make no echo on the wooden floors and my feet are in perfect position as they ought.

"You summoned me, Highness?" I ask with a deep curtsy.

My gown feels heavy on my body. My skin feels as if I could peel it away from the muscles below. I fear torture and the flame.

"Alas, I grieve you were not born a man. Your impassioned words at court may have been heard by many but understood only by me."

"Yes, Highness."

"Have I heard correctly that you brought Count and Countess Langlais together?"

"Yes, Highness. The countess is a dear friend."

He presses his fingers together. "It has been a productive match."

"The countess is a radiant young woman and the count a virile young man. The court claims you've a gift in creating happy unions—a certain magic."

I stiffen. Magic is illegal. "Sire, I simply watch people and listen to their concerns. I only bring God's order and law to the whims of courtiers. I hope you approve of my methods. I've another match in mind, but I'm still studying the man."

"Yet, ma chérie, you are still alone."

"I'll find love one day. It simply has not occurred yet, Sire."

"I might have you sent to a convent."

Hair lifts from the nape of my neck. I hold back the urge to cry. I wonder if he knew my sins. "Sire, no matter what you command me, I beg you to care for Loretta. Allow her to marry the man she loves when she's ready."

The king laughs and steps closer. "I see. No, you shall not go to a convent. Continue your matchmaking and good works because your strange abilities bring in tax dollars. I must admit, I am surprised how much tax can be directly attributed to your meddling. You're a bright star who, I pray, never dims."

"Thank you, Highness."

"As for the other matter, I decided I shall not walk into eternity. I would hate to grovel to lesser men with a higher rank. You are dismissed."

"May I go to my sister's apartment tonight, Highness?"

"Indeed, you should. Versailles is a lonely existence for Madame Loretta. She is surrounded by women who would take her place—and would have—if I were a younger, more foolish man."

I escape, allowing myself to feel the tremble in my legs, which couldn't compete with the exultation of my success at court. I hurry to Loretta's apartment, where I am undressed, bathed, and put in a sleeping shift by her maid, I fall asleep beside my sister for a long time.

Chapter 69

Loretta

16th of November

Cher Journal,

Saturday afternoon, with the fading sunlight of autumn spilling across my lavender, satin tunic, I took in the center of the Hall of Mirrors. I hoped, probably in vain, that Papa might recognize my compromise by making my costume longer than a true hunting tunic and less revealing than many of the images of Atalanta I had seen.

King Louis gestured for me to begin.

I curtsied and faced the audience, and in my soft soprano, called out, *"Remember, Atalanta, abandoned by her father because he wanted a son, and rejoice that she was rescued by a sow bear, who nursed her."*

Yet, even as I called to them, the audience disappeared from my consciousness. Even the king did not matter. All that mattered was my music.

I had become one with music from the first scintillating, ephemeral moment of my performance. This is what I was meant to do, and to have my sister by my side, sharing my greatest pleasure, was more than I could ever have asked for.

Pascaline

I am happy to be undead, to participate in my sister's concert. My fingers fly up the harpsichord, and I wish Andre could see me play at court. I allow my heart to miss him and Celeste but refuse to wallow in the emotion. Instead, I pour it into the music as I oft instruct Loretta.

We pause for the cello. Loretta's soprano and the deep cello argue. The verse ended with:

> *I'll only marry a man who can best me if a footrace.*

I move off the harpsichord with a quick transition and sit upon a swing. As if this was a wonderous opera machina, the swing rises to the ceiling. From my perch, I steal a look at Papa and Charles in the audience to see their reactions. It cannot be lost on them that Loretta has written her own story especially when she cries out in fear:

> *Olympians, why does the world deny me my freedom?*

Charles smiles. I suspect he knows the message is for him, and his expression says he understands. Papa's smile is flat. His face indicates we are making spectacles of ourselves. I find it hard to care.

Loretta's sweet, frightened soprano echoes off the mirrors, and I drop the black cloak to expose a lovely satin toga in rich purple over a thin gossamer taffeta, my hair covered in a golden wig and golden laurels, my body powdered and painted to ensure my reflection.

Grumbles disappear with gasps and murmurs of the

crowd who are not expecting me.

Loretta sings:

Why does Venus come to me?

I croon:

Disciple of Diana, you and I have no quarrel. I am a friend to all those who love.

I shall ensure only the man who could best you is the man who will love you as you are.

My aria continues with words of encouragement and hope and love in marriage.

Once my aria ends, I unclasp my broach. The purple and silver plunge to floor in a luscious silken waterfall to expose Hippomenes's lavender hunting toga. The swing sets me back on the floor; I lift three golden apples hidden in my pockets and toss the laurels on the harpsichord.

The crowd claps. Papa's frown deepens.

Loretta's third song followed Atalanta and Hippomenes's legendary footrace with violins in rising and falling staccatos. Our voices race along with the violins.

Hippomenes wails:

I can never best Atalanta with my speed.

Venus, I pray for you to help me.

At each rise in the music, I drop a golden apple into Loretta's hands.

The music pauses, as the footrace pauses. It begins again. My echoing tone always a step behind until I throw Loretta the last apple. Her voice stops. The laurels are placed upon my head and a veil of red—the color of a Roman bride— upon Loretta's.

Atalanta's aria moved from plaintive to angry to

sorrowful, for Atalanta had lost everything she held dear.

> *I, a disciple of Diana, would die before I am confined to a house!*

I remove the laurels from my head and place the laurels upon hers to begin the final duet:

> *I only bested you with the help of Venus--*

Loretta turns away.

> *I was betrayed but do not taint your triumph.*
>
> *I was once lost on a mountain; I am lost now.*

I placed my hand on her shoulder.

> *I raced you because I love you. Let me guide you.*

She answered:

> *You raced me so you might stand above me.*
>
> *But you are below me, deceiver.*

As Hippomenes, I sink to my knees and embrace her leg:

> *I swear to love you, Beautiful Atalanta, fleet as a cheetah...*

Still in perfect pitch, Loretta spat:

> *You believe you are a lion.*

I sing my next lines: *Strong Atalanta, brave as a bear,*

> *I pray you return my affection—*

Loretta sang:

> *I feel nothing for you.*
>
> *Anymore, than he felt for me.*

Hippomenes pressed on. I let myself feel Andre.

> *Just know I will never abandon our children.*
>
> *Boys and girls will be fattened with venison and boar with you as their mother. Our children will*

not starve with me as their father.

With her back still to me, Loretta sings:

We shall hunt?

I reply:

How could I refuse you?

Since the first time I saw your arrow fly true,

I have loved you.

There was a pause to halt all vibrations as Loretta turns to face me and her lovely soprano admits in the last stanza:

Ingenuity and cunning is also part of the hunting.

Thus, the last notes hang in the air. I kiss her hand and listen to the applause.

Loretta and I curtsy to the king. We gesture toward the court musician, who inclines his head to the king and gestures to the string quintet. We had created something beautiful. As it is late autumn, not everyone will see it. Perhaps there will be an encore next spring.

Jakub

I squeezed my toes in revulsion as I managed to smile at the vision my daughters constructed. The court saw only the beauty of Pascaline's embodiment of Venus. And Loretta, the wild Atalanta. Long silken togas draped their bodies, but they might have well been naked. Ankles, feet, and bare arms exposed to the entirety of the court.

The court applause thudded in my chest. My eardrums thrummed. My daughters are immodest.

The women applaud enthusiastically. Among the men,

Charles clapped. Other men waited until the king stood and clapped. He kissed Loretta's hand.

My daughters curtsied again and left the Hall of Mirrors. I might have followed, but Gunter slid beside us.

"Aren't you glad you did not vanquish that monster?" he asked.

"Ask me when I am done returning the gifts Pascaline is sure to get."

Charles groaned. "We shall be up all night."

"Your daughters are worth a thousand sons. Now Pascaline has mastered her anger, she's even more valuable."

I nodded curtly.

"Tell me, kinsman, will you marry your wild Atalanta?" Gunter asked Charles.

"If she'll have me."

"You still doubt her love though you inspired this operatic triumph?" Gunter asked.

The world spun as the court musician reset his troupe for the actual court performance.

"Charles inspired this outrage?" I asked.

"I've never seen a woman more directly write an opera for one man's ears, even if several might hear it. For the love of God, tell me you understood her message."

"She asked me to love her as she is," Charles said. "All that she has done."

Henri Onfoy approached, politely speaking to me first, then Gunter, before shaking his brother's hand. If Charles were to age, this is how he might look in a decade. Now that he's one of us, my son will keep the hint of youthfulness in his manliness forever.

"Madame Pascaline has someone you must meet," Charles mentioned offhand to Henri.

"Oh no, she believes she can shoot Cupid's arrow into me, too?" Henri feigned disinterest, but I heard his heart rate rise.

"The lady asked if the lieutenant thought you might be a good father to a fatherless boy and a good husband to a semi-wealthy widow," Benoit offered.

"There's no such woman," Henri said.

"If the lady says there is, there must be," Gunter said. "So far, she has not been wrong, Monsieur."

"Everyone has been whispering. Why did you keep her from Versailles?" Henri asked.

"As if I can stop those girls' artistic endeavors. The artistic temperament of the young ladies is beyond me," I said, praying that Agata would forgive my trespass.

"You will be overwintering, then?"

"Only Pascaline. Trying to keep my girls apart is as futile as trying to keep those costumes in check," I told him. "Our kinsman is around to keep an eye on them. They're safer here than anywhere else."

"But are we safe from Madame Pascaline's petitions?" Henri joked. I liked him, even if he never saw the battlefield.

"No one is safe from Madame Pascaline's petitions," Gunter said.

"If you admire her, why don't you marry her?" Henri asked. Now, I really liked him.

"She said no."

"Why? You're wealthy, handsome—"

"I don't love her, and she knows it. Unfortunately for

Monsieur le Count, he and his wife get on famously, so the young ladies know love is possible," Gunter said. "And then Loretta fell in love. It's worse than you think—the groom-to-be is a terrible poet, all brooding, romantic, and battle-scarred."

Henri turned to Charles. "You would marry the king's mistress!"

"I can't pretend I haven't sinned. Loretta explained when she is ready to take on the responsibilities of being a wife, she'll come home."

Henri bowed and said his goodbyes.

I must have frowned because Benoit sucked in his breath beside me. Charles touched the sleeve of my jacket. I ignored both of them because I needed to know if the thing was even possible.

"Love can grow when nurtured. You appear young, handsome," I said to Gunter.

"Unfortunately, I'm not the man to nurture her broken heart. My own heart died long ago on the battlefield. I enjoy the company of my mistresses and provide them with a safe, comfortable place to live. I would do more for my wife, but I never loved anyone except the two children whom Gaius and I raised together. Perhaps my mother. She wept when I left for the army."

"What of the younger brothers?"

"Renee and Jean?" He made a flippant gesture with his hand. "They're grown men. They will learn well, or we will toss them in the sun. Of course, that is why Leon remained with them and I did not."

"Why did you remain in France?"

Gunter laughed. "Jakub, my friend, you're the luckiest

man in all of Europe to have these daughters, otherwise you would've most certainly lost your holding. I mentor your offspring at times, primarily because I am nearby, but I'm here because I must continue to make inroads both with the French Court, your good wife, and other allies—both the strong and the weak.

"I long to return home to know the comforts of my family, but the battle is not yet won or lost. Your daughters feel the same." He inclined his head and left us standing there to stew in our own thoughts, surrounded by music and decadent luxury.

A man came to my side. He whispered, "Count Jakub? I should like to buy some of the shimmering fabric your lovely daughter wore as Venus."

I must have glared because the man quickly added, "I would buy it as a gift for my wife."

Benoit removed a ledger from the bag at his side and had an inked quill at the ready. "May I have your name, Monsieur? Let me see, the corset and toga overskirt Madame Pascaline wore took three and a half yards of fabric."

"Can I order four yards?"

"Certainly."

Benoit took the man's information.

Once he left, I turned to the young cadet. "How did you know that?"

The boy looked discomforted. "Madame Loretta gave me a list, Count de Banquier. She had it all planned, knowing we would have many orders for it. The man obviously wanted to see his wife in a similar garment. They spread love—the way you love the countess."

Something about the lad's tone made me feel like an idiot. The young always think they know everything.

My daughters reentered the hall (thankfully) fully dressed, surrounded by women. The other women protected my daughters, especially Pascaline, from fawning men.

Charles must have noticed as well.

"You're not upset by this attention?" I gestured at Loretta.

He shrugged. "Their schemes have gleaned me an occupation in which I excel, a fine table set by a noble lady to which I am always invited, my cadet is safe, and I am a gifted, young musician's muse."

"Forget not, Lieutenant, the ladies also sang to the cello," Benoit said. The young cadet turned to another man who approached for an order of the shimmering fabric Loretta wore as Atalanta's hunting toga.

"Yes, I can also sell you a pattern if you've a seamstress on staff. Or I can give you the name of the seamstress who created the garments. The filles de Banquier absolutely adore her. She and her women make all the costumes and alterations," Benoit said.

"You know the seamstress, son?" I asked.

"Madame Loretta, my count." The boy's eyes begged Charles and me to notice the many men who wished to speak of business.

Throughout the day, many men purchased ribbons and sashes. Richer men ordered yards of fabric and patterns. Gunter brought them over to speak.

Without a doubt, the seamstress would be pleased by the business, the king would be pleased by the taxes my holding brought in this year, and Charles seemed happy enough. I wondered what would happen when the dye went out of style again. I realized it did not matter. When fashions changed, my faithful daughters, Loretta and Pascaline, would change with them.

Charles leaned over to us and said, "It is too bad Pascaline and Loretta aren't men, and taller. They would've made fine grenadiers."

The king approached with ballet grace. "What is this coterie?"

"Forgive us, Highness. The former grenadier was just complimenting the ladies by calling them grenadiers," Gunter said.

Louis XIV chuckled and said, "What a triumph, Monsieur. You must be beyond proud."

"Thank you, Highness."

"Madame Pascaline shall be overwintering in Versailles, Count de Limousin?"

"Indeed, Highness."

"Excellent. Your comely daughters brighten even the coldest days with their music."

I inclined my head to receive the compliment. "Thank you."

"I discovered art exposes us in ways we do not wish. It is one of the reasons I had to stop performing in the ballet."

"You're a magnificent dancer, Highness. Herr Bach and I both remember."

The king leaned closer. His voice was no softer than a murmur. "I will die as king, and I pray you remember me in kindness for my love of the ballet."

"I will also remember the kindness you offered my children," I said.

"Hardly a kindness to listen to two beautiful women who would have undoubtedly been in the opera if they had not been daughters of a count with ancient views of modesty." The king gave a slight bow of his head and moved on.

I again inclined my head and smiled.

"What is it?" Charles asked.

"Nothing important."

Apparently, my daughters were worth a thousand sons. Even if I had to remind myself every night, I would remember that.

Loretta

16th of November continued

Cher Journal,

After our triumph, the king spent time with his wife, so I was free to walk with Charles into the garden. I wish my experiences had not made me wiser. I still loved him. I wanted more of him in a way I had not before. I wanted him to know me. To know all of me.

I spoke plainly, "Though it pains me that I hurt you both, it was the only way I could sing and protect the holding."

"Was it worth it?" Charles asked.

"I wish I could explain what music means to me, what it has always meant to me. But, please, don't lessen the situation, Lieutenant. Pascaline saw violence coming." I blinked away tears. "And she was right."

"Do you forgive me in my part of that?" Charles asked.

"Pascaline does, so I must." I squared my shoulders. "This time. But the next time, I won't forgive you. And if I am a vampire, you better run fast."

Pascaline

I walk with my fingertips on the arm of Henri Onfoy. Loretta and Charles walk in front of us. I ensure our pace keeps them in sight but allows them privacy. Golden leaves drift down and cover the path below. Thick gray clouds obscure the sky above. I do not need to worry about the immolating sun. Though, of course, I am prepared with my parasol.

"The garden is so beautiful. Next spring, it will be alive in a sea of lavender," I say, happily.

"You wished to speak to me about something, Madame?"

"Yes. Loretta invites you to her table tonight in the Grand Salon. There's someone I wish for you to meet."

"Who?"

"The Viscountess de Fabron—you know of the horrible tragedy that befell House de Fabron this year?"

"The missing viscount, yes."

"The papers are now saying it is likely he was mugged when he entered Paris to visit his mistress. He is in all, likelihood, dead."

Henri sighs. "The papers say things that sell papers."

"Indeed, they do, but Loretta and I are friends with the viscountess. Did you know the viscountess is under the protection of the king this winter? The loss of her husband is not the only tragedy."

"Oh?"

"Château de Fabron was garrisoned two years ago."

Henri crossed himself. "Dear God."

"The young viscount was the youngest of four sons, and the only one who switched religions before it was too late," I explain. "Married a Catholic girl quickly."

"I can only imagine what that family went through. I was not well-acquainted with them. The viscount wasn't much more than a lad, was he?" Henri's voice rises a bit at the question.

"Only twenty-one. The viscountess is also a woman of twenty-one. She is afraid, but it would be hard to be afraid if a widower with a kindly nature and a good head on his shoulders took an interest in her affairs."

Henri steps away from me. "Why would you say that?"

"She has what you need, and you offer her something she does not have. Charles told me if history serves the present, you would be a good, caring father to the little boy. That you wouldn't hurt him or treat him cruelly. When he was a boy, you cared for him kindly."

"What is your interest in this, Madame?"

"I have no interest other than Viscountess de Fabron is a friend. I care deeply for the welfare of all children, and Charles. He worries greatly about you. You've been widowed for nearly a decade. Perhaps being married to a woman who had proven she could bear a son might interest you."

"What can I possibly give a pretty young widow?"

"Stability, kindness, and an aptitude for estate management to rebuild Château de Fabron for the little viscount."

"What do you want for this introduction?"

"Forgive Loretta. In three or four short years, we'll be related through marriage. Charles will be happier if you accept his bride."

Henri smiles. "If you speak the truth, you're too good for this world."

All my worries evaporate. There will be a little back and forth; I see it to the end. "Yet, even if I'm lying, what do you have to lose by accepting my invitation? We only play for ribbons and sou. You won't lose much by sitting down."

"I shall think on it." Henri turns us back toward the palace. "I've been a widower a long time, I might not make a good husband. She'll lose her title—"

"You don't hire rent boys or flaunt a mistress, Monsieur. I've never seen you raise your voice or make mild threats even when you lose an argument over a petition. You're a good advisor to the king and Count Langlais. You know when to listen and when to speak."

"I must say your introduction certainly made the young Count and Countess Langlais happy."

"Thank you for saying so. The knowledge warms my heart to know sweet Catherine is happily married."

"But what of you? You must know Monsieur Bach has eyes for you."

"Bach has eyes for any girl with a big enough dowry. Like Charles, he has known so much war and needs time away from the battlefield before he'd be a good husband."

"Yet, you seem to expect Charles to marry your sister?"

I laugh. "Only after Charles settles into a quiet life without bombs exploding everywhere. Your brother jumps into action if he is startled by loud sounds, but he is a decent, kind man, and I'm happy he will soon be my brother-in-law."

"Do you ever doubt yourself, Madame?"

"All the time."

Shaking his head, Henri asks when he ought to visit Loretta's table. Thus, I win, and so will he.

VERSAILLES
1692

Chapter 70

Loretta

1st of November,

Cher Journal

I watch the many courtiers' carriages pull away from Versailles. Soon my escort would take me home to be Charles's bride and a vampire.

The gracious king came to my apartment. It is hard to imagine this man who I have become fond of within the walls of this palace is the same man who is waging war outside of it. Perhaps it is because I am fond of the man but not the king.

I stood, curtsied, and gave up my dressing stool as expected and required.

"You requested my presence, Madame?" Louis said.

"I wish to marry Captain Charles Onfoy over the winter. I am twenty-two."

"You still wish to gaze at those scars forever?" he asked.

"Yes."

"I vowed to allow this match, though I wish you would reconsider it. You would be safer at the palace where you can continue to write your music and sing—whether or not you are immortal."

"But I love him. You of all people must understand that, Highness."

"Why do you love him?"

"He writes me poetry. He is, and has been, honest with his intentions. He serves France well."

"May I see the poems?"

"Of course, Highness." I scurried to get the ribboned packet.

The king's eyes slipped down the page and frowned. He recited, "Your eyes are blue...like the fountain on a clear day... and your worsted dress—the one your mother made for you— the one you wore while picking rosehips with your sister..."

The king flipped through the poems. "Your voice is like an angel's...I heard God in the tone...the violin bows cut into my heart with their squeal?"

"I did not say Captain Onfoy writes good poetry, Highness, but it's innocent in its way. It's like they are thoughts from his mind. He loves me."

"So do many men. How do you know he will be a faithful husband? Has he not become friends with your sister?"

I blinked away unbidden tears. "Pascaline will never hurt me. If Captain Onfoy has a mistress, it is likely a common woman."

"You've considered Captain Onfoy has been unfaithful in your long engagement."

"I can only assume so, Highness, as I have been, but I'll not concern myself with what happened before our marriage."

"Will you return to Versailles in the spring?"

"Yes."

"May God protect you, Loretta de Banquier. I pray

marriage will not transform you too much. You'll still sing when the days lengthen."

"Captain Onfoy would face my mother or my sister if he tried to tie my voice, Highness."

He chuckled. "We should fear for any man who faces that sister of yours."

"Thank you, Highness."

He inclined his head. I curtsied until he left my room. I was free to marry the man I loved, who attempted to write me poetry, who cared for children, and was a teacher of men.

Chapter 71

Loretta

4th of November

Cher Journal

I gazed across the windswept landscape as horses whinnied and my guards grumbled quietly. The cart in front of my carriage was stuck in the mud. An animalistic howl sounded in the night, and from the other side of the carriage, there was a shout.

I peered out and saw men moving faster than they should. Their feet moved noiselessly over the gravel road. Sour unwashed bodies and rotting meat filled the air. I layered on metal jewelry

I heard muskets.

I supposed vampire peasants might be tired of living under the king's thumb.

Pascaline

I arrange flowers in the room assigned to Charles's mother which overlooks Maman's garden. I cannot wait until Loretta arrives. The inky sky is covered in clouds, and the wind rustles and plucks russet leaves from the branches above us.

"Loretta will be the most beautiful bride," I say to Benoit, who assists me in trimming the thorns from the stems.

"Indeed," he said. He had grown into a fine lad of seventeen. Still three years until he finishes his cadetship and another two before he would face the ultimate decision to become a vampire.

Charles presses himself into the room. "Pascaline, we found more vampires moving across the countryside."

"Negotiation or battle?"

"Depends on what we find. But dress for battle."

Loretta

Cher Journal

A vampire reached into the carriage, and I slipped to the floor. I saw his expanded fangs. Red saliva dripped down his chin. I put my bracelet on my knuckles and tried to strike him. He moved too fast.

I grabbed a cushion and knocked his hand away.

"You royals..." He actually looked at me. His deep voice sounded pleased. "It's you. Count Jakub's whore of a daughter, the spoilt one."

I tried to get even lower as he reached in. "You're the reason the king built a dance school instead of feeding his starving people."

That was not true. The dance school was commissioned long before I was even born. King Louis always had done whatever he wanted. He would continue to do so until his death. Still, I was in no place to argue. Instead, I did my best to burn him with my ornamentation.

He laughed at me; his foul breath filled the carriage.

Horses sounded in the distance.

Over the din and terrible laughter, I heard a deep voice. "By the name of Count de Banquier, we order you away from that carriage," Charles shouted.

He was truly my knight.

Pascaline

I race toward the carriage and snatch the vampire reaching into the window. Healthy peasant vampires have become more antagonistic to the noble vampires since the horde crumbled. Some left for the lands ruled by Protestant kings and princes, but the ones who stayed were hurting and prowled the roads for opportunities.

My dagger slices through the sinew of the vampire's neck and hits bone. His mouth opens as he snaps his fangs at me. I push him to Charles, who slices off his head.

The corner of Charles's eyes crinkle as he fights laughter, watching the vampire's body wandering without the benefit of sight and smell, then stumbling over a hole in the road.

Charles and I advance on the next one.

Three more vampires exit the trees.

One man jumps on my back and tries to grapple me to the ground. I let myself fall backward. I land on him, roll over, and slice him across his snarling mouth. The second slice crosses his throat.

I jump to my feet and gesture to one of the guards.

"Dismember."

The man does so, ignoring the screams of the peasant.

Charles pummels the next vampire with his bare hands. He does not pretend he doesn't enjoy the violence of the action. This is not a battle but a vicious brawl.

Another vampire throws a rock attempting to get Charles to release his friend. It ineffectually hits Charles on the back of the head. I dash to the vampire who threw the rock and take off his head in a single slice of my short sword.

All is quiet.

The human Royal Guard cross themselves as they look at the squirming body parts that Charles and I collect into burlap sacks.

Red saliva covers Charles's tunic, and I warn him about seeing Loretta in such a state. He points at the carriage.

I open the carriage door and find Loretta kneeling on the floor, a knife in hand.

"Were you bitten, chérie?" I ask.

"No," she replies. "What of my guard?"

"One is dead. One is injured…" I glance over my shoulder. "Both drivers are fine. We lost one of the cart horses."

My little sister has grown up, but I still embrace her excitedly. I do not care if I am burned by her jewels as I whisper in her ear. "On the bright side, according to Maman, vampire blood will make you super strong during your transformation so we won't have to sacrifice any humans."

Loretta looks sick. "You planned to sacrifice?"

"I wasn't sure what Maman planned," I whisper. "Do you still want to be a vampire?"

"Yes. I wish to exist with you in strength…and Charles

in love for eternity."

"Good. I planted some roses clippings into pots in Maman's kitchen so you will still have some for the wedding."

Loretta

5th of November

Cher Journal,

Today, I gazed into Charles soft brown eyes. I placed my fan in my left hand to ensure my right hand was free to touch him. He made no move. I rested my right hand upon the velvet arm of his justacorps and smiled.

When he did not lean down, I said, "If I am to be your wife, I'd like you to kiss me now and then."

"Are you to be my wife?"

I pulled the bundle of letters and poems out of my pocket.

"Yes. Every word you wrote to me has shown me your soul. You are the man I love and the one I want to be with."

He smiled; the crowsfeet around his eyes deepened.

I leaned forward and tentatively kissed his lips. The soft skin felt cool against mine. I breathed in his breath. His undead touch was cold on my arms.

His strong hands cupped my cheeks. When he pressed his mouth into mine, I tilted my head back. He encircled my waist, gently pulling me closer. "I dare not go any further. I might infect you," he whispered huskily.

"I'm already infected with Pascaline's blood to ensure I never conceived the king's babe. Gaius said he never knew a vampire living or dead who had a babe. Not in two thousand years."

Charles stopped smiling.

"What's wrong? Did Pascaline never tell you the plan?"

"What do you mean...plan?"

"I thought as you grew closer... I swear I will tell you everything on our wedding night, because then you and I will be one, but I ask you to trust me a little longer. Just know every action Pascaline has made was to ensure that this holding remains as it is and protect the family." I paused. "You were right to think us actresses because that's what we were. For four long years, I played the king's mistress willingly, but he's getting older and has less use for mistresses. Knowing this, do you still want to marry me?"

"No one can remain innocent at Versailles." He gestured at the blackbirds bouncing around Pascaline. "Or even here."

"But we can protect this place and the innocent people within it," I said.

"We?"

"We. If you'll still have me. If not, I hope we remain friends."

"Loretta, I want you to be my wife."

"Do you forgive me?"

"If you forgive me for my trespasses."

I kissed his softly parted lips. He gripped my arms, pulling me closer. I felt the languid heartbeat under his skin. I felt his fangs expand behind his lips. He was holding back. Yet, every inch of my skin trembled from his touch. I leaned back, inhaling Maman's herbal soap and the underlying smell of the man that is Charles.

He released me because we were not yet wed.

Pascaline

The old woman's gummy eyes are upon Loretta as Henri assists his mother out of the carriage, and then his wife. Her posture bends forward, but I can see her as she once was. I do not doubt even as her body failed her mind was sharp.

Charles accepts her kisses as she greets him. "Oh, Charles, you look so pale, and your hands are so cold."

"Fear not, Mother. It's the turning of the weather. I've been training the count's men in the cool evening air.

"May I present, Countess de Banquier, my mother, Madame Dowager Onfoy."

"I am happy to meet your acquaintance and combine our families," Agata said.

Charles reintroduced Henri and introduced us to his second older brother, a monk. (His third brother, Marcel, had perished on the battlefield.)

After introductions, Madame Dowager Onfoy takes Loretta's arm. "Are you not a lovely bride?" She does not kiss her, and something hard revealed itself in the way the woman spoke.

"What a lovely hall!" the younger Madame Onfoy exclaims. "It's just how Charles's letters described."

"Indeed," Madame Dowager Onfoy said. "Don't get too excited, darling, not in your condition."

"Are you with child?" Maman crosses herself.

"Indeed, but it's too early to speak." The younger

Madame Onfoy glows with happiness.

"The midwife told us not to get too excited," Henri adds.

"Always good advice," Maman said. "Allow me to make you rosehip tea to take the road's chill from your bones."

Once Henri establishes his wife and mother's comfort in the house proper, he leaves us to rejoin the men in the bachelor's quarters.

In the privacy of other women, I slip to the floor so I might show my young nephew (who could never know our actual family attachment!) the set of blocks.

Loretta helps serve warm cups of rosehip tea.

Madame Dowager Onfoy says, "So, you're the king's mistress."

The entire room stops moving, except for the little boy.

"Yes, Madame Onfoy, but that time of my life has passed." Loretta says.

"Mother," the younger Madame Onfoy began, "I knew of this...liaison."

"Of course, you did. You're not blind." The old woman hisses. "Henri married a viscountess and my youngest marries the king's whore? Yet, both matches have your touch upon them. What is the game, ladies?"

Loretta straightens. She looks upon her future mother-in-law. "I'm not the king's whore any more than any other lady whom his Highness has set his eyes on, Madame. In the long years of Louis the XIV's sovereignty, there has been many, as no doubt you remember from your time at Versailles."

The old woman stares. "But there's always a game."

"Of course. We needed some way to win the king's favor so we might get dispensation," Loretta says. "He has made his other women duchesses, but Pascaline studied the issue and asked for a different boon."

"Loretta's son will inherit this holding, Madame Onfoy," I say. "I meant to see my sister happy with a man who filled her heart with joy. She has loved your son, and he her, since the first moments they met."

The old woman smiles, then. "I heard the daughters of Banquier were cleverer than most. Yet, you're still unbound, so perhaps you are cleverer than we all. Do you mean to marry Christ?"

"I sincerely doubt Christ would be interested in a woman like me."

The old woman laughs again.

My heart lightens at the sound of horses. I gesture out the window. I recognize the flash of blond hair and pale skin under the rider's cloak, and smile to see the beautiful black horse. Jakub, Charles, and Benoit meet them in the courtyard. "Why look, Herr Bach and his sister are arriving..."

Another danger. I wish with all my might I can bring some sort of peace.

"He's one handsome boy," Madame Dowager Onfoy muses. "Why, dear Pascaline, you're blushing. This Herr Bach has your heart?"

"Herr Bach's life has been filled with war; I'm close friends with his sister."

"Hmmm." Madame Dowager Onfoy turns to Loretta. "Child, you sang for the king. Will you sing for me?"

Loretta moves to the new pedal harp. "Of course, Madame."

Chapter 72

Loretta

8th of November

Cher Journal,

The moment I have waited for has arrived! My wedding was everything I dreamed it might be. Most importantly, I am in love with my noble groom. (Oh, how I love to say the words!)

In a simple pale blue dress of an earlier age, I walked with Papa down the passage of the family chapel, Pascaline behind, assisting my train around corners. I have never loved my chosen father more for the tears in his eyes.

My left hand clutched a bouquet of rosemary, daisybush, marigolds and the last of the roses Pascaline was able to save.

In front of the chapel, Charles looked so handsome in the Banquier livery. My groom stood beside Gunter, who wore the colors of Brandenburg, and near him, Benoit in his uniform. Out in the world, these colors would be fighting. Here they were at peace.

The priest asked, "Who gives this woman in marriage?"

Papa answered and set my hand in Charles's.

I gazed at my groom through my silky veil and found

myself so enraptured, that I almost missed when the priest asked, "Loretta Marie de Banquier, have you come to this chapel with the intention to enter into marriage without coercion, freely and wholeheartedly?"

"I have."

"Charles Louis Onfoy, are you prepared, as you follow the path of marriage, to love and honor each other for as long as you both shall live?"

Charles's voice resounded through the chapel. "I do."

The priest continued. I listened to the words, but I could see only Charles.

"May the Lord in his kindness strengthen the consent you have declared before the Church and graciously bring to fulfillment his blessings within you. May the God of Abraham, the God of Isaac, the God of Jacob, the God who joined together our first parents in paradise, strengthen and bless, in Christ, the consent you have declared before the Church…so what God joins together, no one may put asunder.

"Let us bless the Lord," the assembly said. "Thanks be to God."

The mass continued until the priest sprinkled our golden rings with holy water.

My husband placed the ring on my ring finger, saying, "Loretta, receive this ring as a sign of my love and fidelity. In the name of the Father, and of the Son, and of the Holy Spirit."

I, in turn, pushed his ring onto his finger.

"Charles, receive this ring as a sign of my love and fidelity. In the name of the Father, and of the Son, and of the Holy Spirit."

Charles lifted my veil and gently kissed my lips. I was his

wife and soon I could love him forever.

Then, Cher Journal, as we left the chapel hand in hand, I, and perhaps we, overheard Madame Dowager Onfoy remark to her elder sons. "Strange wedding. Seemed it was missing a few vows."

She was right, of course. Vampires only submit to each other in love. It was time to tell Charles everything.

Charles escorted me to the bridal chamber, where Suzette met us to undress me.

We removed my gown behind the screen, then Suzette kissed my cheeks and left us. When I left the screen, Charles averted his eyes until I was under the blankets.

Charles and I know it is dangerous to consummate the marriage until my fangs erupted, but I admit I want to touch my husband!

"Might we hold hands?"

"As it pleases you," he said, but I could see he wanted to leave.

His fingertips brushed mine. Sitting next to me, his eyes were filled with desire.

"Is this night excruciating to you?"

"I've waited four years; a few more nights are nothing. You?"

"I desire you, but I'm contented as long as you're beside me," I said.

We sat quietly for a time; I broached a new subject.

"Did your mother tell you about the king's dispensation?" I ask brightly. "We wanted to tell you first, but your mother needed to know that your future shall be fortuitous. We told her as a kindness."

Charles gently stroked my cheek. "What are you talking about?"

"I asked you to trust me, and you did. It may sound foolish, but I wanted you to love me."

"You know I do."

"I waited to tell you because I did not want you to marry me for the position or money or anything other than me…but now, thanks to one of Pascaline's most wonderous schemes, our son shall be Jakub's heir!"

"But we cannot have a son."

"Our paper son will be born in approximately a year from now. Of course, he will be called Jakub. Later, Jakub will have a son named Charles," I bit my lip. "You know how French fathers love to keep names going."

"But why?"

"When kings died in battle every decade or so, it was easy for vampires to hide, but with kings living longer, we need to space out the count's visits with different men, or at least different names," I say. "But not any man would do. We needed someone worthy, and you, Charles Onfoy, are the most worthy man we know."

Charles stammered, "You'll have me lie to a king."

"Of course not. That would get us all killed. Pascaline and I will lie. You just have to stand and bow once a generation and return home and help Papa watch over this place. Keep Maman safe."

He cracked his knuckles. "How long can this go on?"

"Don't worry about tomorrow's battles, especially not when you should be kissing me."

Chapter 73

Loretta

11th of November

Cher Journal

Our human wedding guests left. Most of Papa's men escorted them over the border and beyond to ensure the remnants of the horde did not attack. It was time to follow those I loved into death. Charles, Papa, and Gunter prayed for my safety and transformation in the family chapel. Or at least that is what they said they would do.

The fire warmed the room, but I shivered as I lay on the table covered with a thin sheet. Sydella sat next to me and held my hand. Pascaline and Maman busied themselves with the final preparations, wearing only chemises, as it would be a bloody night.

Maman opened my radial artery with her fangs and drank in my blood until I grew pale. I closed my eyes and forced them open again as my consciousness began to fade. I felt thirsty. My mind became full of bubbles and foam. It was hard to think. I panicked. I thrashed and screamed in terror of the oncoming death.

Pascaline sang softly (she always knows what to do). I joined her.

Maman shifted her chemise and opened her breast. "Drink this heart blood. Drink deep, Loretta."

The dark blood spilling from Maman's heart flowed into my mouth. I gagged as I tasted the salt but then swallowed and drank deeply, filling myself with metallic liquid. For the first time, Maman was, in truth, my mother. I loved Pascaline more than ever because my humanity no longer came between us.

I lay back on the table in order to die, listening to Pascaline's sweet song.

Maman stabbed me in the neck.

A tiny pain ripped through my abdomen. I couldn't understand what my stomach had to do with my neck. I laughed. My laughter felt like the rhythm of Mother Earth and Heaven in my mind.

Abruptly, though, I was awash in darkness. The entire bloodline pulsed and opened before me. I entered dark chasms where fully dead vampires resided. I felt them sing to me and was invited to join them. Our music entered my soul, and I became one with the rhythmic heartbeat of all living things in the world.

I saw beyond Maman, to the dark pit, to Gaius.

"You survived," Gaius said.

"I have," I said.

"Excellent. Carry on."

My eyes fluttered open. Pascaline and Maman fed me their blood until I was able to sit without dizziness.

Sydella brought me the detached torso of one of the vampires who attacked the carriage. Maman carved out a slowly beating heart and gave it to me. I bit on the gamey, bloody meat and began to consume it.

Once we bathed and retied ourselves into gowns, Pascaline embraced me tightly. I was happy to be beside my sister and bosom friend.

The men were finally allowed into the room.

Each one of them embraced me in turn—even Gunter—who called me little sister.

The light in Charles's eyes assured me I made the right decision to walk into undeath. Somehow, this girl who believed in the futility of love, within the mercenary institution of marriage, matured into a woman who wanted to exist in tender affection with her husband for all of eternity.

It was simply the most foolish thing I ever heard, yet it made me wish to write an opera.

Pascaline

For the first time since my death, I feel truly alive again. Loretta is contented in her marriage. She is safe. Her boldness, desires, voice, and musical gifts will exist long into the centuries. I look to the spring and Versailles's courtly skirmishes—trading a charity for a song—having the king witness how my good works create industry which brings in taxes.

I visit the crypt where my little Celeste and Greta lay. Neither of their souls remain on the Earthly plane any longer. They went on to Heaven. They deserve to be mourned and remembered, but tonight, my heart is filled with happiness. I evoke their names and tell them all about the wedding. I kiss their brass portraits on the grave markers and put autumn chrysanthemums upon their tombs.

It is late. I meet Sydella in Maman's garden. Even on cold winter nights such as this, there is so much beauty under the frost. Sydella and I embrace. Her skin feels warm. Enraptured, I kiss her hand. Then, meeting her eyes, I put my mouth on her wrist. I kiss it.

Laughing, Sydella offers her blood. I bite.

Even if we cannot linger together for long, Sydella and I shall create beautiful, tender moments for each other. Perhaps, even an enduring peace between our families for eternity.

The End

About the Author-Illustrator

Much to her chagrin, Elizabeth Guizzetti discovered she was not a cyborg and growing up to be an otter would be impractical, so began writing stories at age twelve. Three decades later, Guizzetti is an illustrator and author best known for her demon-poodle based comics, *Out for Souls & Cookies* and *Legends of Walnut Razorfang.* She is also an author who loves vampires, especially their everyday lives!

Guizzetti lives in Seattle with her husband and dog. When not writing or illustrating, she loves hiking and birdwatching.

Follow her work on:

Web: http://www .elizabethguizzetti.com
Instagram: @elizabeth_guizzetti
Facebook: Elizabeth.Guizzetti.Author

Paper Flower Consortium Universe

Honor and Chivalry Among Vampires
(Moldavia and France 1509-12)
Accident Among Vampires
or What Would Dracula Do? (USA, 1951)
Norma's Cleaning Service Mysteries
Immortal House:
A Nightmarish Tale of Vampires and Real Estate
(USA)

Vampires of the Paper Flower Consortium Podcast

More novels to come...

Loyalty Among Vampires

(Set in Brandenburg and France, 1683-86)

A Situation Among Vampires

(Set in England, Oregon Trail, US Territories, 1841-51)

Comics

The Legend of Walnut Razorfang
Faminelands
Out For Souls & Cookies!
Lure

Novels and Novellas

Other Systems
The Light Side of the Moon
The Grove
Chronicles of the Martlet

Illustration Projects

Dear Penpal Belgium 1980
A is for Apex
The Prince of Artemis V

9 781950 708376